WHY READERS LOVE COURTING DEATH & DESIRE

Courting Death & Desire by CB Woods completely captivated me. As a massive fan of *Rift*, I had so many questions about what was happening on Pluto—and this book delivered answers and so much more.

— MINDY LOU WHO, *GOODREADS*

Once again, CB delivers that agonising yearning and tension that just hits so hard. If you loved the "we want each other but absolutely shouldn't" vibes in Rift, get ready for more of that delicious torment. Arcas? Written to perfection. The love/hate dynamic is executed so well. And let's just say it—Mirquios is THAT king. I knew it before, but this book really proves it.

— AMY ADAMS, *GOODREADS*

COURTING DEATH & DESIRE

COURTING DEATH & DESIRE

A COURTS BETWEEN STORY

CB WOODS

For the eldest daughters
wearing crowns of thorns

May you find they were
stars all along

AUTHOR'S NOTE & CONTENT WARNING

Courting Death & Desire is a companion story to *Rift*, the first book in The Courts Between trilogy.

Courting Death & Desire is an interconnected standalones that take place within the events of *The Courts Between Series*, which follow some of our favorite side characters on their own quests throughout the Living Courts.

While you can read this book on its own, you'll be missing out on major context and the stakes may not make as much sense. It does contain *major* spoilers for *Rift*, so I recommend reading Book One of The Courts Between first, *or* tandem reading them with this guide:

cbwoods.net/tandem

There are brief depictions of suicidal ideations and a hefty amount of death-related imagery in this story. Please be careful with your health as you proceed.

THE SYSTEM

THE COURT
ABOVE

THE COURTS
BETWEEN

THE
LIVING
COURTS

THE COURT
BELOW

THE SYSTEM

The system falls into three realms.

The Divine Courts—the Court Above and the Court Below —welcome those who leave their mortal timelines. While all manner of creatures Descend to the Court Below, only the Souls willing to embrace their Shadows can unify themselves and Ascend to the Court Above.

The Living Courts are home to the nine celestial courts, each with their own unique cultures, species, monarchies, and mythology. They devote themselves to their namesakes, the Old Gods in the Court Above.

The Inner Courts are comprised of the Mercurian, Venusian, Earthen, and Maritan Courts.

The Outer Courts include the Jovian, Saturnian, Neptunian, Uranian, and Plutonian Courts.

Resting in the mist between the Divine and the Living are the Courts Between, the Solar and the Lunar Courts. At war for millennia, these mysterious courts of demigods have divided the Living Courts' loyalties as they struggle to grasp whatever power the Divine Courts toss at their feet.

The Rift, a mysterious river made of light and color, weaves the courts together and allows for travel between the gates—whether one would be welcome through that gate is at each monarch's discretion.

CHAPTER
ONE

Of all the feelings in the world to detest, Lunar princess Lunelle Aurellis hated the vibrations of uncertainty most.

She could tolerate a white-hot rage well enough.

Shivering nerves? Not ideal, but nothing she couldn't subdue with a few deep breaths.

A burning jealousy was uncomfortable, of course, but at least it stirred something intriguing within her.

But the back-and-forth icy heat of simply not knowing what to do tingling in her spine was by far the worst of the fluttering emotions battling for dominance as she searched her vanity drawers for nothing in particular. She just needed to keep moving.

"You don't need to do that, Princess, we have it all handled," her maiden, Lura, cooed as she folded a set of impossibly soft silk day dresses into a trunk. Her amethyst gaze watched Lunelle's ticking fingers grasp for air.

"I'm glad one of us does," Lunelle sighed, leaning against the smooth iridescent opal of the vanity. She pulled at the ends

1

of her silver curls, the candlelight of the sconce above casting an amber glow onto the blank canvas of her silk skin.

"It won't be for long," Lura assured her. "And aren't you a *little* excited to see what lies beyond the walls of the Lunar Court?"

Lunelle's pale pink lips folded into a soft pout. "A little. But I don't like leaving Astra. Not with so much up in the air."

Lura squeezed her hand briefly as she moved about the room. "Why don't you bring her in here, hmm? She'll be a great distraction."

Astra certainly was that.

Come pack with me, Lunelle beamed toward the amber energy she'd grown to associate with her sister. She'd missed their shared silent conversations in Astra's exile, but their little trick had snapped back between them with no effort at all.

Astra's raspy velvet tone echoed back. **Be right there.**

Lunelle was wrong. There was a feeling she hated more than uncertainty.

Sorrow.

Astra had spent the last three years exiled at their mother's directive and was hardly home a fortnight before the Solar king's movement in the Outer Courts was ripping them apart once more.

She rolled her shoulders back, attempting to dispel the uncertainty pooling in her chest.

It was in Lunelle's nature as the ever-cautious eldest sister, the heir to the Lunar throne, to remain poised under pressure. Her head shook side to side as she searched for one of her journals in her nightstand.

That wasn't actually true. It wasn't in her nature at all.

It was in the painstaking *nurture* she'd endured those thirty-some-odd years beneath her mother's weighty wing.

Everything from the way she held her chin as courtiers

spoke—angled just so to appear engaged and open to the speaker no matter the subject—to the speed at which she set her fork down—too quickly could be seen as a declaration the meal was over—was carefully curated by thousands of years of women who could never shake the weight of judging eyes on their shoulders.

Lunelle tucked a few leather-bound journals into a bag as several maidens poured into her room, whisking through her things as Lura directed them. Her sister's fiery curls followed, casting a warm glow around the room that almost soothed her nerves.

Almost.

Lunelle could not stop the lingering fear from manifesting in a mumbled, "I'm sure everything will be fine."

"Of course," Astra agreed. Her lips pulled into a tight line as she stretched the muscles in her long legs, wincing as she tried to block out the dark rumblings in Lunelle's chest.

Lunelle envied many things about her younger sister, but her constant vulnerability to the ever-shifting emotions in any given room was not one of them. Some things were better left to interpretation—but Astra had no such luxury as her intuition translated every passing feeling into overwhelming color.

Lunelle tamped her anxiety down, finding that well of swirling ink where she kept most feelings from the time Astra's abilities became clear to the rest of the family.

"I've been training my whole life for this," Lunelle forced through a pained smile. It was true—she *had* spent her entire life navigating the complex politics between the Inner and Outer Courts, she had just always assumed she'd be crowned queen by the time she had to put any of it into practice.

"And you'll have Mother, for better or worse," Astra sighed.

She sat up against the bed, folding her legs beneath her rather like she would when they were just girls.

"Right," Lunelle agreed.

She didn't say she feared it would be for the worse.

"Right," Astra repeated.

In her thirty years of life, Astra had never responded to her in a single word. Dread tugged at Lunelle's heart once more.

"Mother above, Astra. This is it, isn't it?" She reached for a satchel of dried lavender from the nightstand to press into the toes of her favorite boots. Lura slipped behind her, snagging the boots and casting another warning glare. The bile in her stomach rose a touch higher into her throat. "This will be the start of the next intercourt war. It will define my entire reign and I'm not even on the throne yet!"

Astra hopped off the bed and closed the distance between them. Her warm touch as her hands came to rest against Lunelle's shoulders did little to ease the chill settling between vertebrae in her spine. Astra's fiery gaze held hers, widening as Lunelle gently sifted through her fears and found new places to tuck them out of sight.

"Lu," her sister said, squeezing her shoulders. "Mother does not want a war. Mirquios does not want a war. Pluto *certainly* doesn't want a war. The majority of the courts are on our side and will want to settle things peacefully. This is an exercise in diplomacy, nothing more."

"Do you really believe that?" Lunelle asked.

"Absolutely," Astra said with a feigned conviction. It was a lie, and not one of her better ones. Lunelle appreciated the effort all the same. "Solaris has been silent for thirty years! Mother has spent my entire life preparing for her chance to shut Solan down."

That was the truth—whether her nervous system believed it or not. Their mortal enemies a thousand times over, the Solar Court hadn't caused so much trouble since their last attack three decades earlier. But things shifted quickly.

"You're right," Lunelle sighed. She didn't like admitting defeat to anyone other than Astra. "Thank you," she added.

Astra brushed her fingertips against her sister's delicate complexion, the slightest hint of a frown pulling at her lips.

"You'll return home to me in a week or two, and we can forget this whole awful mess."

Molten tears welled against Lunelle's starry eyes—not because she was afraid, but because in all the panic since news had arrived of Pluto's removal from the Outer Courts, Lunelle had nearly managed to forget that this was not a temporary separation for the sisters.

No matter what happened in the Plutonian Court, no matter what resolution they were able to come to, they'd return home, and Astra would marry the King of Mercury and leave her side forever.

Lunelle winced. "Just in time to marry you off," she said.

Astra's shoulders stiffened. "Let's take this hour by hour, shall we?"

Lunelle stepped away from her sister's grip and slid another stack of books into her trunk. She did not even look at their titles or care much at all about what they were. She simply needed something to do with her hands.

The tears made another attempt to spring forth. Biting them back, she leveled her tone.

"I suppose you should go say your goodbyes to your betrothed."

Astra let a tight breath slip between her lips. "I suppose I should." She winked as she patted her sister's shoulder once again. "I had Ameera slip a few satchels of tea into your bags, just in case Pluto is a desolate wasteland."

Astra did not hesitate at the door as she left, off to bid her fiancé farewell.

Mirquios.

Lunelle had yet to speak to the man since his court's arrival in the Lunar Court.

He'd made his intentions clear from the moment he strutted into Astra's birthday ball—he was after a Lunar princess for his throne. She'd understood, of course, it was as strategic an alliance a Living Court could make.

What mere man wouldn't want a Lunar demigoddess at his side in the face of certain war?

Especially one rumored to have such a grip on the Lunarians' mysterious ancient magic. Astra defied its bans simply by existing.

While Lunelle believed the notions of her sister's powers to be greatly misunderstood outside of the bounds of the Lunar Court, all it would take is one conversation, one catch of Astra's incisive gaze across a ballroom even, to know the second-born Lunar princess was something different.

Something *more*.

And even if Lunelle could fault the young king for being charmed by her sister—which though she tried, she couldn't —she certainly could not deny their fate once Astra revealed their union to be ordained by the gods themselves through that godsforsaken Tether.

Lunelle dodged a maiden as she cut through the room. She slipped along the wall and to her window, determined to stay out of the way. Below, in the palace gardens, the Venusians bathed in the soft moonlight, their ethereal bone structures catching and holding onto any light they could.

"Do not forget to pack her long sleeves," a commanding voice cut into the room.

Lunelle spun as her mother, Queen Oestera, strolled into

her bed chambers with High Priestess Tula on her heels, dutifully scribbling notes as the queen spoke.

"It's the middle of Summer," Lunelle protested.

Her mother stopped, her endless celestial gaze searing against Lunelle's skin.

"Pluto may be a great distance away, but they still see the Sun, darling. You've yet to contend with its harsh burn."

"Oh." It was all she had to offer. She hadn't considered how drastically different the Plutonian Court might be from hers. She'd hardly had time to come around to the fact that she was heading away from home at all, let alone as far away as possible. "And you're *certain* you need me there?"

Oestera tilted her head, a soft smile tugging at her lips. "I will not always be here, Lunelle. This war will be fought for years, not months. It's important the Inner Courts see you as the leader you were born to be, and this summit in Pluto is an excellent chance for us to hone your skills as the Lunar queen."

The words settled like stones in her gut.

"The prince—"

Oestera waved her hand. "He is young. Frightened. He has no one to guide him through the disaster he's found himself in. We can be the wisdom he so desperately needs." The queen pointed to a set of delicate pearls, their pale blues and whites swirling on a gilded chain. "Pack those, as well. They bring out her eyes."

Lura darted forward silently and plucked the strand of pearls from Lunelle's vanity to pack away.

"And are we concerned about this prince noticing my eyes?" Lunelle asked, a brow raised.

Her mother shrugged, eyes focused on another sparkling set of gems.

"If we find the prince to be amiable, I don't see why he shouldn't be considered for your coronation trial." Tula and

Oestera exchanged a quick glance, Tula's pen gliding across her parchment as she tracked another string of thoughts. "We'll leave within the hour," Oestera declared, sweeping from the room.

Lunelle sank her hip into the bay beneath her window, her pale complexion somehow holding even less color.

"You forgot about your trial in all the excitement," Lura said quietly, handing Lunelle a cup of warm tea.

"I hadn't forgotten about the trial," Lunelle corrected her. "But perhaps I'd forgotten about the champion aspect."

Forgotten was generous—she'd damn near forced it out of her mind as the day drew nearer. It wasn't that she was opposed to the ritual itself. The coronation trial held a beautiful significance for both her family and her court, but she'd never quite understood why she couldn't go it alone—why champions were forced to participate and compete for her hand.

Lunelle blushed a deep strawberry, annoyed by the image of a man beside her at the end of the trial as if he would bear the same weight in any form.

Lura hummed quietly beside her as the rest of her maidens cleared out, pulling trunks and garment bags behind them.

"Much can change beneath the Summer Sun, Princess," Lura murmured.

Lunelle turned toward the window, watching the Venusians trickle toward the Lunarian Gate. They fell gently into the Rift's myriad of colors whirring beyond the crystalline arch, letting it take their lithe frames up and into the ether—no hesitation, no fears.

None of that godsdamned uncertainty that whispered into her ear, even now.

What do you actually want?

LUNELLE WATCHED her sister dart back into the palace, her shoulders tense as she eyed the Rift humming beyond the gardens.

The Mercurians did not hesitate to slip into the current of colors, falling back into the mystic river from the edge of the Lunar Gate's platform with a frivolity she envied.

"It is simple," her mother assured her. "Not nearly as daunting as it appears."

Lunelle bit her lip, watching the Lunar Sentry and maidens begin their entrances into the Rift.

"You'll fall in, but it cradles you in a way, it doesn't feel like a free fall. You'll locate the Plutonian thread—it's a deep sapphire—and grab hold. It will pull you to the Plutonian Gate, and that's that."

"That's that!" Lunelle chirped, blushing as her mother glared.

"This is the least of your challenges, darling."

She sighed, stepping forward onto the moonstone platform, the amethyst gate arching overhead. "And we'll only be there for a week or two?"

"One can hope," Oestera muttered. "But diplomacy takes time."

"Of course," she huffed.

"At your leisure, my dear," Oestera said, holding her hand before her.

Lunelle edged toward the end of the platform, the Rift's sweeping colors brushing against the toe of her slippers. She held her breath, twisted, and let herself go, soaring across The System with her eyes closed.

"Grab the thread, Lunelle!" Her mother's voice echoed

against the strands of light. She forced her eyes open, two threads over her head in sparkling shades of blue.

"Which blue?" she yelled, but no one answered.

Her eyes darted from the lighter to the darker. Something within her called out to the latter, begging her to touch the dark-as-night sapphire glimmer.

She reached out and wrapped her silver fingers around the thread, and she was gone.

CHAPTER
TWO

wo dozen sapphire roses watched Lunelle from the center of a dazzling floral arrangement as she stepped into what would be the Lunarians' shared study for the foreseeable future.

As far as she could tell, just about everything in the Plutonian palace was some shade of blue—from the oceanic tile of the floor to the deep navy sofas, to the delicate cerulean hue the Plutonians themselves seemed to carry within their complexions.

She did not think the color suited her.

"I meant what I said earlier," her mother hummed, pulling the fingertips of her gloves off as their maidens flooded the room and began unpacking trunks. "The Sun is not to be underestimated. You'll want to stay indoors as much as possible, dear. If you do go out, make sure you're covered."

Oestera sat softly on the plush sofa in the middle of their shared study—a silver star amidst a navy velvet sky—her cheeks still flushed from their jarring trip through the Rift. Lunelle knew she hadn't taken it in years, but some memories

11

never left one's musculature. She had marveled at her mother's gracious fall into the mystical portal she'd only ever heard whispers of, having been forbidden from ever leaving the bounds of the Lunar Court.

Oestera had simply given herself over to the flow of the strange threads, reaching for a deep navy as the colors of each of the courts poured into a ceaseless mirage.

Oestera had landed just as gracefully on the dull gray stone of the last of the Living Courts, Pluto. The Plutonian Gate was much darker and less crystalline than the sparkling amethyst of the Lunarian Gate Lunelle had spent thirty-some years staring at through her window, but there was something embedded in the stones that buzzed against her feet.

Something lurking in the shadows of the halls.

"Princess," Lura said. She slipped an envelope into Lunelle's slender fingers. Under the Moon of the Lunar Court, her silvery complexion sparkled from the celestial energy. Here, she feared she was taking on the morose blues of the palace walls. "It's an invitation to a welcome tea, hosted by the Plutonian princess, Yallara. It seems the younger monarchs will be there."

Oestera looked to Lunelle. The decision was hers.

"I could go for tea," she murmured, her eyes slipping toward the window at the far edge of the room. A sunbeam sliced through the silken curtains and traced a bright line across the dark furniture. "I suppose the sooner I get to know our hosts, the better."

"Tea it is," Oestera nodded. "It would be good to get some face time with the princess. Perhaps the prince will attend."

Lunelle's spine tingled. She'd spent the last two days in meeting after meeting about the prince and his court. Arcas was unmarried, and therefore unable to take the Plutonian throne according to their laws, which would have been fine if his father hadn't passed unexpectedly a few months prior. The instability, combined with Pluto's modest offerings when it came to resources, made them a burden on the Outer Courts as they prepared for war under the Solar king Solan's regime.

He'd hardly gotten his feet under him before Solan removed Pluto from the alliance. Arcas was young, alone, and frightened—a lethal combination in men as far as Lunelle understood.

"Perhaps," she replied flatly, her nerves flaring in rivers along her skin. She reached out to touch a rose petal, marveling at the spread of the bloom under the Sun's touch. At home, the moonblossoms and roses ruffled quietly in the Spring and Summer. Now, she realized, they were mere buds compared to the expansive swirls in the vase, each bigger than her palm.

What else does not reach its full potential, hidden in the dark of night? she thought to herself as Lura preened over her hair, weaving it into an intricate braid.

"Go along," Oestera chirped from the sofa, her eyes already set on her notes from her ambassadors. "And don't be shy, darling, you're just months away from ruling one of the strongest courts in the entire system. Don't let them forget it."

Lunelle sighed, pulling her braid to one side and picking at the silk cord holding it together as she wandered into the hall.

If you were here, you'd have whipped this entire court into shape already, she sent out into the ether. She had no idea if her sister was capable of hearing her over the distance, but it brought her comfort to reach out all the same.

THE PLUTONIAN PALACE was entirely unlike the glittering halls Lunelle grew up in.

Everything in Lunaria was fractured into crystalline angles

and opalescent haze. The Moon's light bounced off odd angles and shiny surfaces, bathing everyone in a mystic glow.

Pluto was all smooth, round stones and sapphire velvet.

She followed Lura and one of Pluto's courtiers, a slim boy easily half her age, through endless twisting paths until she felt a shift in the air—a warmth she did not recognize.

"Oh," she breathed as the courtier drew back flowing white curtains, revealing a Sun-soaked garden rich in the same blue roses she'd marveled at moments ago. Dozens of dignitaries milled about, lounging on wicker furniture and overstuffed cushions on the fluffy grass.

They sipped tea and snacked, relaxed in ways they'd not seemed capable of in the Lunar Court. She lingered at the edge of the garden, unsure how to best insert herself into the small groupings lounging across the lawn. Her eyes fell to a harpist in the corner, her fingers the same shade of the sky above, weaving between cords to sing a soothing melody.

"Princess."

She'd only heard the Mercurian king's deep voice from a distance, and often only in low whispers to her sister over dinner.

They'd crossed paths a few times in Lunaria, but never at her own wishes. She'd avoided him, she was sure Astra had noticed. Mirquios seemed fine enough, but he was still the thing that was going to take her sister away from her far too soon.

At that moment, however, he was a friendly face—and she needed that more than she needed to hold a childish grudge.

"Your Highness," she smiled, stepping closer to him as he plucked a tea cake off a passing tray. She turned to face him, his tall frame hovering over her, wrapped in Mercurian greens that lit up his deep complexion.

She had been surprised when her sister's amber gaze

lingered on the king's broad chest and bright jade eyes at the Solstice ball—not because he wasn't handsome by all definitions of the word, but because Astra had rarely, if ever, given her attention to a man.

But, close up, unable to escape from the gracious lines of his regal posture and his easy warmth, Lunelle understood the appeal.

"How were your travels?" he asked through a bite of the cake.

"Quite the trip," she replied, stretching her shoulders as she spoke. "I'd never taken the Rift before."

Mirquios laughed. "That's right! You and your poor sister, shackled to the palace like that."

She shook her head as a servant offered her something blue on a plate. "I don't know what I expected of Pluto, but I suppose something less... ornate." She gestured to the surrounding garden, dripping in rich colors and opulent fabrics.

"Oh, Arcas certainly has more than he can handle here," Mirquios mumbled. "It's a bit much for those of us who are on the more conservative end with our finances, I suppose."

She arched a silver brow, curious if he would say more.

"Not that Lunaria isn't more than accommodating," he amended. "I admire that you and your mother aren't so ostentatious. Feels ill-advised given the state of things."

"Of course," she said, reaching for a cup of tea from a passing tray, just barely missing the curved handle. The servant turned too quickly, darting away as someone called to them.

Lunelle sighed.

Mirquios sprang forward, cutting across the garden with his long legs, and stopped the servant, snagging a steaming cup and saucer from the tray before turning back to her.

Lunelle's cheeks flushed as she reached for it, uttering her thanks.

"Your sister said she'd never forgive me if I didn't look out for you."

"That sounds like Astra," Lunelle laughed quietly, sipping the strange violet tea. Her head swirled with the porcelain's contents, but she didn't *dislike* it. "I'm not as helpless as she implies, I assure you. I'm just not one to make a scene."

Mirquios rocked forward on his heels. "There is nothing helpless about any of you Lunarian women. Of that, I am certain. There's strength in silence, too, you know."

Lunelle's silver gaze flickered over him before it fixed back on the laughing courtiers on the lawn. "Do you think it's a mistake? Trusting this prince?"

Mirquios considered her question for a moment before answering, the implications hovering in the air between them.

"Princess Lunelle!"

They both turned their heads to address the sweet soprano that rang out behind them. A petite young woman bounded across the gardens, a sheer black gown floating in waves behind her. She looked less like a princess and more akin to a goddess of death, a perfect little creature with a sharp gaze surrounded by shadows. Her pale skin glowed with a cerulean sheen that must have made her the Plutonian princess.

"Princess Yallara," Lunelle returned. "So kind of you to host us."

She bounced on her heels as she grinned. "My brother doesn't have a shred of fun in his bones, so I figured someone had to break the ice."

Yallara sidled up to Lunelle as if they were lifelong friends and not strangers a second ago. Up close, Yallara was not a goddess of death, but a harbinger of mischief. The desire to spark chaos sparkled in the sapphire blues of her eyes.

16

She liked this princess, Lunelle decided. There was something so reminiscent of Astra about the defiance in her chin, the bubbling current of unpredictability in her veins that Lunelle admired.

"And you must be King Mirquios," Yallara said. "I'm delighted to see you here as well!"

Mirquios nodded, his aventurine eyes briefly skimming over her face as he watched his courtiers rumble with laughter across the garden.

"I must know what's in this tea," Lunelle mumbled, her head fogging over as she spoke.

"Oh!" Yallara leaned over her teacup, her eyes dropping to the violet pool swirling in Lunelle's hands. "That's one of the stronger cups. Brave woman," Yallara winked as she watched the tea slosh against the sides of Lunelle's cup.

Lunelle's face heated. "Stronger... than... a chamomile?"

Yallara's lips quirked at the corners. "Well, Princess, it's less of a tea, more of an.... experience," she explained.

Mirquios and Lunelle exchanged a skeptical glance.

Her sloped shoulders shrugged as if reporting on the weather. "Should only be an hour or two. You didn't drink all that much. Oh! Kahlia!" Yallara darted across the courtyard, leaving them to stare silently at the teacup.

"Well," Lunelle said, a tingle slipping over her skin. "This should be interesting."

Mirquios held back a laugh.

Lunelle glared. "This isn't *funny*, Mirquios!"

"I'm so sorry, I didn't know!" He clasped his fingers over his lips, eyes wide as she calculated how long she had before she was a weeping puddle.

"I've been here for an hour and already my mother is going to murder me," she groaned.

"Here," the king murmured, taking the cup from her. In one

swift movement, he threw the entirety of its remains back, wincing as the herbs hit his throat. "If you're going down, at least you won't be alone."

Lunelle gasped, "Your Highness!"

"Foul," he croaked, covering his mouth as he forced the tea to stay down.

Lunelle giggled into her hands, her heart warmed by his attempt at allyship. His lips curled into a smile that reflected hers. She wondered if he was feeling as lightheaded as she was yet.

He cleared his throat, passing the empty cup off to a servant before gesturing to the courtiers before them.

"These diplomacy dinners are always intensely boring, anyway. Perhaps now we'll have a little fun."

CHAPTER
THREE

Dinner was, by all accounts, *not* fun.

The tension at the long table clung to whispered small talk and shifting glances as the dignitaries watched the grand arch at the end of the dining room for the Plutonian prince. Or perhaps Lunelle only imagined it as her head drifted into a vast ocean, her vision hazy at the edges.

There was just so much to look at in the Plutonian palace. The tapestries lining the walls over the flickering lanterns past Yallara's shoulder held her attention for at least ten minutes.

But they were so lovely. She imagined them as the eyes of the divine mothers waiting for her at the Court Above's gates upon her Ascent. They swirled with gentle honey-golds, bronze streaks whispering the secrets of the System to her—

"Lunelle?" her mother asked quietly beside her.

Her shoulders jerked as she turned toward the queen. "Sorry."

"You're quite distracted this evening." Oestera folded her hands in her lap, her eyes darting between Lunelle and the Plutonian princess, stifling a laugh beside her.

"There's just so much... splendor to take in," Lunelle returned, plucking another plump roll from the center of the table.

She'd had at least three, but nothing seemed to quell the ravenous hunger in her stomach.

Her mother sighed. "Perhaps we absorb the splendor later. Or at least, with our mouths closed."

Lunelle's jaw snapped shut. She hadn't realized it was open.

"Better," Oestera muttered.

Yallara's shoulders stiffened as a flurry of movement from the far end of the room stirred the courtiers' attention.

A servant called out, "His Royal Highness, Prince Arcas Hydranos of Pluto."

The room rose in a fluid motion, Lunelle's own frame a beat behind as she shuffled her seat back and tried to straighten her spine against the weight of the tea's haze bearing down on her.

Everything felt suffocating.

The dress, the lights, the eyes of the Inner Court leaders as they ruffled along the table. She followed them to the prince at the head of the table—a pillar of long, slender lines, crowned by a disappointed sneer. His sapphire eyes and pale blue complexion mirrored his younger sister's, but he lacked her self-assuredness, her lightness. Arcas stood with his chest out, though Lunelle could tell by the tension in his shoulders it was not the natural posture he'd preferred. He had to work to maintain it.

He was putting on a show, desperate to reflect the strength and confidence he found in the regents staring back at him.

Arcas sat, catalyzing a wave of courtiers falling to their chairs, and she felt her head swirl again as she plopped unceremoniously back into hers. Her eyes flickered toward Mirquios, seated to her left, and she recognized the same panic in his eyes she was trying to suppress. His lips cracked into a wide grin as she turned away, afraid to start giggling lest she never stop.

"I am honored to host each of you," Prince Arcas declared, his voice tight. Nervous, Lunelle realized. She wondered briefly how her sister would see him—what anxious rainbow clutched at his throat and soaked his shirts. "I hope over the coming weeks we can come to an agreement on how Pluto fits into your alliance."

Oestera raised a glass, prompting the rest of the dignitaries to follow, though Lunelle noticed a considerable amount of wine slip over the edge of Mirquios's glass as he over-extended his arm. She stifled another giggle, drawing a disturbed glare from her mother.

"Sorry," she mouthed, setting her glass down but realizing a second too late that Arcas hadn't given a toast yet. She floated the glass back up as he began speaking again. It was Yallara this time who snorted.

"To forging new loyalties," he said, his eyes glazing over the faces staring back at him.

"Hear, hear!" Mirquios bellowed, the final note sinking quickly to a whisper as he realized he was the only one to cheer as glasses clinked together. Lunelle missed the Martian colonel's glass across from her by a hair. Mirquios gasped at her mistake, quickly dropping his gaze and covering his mouth. Lunelle shot him a glare as her mother's slipper connected with her shin beneath the table.

Dinner could not be over soon enough.

Arcas pressed forward as he sank into the chair at the head of the table. "I would love to hear more about each of your courts and how we can be strong partners as Solan closes in around the Outer Courts, but tonight, let us celebrate."

Chatter rose over the table as wine flowed and dishes began appearing before them.

"This is worse than I thought it would be," Mirquios whispered, leaning close to her.

She only nodded, shoveling her first course into her mouth as quickly as she could without raising alarm. She *had* to soak up that tea before it consumed any sanity left within her.

As she ate, she risked a glance at the prince, his lips downturned as the Venusian High Regent spoke in silky ribbons.

He was not unattractive, she decided.

Though somewhere in her mind, she realized her judgment was not exactly sound. The edge of his jaw cut against his hand as he rested it in his palm before Yallara's tilted head caught his attention. She pulled her shoulders back, sitting up taller against her chair, and Arcas followed, unfolding into a wider, broader posture as he rested his hand against the table.

Lunelle's lips curled into a soft smile, the connection between the siblings warming the space within her saved for her own sister.

"Arcas," Oestera hummed over the table as she leaned forward. "The princess missed the palace tour your lovely sister gave this afternoon. Perhaps you could show her the Plutonian orchards in the morning?"

Arcas turned away from the High Regent and stared at Oestera, and then Lunelle. His eyes widened as they met hers, the deep blues throwing amber glitter as the candlelight reflected in them.

Whatever haze dizzying Lunelle cleared quickly, something about the intensity of his stare more sobering than the food. There was a darkness within them, like a midnight sea.

It was Yallara who answered as words failed to materialize from his tight lips.

"He'd be honored, Your Majesty."

Arcas finally tore his gaze away, releasing her back to her plate, as the herbal swirl of the tea took its revenge and sent her pitching forward and squeezing her eyes against the current.

Whatever sobriety she'd found in the prince's gaze vanished. Lunelle inhaled slowly, desperate to regain control of her senses. Her fingertips grazed the velvet of her dress in an attempt to ground herself.

"Well. Your mother certainly wastes no time," Mirquios whispered, leaning close once more. Her head snapped to the side and a panicked laugh escaped from her chest as his eyes and mouth switched places.

Oestera cleared her throat and leaned forward as Yallara patted Lunelle's knee.

"Get a hold of yourselves," the queen whispered harshly.

Lunelle wondered if Mirquios, too, saw three heads springing from her mother's stately shoulders, or if she was alone in her hallucination as she sank lower into her seat, finding the gilded edge of her plate to be endlessly fascinating.

"Oh!" Yallara gasped beside her, ripping Lunelle from her debate over whether the gold was closest to that of a perfectly sweet honey or of her sister's fiery irises.

"What is it?" Arcas asked, leaning forward in response to his sister's distress. Yallara shook her head, mumbling her dismissal and insisting it was nothing as she signaled to the servant behind her. She grasped for her plate, handing it to the servant quickly, but Arcas held up a hand, curling his fingers in a command to bring it to him.

The servant moved slowly toward the end of the table, Yallara's cerulean complexion deepening into a brilliant fuchsia. The plate landed before the prince with a deafening thud.

Arcas's face matched his sister's as he took in whatever it was.

"Who did it?" he asked, his words fraught with an ill-disguised terror. His eyes scanned the faces of the servants.

"You," he said, pointing a dagger-sharp finger toward the far edge of the room.

Lunelle followed the accusing gesture, landing on a young man in *almost* the right shade of uniform, but not quite. The buttons fastening his vest were silver, not bronze.

His face drained of color as the prince rose from his seat.

Everyone moved in motions that were too quick for her impaired vision to track. The Venusians were gone before she could blink—the sound of metal on metal sent a chill down her spine as she felt the chair behind her ripped away.

Lunelle stumbled forward, a hand gripping her arm tightly and shoving her forward as Yallara screeched her brother's name. Her body raced toward the exit of the room, her silk skirts catching under Mirquios's shoes as he pushed her along. Lunelle reached for the Plutonian princess, her face pale and lips hanging open in horror as she watched whatever was unfolding behind them. Lunelle wrapped a hand around her delicate arm, yanking her into her side.

Mirquios pulled the women forward, but even in the chaos, even as her mind swam beneath wave after wave of crushing confusion, she could not avoid the plate resting at Arcas's now-empty place.

Instead of the lavish dessert she'd been served, Yallara's plate boasted a scarlet mass of tangled vein and muscle, resting in a pool of burgundy blood against the porcelain plate. A small dagger pierced the heart, but she could not make out any detail as Mirquios rushed them away.

Bodies collided as they spilled into the hall, courtiers rushing away as Plutonian guards cut through them and raced toward calamity in the dining room.

"My mother," Lunelle rasped as she stopped to turn, but Oestera was already beside them, waving them forward.

"Get back to our chambers, do not stop," Oestera barked, searching the hall for someone. Her eyes landed on the Venusian High Regent's as they ushered their courtiers toward their wing. "Kahlia!" Oestera called, cutting through the crowd. Lunelle lurched forward to follow, but Mirquios held her back.

"We should get you to safety! Both of you," he yelled over the clamor, his grip tightening on Lunelle's arm.

"Yallara!" Arcas darted from the dining room, his onyx hair falling over his eyes as he pushed past the crowd, weaving between Martian and Earthen dignitaries. "Yallara," he called again. As he drew nearer, Lunelle could see the wet sheen on his black tunic.

She knew if she reached out to touch him, her fingers would come away with red stains.

"Brother," Yallara whispered, pulling away from Lunelle's grasp.

Arcas held his hands up as she went to embrace him, running his hands through his hair to smooth the black curls that clung to his forehead.

"You do not want to touch me, I assure you," he warned, glancing frantically around the hall as courtiers shoved and pushed them into the walls.

"You need to get control of them!" Mirquios yelled over Lunelle's head. "They're panicking!"

Arcas spun, eyes wide as he took in the crush swelling around them. An Earthen councilor slammed into Lunelle's back, pulling at her shoulders as he struggled to right himself. Mirquios shoved the man back, getting between them as best he could, but the crowd was too dense, too uncertain of where to go.

"Arcas!" Mirquios yelled once again. "This is your court! Manage it!"

Yallara glanced between the men, mouthing something inaudible to her brother as he paled. Mirquios pushed Lunelle toward the wall, her back aching as it crashed against the smooth marble. He pulled Yallara away from the prince, handing her off to Lunelle, who held her tightly as the Earthen Court spiraled into itself.

"Is there still a threat?" Mirquios said, gripping Arcas's shoulders and shaking him when he did not respond.

The prince shook his head.

Someone's body fell at Lunelle's feet, bouncing off the tile as the crowd stepped over him.

"Help me get him up!" she hissed to Yallara, stooping as another wave of courtiers poured from the dining room. Yallara gripped the man's hand as Lunelle pushed the crowd back, helping him to his feet as Mirquios's voice boomed above them.

Their eyes snapped forward, finding the Mercurian king perched atop a bust of some ancient Plutonian king, his eyes wild as he screamed over their heads again.

"Do not move another inch!"

Mirquiod cupped his hand over his mouth to amplify his thunderous words.

"People of the Inner Courts! Silence!"

Heads turned, the clamor still rising over his pleas as the edges of the crowd pressed inward.

"Silence!" Mirquios roared, the sound striking something deep within Lunelle's chest and earning the eyes and ears of most of the hall. "This evening's threat has been dealt with, but please be aware of your surroundings as you head back to your chambers for the evening. We will debrief with the monarchs in the western wing library. Go! Calmly," he added, dropping from the statue into the crowd as it slowly shifted away from the dining room doors.

"You should go to bed," Arcas said to Yallara, who was still clinging to Lunelle's arm.

"I will do no such thing," Yallara cried, pushing away from Lunelle.

"I was not asking," Arcas hissed. "You've already been threatened once tonight. Isn't that enough?"

"All the more reason I need to go with you—"

"Enough!" Arcas said, cutting his hand through the space between them. "I will come find you when we're done." Yallara held her brother's gaze, her shoulders set in defiance as his eyes softened. "It is not personal, Yallara, you are in *danger*," he said as he waved a guard forward from the doorway. "See that the princess gets back to her room safely."

Yallara relented, following the crowd as they dissipated.

Arcas looked to Mirquios for a moment, the hesitation clear on his face.

"Go change into something less bloodsoaked," the king muttered. "We'll meet you in the library."

THE LIBRARY WAS quiet as they trickled in.

The walls were draped in ancient maps, peeling at the corners, framed by portraits of eyes that followed Lunelle as she shifted against the black velvet sofa.

Lunelle had not let go of Yallara's hand, though not for lack of trying. The young princess had resisted both times she tried to untangle their fingers. She needed something to hold onto, and Lunelle did not mind being her anchor. Nor did she mind having one in return.

"You cannot be sure of their association," Omnir, the

Martian prince, said as he folded his bronze arms against his chest. He leaned his head back against a densely packed shelf, glaring at the Plutonian prince as he paced between the tufted seats and rows of bookshelves.

"A dagger through the heart might as well be a dagger through a crown," Arcas hissed, pausing in his path just long enough to throw a look at his sister. Yallara stiffened against Lunelle's hand as their eyes passed one another. "The symbology was clear."

Lunelle looked to her mother, her concerned face set in the corner of the room. She'd disappeared with Kahlia, the Venusian High Regent, in the chaos, only to reappear in the library with a marked coolness to her gait.

Oestera was nothing if not calm under pressure.

Mirquios spoke next. "I'm less concerned about their loyalty and more concerned about their singularity. A lone rebel making a statement is one thing, but if your halls are littered with Outer Courtiers attempting to take advantage of our gathering—"

"He was not a rebel," Yallara said, rising suddenly from her perch beside Lunelle.

Every head whipped toward the princess, her pale complexion flushing under the weight of so much attention.

"And how could you possibly know that?" Arcas asked, his pacing rounding the sofa as he loomed over her.

Yallara stepped toward him, rubbing her forefinger to her thumb as her eyes unfocused, as if searching her memory. "His coat was not Plutonian. The buttons. They were Uranian steel, I'd bet my life on it."

Arcas dismissed her. "We cannot be certain of anything, Yallara. The rebels have just as much reason to target a summit of monarchs as the Outer Courtiers—"

"Once again," Mirquios cut in. "It does not matter as of

right now. What matters is being certain there isn't anyone else lingering in the palace—"

"Lunar and Venusian guards are sweeping the halls now," Oestera said. "If anyone is here that shouldn't be, they'll be dealt with swiftly."

Arcas spun on his heel, shame dripping from his tongue in the form of a tense growl. "The Plutonian guard is more than capable of securing our palace!"

"If that were true, we would not have been treated to such a violent scene at dinner," Kahlia said evenly, with a masterful control over their intonation.

"I'm beginning to see why Solan left Pluto to their own devices," Lilah, the Earthen Court's leader, muttered beneath her breath beside Omnir.

"Now, now," Oestera said, waving her hand between them. "Most of you in this room aren't even old enough to remember the devastation of war, let alone be certain what to do when it crosses your threshold. We will return to our courtiers and ensure their safety. We'll get whatever rest we can. Tomorrow, we will begin negotiations with our young prince here, and we will decide how to move forward together."

"Oestera is right," Kahlia said, looking pointedly at the sullen Plutonian prince. "Our people must come first, and I think you have your work cut out for you on that front, Arcas." They brushed behind the prince, resting a hand briefly on his shoulder before disappearing into the hall.

"Brother," Yallara said, her voice still laden with a defiance Lunelle admired. "That man is not a rebel—"

"*Was*," Arcas spat. "Whoever he belonged to, it does not matter. He is no more." He cut a path behind the Martian and Earthen leaders, leaving his sister to watch his frame sulk away into the night. Yallara's midnight skirts swished against

Lunelle's shins as she followed, her chin tucked to her chest in defeat.

"You did well, Mirquios," Oestera said as she stepped between them. She squeezed the king's arm, a gesture so soft and familiar that Lunelle questioned if she saw it right. "The prince could learn a thing or two from you."

Mirquios fell into step beside Oestera, Lunelle a pace behind as they wound their way back through the alarmingly silent halls. She felt a heat prickle at the back of her neck as they rounded a corner, afraid of what might be lurking in the shadows.

"He has the potential to be a good leader, do you not think?"

The king huffed a sigh as they came to a stop before the long hall that the Lunarians had taken over.

"I was a boy on a throne once, too," he finally responded. "Scared shitless, no one to guide me."

"What changed you?" Lunelle asked.

Mirquios leaned against the wall, twin sets of silver eyes falling over him as he thought.

"War," he shrugged. "You mature quickly when enough bodies pile up at the feet of your failings."

Oestera nodded beside him. "He has potential. He needs us."

"But do we need him?" Mirquios asked, his brow raised.

Oestera's eyes bounced from his face to Lunelle, who was eager to hear her mother's assessment.

"Remains to be seen," the queen hummed. She wrapped her fingers around the bronze handle of her bedroom door and stretched her neck as she disappeared through the frame.

Lunelle stepped toward the next door down, her hand stopping to rest on the handle as the king slid along the wall with her.

"Good evening," she said, the words coming out as more of a question than a declaration.

"Your sister would have my head if I didn't ensure you made it into your room safely after all the commotion this evening."

"Ah," she sighed. "Of course." She nudged the door with her shoulder, slipping into the low-lit room, happy to see Lura waiting for her on a plush settee at the end of the bed.

"Goodnight, Lunelle," Mirquios said from the hall.

"Goodnight," she mumbled, already feeling a wave of nausea overtake her without the eyes of every ruler across the Inner Courts suppressing it. Lura wrapped an arm around her shoulder, squeezing her gently before untangling her hair from its braid, humming a song she used to sing when they were much younger girls.

It did little to soothe the well of panic opening within her chest.

CHAPTER
FOUR

Lunelle hardly rested that night.

Between the anxiety keeping her ear tuned to the hall, and the humbling after-effects of Yallara's tea, there was no amount of sleep that could have made climbing out of bed the next morning pleasant.

But duty waited for no hangover, and she was up and being laced into one of her more attractive Summer gowns before the room even came into focus.

The palace halls were still oddly stilted with an icy silence —no one knew what to say in the wake of such a shocking occurrence. She'd half expected the courtiers to stick to their assigned wings for the day, but the Sun had drawn them out of the halls and into the gardens and groves.

To Lunelle's dismay, her mother had not forgotten about Arcas's promise to give her a tour of the grove. They were both restless as they searched for small talk along the twisted trees.

Dense greenery punctuated by crimson bulbs loomed over them, the tangled mass of fruit blocking out the Summer Sun.

Lunelle pulled nervously at the edge of her sleeve as soft cream linen dragged across the rippling grass.

"They do not produce fruit for the first century," Arcas murmured, turning his chin up to the nearest branch. He reached his spindly cerulean knuckles out and brushed the soft underside of an unfurling leaf with a tenderness that surprised her. Everything about him was sharp. He'd been frantic last night, furious.

But this morning he was too tired to maintain his rage.

"It takes them eons to warm up, but once they do..." he trailed off. His fingers wrapped around a plump red fruit, snapping it from the branch. "They'll produce fruit for another six, seven hundred years. Maybe more if they're from a particularly strong lineage."

Lunelle lagged behind him as he moved from tree to tree, his hands whispering amongst the leaves as they moved along. Her mother's stare burned against her back, watching them weave through the grove from a lavish tent on the palace lawn. She'd stayed close all morning, uneasy after last night's attack. When Arcas greeted them over breakfast in the tent, Lunelle expected her mother would join them.

She glanced over her shoulder, covered by the light fabric of her dress in an effort to prevent burns to her pale skin, watching the Inner Courtiers stretch out in the Sun, basking in its sacred light. They held no reservations as they let the warm rays spill across the bridges of their noses, freckling them with shimmering spots.

A golden beam slipped through the trees, toasting a perfect circle against her palm. She twisted her hand one way and the next, watching the sunlight chase her blood across icy skin.

She thought it would hurt—the Sun. But it was not pain that she felt. It was something much more frightening that took hold across her chest.

Desire.

Desire was not something Lunelle had much experience feeding, but plenty of practice ignoring. She'd certainly encountered its hungry mouth in her younger years when crowns were merely an accessory, the very notion of thrones reserved for her mother alone.

Lunelle had let it wash over her in midnight meetings in palace gardens against the unsteady hands of councilwomen's sons. She'd felt it climb her spine as thick-lashed eyes flashed toward hers across ballrooms, courtiers spinning out in moonshine clouds. She'd given herself over to it a time or two when she was simply unable to distract herself. But mostly, she'd shoved it deep down under rocky shores where she didn't have to stare it full in the face.

As was her duty.

She was the heir to a crown of stars, as ancient as the spray of glittering bodies that inspired it, and she had too much resting on her shoulders to risk distraction.

In the Plutonian Court, though, she found the thought of stepping into the gilded light more than pleasant. It was downright tempting.

"Which one is the oldest?" Lunelle asked, her swirling gaze sweeping the orchard. There must have been a hundred rows of trees, easily. They stretched into oblivion as far as she could tell.

Arcas's lips tilted into a crooked smile. "This way."

He dodged quickly into the thick walls of the pomegranate trees, cutting across a dozen neatly marked rows as she skipped over fallen limbs and rotting fruit to keep up.

"This one," he breathed, stopping short in the middle of a row, his boots crunching against decaying leaves. Lunelle steadied herself at his side, looking up at a towering tree twice the size of the rest, its roots tangled and popping up from the ground.

Her heart twisted as she traced the curled and peeling lines of the bark.

"It's incredible."

Arcas reached for a branch, pulling it gently and letting it spring back up. The night before, he'd been stiff, inhibited by his obvious nerves, and then, of course, panic-stricken as things devolved. But here, hidden between shadows, he was lighter in his step. *Almost* amiable, but she hesitated to bestow him too much generosity too soon.

He was, after all, an enemy to her court until mere days ago, and revealed himself to be far from a seasoned leader last night.

"How is your sister?" Lunelle asked, her voice hardly a whisper.

Arcas glanced at her in the space of a breath, his eyes returning to the tree just as quickly. He tucked his hands behind his back as he stepped closer.

"She is all right," he said. "As well as she can be. I'm not sure she fully understands the threat laid before her."

"I'm certain she does," Lunelle said. "She's a smart girl."

"That she is," he agreed.

Lunelle rubbed the lace of her sleeve between her thumb and forefinger. "And you? Are you all right?"

Arcas did not turn to look at her, his silence loaded with a myriad of emotions she did not understand.

"They say the tree grew from Proserpina's tears as Pluto stole her away."

"Proserpina?" Lunelle asked, unsurprised that he'd avoided her question.

His lips ticked upward in what was dangerously close to a smile as he turned those deep blue eyes on her.

35

"The Goddess of Death. Pluto's bride, though the myths tend to glamorize their marriage. He kidnapped her from her family's orchard and forced her to take his throne."

Lunelle sighed. "That's terrible. Her poor family must have been devastated."

Arcas nodded. "Her mother spent the rest of her days searching for her. But Proserpina grew to tolerate the marriage."

"Until Mercury spotted her."

Mirquios's deep voice shook both Lunelle and Arcas as they moved apart from one another. The tension in the prince's shoulders snapped together immediately, holding him in a rigid grasp as the king edged his way into their conversation.

"Yes," Arcas said, his lips pressing together. "Mercury found her as he traveled the courts."

"He saved her," Mirquios explained to Lunelle, touching the tip of his finger to his lips. "Pluto was selfish—grasping for power he did not understand."

Arcas snorted. "Pluto was a lonely deity, he merely desired to find partnership—"

"Ah, yes, and his selfish desires justified forcing a young woman to wear a crown of bones—"

"I wonder," Lunelle interjected, stepping away from them as she stroked the taut flesh of the nearest pomegranate, "what either of you knows about Proserpina's desires?"

She unleashed a starry glare on the men, the silence following as endless as the gnarled roots dancing between them, reaching for anything to consume, tearing paths through the dust to find any life.

Arcas glanced back toward the palace, his lips parting as if he had something more to add as he rocked forward on his heels, but he gave up. He bowed to her quickly before disappearing into the thicket.

"Predictable retreat," the king muttered.

Lunelle strolled toward the tent, her linen skirts swishing behind her as the king trailed. His dizzying eyes scanned the orchard as they walked—checking the shadows, she realized.

"Are you feeling okay this morning, Princess?"

Lunelle winced. She'd attempted to forget the bulk of last night's activities, but the surge of energy in her veins had kept her up until the Sun made its return, beckoning her to the window as it bled vibrant oranges and reds onto the terrace below her window.

"I've been better," she confessed. "I do not know which took a worse toll—the attacker, or the tea."

Mirquios laughed, the low rumble of it settling between the trees like an early morning fog. "I've had plenty of rough mornings in my day, but this one was particularly horrendous. I think both share the blame."

"I do not think I'll be partaking in any more of the princess's tea parties."

He smiled softly, a genuine thing, but his eyes remained elsewhere. "Certainly not."

They continued slowly, meandering across the orchard. She preferred his company to that of the tent, where half the courtiers were rehashing everything they thought they saw, and the other half were too exhausted to engage beyond tacit smiles.

But the silence between them was surprisingly tolerable, Lunelle noted, irritated at her growing affinity for her sister's fiancé. It was so much easier to dislike him for stealing Astra away, and yet, there was such an easy charm about him, she found it damn near impossible to hold him accountable for it.

And after watching him take control of the courtiers in the hall, she'd grown an ever more regrettable feeling toward the man—respect.

Lunelle picked up her skirt as she hopped over a twisted section of roots, the edges of the pale linen stained with Plutonian dust.

"She wanted to be seen," Mirquios said, tucking his chin toward his chest as he stepped over the roots.

"Pardon?" Lunelle asked.

"Proserpina."

Lunelle shook her head, finding it a tad bit easier to dislike him again. "Of course, because all women naturally desire to be the center of men's attention."

A slow grin cracked over his face as those bright eyes stared back toward the massive tree they'd left behind, rising above the rest of the grove.

"She wanted to be *seen*. Pluto only ever *looked* at her. He never saw her for who she truly was."

Lunelle mulled over his point as they began walking again, the quick anger that rose in her chest dissipating with each step. He plucked a pomegranate from the last tree at the far edge, her mother's stare once again finding her from the tent now that she'd emerged once again.

"You cannot court him," Mirquios said as plainly as one might state the direction of the wind. He pulled at the end of the fruit, struggling to get hold of it.

Lunelle cleared her throat, still stuck on what he'd risen within her mind about Proserpina.

"I'm sorry?"

"Arcas. He's a disaster, Lunelle, you saw so last night. He cannot lead his own modest court, let alone a court as powerful as yours."

She looked away from him, searching the tent, spotting her mother as she laughed with Kahlia. The pomegranate slipped from Mirquios's hands, landing in the grass below with a thud. Lunelle quickly bent at her knees and scooped it up.

She tilted her head, watching the prince as he slinked between tables, a dark cloud rolling between the courtiers. Searching for his sister, she assumed.

"Arcas is green, I'll give you that. But I'm not sure he's a *disaster*."

"There's something dark within him, Lunelle. Something I don't trust."

"I feel it," Lunelle admitted, cracking the pomegranate in half in one quick twist. She handed half to the king, his eyes darting from her hands to her face.

"I loosened it," he said, eyebrows arched as he pointed to her pale hands now stained in blood reds.

"Perhaps Proserpina did not want to be looked at *or* seen," Lunelle mused, flinging the ruby splatter from her fingertips. Mirquios's eyes narrowed, watching as she popped a handful of weeping seeds into her mouth.

"Oh?"

She nodded, shoving the second half into his hands.

"Perhaps she wanted to be feared."

LUNELLE RARELY LET herself slip into such an unbecoming posture, but given the seclusion of the tiny courtyard garden between her chambers and the dining hall, she let herself relax.

She pulled one knee up onto the stone edge above a rippling fountain, adjusting her skirts so they covered anything necessary as she swung the other leg back and forth across the pavers. A wall of lush sapphire roses climbed over her, dripping deep blue petals into the fountain's water.

She counted them as they fell, allowing her mind to focus

on nothing but their spiraling paths lest she devolve into panic.

A shuffling of boots ripped her from petal seventeen.

"Apologies," Arcas offered, holding his palms up before backing toward a marble arch separating the palace from the small paradise.

"Don't apologize! I should be going, anyway," Lunelle said, rising from her perch.

His eyes fell over the cobblestone between them, a softness to his gaze when he wasn't in a dead panic. "I didn't mean to frighten you off," he mumbled, running his fingers through his hair.

Lunelle rolled her eyes as he stepped closer beneath the rose canopy.

"Very little could frighten me off."

Arcas snorted, shrugging his shoulders as he focused his attention on the intricacies of a particularly large bloom near his face.

"I believe it," he said quietly into the petals.

"You avoided my question earlier."

"What question?"

Lunelle wrapped her arms across her body, rocking side to side as she ventured closer.

"I asked if you were okay."

"Ah," he hummed, the pale column of his throat tightening against a response.

"Well," she sighed. Lunelle turned to leave him to his sulking, void of any patience for it. Before she crossed through the arch, she turned, resting her hand on the alabaster marble. "I will not bother asking a third time, if that eases your mind."

Back in her room, she pulled the curtain away from her window to find he was still standing in the same spot, overlooking the swaying roses.

"What is he doing out there?" Lura asked, craning her neck between Lunelle and the glass.

"What all men do when they cannot express a feeling," she scoffed. "He's plotting."

Her tea was cold.

Lunelle had stared at the same page in her novel for far too long, fixated on a turn of phrase she hadn't been able to untangle as her mind swirled with thoughts.

"What do you think?" her mother asked, appearing in her evening wear. Several maidens trailed her, fussing with the buttons on the high neck.

"I think it's a bit overwrought," Lunelle whispered, laying the book on the table before her. "The love interest isn't very believable. He falls for the princess far too quickly."

Oestera paused beside her daughter, laying a hand on her shoulder. As she stopped, so did everything in the room, the chaotic flitting about of maidens pausing for a moment.

"I meant about the prince."

"Arcas?"

Oestera laughed. "Is there another?"

"No," Lunelle breathed. "He's... fine? I suppose? I can't say I'm impressed with how he handled things last night, and he was only slightly more tolerable today."

Oestera sighed. "It wasn't exactly a show of strength, was it? But perhaps with the right leader by his side, he might make better decisions." Oestera's delicate brow curved upward, her thinning skin lifting with plenty of implication.

"I believe Mirquios is spoken for," Lunelle whispered to herself, snorting at her joke. Oestera did not return the amusement, her eyes locked on her daughter's flippant face.

CB WOODS

"Oh," Lunelle said before she could stop herself, sitting at attention. Her movement was so sudden it shook Oestera's hand from her shoulder. "Mother, I—"

"Breathe, darling. We have plenty of time to get to know him. There's still so much to understand about their potential allyship. I did not mean to panic you."

Lunelle's cheeks heated. "Are you not afraid of his lack of..." She searched for the word, her eyes landing on her book as if it might fly off the page. "Refinement? His court is in shambles, and he crumbled the second things got tense. Even Mirquios thinks him a mess."

"Mirquios has been on his own throne for not even five years. You are all young and reckless in your own unique ways. And when he brings your sister back to his court, he'll have his own shambles to contend with."

Lunelle's lips drew into a tight line. "I do not think that's fair—"

"You mistake my remark for criticism," Oestera said. She did not elaborate as Lunelle waited in the silence.

She leaned her chin on her palm. "I will court him if you truly think it the most strategic option, but I do not find him to be a particularly compelling ruler, Mother."

Oestera exhaled, something stirring within her gaze as she moved back toward the maidens waiting patiently.

She did not offer anything more to her daughter before dinner.

42

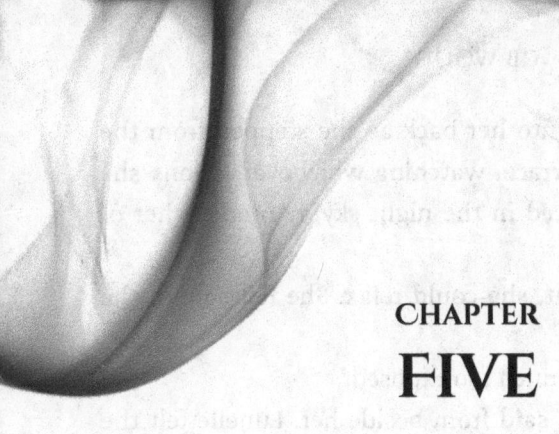

L unelle's neck ached as she forced herself to listen to another round of debate between the courtiers.

They dined in the ballroom that evening, the doors scrolled back to let the pleasant breeze act as a sort of current, carrying them through the night despite the near-constant darting looks from guards and sentries of all backgrounds watching every door.

They had been deep in discussion all day, broken for the afternoon, and immediately resumed as dinner plates hit the table. Intercourt battalion placements, preemptive strikes, and intelligence gathered through any means necessary. All important considerations, of course, but not once had anyone brought up the glaring factor that kept her from being able to pull in a full breath.

War was going to cost lives, no matter how well-aligned their allegiances were.

She'd sat and listened to them argue back and forth all night before she finally caved and scooted her chair back from the table, ready to escape the tension for just a moment. Her mother's eyes pressed into her back as she stepped from the dining hall onto the terrace, watching whichever Moons she could find as they danced in the night sky, reminding her of home.

In the cover of night, she could relax. She felt safe in the darkness.

In the Sun, she was much too exposed.

"I am better," Arcas said from beside her. Lunelle felt the air tighten with his unnerving energy a moment ago, but she'd done her best to ignore it.

"What?" she asked, twisting to lean against the delicately carved marble banister overlooking another lush orchard.

His sapphire eyes did not meet hers, and instead examined the curled hem of her gown.

"You asked how I was. I am better. Not great, but better."

Lunelle's chin dipped in a shallow nod, processing the asynchronous conversation.

"You seem to be the troubled one this evening," Arcas said.

"I fear we're all too wrapped up in how to hold onto our power that we've neglected to consider who will pay the price of our war," she said quietly, staring at her fingers as she twisted them around one another. "Not once has anyone ventured to discuss what allying with your court means for the Inner Court Army. They'll suffer beyond anything the monarchs at that table ever will."

The prince's lips lifted in a crooked grin, so similar to that of her sister's when she sensed something Lunelle couldn't.

"I'm curious," he said, pulling at the edge of his sleeve. "When you take the throne, what will be your first act?"

Lunelle's eyes narrowed as Arcas circled her. "I suppose that depends on what happens here."

"I suppose it does."

Arcas leaned beside Lunelle, far enough away that he did

not encroach on her space, a consideration she appreciated. His eyes swept the trees below, something she couldn't identify bubbling just under the surface of his skin.

"What would *your* first act be? If you ruled over all the sentiments and spirits of the Living Courts, if anything you did had a ripple effect across dreams and nightmares... what would it be?"

Arcas closed his eyes, just for a moment. His sky-blue knuckles rapped against the stone banister, gentle thuds matching the pace of her heart. Just when the silence became so heavy, so unbearably long that she was about to answer for him, he spoke.

"I'd crown someone else."

A wide smile broke across his lips, but it burned out quickly as Lunelle's eyes turned on him, lit with a disgust that forced him back a step.

"You hold your cities, your people in such little regard that you'd rather pawn them off on someone else than work hard for them? Nearly unchecked power, and instead of using it for good, you throw it away because what? It's *scary*?"

Arcas tilted his head. "You do not know *scary*, Princess." He stepped closer. "Look at me. Look at my court. Do you think I'm ignorant of my situation? Blind to my ineptitude? My father pillaged these cities and left entire villages for dead rather than go without a single luxury. Do you know how I ended up on the throne, Lunelle? Has the gossip reached the Lunar Court's lofty halls?"

He paced around her in a wide arc, his lips curled in a snarl as he spoke.

"I am my father's *third* son. My father, my *merciless* father, beheaded my eldest brother for treason, and the next, he poisoned slowly over the course of a year just to prove he was weak. And do you know their crimes? Their grave missteps that cost them their lives at the hands of their own flesh? They wanted to grant citizenship to the Sirens of Sephonia, but because they were all female, my father did not see the point. So he *killed* them."

He stopped beside her again, leaning his back against the rail and folding his arms. The bronze buttons at the end of his sleeve caught their matching pairs at his chest, tugging the dense navy velvet.

"I should have been an ambassador somewhere, just interesting enough to make me forget my rotten luck at being born the last son, and yet here I stand, crumbling under a crown I never wanted to touch." His eyes glazed over as he looked over his shoulder at the orchard. "It digs into my skull and whispers nightmarish cruelties to me in every damned reflection I have the misfortune of coming across."

Lunelle swallowed. "Arcas—"

"And now," he continued, fighting for a steady breath. "Now, I've been cast aside by the Outer Courts, forced to beg my way into the Inner Courts, and instead of focusing on improving things for my people, I'm going to be thrust into a war we cannot afford in riches or in bodies. I set aside my pride and invite the most powerful people in the entire system to my home and, on the first night, I leave dinner soaked in blood with my tail between my legs."

He exhaled, waving a hand between them.

"So yes, Princess, I'd crown someone else. Perhaps the Mercurian king. He seems more than suitable for the job."

"I'm sorry," Lunelle whispered. Her pulse raced beneath her skin. She moved toward the ballroom, needing a few steps to shake off some of the energy she'd absorbed from him. It was a dark thing, soaked in ancient lust and wrath. "I did not know—"

"No. You didn't. Apologies, Lunelle, I should not have been so free with my words—"

"No! No, don't apologize. I actually appreciate seeing a side of you that isn't so... stiff." She frowned. It wasn't the right word. But he seemed to understand.

"The last season has been hard. I was blindsided by my father's sudden Descent. I was unprepared for every aspect of the throne before the Solar Court began their plans. And then the rebellion took root—I feel as if I'm floundering at every turn."

He inhaled, the tip of the breath shuddering under his anxieties, the misery of his station carved into shallow lines around his eyes.

Lunelle took in the real Arcas for the first time. Not just the misguided prince who couldn't seem to get his priorities straight, but the little boy within him, terrified to be in any position of power. His lips twisted into a worried knot, and his chest sank in. She paced toward him, her sparkling lavender train dragging softly against the stones of the terrace.

"Arcas?"

His head snapped toward her, a softness at the edge of his eyes that betrayed his brooding exterior. He was not all Shadow. There was a lightness within him, wrestling with the weight of his lineage.

She edged closer, waiting for his eyes to pour into hers, waiting for him to shake the swirling thoughts distracting him so he'd hear her clearly.

"You need to look the child within you in the eyes and tell him to grow up."

The prince's nostrils flared, his gaze widening as her words bounced against his chest.

"Oh," he said, clearly taken aback. "I... I suppose I was expecting something... something—"

"Soft?" Lunelle asked, her delicate brow carving into an amused arch.

"No," he started. "No, well, perhaps a bit less harsh. You've been much less... blunt in our meetings."

Lunelle's jaw snapped, the threads she wove so carefully between her lips in the name of peace unraveling.

"I am quiet, Arcas, but it is not because I do not have anything to say." She rolled her shoulders back, breathing into a space between the strong muscles she'd neglected to stretch for too long. "There is an advantage in keeping your mouth shut and your ears open—in watching. Waiting. You can learn so much in the number of breaths someone can tolerate without speaking, in the way their hands tick as they itch for their turn to speak. It's shocking how much a single glance can give away."

She inhaled, watching the curl of his fingers against his thigh as he made the calculations of what she'd seen, what she knew about him that even he didn't.

She continued, "Someone told me recently there is strength in silence, but I don't think he realized how right he was. There is truth in silence, and truth is power."

Arcas glanced over her shoulders, the muscles in the side of his neck tightening as he searched for words. After grasping at a billion rebuttals, he settled on a simple, "Thank you."

Lunelle's head cocked to one side. It was her turn to be surprised.

"You're welcome," she said reflexively.

"No, truly, Lunelle. Thank you for rattling me." He leaned onto his elbows against the railing. "You are right, about many things, but especially about my need to grow up. I'm not a child. I'm a leader, and I've been scrambling to prove that to everyone but myself. If I don't believe in myself, who should?"

Lunelle nodded, her eyes darting across the terrace as

dinner ended and moved into more spirited pursuits. The high lilt of a flute bounced off the domed hall within, tickling something in her spine.

Arcas straightened, taller than she'd seen him before, his lips parting as he strung a question together.

"Would you like to dance, Princess?"

She glanced at his palm, reflecting the dark blues of the roses swimming against the night sky above, and surprised herself by resting her hand in his. She imagined he'd pull her into the hall, under the glimmering lanterns, but instead, he fell back on his heel, pulling her forward in a soft initiation, his hand gliding hers through the air in a wide circle as he spun her.

It was harder to hear any of the percussive elements of the music inside, but Lunelle did not have to fret about that.

Arcas was surprisingly capable of keeping time.

He wound her around and into him, carrying her hands on the slope of his forearms as he turned them about.

"I must admit, I'm curious. What else has the quiet taught you about me?"

Lunelle thought about this as he swept her away from the banister and into the shadows beyond the ballroom.

Where no one would stare, she realized.

"Do you really want to know?" she asked, her eyes locked to his.

"It's hard to hurt a third son's feelings, though you've come close this evening," he chuckled.

She swayed along with him, turning over the notes she'd carefully collected in her head for anything particularly interesting. Yallara's wounded face appeared in her mind, desperate for her brother to hear her out.

"You love your sister too much," she shared, observing the flex in his jaw. "You inhibit her with your protective instincts.

Any time she opens her mouth to speak, you dismiss her. But I believe it's to keep her safe, not silent."

Arcas snorted, his lips pulling into a crooked smile. "She hates it."

"I know the temptation. I am an elder sibling, too. She's young, but she cares, Arcas. Let her test the waters, she'll learn to swim."

He nodded as he spun her away from him, the delicate lace along her hem sweeping over his boots.

"What else?"

She chewed on her lip. "Hmm. Kahlia doesn't respect you. You haven't spent enough time appealing to their softer sensibilities. The Venusians are a people who worship at the altar of love herself, they need to see passion from you, they need to know you care deeply about your court and our cause."

He considered this, his hand dropping around her waist as he twisted her in a tight arc, looping her arm over her head and spinning her again.

"One more," he murmured.

"You're a glutton for punishment," Lunelle laughed.

Arcas stopped her spin, holding her crystalline gaze as his fingertips grazed the seam at her waist.

"Perhaps," he admitted. "Punish me, then."

"I am sorry you lost your brothers," Lunelle said quietly. "But the moment they Descended, you ceased to be a third son. The crown of Pluto rests on your head. You need to show us it rests on more than desperation."

Arcas tucked his hands behind his back, his eyes flickering over the terrace as a quiet slope overtook his lips. The shadows from before retreated, giving way to the lights of the ballroom.

He swallowed, brushing his coat as he looked away from her.

"Thank you for the dance."

He gestured toward the ballroom, where her mother was hovering with two glasses of wine, attempting to appear uninterested in whatever Lunelle was doing.

He cleared his throat as she stepped away, drawing her attention over her shoulder.

"For the record, you may hurt my feelings anytime, Lunelle."

She sighed, a gentle smile threatening to reveal the tingle she felt in her spine.

"Remember you said that, Your Highness."

SHE WAS NEARLY BACK to her chambers when her mother caught her arm.

"You didn't want to stay for another round of cards?" Oestera's eyes glowed with a delight Lunelle recognized. One that made her uneasy.

"I am quite exhausted," she said.

"All that dancing, I suppose," Oestera mused, her brows raised as they wandered through the dark hall.

"Do you think you're being subtle?" Lunelle asked, the ache in her neck returning.

Oestera stopped walking, her face falling as she looked her daughter over.

"I was not trying to be. You know, Lunelle, duty does not always have to be painful. If you can find even a little joy in this, seize it."

Lunelle chewed on her lower lip, stretching that knot in her neck, begging it to release.

"We can discuss it more tomorrow, darling. Get some rest," her mother said, disappearing into her bedroom.

As Lunelle pushed her own door inward, the heavy boots of

the Mercurians echoed through the hall, buzzing in a large group as they returned to their chambers.

"Princess!" Mirquios called, his bright eyes mellowed by the haze of a few too many glasses of wine.

"Good evening," she said quietly as he broke away from his court. He leaned against the meticulously tiled wall outside of her door and folded his arms, a playful smile tugging at his full lips.

It was irritating, actually, how ridiculously handsome he was. It should have been enough to be born a king, but she knew all too well that monarchs had a tendency toward greed.

Mirquios spoke in a low tone, laced with an amusement she resented immediately.

"I hope you'll forgive me for eavesdropping earlier. I stepped onto the terrace for some fresh air, and I couldn't help but overhear a rather vicious execution of a certain prince."

Lunelle's cheeks heated, trying to think back to what exactly she might have said to Arcas.

She waved her hand between them, clearing her conscience. "He insisted I tell him what I really think!"

The king chuckled. "I was not judging. I rather enjoyed it."

"Oh, well, if *you* enjoyed it, then I suppose I should just go around dressing down every dignitary I find," she huffed, rubbing at the pain in her neck. "I could start with you, if you so desire, Your Majesty?"

An even deeper laugh rumbled in his broad chest.

Ridiculously broad, Lunelle thought.

"You and your sister have a talent for eviscerating men, you know that?"

Her heart twisted around itself, an angry tide crashing against her ribs. "Fire and ice both burn in the right circumstances."

"I did not mean to offend—"

Lunelle's frigid glare silenced him. She shoved her door open with her hip, backing into the slim opening.

"You made a good point with him this evening, for what it's worth," he said, pushing against the wall and stepping away. "When I told you there was strength in silence, I had no idea how right I was."

Lunelle huffed. *I imagine the list of things you do not know is long, indeed,* she thought as she pushed the door closed.

Astra would have said it, loudly and without hesitation.

They were different in at least that way.

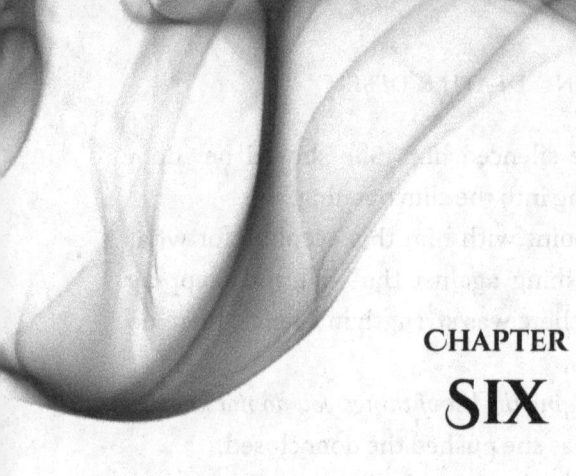

CHAPTER
SIX

L unelle rushed so quickly into her chambers that she failed to see the unnerved look on Lura's face.

She flopped onto her bed, feeling rather like a petulant teenager instead of a fully grown soon-to-be-queen as she shook off Mirquios's prideful grin. She'd resented being compared to her sister—that's what bothered her, she realized. It was natural, of course, for people to do it.

Gods knew the Lunar Courtiers loved nothing more than to hold them up beside one another, but it was a game they both lost.

Astra was nothing like Lunelle, and Lunelle was nothing like Astra, and the court was all the better for it. They would never understand the talents each of them possessed, forever reducing them both to Fire and Ice.

She could have told him so. She could have given him the same treatment Arcas received—she'd kept a litany of observations about the Mercurians' behaviors should Astra ever need a reason to change her mind.

Not that minds changed once Tethered, of course.

She resented something else almost as much as the comparison—the lilt to his tone, the suggestion that he was special for seeing something within her she'd always known about herself.

He may have been the first person to say it aloud, but she'd realized years ago her power was in the held breaths of courtiers, in the things they do not say.

"This is useless to dwell on," she muttered to herself as she rolled over, flipping her metallic locks across her shoulders. Something crunched beneath her as she tossed. She sat up, sliding her hand between the bedspread and her stomach, finding a small envelope with her name scrawled across the front.

Her eyes darted to the two maidens by the door.

"Would you like a moment, Princess?" Lura asked. Her pale amethyst eyes fell directly on the envelope.

She'd been waiting for Lunelle to discover it.

Lunelle would have liked a moment. She would have liked several moments.

"Yes, Lura. Thank you," Lunelle said. Her finger was already midway across the seal, cracking the navy wax with one quick swipe as they shuffled into the next room.

Princess Lunelle Aurellis,

It is with great honor that the Plutonian Court receives the next Lunar queen. We've heard promising things about your wise heart. Surely, you must realize, all is not well within the courts. It is up to the future generation of leaders to right the wrongs.

Meet us at midnight tomorrow at The Underworld and see a side of the courts you've never dreamed of.

55

Beneath the elegant script bled an inked dagger pierced through a crown and a short line in a language Lunelle did not recognize, though she was fluent in several.

She pursed her lips, a flicker of something heated within her and caught her off guard. Folding the parchment inward, she found a space between her journals to slip the note. Though she wasn't sure how she knew, she was certain it wasn't for public consumption. *The Underworld*, she thought, a chill racing between the tissue of her spine like a fish swimming upriver.

She shook her head. Nothing good could come of anything of the sort, especially after last night's showing.

"Lura," she called. "Can you draw a bath for me?" She rolled her shoulders back, stretching her neck, trying to find somewhere to keep all of the tension. It was always moments like those she wondered how her sister kept from burning down entire cities—the tension within her certainly felt flammable enough to ignite fires.

"Already drawn, Princess," Lura smiled as she poked her head back into the room.

"You're an angel," Lunelle said quietly, chewing on the edge of her thumb.

"Princess?" Lura stepped into the room, glancing over her shoulder for any other ears as she dropped her tone. She pulled nervously at the edge of her robes.

"What is it, Lura?" Lunelle's eyes softened as she stood.

"I wasn't being nosy, I promise," Lura started. She folded her knee beneath her as she sank onto the arm of a chair across from Lunelle. "But I saw who dropped the note, and, well, I recognized the insignia on her vest."

Lunelle's lips parted, but she held her question.

Lura's eyes darted across the room toward the door.

"She was a rebel, Princess. A Nova Rebel."

Lunelle sat back on her bed. She'd heard of the Nova Rebels in whispers during meetings with her mother—they were causing quite the problem down in Ellume, back in the Lunar Court. She would never admit it to the queen, but she had been curious more than once about their mission.

And whether, given the opportunity to hear them out, she might actually agree with a portion of it.

Arcas had mentioned the rebels last night, but Yallara hadn't seemed convinced their attacker was part of the group. The heat rose along her spine at the very notion of subverting her mother—her court—to take a meeting with them. The thought had simmered in her muscles for years now, but this note—this invitation—forced them to scream to the surface of her skin.

She'd seen the rot within her own court and knew how it spread to the rest.

"A rebel," she repeated, avoiding Lura's face.

She whispered, "I know your mother and Ivonne are against them—"

Lunelle held up a hand. "My mother and I share many similarities, but not all," she said aloud for perhaps the first time in her entire life. But she felt it then—taking hold somewhere between lung and heart—it would not be the last.

"How *much* do you know about the Novas, Lura?"

Lura looked toward the stack of journals on her nightstand, finding the one that contained the note. "Enough."

"I try not to pit our maidens against one another..." Lunelle drew her knees to her chest, her mind turning over. "So do not feel pressured to answer. But you speak with Ameera often—if there's any whiff of rebellion in the Lunar Court, surely my sister is involved, no?"

Lura considered this. Of course, maidens talked, but Ameera had always been tight-lipped about Astra's comings and goings—no matter how much the other maidens begged for even a morsel of the Fire Queen's antics.

"I can't be sure," she said. "I could inquire?"

"No," Lunelle sighed. "I'll write to her. Not that she's any good at keeping up with her correspondence." She chuckled. "Perhaps I should write to Ameera after all."

Lura shrugged—though Ameera was loyal to her princess, she and Lunelle had developed a kinship in Astra's absence.

"Be considerate of what you commit to ink, Princess. The Rift is not as safe as it once was."

Lunelle nodded. "Do not speak of this to anyone else."

"Of course."

Lunelle slipped under the warm water in the tub, letting her stiff shoulders soften despite her mind only tangling into a deeper knot. She closed her eyes, resting her neck against the bronze edge, feeling a pull on her mind as she spiraled downward.

She was unable to resist the sweet melody that pulled her further within herself.

Her eyes fluttered open, a busy tavern materializing around her. The scent of thick mead and sweet wine tickled her nostrils as the dimly lit room faded into her consciousness. A few men sat at the table before her, plucking away at plates of something that smelled like home.

"Princess?"

Lunelle spun, face to face with a broad set of shoulders. A warm gaze settled softly over cerulean skin. She jolted, unsure where she was or how she'd arrived there.

Or how in the Nether the man before her could see her.

The sharp start to her heart shoved her back through space and time and plopped her unceremoniously back into the water, surprisingly cold to her after just a few moments.

"Princess?" Lura asked again. "Is everything well?"

Lunelle must have looked as drained of color as she felt. "Um, yes. Yes, of course. I think I fell asleep."

She spent the rest of her evening allowing her eyelids to flutter shut, waiting for the spiraling drain to begin.

To her disappointment or relief—she had no way of telling —she remained firmly in her bed, staring at the journals on her nightstand, the slightly larger gap between the middle volume taunting her with its tempting ideas.

CHAPTER
SEVEN

"Yallara!"

Lunelle hadn't expected to see anyone in the far wing of the palace, but she was delighted to see the princess back out and about. She'd only briefly seen her at meals and, even then, Yallara had avoided speaking with anyone.

Not that Lunelle had been much more sociable. She'd spent her last few mornings tucked into the corner of a small library, lost in one of her novels, enjoying the peace and quiet.

Yallara swept into the room with her own book, clearly surprised to find her favorite room in the palace occupied.

"I see I've been found out. This room has the *best* view of the Plutonian silver pools."

Lunelle glanced out the window. A dozen small pools ran from the window down the hill, liquid moonlight slipping from one to another in a rhythmic breath. She found herself lost in their whispers for nearly an hour on her first morning there.

"They are quite something."

"I'm sure nothing compared to the Lunar Court's views."

"We're both quite fortunate, I think," Lunelle returned. She leaned back in the soft armchair as Yallara settled into the settee across from her.

"Do you mind if I join you?"

"Not at all," she said. Astra would have leaned over, demanding to know what Yallara was reading. If she liked it, should she read it too? But Lunelle was happy to let the princess live in her own world as she stared at the map, distracting herself from the weight of her decisions as a certain invitation came to mind.

"Can I ask you something?"

"Of course," Lunelle said.

Yallara tucked her legs beneath her in a soft posture that immediately eased Lunelle's tension. She was shaken, of course, but she was still the bubbly princess Lunelle had met in the garden upon her arrival.

"I've heard rumors about the Lunar Court."

Lunelle twisted toward her. "We can't read minds," she said stoically. It was always the first question anyone asked.

Yallara's chin dropped as a shocked gasp slipped between her lips. "Are you sure?"

Lunelle giggled, crossing one leg over the other.

"Well, I suppose in some ways we can. My sister and I, for example, are able to communicate within the confines of our minds. But that's quite uncommon these days."

"It wasn't always?" Yallara asked.

"No," Lunelle said, her eyes dropping to her hands as she twisted her fingers. "It wasn't."

"Your sister..." Yallara looked toward the door of the study, half open to the hall. They were far enough away from most of the action, but Lunelle appreciated her discretion. "Is it true she breathes fire?"

"She's not a dragon," Lunelle scoffed. "But she does have some... heated tendencies. Yes."

Yallara sighed. "Fascinating."

"Plutonians have their own peculiarities, I'm sure."

Yallara set her book aside, leaning her elbow on the back of the couch.

"We've all sorts of strange creatures, I suppose. The Sirens, the Harpies. There are occultists in the city. The proximity to death draws them from all over the courts. The Descendants reside in caves along the cliffs."

"The Descendants?"

Yallara's eyes moved toward the window, searching for the words.

"They are not human, but nor are they gods. They're believed to come from somewhere between here and the Court Below—half alive, half dead. They have a foot in each world."

Lunelle held her breath, the thought quite paralyzing.

Yallara's sapphire eyes wandered back toward her. "Things seem to be shifting quickly, don't you think? Every morning I wake up and it feels like another piece of some horrible puzzle has fallen into place."

Lunelle nodded, understanding her all too well. She decided now was as good a time as any to test the waters.

"We've had an increase in rebel activity in our cities. Our courtiers are unsettled, to say the least." And she had done exactly that, said the least she could on the subject in the hopes that it might spark something within Yallara worth noting.

"What sort of rebels?" Her onyx brows tucked inward, her eyes darting to the door.

Lunelle ran her finger over her invitation's severed seal, letting the cracked wax warm against her fingertip.

"I'm not sure," Lunelle lied. "We haven't been able to infiltrate and identify who they're in service to."

Yallara's tongue pushed at the edge of her lips, debating on how much to reveal to the demigoddess before her.

"My brother is cautious with my exposure to what happens outside of these opulent walls." She stretched her neck, eyes slipping from the window to Lunelle's face. "But I hear things, of course."

Lunelle expected more to flow from the young princess's mind, but she seemed hesitant to divulge more.

So Lunelle did what she did best.

She waited.

"He thinks I don't hear the whispers amongst the soldiers as they return from our southern territories," Yallara finally admitted, her velvet voice falling into a hushed whisper. "We've lost control of Charon and Sephonia. It's why he was so sure that the man the other night—"

"Hold that thought," Lunelle said, the hair on the back of her neck prickling as she heard the clamor she'd learned to associate with Arcas and his unending posse of advisors and bodyguards bouncing off the hall. She rose from her seat and crossed the library slowly, like a beam of moonlight brushing silently over the ornate rug. She wrapped her fingers around the bronze handle and pushed it shut slowly, aware that a slamming door drew more ears than hushed gossip.

She turned to Yallara. "Your brother and his council certainly make their presence known."

Yallara giggled. "Arcas is not what one would call... graceful."

Lunelle tucked herself onto the plush couch across from Yallara, mirroring her relaxed position in the hopes it would ingratiate her to the young princess. She wouldn't call the prince gracious, she supposed, but he wasn't without a certain air about him.

"What *would* you call him?" Lunelle asked.

"Scared," Yallara laughed, her gemstone gaze hardening as she stretched her shoulders. "I'm curious what *you* would call him?"

Lunelle folded her hands in her lap, weaving her fingers together as she thought about the smartest answer. The answer her mother would give.

"I think your brother is up against a myriad of forces that would scare any man."

"But not a demigoddess," Yallara snorted. "Excellent, Princess. Your mother would be proud."

Lunelle dropped her shoulders, melting her posture into something less curated, less calculated.

"Scared leaders make brash choices in order to appear decisive."

"So you agree, then? You think he's scared?"

"I know he is," Lunelle sighed. "Because we all are, Yallara. Anyone who claims otherwise is worse than scared—they're arrogant. Arrogant leaders get innocent people killed."

The notion seemed to appease Yallara and unlock a small chamber within her chest, the secrets flowing much more easily.

"There are rebels in the palace," she whispered. "He cannot purge them no matter how hard he tries."

Lunelle's neck flushed. "Why get rid of them? Is he so unwilling to hear them out?"

Yallara's eyes widened. "And start a civil war on the back of an inter-court conflict? The city streets would be soaked in blood by the Solstice."

"Not necessarily," Lunelle countered, squeezing her nails

into her palms. "Couldn't there be a peaceful transition brokered? Work with the rebels and not against them?"

"The Plutonian elite have squashed any whiff of rebellion for centuries, Lunelle. This is not a new battle. Think of your own court's nobility. Would the demigoddesses of Lunaria release their power quietly?"

Lunelle inhaled slowly. *No*, she knew, *they would not.*

"He has a good heart," Yallara murmured, her eyes falling again to the window beside them. "I hope you see that."

"Does it matter how good his heart is if it never circulates to his mind?" Lunelle asked.

The princess tossed her a crooked smile—so similar to her brother's bemused smirk.

"Perhaps if someone could quicken his pulse," she whispered.

A warmth spread over Lunelle's chest, blossoming through her lungs and into her ribs. She'd suspected, of course, when they came here that things would move in this direction, but it still felt strange to imagine.

"You *are* going to court him, aren't you?"

Lunelle thought about this. The word *court* felt silly. It implied action on her part, but she knew—and she was sure Yallara did, too—that her mother would ultimately make the call. Oestera was still on the throne, still the queen. Whatever she decided would go.

The library door cracked inward as Arcas slithered through —his face pale, his breath rapid.

"Oh," he sighed, catching Lunelle's eyes. "Apologies, ladies, this room is usually unoccupied."

"As it will be again soon," Yallara teased, rising from her seat. "I've business to attend to," she announced, winking at Lunelle as she skipped lightly from the room. Lunelle sat straighter in her chair, sliding her ankles toward the floor slowly, as if the prince might not notice her relaxed posture.

"I can arrange for a chaperone," Arcas said quietly, tilting his head toward the library door.

"A chaperone?" Lunelle asked. "Are we going somewhere?"

"No," Arcas answered, setting his books on the writing desk against the wall. "Only, I thought, if we're to be here together..."

Lunelle's eyes flitted about the room. "Are you threatened by me, Your Highness?"

Arcas's pale blue lips tightened into a flat line. "Of course not, Princess, I—"

"I am teasing," she said softly, blushing as she realized her humor did not land. "We do not require chaperones in the Lunar Court. I was unaware the Plutonians had such customs."

Arcas arched his onyx brows, settling into an armchair across from her, still posed as if someone might show up to paint a portrait, but his lips relaxed.

"We do not," he said. "I was always told that Lunarian women practice strict rules of engagement within courtships—"

Lunelle jolted. Yallara suggesting it was one thing, but Arcas was another entirely.

"Courtships?"

"I am not implying—well, I suppose I am. Gods above," he muttered. "Forget I said it."

Lunelle turned her eyes away from him, afraid that his bumbling nature was beginning to warm to her as endearing.

"If I *were* to court you, not saying that I am..."

"Understood."

"...I'm afraid I've no clue what you're referencing as far as rules of engagement."

Arcas rose from his seat, darting to the wall of bookshelves behind her.

"It's somewhere here," he whispered as he scanned dozens of bound spines. "Ah! Yes." He tilted a deep amethyst volume from a shelf packed with Inner Court writings and handed it to her.

"*A Delicate Dance: A Complete History of Lunarian Courtship Rituals,*" Lunelle read as she thumbed through the pages. "Arcas, where in the Nether did you get this?"

Arcas shrugged, settling back into his chair. "It's a commonly referenced text amongst the nobility here."

Lunelle battled back an unbecoming laugh as she read the section headings, dozens of strange rules she'd never heard of before, documented in bold lettering.

"We don't practice a single one of these," Lunelle said through a stunned giggle.

Chaperones are required in any room in which a Lunarian woman is present. If a Lunarian woman is found to have touched a suitor with her bare hand, she must engage in ritualistic cleansing until her next completed cycle in the Lunar Temple. Lunarian women are docile in nature and easily frightened, one must always send a female attending into the room to signal your presence before following.

"None of this is even remotely true, Arcas."

"I thought it was strange that you danced with me so willingly," he admitted. "But I thought perhaps since we were outdoors and within view of others—"

"Where is this from?" she asked, rotating the book in her hands. A gilded icon shimmered at the base of the spine. She held it close, rotating it to catch the light from the window. Lunelle snorted.

"Arcas, this was written by an Ellumian satirist." She held the book up and flipped to the final page, where the author had included a brief biography and explanation. "This author must warn any readers of this handbook that attempting to abide by these rules will only result in one of the deepest wounds known to the Living Courts—a Lunarian woman's pity."

His pale blue complexion flushed violet as blood rushed to his cheeks.

"I am late for a meeting," he mumbled, snatching the book from her hands and tossing it into a bronze basket beside the desk. He hadn't been the subject of her pity before—but he certainly forced it from her as he stomped out of the room rather like a child.

G*ods*, she was tired.

The only thing keeping her eyes open was finally receiving a letter from her sister after weeks of disconcerting silence. Lunelle knew her mother received a detailed report from the High Priestess and her many eyes and ears each morning, but she also knew her sister.

If eyes were watching her, Astra was well aware and acted accordingly.

It was a sparse communication at best, rife with complaints of the king's commander, Luxuros, which was not the least bit surprising. She'd watched their few interactions closely, alarmed by the heat searing beneath the commander's skin.

But if Astra hadn't beheaded him upon entry into the palace, Lunelle trusted he wasn't a threat.

Yet.

She'd just finished her final grievance in a lengthy list—*the commander doesn't even laugh at her jokes, for gods' sakes*—when the swift movement of a pale green cape caught her eye.

Mirquios rushed past the library, his boots shuffling against the slick marble of the Plutonian halls. Something in the way he held his shoulders raised the hair on the back of her neck, tickling that space in her soul reserved for truly emergent situations. She argued with herself as she attempted to drag the pen along her response, but an insistent tug within her chest drew her from her seat.

He was in a hurry, that much was clear. As she left the comfort of the library, she saw but a mere slip of his cape curl around the corner. Lunelle followed, her eyes scraping the halls as he darted from the safety of the palace through a side door.

"Princess!"

Lunelle jerked, a silent swear ramming against the side of her head as she found Lura's wide eyes peering at her from the Divine Mother's altar at the end of the hall. She stopped as Mirquios disappeared into the night air.

"You seem shaken," Lura observed.

"I am... not. I was... where do you think the Mercurian king is off to in such a panic?"

Lura's irises flashed toward the door. She'd heard a pair of boots scuffling by quite hurriedly as she prayed, but she hadn't caught who they belonged to.

"I'm sure I do not know," she said, suspicion crawling over her. In all her years serving at Lunelle's side, she'd never once seen her so agitated.

Lunelle's heart raced against her judgment, and her judgment was losing its lead.

"I think he's in trouble."

"Princess, you should get back to your—"

"No, thank you," she said simply. Her heart gave a satisfied leap at the decision resolving in her mind. She twisted from

Lura and took off for the door, the night air greeting her with a balmy kiss on her bare shoulders.

"Princess!" Lura hissed. "*Lunelle*," she tried as her careful politeness failed.

"Either forget you saw me or come along," Lunelle called over her shoulder, a rush so unfamiliar within her she nearly felt as if she'd had another cup of Yallara's tea.

Lura sighed, glancing toward the guard at the door.

"I need your cloak," she said flatly. Their nose scrunched, sapphire eyes narrowing. "Do *you* want to be the one dealing with the Lunar queen when the princess has been ambushed in the middle of your city?"

The guard looked at Lura's outstretched hand, then over to Lunelle, who cut a quick path through the garden, and came back to Lura, their shoulders sinking as they shimmied off their black cloak.

"Your service to the Lunar Crown will be remembered," Lura said quickly as she broke into a sprint to catch up with her charge.

Lunelle's pulse drummed against her wrists as the evening breeze seemed to sweep up from behind her and bless her first step from the palace garden and into the cobbled streets of Pluto's sprawling city, Charon. Guards eyed her as Lura chased on her tail, nearly toppling over her when she stopped to search for any sign of Mirquios in the darkened streets.

Blue flames danced within lamps against gray stone buildings as her eyes locked on that cape, now joined with two others. The Mercurians hustled down a dark alley.

"Princess, *what* are we doing?"

Two sets of sapphire eyes glanced at the Lunarians from across the street. They stuck out terribly. Lura tossed the Plutonian's cloak out in a gentle arc, pulling it over Lunelle's shoulders.

She inhaled sharply as Lura's fingers wove the ribbon into a tight bow.

"If my sister is going to be married to the king, we should know what sort of dealings he's involved in, shouldn't we?"

Lura stared silently at her princess.

"I'm not a madwoman, Lura, I felt what I felt and I listened to it!"

Her maiden's lips wobbled into a smile.

"I don't believe I've ever once related to the bags under Ameera's eyes before today." Lura held Lunelle's gaze, searching for anything to hold onto. It was there, buried between her duties to her throne and her sister, the need to see this through. "Let's go, then, we're losing them."

Lura followed Lunelle through the streets, slipping into shadows and hazy fog as it settled over the city like a thick blanket. Plutonians still out at this hour tracked them as they jogged, wondering what in the worlds they may be witnessing.

The Mercurians were nearly out of sight ahead, but Lunelle and Lura pressed on. When they banked left down a street bellowing with loud laughter and distant music, they stopped behind a crumbling building, the sour scent of old hops and ale floating over them. Mirquios's courtiers stepped through an ancient wooden door first, his eyes sweeping over the street before he disappeared.

"It's a tavern," Lura said as they scooted down the uneven stone path. "They're just having a night out."

Lunelle shook her head, that strange gnaw in her soul still begging her forward.

"No, I don't believe so. The way he was looking at who might see him, something must be happening inside."

"We *cannot* go in there," Lura declared.

"I thought it was just a tavern," Lunelle whispered.

Lura snorted, crossing her delicate arms.

"Princess, have you ever set foot in a city tavern before?"

Lunelle glared at her but moved another breath closer still to the door. She could smell the warm caress of bread, the music grew louder with each step. Lura snatched her elbow, begging her to come back away from the door, where anyone could step out at any moment.

"There are dangers in these streets, Lunelle. We shouldn't be here."

Lunelle, for perhaps the first time in her entire life, ignored someone warning her. She edged toward the tavern, a wave of laughter rising from the window carved in the side. Lunelle tucked herself against the pane, allowing one eye to slip around the opening. In the middle, Mirquios sat at a table piled high with plates and pitchers, several folks in black leather speaking in quiet tones. Or perhaps they spoke at a normal level, but the music from the stage in the corner drowned them out.

Mirquios listened intently, his bright eyes transfixed by whatever the man with a thick sheet of black hair said, their heads both nodding in agreement.

She recognized the man beside him.

Luxuros.

Mirquios raised a hand and gestured toward a colorful map on the far wall, and that's when she caught it.

The dagger-pierced crown was emblazoned on his wrist in red ink.

"Lura," Lunelle gasped, looking for her maiden. Lura remained rooted to the corner of the street, unwilling to further entangle herself. Lunelle rushed toward her, pointing toward the window.

"They're *rebels*," Lunelle hissed, confused by the delight that simmered against her skin.

To Lunelle's surprise, Lura relaxed her stance.

"Of course," she said. "The Underground," Lura pointed at the swinging board hanging above the door, the name of the tavern scrawled in Plutonian runes. "The curved arrow is one of the god Pluto's symbols. They use it in jest to the gods," Lura explained.

"I wonder if Astra knows about this," Lunelle whispered to herself.

"Surely he's told her—they're Tethered, it's not as if he could hide it if he wanted to."

Lunelle's brows creased. "What do you mean?"

"I'm only assuming, Lunelle, but your sister's sensibilities are powerful enough, and with the added connection of a Tether? I imagine she'd be able to see every shred of him, past, present, and future."

"And she still agreed to marry him," Lunelle thought aloud. "She *must* be involved."

"Wouldn't surprise me if your sister wasn't running the rebellion by now," Lura laughed.

"No," Lunelle breathed. "It would not. The commander is in there as well."

She glanced back over her shoulder, feeling that ache within her again, and realized that perhaps it had nothing to do with Mirquios, but everything to do with the rebels sitting across from him.

She'd hidden that invitation away, afraid of what it might mean. But if the king was here, if his commander was here, if her sister was aware of their movements...

Lunelle set her shoulders back and nodded, bringing a ceasefire to the war within her.

"I'm going to speak with them," she announced.

"Lu—"

COURTING DEATH & DESIRE

The princess held up her hand, a mirror image of her mother, and arched a brow.

"As soon as Mirquios leaves, I'm going in. You do not have to come with me, but I need to find out for myself what's going on."

Lura fought the smile tugging at her lips as she watched Lunelle's spine straighten beneath her cloak.

"Yes, Princess."

The sudden shuffle of boots and scraping of chairs jarred her from her perch at the tavern window.

The Mercurians rose in a wave of broad shoulders and bright eyes, Mirquios leading the charge beside Luxuros as they filed into the alleyway, pulling their jade hoods over their eyes. As the last of them faded from view, she inhaled slowly.

Once.

Twice.

Three times.

Oh, gods, just do it, she told herself as she stepped up onto the aged wooden stairs and pushed the swinging door inward. Dozens of eyes turned toward her at once, the dim lighting and dusty hall coming to a standstill as she lowered her hood and released her gleaming silver features upon them. She searched the faces, for whom, she did not know, but hoped that some-one, anyone, would direct her.

"Princess?" a voice mumbled, appearing from behind a particularly raucous table of Plutonian guards. She turned her gaze in his direction, landing on the cerulean face of the man she'd seen just the night before.

"We were wondering where you came from the other night," he chuckled. "And where you popped off to just as suddenly. Kwan Alinu, Captain of the Plutonian Novas."

He stuck out a bare hand, warm in her cool grasp, shaking hers firmly before pointing to a scarlet door at the back of the tavern.

"It's quieter upstairs."

Lunelle cut across the bustle of the room and slipped between the door and the staircase, Kwan trailing behind her as she climbed. The skirt had been a bold choice, she realized, as she hit the midway point.

"To your right," Kwan mumbled behind her as she stepped onto a dim landing. She stopped outside another scarlet door, looking at the captain. He seemed to recognize that she was not used to walking into a room blindly, as she almost always had several guards and maidens around her. He slid past her to enter a small study that was teeming with crooked bookcases and dozens of maps.

Kwan sat behind a writing desk overflowing with letters and ink stains, gesturing to the tattered chair across from him.

Lunelle sat, her eyes taking in one map after another, each pinned with slips of fabric in various colors. She tried to find a pattern, to make sense of the faded blues and reds, but nothing sprang forward.

"I must say, I'm delighted you came to speak with me, but I'm shocked to see you alone."

"I'm not alone," she replied, though she did not elaborate that she'd managed to bring but one maiden waiting in the alley, her hands soft from years of dressing hair and selecting silks for gowns.

If pressed, Lunelle was sure Lura could find it within her to defend herself. They both could.

Probably.

"You were quite alone last night," he said, pulling his lengths of raven hair into a thick knot at the nape of his neck. "Scared our patrons half to death—they thought they were seeing spirits."

Lunelle blushed. "Hard to say which of us was more disturbed," she muttered.

"I'd like to know how much you know about us before I give you the whole spiel," he laughed.

"Not much, I must confess. Our Southern city, Ellume, is overrun with rebels from what I understand, but it's been unclear who they're in service to. I thought Solan, and now suspect I am being kept in the dark deliberately."

Kwan nodded, leaning back in his chair. "That's likely the case, Princess. The old guard never gives up their power easily. The Lunar Captain has been hard at work trying to undo the damage your High Priestess, Ivonne, has wrecked across Ellume."

Lunelle's hands fidgeted. "Ivonne?"

Kwan nodded. "When was the last time you left your crystal tower, I wonder?"

A sigh slipped over her lips. "This is the first time I've left home in a decade, at least. We used to travel to Ellume on the Equinoxes, but my mother—the queen—has since moved the celebrations to Lunaria."

"Ellume has fallen into Nova control. Ivonne has been working to convince your mother that isn't the case, but like many major cities across the court, there's a movement growing, a movement that will not be stopped. A movement we'd like you to support, not suppress."

Lunelle watched as he pulled a stack of parchment, neatly bound with leather lacing, from his desk.

"This is our creed, our vision for a new world. I won't ask you to make up your mind today, but I do implore you to understand that people are starved for action, and if you don't take it, they will."

Lunelle reached for the booklet, running her finger along the title page. "*The Gods Have Gods*," she read aloud. "*A Perspective on Dismantling the Oppressive Rulership of the Court Above.*"

"The Living Courts and the Courts Between are our starting points, but our sights are aimed even higher."

She wanted to ask who the gods of the gods were, who the Court Above answers to, but her blood rushed against her ears.

"All of those questions," Kwan said, swirling his fingers in the space between them. "They have answers, Lunelle, but those answers may be hard to digest. The Lunar Court has more secrets than you realize."

"The Lunar Court?" she asked, unable to bite it back.

Kwan gave her a soft smile. She certainly was not the first regent to bristle at the notion that everything they knew was wrong.

"We have reason to believe that Solan and Leona were not enemies, Lunelle. We suspect they were trying to broker a treaty, and that the Court Above put an end to it. They *thrive* when the Inner and Outer Courts feud."

Lunelle's heart stuttered. Sitting higher against the desk, her fingers curled around the paper in her hands.

"What do you mean—how would... how would that be?"

Kwan lowered his gaze, softening under her panic.

"You've been kept in a bubble for over thirty years, Lunelle. Ask yourself *why*—what does your mother stand to gain by

79

keeping you from forging your own alliances, your own relationships?"

Lunelle shook her head. Her mother was overprotective, she always had been—losing her own sister to the Solar king's wrath had shattered any illusions that her daughters' might alone could prevent them from succumbing to the Solar Court. Lunelle had always been understanding of her mother's tight grip in response.

"What evidence do you have?" she barked.

"It's in the book, Lunelle. Detailed accounts by fellow rebels from across the courts, even your own. Selenia was spotted in Solaris just before The Flare—there has to be a reason. The gods only benefit from sowing division, and that's as true as it is between Pluto and Venus as it is between Sun and Moon."

Lunelle's teeth held tightly to her tongue, her confusion battling for an outlet, a place to run.

"Take a few nights. Read. Ask yourself some hard questions. But when you resurface, and when the kind heart we've heard so much about swells with the injustices your courtiers have borne the burden of, I will be here. The Novas will be here."

Lunelle sank, her shoulders crashing into the wooden back of the chair.

"Thank you," she said, hardly above a whisper. "I appreciate you seeking me out."

"Be careful in the city, Princess. The gods have gods, but they also have demons."

Her eyes narrowed.

"I'm happy to provide an escort service."

"No," she said, gathering the text and her cloak. "I can manage. We'll speak soon, Kwan."

"Take your time," he said quietly, rising as she made to

leave. "But do not take theirs," he sighed, waving toward the city outside. His implication settled over her shoulders like a heavy Summer rain, thick with a darkness she could not shake.

Should not shake, she corrected herself as she descended the stairs, pulling her hood over her delicate features and tucking her evening reading assignment under her arm.

"How was it?" Lura barked as she skipped over herself to keep up with Lunelle's trot down the quiet street.

"Very interesting," Lunelle returned, flashing the manuscript beneath her cloak. "We have some homework to do, Lura. Nothing is what I thought it was, but we mustn't let Mother catch wind of any of this. Do you understand?"

Her maiden nodded, falling behind just a step, tugging the neckline of her gown.

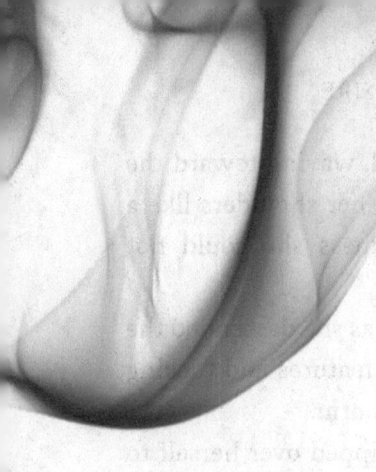

A tight grip around her wrist yanked Lunelle from a fitful sleep.

She yelped as two sapphire eyes peered back at her, the haze of her dream still brushing against her back as she tried to understand where she was.

"Sorry," Yallara chirped, pulling her upright. "We're going to be late!"

"Late for what?" Lunelle asked tiredly, batting Yallara away as if she were a moth lost in the dark.

"You'll see. Did you bring anything white?" Yallara released Lunelle's wrist and dug into the trunk at the foot of her bed, flinging gowns and lace across her room.

"Yallara!" Lunelle stood, gathering the floating slips of silk, shaking off whatever sleep clung to her head. Yallara popped up from the trunk with a silver-beaded gown in her hands, one of Lunelle's favorites.

"Oh, this is perfect," she chirped, tossing it toward the bewildered princess.

"Yallara, it's the middle of the night," Lunelle moaned as

she glanced out her window. She wasn't sure what was more disturbing—Yallara's frantic intrusion or that she'd been in Pluto long enough to recognize time by the state of the sky.

"Exactly," Yallara said. "We haven't got a moment to lose. Put that on!"

Lunelle turned to look at the spritely princess, her obsidian hair piled high on her head in intricate loops, framed by iridescent pearls twisted into the spirals. She was in a gossamer white gown, floating off her slight frame in wisps of thin smoke.

Yallara blinked and waved at her again. "Put it on!"

Something about the earnestness in her tone, the excitement in her eyes, loosened the knot in Lunelle's spine. Her mind wandered back to a time in her youth, when Astra was still just a rebellious teenager, shaking her awake hours before the Moon would rise. She'd been wrapped in black leather, tossing a pair of riding pants to Lunelle.

"It's a full Moon," Astra whispered, glancing over her shoulder as if their mother might be outside the door. "Riverion is already saddled. Come with me!"

"Come with you where?" Lunelle asked, her eyes wide as Astra's shoulders fell, hearing the apprehension in Lunelle's tone.

"Do not ask me where, just come with me! Please. We'll be back before Mother wakes."

"I cannot just leave, As! And neither should you."

She watched Astra's heart break, heard it between breaths as the wind that brought her into Lunelle's room quieted. She did not push. She did not insist.

She returned to her bedroom—or perhaps she didn't.

Lunelle would never know.

"Hand me the white boots," Lunelle sighed, gesturing to her trunk. "They look better with the silver."

Yallara clapped her hands together and dug into the trunk,

squealing as quietly as she could manage as she fished for Lunelle's pristine white boots, handing them over and bouncing on her heels. The moment Lunelle's fingers left the laces, she reached for her wrist again, pulling her into the hallway where several other courtiers waited, each dressed in shades of cream, beige, and silver.

"And that makes a dozen of us!" Yallara reached for something from one of the Venusians and handed it to Lunelle—an intricate mask made of lace curled in delicate florals around shimmering opalescent pearls. Long white feathers burst from the sides of the mask, trailing down her shoulders as she held it to her face for Yallara's approval. The group fastened their own masks over their eyes, each one a beautiful representation of their home court, Lunelle realized.

She eyed hers again, the phases of the Moon shimmering beneath the flickering sconce painted in some sort of iridescent glitter.

Yallara charged ahead, and Lunelle marveled as no one seemed to question her, even though she herself did not seem to have questions. She led them down the hall and into a dimly lit staircase, plunging beneath the palace for what felt like an eternity, the air pulling tight with a crisp edge.

When the staircase finally spit them out, they piled into the mouth of an underground cavern, sparkling dark crystals climbing the walls. Lunelle leaned closer to a cluster to examine them, the sound of footsteps echoing off the arched walls punctuating the brisk air.

"Are they sapphires?" a deep voice asked.

"No," Lunelle replied without meeting the inquirer's gaze. "Stibnite." She ran her fingers against the cool edge of the nearest crystal, enjoying the pleasant buzz against her fingertips at its energy. "They connect you to your ancestors, your past lives."

"Precisely!" Yallara pointed toward the end of the cavern in the distance, a shuffling sea of white pouring into the next room. "Tonight is the Feast of Proserpina. Every year, we dress in white and don masks to confuse Pluto, so that he might not realize if we're living or dead, and give Proserpina the chance to escape. It is the one night a year when we might get a taste of death—we parade through the Plutonion catacombs to the Cliffs of Descent over the sea. If you're brave enough to face your Descent and leap from the cliffs, they say Proserpina will grant you a blessing."

"A bit macabre," the voice next to her said quietly. She glanced at him, bright jade eyes flickering behind his mask.

"I like it," Lunelle said, straightening beside Mirquios.

"I thought you might." Yallara winked and grabbed Lunelle's hand, pulling her into the fray of Plutonians pouring into the catacombs from the streets above. The courtiers fell into line behind them, the rhythmic sound of their steps echoing against the caverns, sending Lunelle's heart into a stilted rhythm.

Yallara pulled her through a small carved door in the crystal-coated wall, and they stepped into a thrumming sea of white and blue, flowing down an ancient hall made of alabaster skulls encrusted with stibnite crowns. Ribs and spines laddered up toward the domed ceiling. Thousands and thousands of Plutonians passed and watched as they fell into the crowd.

Plutonians danced to dozens of drums, skipping and turning in circles as they rippled along the city's underbelly. Masks made of lace and leather and linen watched Lunelle as her silver waves twisted and turned under Yallara's arms.

The drumbeat was hypnotic, so unlike the delicate strings Lunelle was used to waltzing against. The percussive pulse came from somewhere otherworldly, but not unfamiliar. She felt it seep into her muscle and bone, finding spaces to hide she hadn't noticed before.

As the crowd danced on, she felt herself bloom into the movement, shedding a thick layer of regal posture, taking up behind Yallara and amongst the Venusians and Earthens. The catacombs teemed with life that once was and life that still would be, a thought that simmered against her skin as they passed under the heart of the city and beyond the walls, climbing cobbled steps into the night and onto the rocky shores of the Hydranian Sea.

The drums faded into the sea breeze and crashing waves beneath the cliffs. Hundreds, maybe thousands of festival goers—Lunelle could hardly see the edge of the crowd—danced along the edges. Goblets of wine and fruit lay on tables adorned with white blossoms, releasing sweet perfume into the air, mingling with sweat and sea and starlight. Blue-flamed bonfires freckled the cliffside, sending sparkling sapphire embers into the velvet sky.

Yallara giggled as she led her guests to a table at the edge of the cliffs overlooking the black sea below. Lunelle's stomach churned, a dark thought rattling around in her lungs. What might it feel like to leave the edge of this world for the next?

She slid into a chair decorated with runes and a garland of white blossoms spilling to the dark dust beneath them. Yallara hardly touched her chair before she was up again, falling into the arms of a masked courtier and spinning with him into the center of the festival, where dozens of couples twirled to a more robust offering of sounds now. Strings, drums, flutes, a harp. They sang together into one hypnotic melody.

Lunelle reached across the table and grabbed a large chunk of stibnite, heavy in her palm. It sparked against her, two forces between them colliding.

"It's quite something," Mirquios said as he sat beside her,

waving over the cliff's edge and to the dancers. She watched the fire inside her crystal dance, wondering if he saw it too, or if it was all in her head. "The Plutonians in my court do their own version of this, though on a much less grand scale."

Lunelle twisted toward him, the white of his mask contrasting beautifully against his dark complexion. She'd understood her sister's initial attraction to the king, but she hadn't ever really taken a moment to observe the way his eyes lit from somewhere deep within, much like her crystal. She held it up to him.

"Do you see that?"

The king leaned forward, tilting his head. "The glow?"

She smiled. She was not losing her wits, then. He stretched out his hand and she set it into his palm as his lips parted. The king laughed.

"I was going to ask if you wanted to dance, but I appreciate your willingness to share your trinkets."

Her nose scrunched, the pale silver spots across the bridge of it contracting and exploding into a constellation across her blushing cheeks.

"Do you have pockets?" she asked.

"Pardon, Princess?"

"I like this crystal. I don't want to lose it, but I do want to dance."

Mirquios nodded, rising and stuffing the iridescent stone into his silver jacket pocket and holding out his hand once more. His touch was warmer than Arcas and Yallara's, their proximity to death pushing them closer to her own chilled nerves, she suspected.

She wove them through the dense crowd, finding a space near Yallara as the drums picked up. Mirquios waited for her to lead, but her eyes widened as she watched the other dancers.

"I'm afraid I've spent my entire life learning every dance

known to the courts... but this one does not seem to have rules!"

Mirquios watched Yallara for a moment, recognizing one of the folk dances he'd seen time and again in his Earthen station.

"Follow me," he called out over the drums, taking her hand and walking her in a wide circle around him. As she passed before him, he spun her quickly, her silver waves loose around her face instead of bound tightly into a braid. He released her hand and held his palm up between them, his eyes darting quickly to hers. They clasped their hands together as they circled one another before he closed his hand over hers and twirled her again, catching her in his arms.

Mirquios pulled her close—closer than she was prepared for. He leaned forward, dropping her back into a slow fall, her stomach tying itself into a knot. He paused for just a breath before sweeping her up and into a series of rapid spins around the swirling crowd.

"It's so fast!" Lunelle giggled as he held one hand over his head and the other to their sides, twisting her so she faced away from him as they hopped toward and away from one another in time with the drums.

"Hold on," Mirquios bellowed as he threw her into another series of bouncing spins in the opposite direction. Lunelle's foot wobbled in the dust as they raced toward the center, a laugh escaping her chest as the king caught her, pulling her by the elbow into his chest.

"Sorry," she mumbled, trying to right herself as dancers brushed against them.

"Do not apologize, Princess. I was wondering if you Lunarians had any flaws—it seems you're half-human after all."

The king grinned at her, her eyes stuck on his, something

foreign in her chest clicking into place and releasing a chill over her lungs.

A chill that soured the moment she registered its implications.

"Lunelle!" Yallara cut through the dancers, reaching for her hand. "They're going to Descend!"

"What?" she gasped.

"The divers!" she yelled, pointing toward the cliffs.

Lunelle dropped her hand from the king's, trailing Yallara to the edge of the crowd where a dozen Plutonians in their festival whites teetered on the edge of the cliffs.

A priestess chanted from the far side, incense floating into the fathomless black below, her voice hardly rising over the surf.

Yallara leaned closer to her, looping her arm through Lunelle's elbow.

In the way a sister might, she realized.

She closed her eyes as Yallara explained. "The Cliffs of Descent are a holy ground, where Proserpina tried to liberate herself from Pluto by jumping, only to drown and wake up right back in the underworld with him. Only those who are brave enough to risk the violent sea below get their reward from her spirit. They say it feels just like Descending. One horrifying step into the ether, and then the rest is just falling softly into the Mother's arms."

Lunelle bit her lip, twisting her fingers together as she watched the divers shed their masks, revealing themselves to Pluto as they faced his wrath in the hopes of earning Proserpina's mercy.

The priestess stopped her song, and they tumbled like falling trees off the edge, a collective inhale from the crowd forcing her breath to stick in her throat.

She wondered as she watched their feet leave all they'd ever known behind for just a chance at what they wanted, if they felt terror shredding at their lungs, or if just the act of taking what they so desired was enough to quell it.

To silence the screaming.

She was still wondering as she stumbled back toward her bedchambers, her boots in her hands and mask askew as the Sun threatened to make its return.

"Lunelle!" The deep bass notes rattled in her chest as she twisted toward the king, that same thing against her ribs catching her off guard.

"Mirquios?"

"You forgot your rock," he said, digging into his pocket and producing the shimmering jagged gem.

"It's not just a rock," she sighed, taking it.

He flashed a smile. "No, it's stibnite. Connects you with your ancestors and past lives. Glows when certain Lunar demigoddesses touch it."

She turned her gaze to his as he pulled his mask off.

"Goodnight," she said, the crystal whirring to life in her hand.

"Good morning," he chuckled, fading down the hall.

Lunelle forced a hard swallow, the lingering chill in her bones sending icy rivulets across her skin as she made her way into her bedroom. She collapsed onto the bed in a heap of silk and sparkle, feeling every bit a petulant child and not the grown leader she'd come to Pluto as.

Her final thoughts before succumbing to the thrill of the night's activities returned to the divers and their desperation.

Perhaps tumbling over a cliff's edge was preferable to the quiet betrayal she'd flirted with in the hall.

THE PLUTONIAN PALACE was even more blue in her dreams.

The walls sparkled as she wandered through them, the silver dress she hadn't had the energy to strip off clinging to her curves. She ran her fingertips along the ancient stones, following a path she now knew well.

The library was empty, and she was somewhat annoyed at her own disappointment. She sat in the bay of the window, watching the silver pools trickle down the hill.

"Quite the gown," he said.

Lunelle's eyes slipped from the flowing silver pools to the library's door, the pale blues of his face darkened by the late hour.

"You missed out on all the festivities," Lunelle said, twisting in the cushioned bay to tuck her knees to her chest.

Arcas leaned against the doorway, crossing one ankle over the other.

"I find it... refreshing that you give my sister so much of your attention," he said, brushing his fingertips along the soft gray linen of his shirt.

"No, you don't," Lunelle retorted, smirking as he mirrored her bemusement.

"You're right. I'm actually mad with envy," he murmured.

"Envy that you did not get invited or envy that I split my attention?"

Arcas sighed, stepping into the library, but leaving the door open.

"I do not need to compete for your attention, Lunelle. You're a grown woman. You should bestow it on whomever you please—even on spoiled princesses and self-righteous kings."

She swallowed a defensiveness sparking in her chest.

"He isn't nearly as self-righteous as you are—"

"Let's not fight." Arcas sat beside her.

"Fair enough. I meant to ask... what flows through the pools?"

Arcas raised his brows. "Yallara hasn't bored you to death with the legends? I'm surprised. She loves talking about them."

Lunelle shook her head. "She has not."

Arcas twisted so his long legs fell over the edge and made space for her to move closer. Lunelle kneeled against the glass, looking over the pools as they whispered into a river of starlight.

"They are Souls," Arcas whispered, watching her brows as they furrowed.

"How—"

"At least, that's what people say," Arcas amended, grinning as she sighed. "But the liquid itself is only water. It's actually the stibnite below, the crystals in the catacombs, that give the metallic effect. The water catches the light, and it bounces off the crystals." He stood, offering her a hand. "You should see them up close."

Lunelle stared at his fingertips, hovering only inches from her lips.

"They're even lovelier to touch," he said, his hand shifting closer. Lunelle rested her palm in his, and he pulled her gently to her feet, winding her through the library's dense shelves and to a window toward the back corner. He released her hand to pop the frame of the window out of the wall, the pane coming free with minimal effort on his part.

His eyes bounced between Lunelle and the window, only a few feet off the ground.

"Can you make it in that dress?"

"This feels like a contrived trick to get me out of it," Lunelle muttered as she eyed the frame.

Arcas drew nearer to her, his fingertips skimming her hip. He leaned in, his breath warm on her neck.

"Do you really think I'd have to trick you?"

Lunelle swatted his arm, scoffing despite the thrill running through her spine. In an effort not to give into it, she darted forward, hiking her skirt up over her knees and stepping gingerly over the barrier. She ducked her head beneath the top of the frame and swung her second leg up, dropping to the soft ground below.

The grass swished against her bare feet as she ran along the outside of the ivy-coated palace, her fingers brushing the dense leaves as Arcas hit the ground behind her.

Lunelle jogged forward, heading for the stream of liquid starlight running from below the window she'd been seated beneath and into the gardens.

Arcas caught up to her, falling to his knees at the edge of the pools and holding his hand to her once more. As he helped her to the ground, he reached into the water with his other hand, cupping the silver and bringing it to her face.

"See? Clear."

Lunelle leaned out over the babbling stream, her reflection warped in this astral version of the palace.

"It's all an illusion, then?"

"Isn't everything, to an extent?"

Lunelle looked back toward the prince as he leaned into the garden grounds on his elbow, one leg propped up as if at the beach.

He looked godsdamned peaceful, for once.

Lunelle fell back over her feet, swinging her legs out to stretch along his. She leaned close to him, in a way she wouldn't have done anywhere else, the buzz between them exaggerated in this space.

She wondered for a moment where he really was—if he was in bed, thinking of her, and somehow the cosmos pushed them together. She lay back in the grass, the skies above rippled with rainbow threads and glittering stars.

"Lunelle?"

"Hmm?" she hummed as she ran her fingertips over the silk of her gown, letting the gentle breeze and whispering of the stream lull her into a second sleep.

"Never mind," Arcas whispered, leaning closer to her, his hand just brushing the silk piled between them.

When she woke, she half expected to find him in her bed, but the space remained empty, producing a strange ache in her stomach she did not have time to unravel.

CHAPTER
ELEVEN

Lunelle ran her hands along the cover of Kwan's manuscript, the steam from her tea rising over the first section.

A People's History of The Flare.

She had stared at the words for an hour already, hoping to enjoy the palace to herself at the late hour. She'd spent much of the day unfocused, and a lengthy conversation between her mother and Arcas after dinner had only left her even more unsettled.

She had also *attempted* to sleep to make up for the prior evening's interruptions, but it was of no use. There were too many questions and so very few answers.

"I'll be along soon."

Lunelle looked up from the manuscript, setting her pen down as she waved the steam rolling off her cup away from her. She tugged a half-drafted letter to Astra over Kwan's book.

"Good evening, Mirquios," she said, stretching her back lightly over the chair.

"Evening? It's the middle of the night. Shouldn't you be sleeping?"

Lunelle shrugged. He stopped at the edge of her table, pulling his cloak off and laying it over his forearm.

"My sense of time is completely thrown off with the Sun and all of Pluto's Moons. Add in an all-nighter with Yallara and I'm afraid, to be frank, I'm fucked."

Mirquios barked a laugh at this, his eyes lighting up at her harsh language.

"I don't think I've slept properly since leaving Mercury," he confessed. "May I join you?"

"Please," she said, straightening up her pile of parchment. She signaled to Lura across the terrace for another teacup. She'd tried to send her maiden to bed hours ago, but after carefully watching her all day, Lura's concern was clear.

Mirquios eyed the teapot suspiciously.

"Merely chamomile this time," Lunelle assured him.

"How boring." He draped his cloak over the seat across from her and slid into the chair.

"My sister hasn't responded to a single letter this week," Lunelle muttered under her breath, gesturing to her unfinished missive.

The king nodded. "I haven't had much luck, either."

Lunelle watched him, his bright eyes half closed at the late hour.

"She's always been bad at keeping up with her correspondence. If I know her, she's not even in Lunaria at this point. The second my mother left the court, she probably darted off to gods know where."

"Luxuros is with her, he doesn't tolerate trouble." He took the cup Lura offered him and slowly inhaled the floral steam.

Lunelle snorted. "I fear my sister won't tolerate *him*."

Mirquios released a held breath. "The commander did

seem a bit... apprehensive about staying back with her. I've watched the man charge headfirst into armies thick as night, but your sister gave him pause."

Lunelle smiled against the rim of her teacup. "Good."

Their eyes met, holding onto one another's secrets across the table.

"You and your sister both have a way of looking right through men, don't you?" Mirquios asked as Lura set cream and sugar between them before fading back into the terrace shadows.

"Have you met our mother?" Lunelle giggled.

For the first time since leaving the Lunar Court, a lightness welled within her, the weight of the worlds falling from her shoulders. Her eyes dropped to his folded gloves on the table as he poured his tea.

"Where were you coming from?"

He paused for a moment, seemingly debating with himself on the best answer. Or, she realized, if he could trust her with the truth.

"How much do you know about the political tension in Pluto, Princess?"

Her fingers clutched her teacup tighter, fighting the urge to drop her gaze to the pile of writings below her letter.

"Enough to know that wherever you were, the prince wouldn't have been happy."

Mirquios nodded. She waited for him to confess his association—to let her in—but he left it at that.

"How much influence do you think you have over him? The prince?"

Lunelle unconsciously checked over her shoulder for her mother's watchful stare as if Mirquios had been sent to test her.

"Me?"

He tilted his head. "He seems to seek out your opinion. That has to be worth something."

"Once," she said. "But that doesn't mean he'd listen again."

Mirquios shook his head. "Not just once. I've watched him carefully, Lunelle. In every room, he looks for you. When he speaks, he waits to see if you nod."

Lunelle's cheeks flushed pink. "I hadn't noticed."

"I don't believe that for a second," Mirquios laughed. "You're far too observant. If I've noticed, surely you have."

Lunelle deflected. "He does not seem interested in anything that threatens what little stability he can cling to. From what I've gathered, the... unrest... is just another thing he doesn't have a clue how to handle. And despite your implications, I don't think he takes me all that seriously. I am a way out of trouble for him, nothing more."

"Then he's even more of a fool than I originally suspected," Mirquios said through sips of tea, stretching his neck gently.

"I always knew it would happen—that I'd be on the throne, *married*," she sighed. "But I suppose I imagined it happening on my own terms. Not because of a war."

His brows floated upward in surprise. "You wished for romance?"

She bit back a laugh. "No. Of course not. Romance is for the less fortunate," she sighed. "I just thought I'd feel more ready for it. And transparently, I thought I'd settle down well before Astra. Then you came along." She waved at him from across the table. "You've completely thrown my timeline."

"Oh, well, my sincerest apologies, Princess," he mocked.

She dropped her gaze, tucking her brows together.

"I do not mean it as an insult. I just... I thought when Astra finally came home, we'd have some time together. I lost three years with her. I never dreamed she'd leave Lunaria for good."

Mirquios nodded, his fingers crawling over his chest as she spoke.

"I want my sister to be happy, but I also do not wish to deprive the world of the good she could do if she had the right resources. The right freedoms. I always imagined that I'd take the throne and restore my court to the paradise it once was—to bring back the magic we've all been barred from. I've spent years dreaming of unleashing Astra in all her glory. I'm envious that you'll be the one to witness the Fire Queen's Phoenician rise."

He took this in, his eyes examining the teacups between them.

"Does your sister know of your plans, Lunelle? Does she realize how you see her?"

Lunelle let a long, dark breath loose. A silver tear pooled at the corner of her eye, and she fought the urge to flick it away.

"Does any little sister know the lengths their eldest would go to let them shine?"

"Your sister is not the only one worthy of having what they want, Lunelle."

She twisted her fingers against her dress. "My sister will get what she wants because she *knows* what she wants."

"And you do not?"

Her eyes fell once again onto her stack of papers, at the ghost of the strange tome she'd been given.

"Or, are you simply too afraid to admit it?" he added.

Lunelle blinked, lifting her tea to her lips. It was decidedly that one, wasn't it? She knew it as she watched his inescapable eyes blaze into her. In the very far recesses of her mind, she wondered if Astra noticed the lines at the corners of his eyes, the ones that promised a lightness at the ends of hard evenings.

For a moment, she wasn't sure what was more of a threat

to her. The manuscript within her reach, or the king just out of it.

"Does it hurt?" she asked, pointing to his chest as he pushed against the space between his lungs.

Mirquios tilted his head.

"Does what hurt?" he asked.

"The Tether?"

His hand dropped from his chest and wrapped around his teacup.

"Yes," he settled. "I suppose it does."

"I'm sorry," she offered, though she wasn't sure she meant it.

They fell into a comfortable silence as she focused back on her letter, his eyes watching her hands float across the page.

"You're tired," Lunelle said without looking up. She could feel the energy shift in the air. "Or perhaps I'm boring you."

Mirquios chuckled, setting down his teacup.

"I find you... peaceful. Never boring."

She allowed one side of her mouth to accept the compliment in the form of a half smile, the letters making less and less sense as she rambled. She squeezed her eyes shut.

"Perhaps we both should stop fighting it," the king said.

Lunelle's eyes snapped up to his from her parchment. "Pardon?"

"Sleep."

"Ah. Yes," she mumbled. "Perhaps you're right."

She quickly gathered her things, hardly giving him an audible farewell before disappearing from the terrace.

SHE'D ALMOST MADE it back to her room, half asleep already, but a shadow moving in the library caught her eye.

Lunelle poked her head in through the door to see a set of hunched shoulders wrapped in blue velvet.

"Does the prince not sleep?" she asked, setting her things down on the table nearest her. Arcas was tucked in the window's cushioned seat, a book in his lap as he stared at the flowing silver pools beneath.

"The prince does not sleep *well*," he laughed. His eyes flickered to hers. "Are you all right?"

Lunelle wanted to laugh. She was *not* all right. Not the least bit. The panic in her chest as she'd realized she felt anything but a casual disinterest in her sister's fiancé set her on edge, and she was more interested in throwing herself into the silver pools for relief than she was in admitting it. She moved closer to the window, maintaining an acceptable amount of space between them.

In her dream the other night, the pools sparkled in a way that felt otherworldly, and she was pleased to find they held their shine.

"They're so beautiful," she whispered.

"They're a dream," he sighed. She turned, his eyes fixed on her face. Arcas tossed her a tilted smile and held up his hands in surrender. "I don't know how it works."

Lunelle blushed a deep crimson. If he'd really been there in her dream, where else could he be?

"But I did not mind it," he said softly.

Something about the way he stared at her hit a release valve in her chest. She *liked* the hunger in his eyes. It made her forget what a fool she'd been just moments ago.

"At least you mostly behaved yourself," Lunelle laughed, her brow arched as she sat back on her heels. "Though perhaps I'm a little disappointed in that."

Arcas sighed, leaning his head back on the wall behind him.

"You always say the exact opposite of what I expect."

"That's because you've painted a portrait of me in your mind that is not remotely accurate."

"How do you figure?" He crossed his arms, eyeing her as she relaxed against her side of the window.

"You think me a stiff princess, groomed to be perfectly compliant to her mother's wishes. Here to smile demurely and court befuddled princes."

"Befuddled," he scoffed. "That's generous."

Lunelle only tilted her head in response.

"You are none of those things, then?"

"I'm *some* of those things," Lunelle sighed. "But I am so much more."

Arcas thought about that for a moment.

"What is it you really want, Princess?" he asked. The question needled at her, like a sharp breath caught between her ribs.

"I want people to stop asking me that," she huffed.

Arcas leaned forward, the smoky scent of him wafting over her, tempting her to sort through the layers of it.

"Perhaps... if you just took what you wanted, no one would have to ask."

His eyes fell over her lips—she watched the calculations flash across his face as he measured the distance between them. On any other night, she might have excused herself and retired for bed, the weight of her exhaustion dragging her down. She might have come up with a clever way to turn the conversation on its head and left him pondering the many facets of her.

She might have at least leaned away from him, silently dismissing the plans he drew against his knee, his fingers nervously twitching against the fabric.

But tonight, she rather liked the idea of taking something

she wanted. And she wanted to know if the venom in his heart tasted as bitter as she suspected.

Arcas leaned forward, sending her back against the wall. Her heart stuttered as his eyes seared into her.

She warred with herself. Perhaps her dream had been in pursuit of *something* romantic, and the foreign nature of admitting she might actually enjoy that simply confused her senses.

What if all those feelings Mirquios stirred within her were merely that—a yearning for any of it? Not with him specifically, but a jealousy for what he surely had with her sister.

It made sense, didn't it?

Arcas could be a sort of release for her—but what if she *did* feel more for him? The shock of it alone might have muddled her mind in her dreams.

Arcas edged in closer, the smoky scent of him drowning her now.

"Your mother seems to think we'd make an advantageous match."

"Of course," she said quietly, his heartbeat picking up as he moved closer still.

"I think we've got the physical chemistry for it."

Arcas leaned over her, his long lines stretching against her soft curves. She had to crane her neck to hold onto his gaze, a light pink blush rising over her as she wondered what the muscles in his neck felt like flexing against her hold.

He exhaled. "But, I cannot tell how you *feel*... and I've found I'm rather fond of hearing what you think."

He was too close now, too near for her to concentrate on assembling the scattered thoughts that floated away from her. Perhaps she would have felt differently in a garden where the air blossomed with early sweet florals instead of the curling heat between their mouths.

Perhaps she wouldn't have felt her pulse quicken beneath her skin, just a breath away from his fingertips.

But then again, even in her dreams, hadn't she choked on the same suffocating tension?

And at any rate, she wasn't there now.

She was very much *inside*, pinned against a wall, drowning in the strange alchemy of the Plutonian prince once again.

"I will not come any closer," Arcas murmured, his voice dropping into a devastatingly low register. "Unless you ask me to."

Blood rushed to the surface of Lunelle's skin, painting her in a pale pink as she sifted through an explosion of racing thoughts.

Maybe Arcas *was* exactly what she needed.

He wasn't tied to her by Fate's mysterious strings, but just maybe the freedom to move forward and crash into him was worth more to her in that moment than the gods making the choice for her.

He must have felt it course through the slip of space between them. The decision she made, the giving over of herself. He must have heard it in the way her breath caught against her throat—his crooked grin certainly implied he'd noticed the shift.

"Your move, starling," he whispered.

Lunelle pushed into her knees, rising to meet him with a slow caution that dissolved entirely by the time their lips met.

Arcas found her hip through her dress, wrapping gently around her as she leaned into his touch. She let him rain over her, wandering over his chest, dancing quietly along his neck, searching for any space to hold onto him.

The crawling sear of his kiss sent all but one thought scrambling off into the ether as he backed her further into the wall—a near-silent whine leaving his throat that lit

104

something inside her she had not kindled in a very long time.

It was that last remaining thought, however, that stopped her from inviting him into her bed—or hells, throwing her dress off in the library—that pushed her away from him after another moment of indulging his kneading fingers and hungry kiss.

That final thought—an unmovable, demanding thing— echoed off her skull as she bid him goodnight and darted into the hallway, letting the dark consume her.

The thought that as long as she did not open her eyes, she would not have to mourn the sapphire gaze staring back at her when she might have preferred emeralds.

THE SEAMS *of the terrace warped and rolled in on one another as she moved across the glittering stone patio. The lanterns were not blue, but a softer, quieter lilac.*

"Lunelle!" Mirquios said, setting down his pen. "It's the middle of the night."

It was indeed silent in the hall behind them. Not even Lura or one of the king's many courtiers lurked in the shadows. But Lunelle was on guard after her interaction with Arcas.

"I'm too tired to sleep," she said, a weak smile unfolding as he stood.

"I wish I did not understand what you mean. I was thinking of taking a walk to clear my mind. Would you like to join me?"

Lunelle resented how much she did want to accompany him.

She paced beside him in a silence she soon resented, too. Not because it was uncomfortable, or even unwanted, but because there was only one other person in the world she felt so at ease in the quiet with, and she bore the king's ring on her left hand.

But maybe here, in the safety of her subconscious, she could forgive herself for the transgressions bubbling against her fingertips.

They strolled beneath the cerulean haze of Pluto's night sky. The rose bushes whispered to one another, gossiping about what a traitorous fool the Lunar princess was.

At least, that's what Lunelle assumed they might say.

"My advisor overheard your mother and Arcas making plans today," Mirquois admitted, his words tense with the tone of a man who told himself he wouldn't get involved.

"Did they?"

"It seems he is to be a Lunar champion."

"Oh," Lunelle sighed, a rush of heat in her cheeks softer here, but she was sure she'd be consumed in flames if they were in a real garden. "Of course. You know, with so much up in the air, I'd almost convinced myself that my trial would be delayed."

Mirquios nodded, slowing his pace as they stepped under a meandering tree spilling gentle pink blossoms onto the pavers below.

"He's not the worst fate, Mirquios—"

She searched the king's bright gaze, somehow even brighter here. She shrugged, unsure how she felt about anything at this point.

"So, you'll marry him, then?"

"If that's what's best for the courts—"

"What about what's best for you?"

Lunelle sighed. "What about it? You bear the same weight I do, Mirquios. You know desire and duty rarely intersect. You are fortunate that Fate chose to bless you."

"So you do have desires?" His lips curled upward.

She turned away from him, her arms crossing at her chest.

"It does not matter whether I do or don't."

She felt him, even through the misty waves of this plane, as he hovered just behind her.

"*What is it you dream of? Is it Arcas? Because if you want to be with him, who would I be to interfere—*"

Lunelle spun to face him—she knew how close he was, but it still somehow took her by surprise, the crackling of static between them.

"*Who would you be to interfere with anything about my life or my court?*"

The king started, raising his hand to his chest.

"*Lunelle, I am your friend—*"

"*You are no such thing, Mirquios. You are a foreign king whom I've known just as long as I've known the Plutonian prince. You are my sister's betrothed, but that does not make you somehow all-knowing of my desires or what is best for me or anything of the matter!*"

She battled the urge to stomp her foot, maintaining her balanced posture despite the voice in her head screaming.

Mirquios took a moment, his eyes dropping over her face, watching for the truth of her. He leaned forward, dropping his voice to a whisper as if someone might interrupt them.

"*I would keep your secrets, Lunelle.*"

Her nose scrunched. He thought he would keep her secrets because he did not know how deeply buried they were. He did not know the ache forming in her Soul. He did not know she was beginning to fear he and her secrets were one and the same.

Did she imagine it? The way he rocked forward in his boots?

Surely, it was the nature of dreaming of men in gardens—the lines of time wobbled and blurred, imparting a subsequent effect on the lines between sisters and their betrothed kings.

"*Lunelle,*" he breathed, a fingertip brushing against hers.

It was enough—the heat of such a betrayal—to shove her back into reality, where she wished desperately to unknow what she now firmly understood about her own Soul.

CHAPTER

TWELVE

"You look tired, darling," Oestera said over a quiet lunch in their shared study.

Lunelle fended off a yawn, pouring a third cup of tea as she poked at the strange fruits on her plate.

"Were you up late?"

She glanced at her mother, jaw set in a posture that discouraged further investigations on Oestera's part.

"I have struggled to sleep lately. Yallara took me to a festival a few nights ago and I've been a mess since," she confessed. She did not find it necessary to share what kept her up last night, or the nights that followed. Between poring over the rebels' manifesto and battling the near-ravenous curiosity within her to seek out a certain prince after dinner, she'd lost out on a week's worth of rest, at least.

Though she hadn't given in to that temptation again, she'd driven herself mad fighting the urge.

And, perhaps, she was afraid to sleep, should she find herself beneath a jade gaze.

"Oh," Oestera said. "Did you enjoy yourself?

108

Lunelle tried not to let the surprise show on her face.

"I did. I find the Plutonian customs beautiful. They honor death in such loud and interesting ways."

Oestera nodded curtly, returning to her morning communications. Lunelle watched her mother for a moment, taking in the creases beneath her eyes. She looked as tired as Lunelle felt—it had been the longest she'd been away from home in more than thirty years, and the discussions amongst the monarchs were not getting any less convoluted.

In fact, they'd only uncovered more and more knots to untangle as the days wore on.

"You miss Father."

Oestera's eyes slipped from her correspondence to Lunelle's face, her shoulders sinking just slightly.

"Do you know I have not spent more than a few hours away from that man since we met?"

Lunelle giggled.

"Don't you ever tire of one another?"

Oestera thought about this for a moment.

"I tire of most things, but never him."

All at once, Lunelle realized how deeply she envied her mother in nearly all facets, but especially that one. Prior to that moment, she might have thought it was her mother's confidence or her resilience in the face of adversity that she wished she possessed more of.

But there, painted in the gleam of her mother's eyes, she saw what she'd wanted most.

Someone to never tire of her.

THE LIBRARY no longer felt like somewhere she could hide.

Not after the way he'd touched her the other night. After the way she'd touched him.

It was dangerous, how distracting all of it was. She was too godsdamned old to be driven to such wandering thoughts over any man, let alone two.

It's not that she was ashamed of it, or wasn't interested in a repeat experience... but it had only left her head cloudier in the end.

It was inexcusable, she knew, to be so selfish. Courts were on the brink of war, and she was sitting in a foreign court fending off thoughts of velvet skin and bright eyes.

Eyes that were not hers to gaze into.

Velvet skin that could be hers if she simply said the word. She wouldn't even need to say it out loud—she'd just need to glance at Arcas in front of her mother for the deal to be signed in blood. It was obvious, the way Oestera watched them at meals and as they stood in comfortable silence on the terrace after card games.

But there was so much Oestera didn't see.

Lunelle shook her head, desperate to rid herself of these terrible thoughts.

So she took her tea in the atrium, the delicate glass architecture stretching into the sky and filtering gentle sunbeams across the circular room. She swirled her spoon against the sapphire teacup, letting the warmth of the Sun caress her as she enjoyed a quiet moment.

The boots of the Plutonians echoed off the halls midway through her tea.

They passed in one massive wave of blue, circling the atrium on their way to lunch. She attempted to keep her eyes on her tea, but Arcas caught hers from across the room. She forced a soft smile, but found she wished he hadn't seen her at all when she saw the frown developing at the corner of his mouth at something one of his advisors whispered to him.

She returned to her tea as he moved into her peripheral vision, crossing the atrium and stopping beside her.

"Princess," he said.

"Arcas," she returned, setting her cup down on the table.

"I trust I'll see you at dinner."

Lunelle arched a brow. "Uh, well, yes."

He nodded. "Excellent."

"I suppose," she mumbled, brows knitting together.

Arcas was gone before she could gather anything else into a coherent sentence.

"You know," Mirquios said, sliding into the chair across from her as she flipped another trio of cards over for Yallara. "Your sister did a reading for me before we left. It was not all that encouraging."

Yallara turned her eyes toward the king, her gaze fogged by wine and the late hour. Lunelle made a concerted effort to avoid looking at him, for fear he might look back.

She'd been unsuccessful at shaking her dream all week.

"What was so alarming about it?" Yallara asked.

Lunelle listened as she lined up the cards over the previous draw, finding the threads that wove them together.

"It was decidedly bleak," Mirquios mumbled.

"Not everything has to mean something," Lunelle said.

The king snorted. "That's exactly what Astra told me."

Lunelle pulled a final card, laying it in the middle of her spread. She leaned back, taking it all in and absorbing the artwork as she let their meanings mingle together, desperately trying to push anything Astra may or may not have said to him out of her head.

She twisted her lips into a smirk. "You got the Nether Queen card, didn't you?"

Mirquios leaned away from her, startled. "How did you know?"

"No one likes to see her in a reading, but it's because they look at her all wrong." Lunelle took a sip of her wine, tilting her head as she read the cards one more time to herself. "She does not represent a finite end, but the beginning of the next."

Mirquios touched his fingers to his chin, taking the message for a second time and deciding what to do about it. She blushed, thinking of just how strange the heat from those fingertips had been in her dream.

"Well, then, what's my Fate?" Yallara asked.

"Hmm," Lunelle said, pointing to the first row, nearest Yallara. "I see swift change coming for you—you see all these daggers? They cut ties. They unleash you. But over here," Lunelle tapped a card featuring a man with broad shoulders and a bejeweled crown. "You're blocked by the weight of expectations. Imposed by others, but also by yourself. You can't get to here—" she pointed to the Divine Queen in the middle, "—without shedding all that extra weight."

"So you're saying I'm well on my way to becoming queen of the universe." Yallara's lips cut into a wicked grin over her glass. "As long as a certain... *weight*... were to take his boot off my neck."

"Precisely," Lunelle giggled.

"What do you see for me?"

Three heads swiveled to Arcas at the end of the table, watching silently.

Lunelle stiffened. She hadn't seen him since their uncomfortable interaction—if she could call it that—in the atrium. She gathered the cards before her and gestured to Mirquios, shooing him to another seat. The king moved aside, making room for Arcas to settle like a heavy fog over the table.

"Have you had your cards read before?" she asked.

Yallara laughed behind him. "Be gentle, Princess, it's his first time."

Arcas glared over his shoulder at his sister and sat straighter.

"I have not," he confirmed.

"There are a few rules," Lunelle said, pushing through the faint pink heat Yallara's comment summoned. "While Lunarians are blessed by the Mother with an intense intuition, I cannot tell the future, and neither can these cards. Anything I say is for you to reflect on and take what makes sense—leave anything else."

Arcas nodded.

Lunelle turned over three cards, letting him absorb them before she made any commentary.

"What do you see first?" she asked.

Arcas leaned over the table, his eyes searching the cards.

"Stars," he said. "Many stars."

Lunelle nodded. "What else?"

A crooked grin pulled at his lips. "The Moon."

Lunelle felt the slightest hint of something burn against her ribs.

"The last one?"

"The High Priestess."

"She's a teacher," Lunelle explained. "Above all her duties to serve her court, her priority is to impart wisdom through grace. *Perhaps* there's a feminine presence in your life you could learn from."

She tilted her chin toward Yallara, but Arcas was staring at the third card, a cluster of celestial bodies with no name.

"What is this one?"

"That's The Void," Lunelle said. "It's meant as a place-holder of sorts. It appears when you're missing something—an answer or insight you have not been able to grasp."

The prince eyed her, a softening within his gaze that Lunelle was starting to recognize.

"What do you think I'm missing, Lunelle?"

The air pulled between them, a tightness she couldn't explain—something in the way he said her name.

"Only you can answer that."

Lunelle leaned back against her chair, gathering her cards as a yawn overtook her.

"You still haven't recovered from the festival," Yallara laughed.

"Indeed," Lunelle returned, rising.

"I'll walk you to your room," Arcas said quickly, drawing a look from Yallara.

Lunelle tucked her cards back into the silk pouch she'd found for them last Summer at the village markets, looping the drawstrings over her fingers as the table dispersed. She felt that *thing*—whatever it was—that shifts between two people when a glimpse of the future passes between both their minds.

The pair only made it into the hall before Arcas fumbled for an apology.

"I've been thinking about my behavior in the atrium this morning."

"That makes two of us," Lunelle said gently, her cards bouncing against her gown as they turned the corner, the hall's silence embracing them.

"I assure you it had nothing to do with the other night," he said, wandering slowly along the wing she stayed in. "I was in a bit of a mood."

Lunelle nodded. "I see."

Arcas tucked his hands behind his back.

"One of our cities has fallen to rebel forces."

Lunelle weighed her response options, unsure how to navigate this topic with him. Her lips parted, and she almost asked how he felt about it, but she realized that the only thing more frightening than not knowing his opinion would be knowing they stood on opposite sides.

So she held her question—and her breath as it rotted within her immediately.

Another thought festered beside it.

Astra would have asked.

They came to a stop outside her door, and just as she was about to bid him goodnight, his dark eyes dropped to her lips in what seemed to be his tell.

"I find I must ask you to be blunt with me once more."

He rocked on his heels, his eyes darting down the hall before returning to hers.

"I think we both know what I'm missing, Lunelle."

It was the softness in how he said her name that broke her.

She pushed forward, pulling his parted lips to hers. He paused for only a second, his arms clasping around her lower back as she settled into him. He ran his fingers over the soft fabric of her dress as her lips came down over his.

He released a slow breath as she explored the space of him, hypnotized by the way their bodies pressed together. His lips closed over hers as he touched her soft waves, inviting her mouth to do more than just dance with his. She was happy to let him consume her—to drag her as far down as she could stand.

To distract her from the awful pit in her stomach.

"Is this what you want?" he asked as she slipped beneath the surface of him, tasting the salty skin of his neck, his hands tightening against her back.

Lunelle sighed, craning her neck back. "What did I say about asking me what I want?"

Arcas leaned his hand against the wall behind her, closing his eyes as she returned to her mission to taste every tensed stretch of muscle along his neck, her fingers threading under his shirt and touching bare skin. She'd expected him to feel colder, but pinned between her body and the wall, she only felt flames.

"Lunelle," he whispered, her nails skimming over his chest in a way that made it hard to say anything other than quiet praises.

"You told me to take what I wanted the other night. Do not get in the way of that now," she murmured, dropping her hand to the buttons on his shirt.

His eyes were no longer sapphires, but two obsidian portals that ran her blood cooler as she arched away from him.

"I will give you anything you desire, starling," he laughed. "But perhaps somewhere more private?"

A blush crept over Lunelle's pale face as her eyes followed his down the hall. It was late enough that hardly anyone was wandering the palace, but the servants didn't need to bear witness to her bad decisions. He backed away from her as she fussed with her handle, pushing him into her bed chambers as she glanced over her shoulder. Arcas was already halfway across to her bed when she turned around.

He paused, his long arms snapping around her waist, drawing her into him.

His lips found hers again, pulling and tugging across her body she whined at the pressure between their hips. She leaned back against the writing desk she'd left covered in musings her sister would never read, making room for him to settle between her legs. His tongue found hers while her fingers desperately wrestled his trousers.

Arcas laughed as she shoved his pants away from his waist, breaking the spell that had settled over her.

"What?" she asked, her eyes widening as she caught sight of him.

"The last time we were alone, I thought you needed a chaperone, and I daresay that book was right."

Arcas grabbed the back of her head, pulling gently at her hair and exposing her neck to his mouth as her fingers reached for his sensitive skin.

"Gods," he hissed. She found a firm hold on him, swallowing hard as he fought for a deep breath. He pressed into her lips with his thumb, stroking the swollen petal pink of them. "Should have expected you'd show no mercy."

Lunelle swallowed, the intensity of his gaze almost too much to carry. She moved her hand slowly, letting the velvet of him slip through her fingers and admiring the length of his lashes as his eyes closed and his breathing quickened. He braced himself on the wall behind her, gasping softly with each stroke.

She'd let their first night paint an underwhelming portrait of him in her mind. Here, stuttering at her touch, she could admit she'd neglected to see the strength in his jaw, or the statuesque curve of his nose. She'd ignored the soothing tenor of his voice, even more attractive to her as it fell into taut notes as he lost the ability to suppress his pleasure.

He was not nearly as pathetic as she'd imagined, despite the near whimper building at the back of his throat.

She quite liked drawing the desperation from him.

"I will not last, Princess," he warned, gripping the back of her neck as she watched his teeth crush his lower lip. Lunelle did not slow her pace, merely pulling him down to her lips to take advantage of how lost he was in her.

"Princess," he hissed between increasingly rapid breaths.

It was the undercurrent beneath his intriguing angles and lines that really enchanted her, she realized as he choked on a soft moan, his jaw clenching against his release. A shadowy depth she did not fully understand, but enjoyed watching dissipate when she drew near.

"Give me what I want," she hummed, his eyes closing tightly.

"Fuck," he groaned, gripping her shoulder as he arrived. Lunelle didn't speak as she wiped away the evidence of his lost control on her skirt, her spine straightening with the power she found in bringing him to such a quick finish. He refastened his trousers, unable to look her in the eyes.

"I'm no maiden, Arcas," she said, brushing her hands against his waistband. Her silver gaze captured his as her lips curled into a sly smile. "That was exactly what I wanted, there's no shame in giving me what I want in a timely manner."

"And what about what I want?" he asked, leaning over her and cradling her neck. Lunelle rested her hand on his wrist, staring up at him as she stroked the pale blues of his skin.

"I'm afraid to know what you want," she confessed.

Arcas chuckled, trailing his hand down her sleeve and pulling gently, exposing her gleaming shoulder to his haunting touch. She leaned into the sensation, urging him silently to reveal more of her. He slipped the fabric away, her breasts falling freely into the cool air.

"I want to know what a Lunar goddess sounds like when she comes."

Lunelle gasped quietly as he claimed her mouth again,

dropping his hands from her neck to the exposed curves of her breasts and massaging gently, slowly, reverently.

She broke from his touch, standing to pull the rest of her dress over her head and sending it to the floor as he watched the slopes and valleys of her twist in the low light.

She *liked* drawing those strained sounds from him. She *liked* knowing he couldn't take his eyes off her. She *liked* the tightening of his throat when she gripped his hand and brought him to the soft cloud of her bed, lying back so he had full access to her as he kneeled between her legs.

He did not hesitate to push her thighs open, his breath hitching at the sight before him, and she *liked* that, too.

"Demigoddess is an understatement—"

"Less talking," she dismissed him.

Arcas rolled his eyes and crawled his fingers over her thigh, just brushing her center as she twitched in response. Lunelle gripped the back of his head, forcing him to her, a low rumble of laughter reverberating in his chest as he began stroking her slowly.

Her head fell back, crashing against the fluffy pillows behind her, enjoying the shift of weight off her chest for a moment as his movements distracted her from any thought that wasn't the praise of his tongue against her. She reached for his hand, resting lazily on her leg, and pulled it toward her breast, squeezing his fingers around her soft skin. He took the note eagerly, desperate to make her feel even a drop of the pleasure she'd drawn from him.

"There," she gasped as he hit a pace that made the edges of her vision sparkle with the threat of release. She sighed as he found the spot again. His hands squeezed her, giving her everything he could offer as she wound her hips against him. The tension simmered, the space between them buzzing with an energy she'd seldom felt with another partner. There was something so dark about him, so unidentifiable, and it bled into her as she raced toward her intention.

Arcas moaned against her as her cries grew less predictable, less controlled.

"Do not stop, Prince," she whined, clutching his hand. That sacred space within her opened up, filling with lust and smoke and sapphire stars, shimmering at the edge as she bucked against his mouth. Arcas dug his hands into her body, begging her to give him what he'd worked so hard for.

She broke—splintering from the inside out, bursting against all the lingering guilt and doubt she'd brought into the room. Arcas did not stop until she was writhing in his hands, gasping for breath, and pulling sharply at his hair. He fell over her as she slipped back into her body.

Lunelle pushed him away, too alert to every brush of skin against hers, too sensitive to it. Her chest heaved as she found her breath again, the brazen decisions she'd made since leaving dinner crashing around her.

Arcas rose, snagging her dress from the floor and handing it to her gently.

Lunelle pulled it over her head, not caring to properly adjust the lacings to her soft curves. She stood and planted a hand on the prince's chest, his eyes wild with all sorts of conflicting ideas.

"So?"

"So?" he echoed.

"Did I sound like you imagined?"

Arcas snorted, adjusting the shoulder of her dress.

"Hmm. I'm not sure. Perhaps I should try again."

Lunelle glared at him as she pushed his hand away and tapped his cheek with her palm.

"If you're a good boy, maybe I'll let you."

She made no secret about shoving him toward the door.

Her need to be alone—utterly alone—climbed her spine and gnawed at her skin.

By the time she was back in her bed, the rush of his touch was already gone, and she was left once again to contend with the terrifying thought that no matter how intriguing of a distraction Arcas was, it might never be enough.

S leep would not release her from her misery.

She gave up after an hour of desperately trying to control her breath.

Lunelle swung her legs over the edge of the bed and pulled on a dense pair of wool leggings and a black sweater to ward off the slight chill settling over the courts.

Before she left her room, she plucked a ripe pomegranate off the top of the fruit basket on the desk, tucking it into her cloak.

If she was going to beg a goddess for relief, she might as well bring her an offering.

She was a silent breeze as she quickly cut through the halls, searching for the door Yallara had taken them through. She pushed gently along the walls, waiting for that raised edge she knew would fall into the stairs.

It took three hallways before she finally recognized a painting of a centuries-old Plutonian queen, her gaze fixed on her shoulders as she disappeared into the wall.

It was colder than just a week ago, though Lunelle realized

she wasn't tucked into the middle of a cantering crowd. There was no body heat to buzz against her as she skipped through the near-empty catacombs beneath the city. The occasional creature skittered away from her as she approached, but it was as if she had the entire city to herself at this hour.

Her footsteps echoed against the crystalline cavern, bouncing off bones and glittering stibnite as she wandered down the same route they'd taken before. She hadn't noticed just how high the ceilings were when she'd been consumed by the crowd, or how hollow the eye sockets of the ever-watching guardians in the walls had been.

When she began her climb to the top of the stairs beyond the city, the echo of the wind whipping outside inspired a quiet dread in her chest.

Maybe this had been a ridiculous idea.

But as she closed her eyes and was met with two floating green orbs, she was reassured that if she didn't do something —beg *someone* for relief—she was going to make a mess the likes of which might never be untangled.

She was not a silly girl, she reminded herself as she stepped out onto the rocky cliffs, now desolate after teeming with so much life and so much death.

She was not in denial. She knew what was happening.

She was falling for a man who was not available to her, and she saw and felt it as clearly as a full Moon.

She'd felt it the moment they arrived, really, that he was not just another courtier to fool into believing she knew what she was doing here. He was smart, but perhaps not smart enough to realize the precarious position they were in.

Her sister did not deserve her betrayal, and neither did Arcas or Mirquios.

As she settled on the edge of the cliffs and rooted herself into the blue-gray dust, she forced herself to lean forward, for just a moment. The black sea churned below—not all that different from the one she'd grown up over in the Lunar Court —but everything felt unknown here.

She felt unknown here.

Her entire life, she'd been so certain of who she was and the role she played in her court, in her family, in her relationship with her mother, her sister, her father.

Her people.

But a single dance, a few compliments, and now she was slipping under those black waves, unable to keep her head up.

It was pathetic.

Worse than pathetic.

Lunelle lay back, letting her bones settle in the Plutonian dust like so many who came before her, staring at the sky above. The infinite swirl of stars and Moons, the winking pastels of the Rift—it all stared back.

Watching.

Judging.

She closed her eyes, if only to escape their criticisms, and perhaps to gain the courage to do as the divers had done at the festival—but there it was again.

That slip-sliding feeling at the base of her neck, the temptation to let her entire mind drain within her and tumble into another universe.

Had she not been so disturbed, she would have ignored it. But its insistence took her along—another distraction she couldn't deny.

Lunelle fell into her soul, spinning and whirring amongst a Rift of her own doing, landing with a harsh jolt on a soft bed of moss and moonblossoms, unfurling in a delicate Spring rainstorm. She could taste the sea on the raindrops as they landed on her rose-petal lips. She sat up, pushing against the damp moss and shaking off the mist clinging to her.

"Princess," a velvet tone hummed.

Her eyes searched for the harmonic sound but found only a deep forest to peer into.

"Hello?" Lunelle whispered.

"What a heavy heart," the voice cooed. Lunelle could feel it then, the weight of the words, coming from behind her. She spun on the moss, raising to her knees.

The goddess before her was no one she recognized, but pieces of them seemed to be acquainted.

Her hair fell in delicate pink curls, the shade of strawberries when they first popped from their leaves, unripened but full of promise. Her hazy eyes were wide set, seeing everything around them at once, the kind of eyes that had seen everything. She was long and curved, a strength running in her thighs as she gazed upon Lunelle's hands.

She kneeled just a short distance from Lunelle, her long hair falling over bare breasts and pooling into her lap. Her arms were adorned with strange tattoos, rippling in navy ink, Plutonian runes running the length of her olive skin.

"You brought me a gift," she said, her voice singular but laced with the wisdom of a million women. Lunelle looked at her hands, fitted gently around the swollen red fruit she'd nabbed before leaving the palace.

"Proserpina," Lunelle breathed, her heart stopping as the goddess stretched her hand toward her. She reached forward, placing the offering in her iridescent palm.

"Thank you for this," the goddess said. "But what did you hope to receive in exchange for it?"

Lunelle shook her head, her silver waves glistening in the misting rain.

"Nothing. I just... I thought maybe it was lonely, in the days following your celebration. That everyone moved on and thinks one night was enough."

The slightest glint of admiration warmed Proserpina's eyes.

"You were not one of the divers," she observed. "You did not seek a blessing from me, yet you still thought of me in your hour of need."

"Is it my hour of need?" Lunelle asked, her hands so empty now, she was unsure what to do with them.

"You're here, no?"

Lunelle nodded. "I came to the cliffs to confess something, I think. To purge myself of it."

Proserpina grinned. "Shall I leave you to it, then? Shouting your sins to the crests of the sea?"

"I'm sure you have better things to do than to listen to pathetic whims of the heart."

Proserpina shrugged, her eyes raking over Lunelle.

"You know, people offer the gods all sorts of strange things, but rarely gossip."

Lunelle could not stop herself. She laughed. Because it *was* trite gossip in the end. People were dying, wars were starting— and here she was, seeking the ear of a goddess to tell her to get her head out of the clouds.

"I fear I'm losing myself to a man I can never claim."

Proserpina nodded, forcing her thumbs between the skin and tissue of the pomegranate.

"A woman can never lose herself to a man, she merely loans him her splendor."

Lunelle huffed a shallow sigh, staring at her fingertips.

"What if it's his splendor I'm after?"

The goddess pursed her lips. "What stops a Lunar queen from taking what's hers?"

"He is engaged to my sister."

Proserpina considered this. "And you like her?"

Lunelle giggled. "I love her very much."

Proserpina dug a few seeds from the flesh of the pomegranate, popping them into her mouth and staining her lips a deep red.

"No man is in possession of enough splendor to come between sisters, dear girl. But you know that."

Lunelle nodded.

"You know," the goddess sank back onto her heels, loosening her divine posture. "They tell a story about me—that Pluto ripped me away from the arms of my mother, that he dragged me to the edge of the universe, that I sought Descent rather than spend eternity in his hold."

Lunelle moved her hair from one side of her neck to the other, shaking the rain from the ends.

"Is that not so?"

"No," Proserpina said, a sorrow seeping into her words. "It's not so." Her eyes drifted into the deep black of the fathomless forest behind Lunelle. "I went willingly, but my mother did not want to give me up. She did not think I was ready to be a wife, and perhaps I wasn't. My life was not a happy affair, Princess. It was rife with suffering. I prayed to Pluto, to the God of Death himself and asked him to take me. It was the shame of getting what I wanted that allowed the rumors to spread."

"I don't understand—"

"Pluto granted me exactly what I begged for, what I knew my heart craved, and I let my mother, my sisters, and the rest of the gods believe he'd done it out of selfishness to save face. But I was born yearning for death—not of my body, but his. Our Souls... they were crafted from the same speckled light, never pure enough for the day. It took centuries to admit it— eons of wasted time."

Proserpina cast her eyes toward the forest once more, and Lunelle wondered where he was—where death lurked when no one needed his escort services.

"What about Mercury?"

Proserpina scoffed. "Mercury did not know what he did not know. He thought he was saving me. He thought he was protecting me. But all he did was delay the inevitable."

She offered half her pomegranate to Lunelle.

"How did you know what to ask for?" Lunelle took a handful of seeds and let them rest on her tongue, enjoying the tart juice as it burst along her lips.

"The most important things in life you can never know for certain."

Proserpina's eyes wandered back from the trees to Lunelle's face, the depth of her stare sending a shiver over Lunelle's body.

"So there is no fighting it then? Fate?"

Proserpina's lashes fluttered against her tan skin, an easy smile closing over her lips.

"Has it worked for you so far?"

The goddess leaned toward her, pressing her pome-granate-stained lips to Lunelle's forehead, sending her cata-pulting back through herself and into the dust of the cliffs, the sea crashing below her. Her eyes shot open, and she scrambled back from the cliff's edge, climbing to her feet as she shook the strange hypnosis she'd fallen into.

It took until she was back in the catacombs, outside of the palace passageway, to get the taste of pomegranate out of her mouth.

CHAPTER

FOURTEEN

When she woke the next morning, Lunelle had made two decisions.

The first was that Proserpina had a good point. Pluto was not the villain in either of their stories, and Mercury did not know what he did not know.

She'd been silly to think her delusions about the king were anything other than fear of letting herself want what she knew she *should*—Arcas was not her enemy.

He was what made sense.

He was what she'd asked for.

The second decision was that she could no longer waver on what to do about the rebellion. She needed to put her feet on the ground and move, one way or another.

The further she got into her morning, the more she realized she hadn't actually made two decisions so much as decided to make two decisions, but that was enough progress to push her through breakfast with the courtiers and a long round of debates on the merits of absorbing Pluto's infantry into the

Inner Court army, versus leaving them in Pluto as a secondary wave in closer proximity to Solan.

She knew she only had an hour before the courts were to convene for yet another lengthy debate, this time on gods knew what, but she hoped to get a break before dinner.

"Lura?"

Her maiden poked her head through the door, eyes wide.

"Will you tell me when my mother returns from her lunch with the Venusians?"

Lura nodded. "Of course, Princess."

Lunelle dug in her trunk for the manuscript Kwan had lent her, diving back into the article she'd left off on.

The People's History of The Flare

The events surrounding the Solar Court's lethal attack are not entirely clear, but of two things we can be certain:

1. The Solar Court only benefits from confusion around the king's motives and,

2. The Lunar Court's deity, Selenia, was spotted within the gates of Solaris on the morning of the incident.

Lunelle's heart raced as she read the name—Selenia. It had been nearly a decade since she'd seen her mother's mother. She did not leave her throne in the Court Above often. Even when she did, it was always fraught with stress and tension on her mother's behalf.

She leaned toward the fire as she read, something about just seeing Selenia's name in conjunction with The Flare chilled her to her bones.

"Princess," Lura whispered, but it was too late, someone was already bursting into her room.

"Arcas!" Lunelle gasped, shoving her book aside and flipping it face down on the coffee table by the fire. The prince was paler than usual, his cerulean hues retreating for an icy shade.

"Might I speak with you privately, Princess?" His eyes flickered to Lura, who gracefully bowed her head and backed out of the room.

Lunelle rose from the sofa, smoothing her gown. She'd seen him at breakfast, a quiet smile passing between them, but he'd given her generous space—unlike the night before.

She supposed it was time to put her first decision to work.

"Lunelle," Arcas said, tightly. "I was going to wait until I discussed this with the queen, however, I was hoping to get clarity from you last night, and we got distracted..."

Arcas moved closer to her, his hands clenched at the adrenaline coursing through his veins. She could sense it, nearly see it rippling from him.

"I seem to always be distracted by you in some sense."

She braced herself—and vaguely wondered if bracing oneself for a marriage proposal was a good omen—but the question did not come.

His gaze swept over the table, catching on something Lunelle's had not.

A dagger piercing a crown, lightly etched over the back page, dancing beneath the firelight.

"What is that?"

His tone was frigid, every muscle in his back pulled taut as he stepped toward the table.

"Arcas—"

Lunelle was unsure of the smart thing to do—what her mother would do.

Her mother, she realized, would have been too smart to be speaking to the rebels in the first place.

"Where did you get this?" His cold gaze turned on her, sending a bolt of ice straight to her heart.

"I-I was sent it. It piqued my curiosity."

Arcas tilted his head. "Do you have any idea how dangerous these people are, Lunelle?"

She snorted. There it was—the way out of this.

Play dumb, as if she were just a clueless princess—because that's all she was to him in the end.

"It was left for me, Arcas. I was merely curious. Don't you wish to know what your people are reading?"

"I wish to purge my city of every last one of these arrogant fools," he muttered, snatching the manuscript from the table. "This is a curse upon our necks, Lunelle. It will be what sends us both to our graves. Don't you see that?"

Lunelle shook her head. "Aren't you even a little sympathetic to their perspective?"

His head tilted, his entire view of her crumbling in a moment—she could see it in his eyes.

"How many pages did it take to poison your mind? You, who knows so much more than the average citizen. You, the steward of sentiment and feeling—and a few pieces of propaganda is all it takes. Imagine what will happen if we continue to let the poison spread!"

He stepped closer, the anger fading from his bones, but it only seeped out into the space between them. His hand dropped, and a flutter of pages and flame flared beside them as the manuscript landed in the fire with a hiss.

She held her breath, her face frozen in the careful mask her mother had sculpted out of her for years.

"For centuries, people have cried out against injustice because they think there is some mythical happiness that lies on the other side of revolution. But they fail to account for so much, Princess. They've no respect for what the crown sacrifices on their behalf. The damage to our shoulders that the weight of the worlds does over time. They think it must be easy, a life of luxury. But you've seen how untrue that is, I'm sure."

"Of course," she whispered, hating each letter as it left her lips. "You're right."

He held her stare for a moment longer, the edges of him softening as he found no threat on her tongue.

"This evening," Arcas said, exhaling as he reached for her hand. "If you find yourself not sleeping again..."

Lunelle flinched as he said it, but she nodded despite it. It was better than the question she feared he'd come to ask. She nodded anyway.

"Excellent," he said quietly, sliding closer to her. He pitched forward, dropping his lips to hers in a kiss not much warmer than his tone had been just moments before.

Last night, she'd allowed herself to believe he was something else—something salvageable.

But as he kissed her, her decision crystallized in her chest. Arcas had no place in her court—but the people he'd just thrown into the fire did.

And she'd be damned to the Nether for eternity before finding herself on the side that burned the truth to keep their boots on the necks of the people who served them.

"Lunelle," Oestera called as they passed one another in the hall. "I've not seen you all day!"

"Sorry, Mother," Lunelle said, spinning on her heels to walk with her, wherever she was headed.

"You seem tense, darling."

The term of endearment made her flinch.

"I've been listening to men bark at one another for weeks over minute issues that don't serve anyone at large. What else should I be?"

Oestera snorted but quickly settled herself. "I hope we're

returning home soon. I don't know how much more I can take, either."

"Mother?" Lunelle stopped in the hallway, her mother turning with an arched brow. Her maidens stopped and stepped back, giving them space. "Are you certain about Arcas?"

Oestera's eyes measured all the things Lunelle wasn't saying, weighing them one by one.

"Are you not?"

"No," she said. "I'm not."

"We don't have to make any decisions today, Lunelle. Perhaps we need more time to better understand your hesitations."

Lunelle hadn't expected such a reasonable answer from her.

"Thank you," she whispered.

Oestera rested a hand on Lunelle's shoulder.

"My conversations with the prince have been promising, for what it's worth."

Lunelle wanted to shout that it was worth nothing, that he was too arrogant, too scared, too rooted in his father's ways to be reasoned with, but how could she explain all of that to her mother without confessing to her newfound affinity for the rebels?

"I had another question," Lunelle said, barely audible. She leaned close to her mother, aware that the hall was not the ideal place to discuss Selenia. "The Flare..."

Oestera's face drained of color. It was such a sensitive topic —one they hardly broached, despite Lunelle's earliest memories forged in its blinding light.

"The Plutonians seem to believe that your mother was present in Solaris—"

"Princess!" Yallara moved through the hall, a billowing

sapphire gown flowing behind her as her courtiers chased her. "You must come with us, we have a Descendant here!"

Lunelle glanced at her mother, who squeezed her arm and bowed out of the conversation.

Godsdammit.

"A Descendant?" Lunelle asked.

Yallara clapped her hands together. "They're Pluto's devotees! They can tell you about your past Descents!"

"Oh," Lunelle whispered, unsure if that was information she wanted. Yallara grabbed her hands and dragged her toward the palace gardens, where a table had been set with a black tablecloth and an elderly figure was setting out crystals in varying colors and cuts.

They—the Descendant, Lunelle realized—wore black head to toe, with a smoky veil covering their head, their eyes hardly visible through the thin fabric.

"Who is first?" the Descendant asked, their voice rough as they finished their spread.

"Me," Lunelle said, surprising herself. Yallara pushed her forward, standing behind her as she sank onto the iron chair across from the reader.

The Descendant's energy was that of death itself, Lunelle thought. A drifting chill rolled from their shoulders, pushing her away as they stared at her with unseeing eyes.

"Pick one," they said, gesturing vaguely to the crystals between them, waving a withered hand over the stones.

Lunelle surveyed them but did not need long to decide. She reached for the small, oblong stone that shone with a rainbow gleam that reminded her of the Rift.

The stibnite.

"Mmm," the Descendant hummed, holding Lunelle's palm flat with the stone resting in the center. "Fascinating," they breathed as they observed her.

The crystal whirred in her hand with the same strange turning of inner light as the piece she stole from Proserpina's festival.

The Descendant held their breath for a moment, leaning back from her, as if she were the one to be frightened of.

"What strange magic you possess," the Descendant said quietly.

"Magic?" Lunelle asked.

"She does not know," they whispered to whoever it was they called to.

"What doesn't she know?" Yallara asked.

The Descendant hissed in her direction, the black veil ruffling on the breeze. Yallara stepped back, no longer her playful self.

"Who will tell her?" they asked again, but Lunelle could not follow the thread of their thoughts.

She leaned forward. "Tell me—"

The Descendant jerked her hand closer, holding the stone up to Lunelle's eyes.

"*They* will tell you."

"They?" Lunelle closed her palm over the stone, feeling the insides stutter and disappear.

"You woke your dead, Princess. Ask them."

Lunelle blinked, a shiver running down her spine. Proserpina's gaze flashed to her mind—perhaps that was what they meant.

"There is a star," the Descendant whispered, their breath rolling over Lunelle's fingers like a morning fog. "You must embrace it."

Lunelle felt that second decision straining to the surface of her skin.

"If you don't, it will embrace you, and it will be all-consuming."

The Descendant dropped her hand, folding her fingers over the stone and leaning back, turning their eyes to Yallara.

"Pick a stone," they said, dismissing Lunelle with little more than a dusty breath.

She made it through Yallara's first three lifetimes before she quietly slipped away, the stone burning a hole in her pocket.

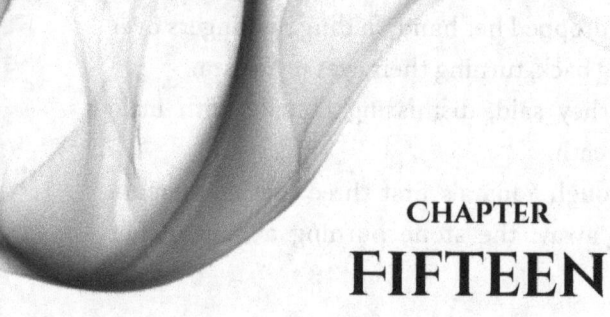

CHAPTER
FIFTEEN

The stone was all she could think of.

It was all she saw the rest of the evening, those strange undulating waves within, taunting her. When she closed her eyes in her bed, the sharp edges found her, carving shallow scratches into her skin. She'd prayed to Proserpina, and to any other gods who might be listening, to give her the push she needed, but now that it was here, she was rooted and withering.

If she were younger, perhaps—a bit more brash, a bit less jaded—she wouldn't have hesitated.

If she were Astra.

Fuck it, Lunelle thought as she swung her legs over the edge of the bed and slipped on the boots she'd never tucked away after Proserpina's feast. She pulled a cloak from her trunk, yanking the hood low over her face.

"Lunelle?" Lura asked as the princess tied the ribbon.

"Do not stop me," Lunelle said.

Lura grabbed her by the shoulders, her amethyst eyes fixed on her princess.

"I will not stop you, but I also must urge you to please be careful. Let me come—"

"No. No," Lunelle insisted. "I will do this alone. You saw how Arcas responded to the manuscript and the man from the first night. Imagine what he'd do to you—I cannot ask you to take that sort of risk."

Lura relented, but Lunelle could feel her hesitation gnawing at her.

"Please, be careful."

Lunelle only nodded, sweeping from the room as quickly as possible. The palace was quiet. It wasn't so late that everyone had turned in for the night, but most eyes were either bleary with the sleep they craved or a haze of wine as they finished their card games and danced lazily under lowered lanterns.

It was easy for her to slip away, a shadow curling through the garden and onto the streets of Charon.

She took the same path she'd taken before, staying close to the sides of buildings and avoiding the streetlamps as much as possible. When she came to The Underground's door, she released a tense breath. It was as if her body knew she was making the right choice, even if her heart was still bound by fearful black ribbons.

Kwan did not seem surprised to see her as she blew into the tavern, but he *did* seem surprised by the wave of fury that preceded her as she held out her arm.

"I want in," she barked.

"Good evening, Princess," Kwan said quietly, his eyes flashing toward the door. Lunelle sank back on her hip, drawing her arm into her side. She'd assumed this was a safe house of sorts, which was a big assumption to make.

"Did you enjoy your reading material?" Kwan tilted his head toward the door to the stairs, walking slowly across the tavern as she followed.

"I didn't get far before the prince destroyed it," she said softly as they ascended the steps. As they crested the landing outside of his study, Lunelle set her face and balanced her shoulders. "I figure that anything which produces so much anxiety to those in power must be worth fighting for."

"I feared what might happen if Arcas got his hands on it. I was foolish to think he might be tempted to educate himself," Kwan said, tucking himself behind his desk.

"It's a good thing we make copies."

He smiled, pulling the drawer of his desk open, a dozen neatly copied manuscripts tucked beside one another.

"What do I need to do to take the oath?" she asked, afraid that if she slowed her breath, she might come to her senses.

"You're here, that's a good start." Kwan reached to his side, slowly unsheathing a small dagger and resting it in the space between them. "The Nova oath is simple. You can never reveal your participation or anyone else's outside of the rebellion. The blood oath protects us. Most of us have found ways to signal our allegiance without stating it outright. You'll pick it up."

Lunelle nodded.

"You'll have to find someone to initiate you," Kwan said.

Lunelle's brows arched. "You cannot?"

"I will not," Kwan returned. "It's not personal, Princess. You've just scratched the surface—if you really want to join, you'll find your way in."

Lunelle pointed to the slim dagger between them.

"Was this for show, then?"

He pushed it toward her, folding the blade into a slot in the handle.

"It's yours now. My Plutonian captain's insignia is carved into the handle. Whomever you bind yourself to will recognize it and know you can be trusted."

She took the blade, turning it over in her hand. It was lighter than she expected, a scrawling rose piercing a crown carved into the handle.

"And once I'm oathbound?"

"You find your Lunar captain, and you prepare yourself. Revolutions are never bloodless endeavors, Lunelle."

She rubbed her thumb against the intricate carving, letting it warm to her touch.

"Thank you," she said, tucking it into her cloak. "I'll see you again soon."

"I hope that's true," Kwan said.

"AND WHERE WERE you at such a late hour?"

She heard her mother's voice before she saw her proud shoulders held gracefully as she read from one of her daily reports.

"I was out with Yallara," Lunelle said.

"Of course," Oestera sighed, but did not push her further. "Your sister is up to no good, as usual." She waved one of Tula's missives in the air between them. "Seems she injured herself falling off a horse."

"Astra?" Lunelle asked as she peeled her cloak from her shoulders and handed it to Lura, who waited at the door. "What happened to spook the horse? It must have been extreme if Astra couldn't handle it."

Oestera cast a glare at her eldest daughter. "Tula believes there was a snake. But Tula, unfortunately, is a fool."

"She's not a *fool*," Lunelle insisted, sitting across from her mother. "She trusts my sister. Something you might consider trying one day."

141

She smiled, attempting to keep her tone light and playful, but she heard the edge forming on her tongue.

"I trust your sister," Oestera said, leaning back in her seat and pursing her lips. "I trust her to lie straight to Tula's face so convincingly she doesn't think twice. Your father... however... knows her better. She went to Ellume with the Mercurian commander."

"Luxuros?" Lunelle asked, trying to think of her sister's most recent mention of him. They were all quite critical.

"Yes, the Solarian."

Lunelle bristled. "That's quite the accusation, Mother."

"It's not an accusation, it's a fact. And if you couldn't sense it on him the moment he entered the palace, I've failed as your mother."

Lunelle rose from her seat, a veil of sweat forming against her skin.

"And you're just fine with this? You're perfectly content to sell Astra to a king who keeps that kind of company?"

"Sell is a harsh term," Oestera said, laying her book on the cushion beside her. "I merely created the right circumstances for them to meet."

"You forced her hand, you *know* you did! I don't understand how you could do this—"

"Lunelle," Oestera said, a command. *Stand down.* "Your defense of your sister is admirable, but do not fret. I have plans in place for Astra that you do not *want* to understand right now. One day, it will all be clear."

Lunelle's chest tightened—the fabric of her dress felt much stiffer than it had moments ago.

"You always have it all planned, don't you? You brought me here for the same reason. A bargaining chip! And to that awful prince—"

"Think what you want of me, Lunelle. Tell yourself whatever story you need to. But I am doing what's best for all of us, I can assure you of that. I've given you plenty of outs with Arcas. The only one forcing *your* hand is you." Oestera stood, brushing past her daughter as she aimed to disappear into her side of their rooms.

Lunelle was panicked, angry, and flush with a rage she'd never felt before.

A rage she knew her sister felt frequently.

"And what of your mother? Selenia?"

Oestera froze.

"What of her?" she asked without turning.

"Is she where you've learned all your tricks—your *planning*?"

Oestera released a heavy sigh, a sour grin spreading over her lips.

"Selenia is precisely where I learned every move I make, Lunelle. For better or worse."

Oestera pushed into her bedroom, shoving the door shut behind her without an ounce of the grace she held so dearly.

Lunelle stood in the silence, but only briefly.

"Princess," Lura whispered, hovering near her. "Are you all right?"

Lunelle smoothed her skirts and set off for the door.

"I'm staying in the palace," she assured Lura before taking off through the Plutonian halls.

She let her revulsion at her mother's convoluted plans propel her across the palace, through the quiet halls as most of the courtiers slept, and around the corner into the chambers of the Mercurians.

She did not care about the implications as she knocked on his door, nor did she offer any explanation to the baffled servant who answered.

"Where is he?"

"Princess Lunelle—"

She pushed past him. "Where is the king?"

The servant eyed her, his Mercurian greens contrasting with the rich sapphires of the walls.

"Lunelle?"

Mirquios appeared in the doorway, pulling a thin shirt over his shoulders.

"Are you all right?" He stepped closer, his feet bare against the plush rug beneath them as her chest heaved. "Is Astra okay?"

Lunelle's eyes fell to the servant beside them.

"Leave us," Mirquios commanded.

The servant resisted, uncomfortable with Lunelle's vibrating energy.

"Your High—"

"Now!" Mirquios bellowed.

The man faded away through the door Lunelle had just stormed. Mirquios reached for her elbow, a touch she was sure was meant to be comforting, but in her anger, it was irritating. She jerked her arm away.

"He's *Solarian*," she finally growled, three decades of wishing she'd defended her sister louder falling out of her at once. "You left my sister with a godsdamned *Solarian?*"

He reached for her arm again, and she pushed him away, shocking the king.

"Lunelle—"

"Have you lost your wits, Your Highness? Do you've any idea the danger you've put her in? He could, he could, he—"

Mirquios closed the distance between them, towering over her as she struggled to put her fears into words.

"What? He could what? Tell me, Princess, what is it you fear my commander will do? My best friend? My *brother?*"

Lunelle's voice caught in her chest, unsure how to navigate

the weight of a man's seething—she'd been exposed to it so infrequently.

"Speak *up*, Princess."

The spite with which the words leaped from his tongue unraveled something within her that would not return to its spool.

"You know, perhaps my anger has been misplaced," she hissed through her teeth. "Perhaps, *you* are the one I should be suspicious of. From the moment you arrived at my court, you've had nothing but my sister's power in your sights, and I wonder what you *wouldn't* do to ensure she was on your side or unable to stand against you—"

"Lunelle," Mirquios said, his face falling. His hand reached for his chest as he stepped back from her. "Is that what you think of me? That I would con your sister into an attachment with the intention of harming her?"

"I don't know what to think!" Lunelle cried, throwing her hands up. "You are the King of Mercury, but you are also in leagues with the rebels, you are my sister's betrothed, but you cannot deny that you've been on several occasions a bit too comfortable with me—"

"What did you say?" His sparkling eyes burned into her.

"I am not a child, Mirquios, I know when a man has more on his mind than—"

"Not that," Mirquios breathed. He gripped his chest as he moved closer to her. "But trust that we'll get back to *that*."

Lunelle inhaled slowly, trying to gather the thoughts that had exploded from her mind across the room.

The king eased further into her space, consuming her.

"Who am I in leagues with, Princess?"

She swallowed. "I—"

His head tilted. "Come now, Lunelle. You're far too wise to accuse without evidence."

She folded her arms, swallowing against the heat of his stare.

"I followed you," she admitted. "To The Underground."

Mirquios nodded. "Keep going."

"I spoke with Kwan," she continued, her nerves beginning to seep back into her speech. Mirquios circled his finger between them, begging her to keep pulling at the thread.

"And what did you discuss?"

Kwan's words clicked into a linear thought in her mind—the king was oathbound to someone, and forbidden from revealing himself to her.

"You cannot tell me," Lunelle breathed.

His eyes widened, a slow smile breaking across his jaw. Lunelle reached into her cloak and felt for the blade Kwan gifted her, shoving it into the king's hands.

"Bind me," she gasped. "You can bind me, can't you?"

Mirquios examined her with those all-seeing eyes, a blush spreading across her neck as she feared he saw more than she intended to display.

"And you understand fully what you're getting yourself into?"

"Absolutely not," she sighed.

The king laughed, bursting through the tension between them.

"Good, that was a test of your arrogance. But you've read the manifesto?"

She frowned. "Partially. Arcas found it. He burned it."

"Bastard," Mirquios muttered. "But you're genuine—you want to bring about the end of the monarchies? You understand that the end goal aims even higher?" His eyes swept upward.

Lunelle nodded, for the first time in her entire life, she felt it deep within her, emanating from the very marrow in her bones—she had found it. The *thing* she was chasing.

"Hold out your hand."

She extended her pale palm, glimmering under the low lanterns, as he unfolded the blade.

"A shallow cut will do," he said, his voice steady as he dragged the sharp tip across her flesh, carving a delicate arc in the shape of a crescent moon. "Might as well make you the Lunar queen in your scars, since you may never reign on the throne."

Lunelle's lips twisted into a smile, her breath catching as the sting in her flesh sank between tendons, returning a bloody blossom from the wound. A bronze glimmer flickered in the swirling crimsons, the goddess blood within her lurching to the surface of her skin. Mirquios repeated the movement against his own palm, creating a mirrored moon to hers.

"Lunelle Aurellis, Princess of Lunaria, you will fight for the people who serve the courts alongside them, never over them. You will protect peace and reject oppression. You will never reveal your association or another Nova's as long as we both breathe."

He held out his palm, stained with a rush of red. She averted her eyes as she rested her hand over his, unable to hold their intensity.

The king closed his fingers around hers, pressing their cuts together. He squeezed to ensure their blood intertwined, a searing heat gripping the nerves of their palms and fusing them together.

Lunelle drew in a sharp breath at the pain, wondering if she would feel any different now that she'd taken such a large step into the ether.

Mirquios stared at their entangled hands. "Now, the other thing you said—"

A flush of embarrassment crawled over her neck, pushing her back a step. She'd hoped he would forget the other accusation she'd made, as she hadn't meant to let it slip out.

She hadn't meant for many of the things she said lately to slip out.

Lunelle sighed, preparing to face the cursed greens of his eyes, impossible to tolerate at such a close distance.

"I shouldn't have said that," she admitted quietly, staring at their hands still resting together, the sting racing around her flesh. "I was angry at you, I'm *still* angry, by the way. But I was being ridiculous—"

"Were you?" he asked, his low voice slipping into a hushed whisper across her lips.

The king's other hand reached forward, catching her chin and forcing her to look at him.

To *see* him.

Her eyes flickered to his, and she swore she heard the entire realm draw a breath as that *thing* in her chest she'd wrestled with so many times broke free, shattering bone and blood vessels as it tore through her.

She reached for it, attempting to capture the rush, but there was no containing it.

The king's hand tightened around hers as time crashed to a halt, the static between them popping into an iridescent shimmer that dimmed the rest of the world, leaving only them.

Only that single second.

Oh, gods.

Lunelle searched for a breath. She did not find it within herself, but rather between them, pulled from an impossible, invisible thread she'd only ever heard stories of.

"H-how? No," she sputtered, backing away from him, but that only sealed their Fate—it was undeniable as she rocked back and felt the Tether pull at her ribs, begging her to return to him.

"Lunelle," Mirquios whispered, his eyes as wide as hers, breath just as stilted.

"I don't—I don't understand! Oh," she gasped. "Oh, my gods, how? My sister! You're Tethered to Astra!"

Lunelle grasped at the space between them, sure she'd be able to pluck it away from her like a piece of lint.

"Right," Mirquios said, a hesitation beneath his words she could not unhear. "No, Lunelle, wait. I can explain—"

"There is nothing to explain, Your Highness," she said through clenched teeth, backing away from him. "This—this is impossible. This cannot happen. You belong to my sister, no matter what you two have agreed upon, this does not change that."

Lunelle fought back a sob, the overwhelm of the Tether setting her entire Soul on fire.

"Yes," he agreed, his hand rubbing at the bruise on his chest.

Lunelle did not bid him farewell.

She did not ask questions she did not want to know the answers to.

She did not risk looking into those dazzling eyes once more as she opened his door.

She felt it, the release on the cord between them as he moved to follow her.

"Do not," she choked. "Please."

She felt every ragged breath he released as she ran, fighting every instinct that begged her to retreat, to run back into his arms the entire way.

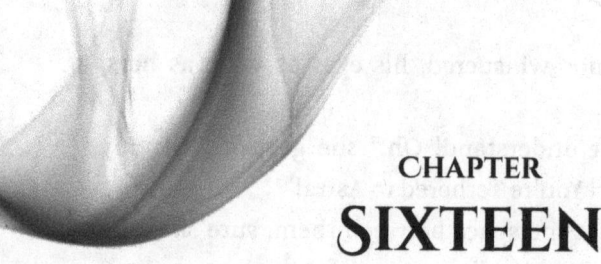

CHAPTER
SIXTEEN

L unelle aimed to get back to her room, where she could panic in private.

And yet, the madness within her pushed her feet toward the eastern wing of the palace, where two guards flanked the ornate bronze doors of the prince's chambers.

As she approached, they did not ask questions. They merely pulled back the heavy door, welcoming her in.

She'd been expected.

She wasn't sure what disturbed her more, that she'd made herself into the prince's plaything or that she'd just committed the deepest betrayal of her sister without intending to.

It did not matter.

Both suffocated her as she entered his chambers.

Arcas was not in the massive bed to her right, layered with plush quilts and pillows. Candlelight flickered on one night-stand—that must have been his side, she noted.

Her stomach twisted in knots as she stepped further into the room, deep blue velvets and black silks creating a dark, lush space. The doors at the far end were flung open, letting the Autumn air float across the dark marble. His slender frame appeared in the doorway, lit by the rainbow aurora of the Rift behind him.

He looked more like a deity than a man.

And that was a dangerous line of thinking.

He was only in a pair of soft sleep pants, the rest of him exposed to the starry sky above.

"Lunelle."

"Arcas," she muttered. His name was a curse—a means to an end. She was so utterly thrown by the Tether in her chest, so miserable under its strain that she would have done anything to forget about it.

And she was about to.

"I wasn't sure if I'd see you tonight."

She only nodded, fiddling with the lace of her sleeve.

"What's wrong?" Arcas squinted in the dim lighting, tilting his head. His jaw flexed, an irritation there she could not identify. "What do you need from me, Princess?"

She took a breath. And then another.

And a third for good measure.

And then she hauled herself to him, praying to any god that might be listening that it would take away the stone settling in her stomach for just a moment.

Their bodies clashed together, a low grunt leaving his bare chest as she pulled at him. This was not the controlled exploration of her desires before, where she knew exactly what she wanted and how to get it.

This was a woman unhinged, desperate to numb many types of pain at once. She roamed her hands over his torso, his fingers finding their place on her hips and in her hair, pulling harder than he might have had she not swept in with such a fury at her back.

Arcas did not ask another question—perhaps afraid of

what the answers might be—as he backed her into the glass of his balcony door, bracing himself before pulling against her backside and wrapping her legs around his waist. He never broke contact with her mouth, taking anything she would give him as he walked her toward his bed.

She was slipping under the waves of him before her back even hit the silk of his bedding, surprised when she was suddenly horizontal. He reached for her braid, tugging at the leather band and releasing her long white waves.

He crashed over her, the weight of him a welcome anchor to her heavy heart.

She could feel him between her legs, already hardened at the thought of her seeking him out once more, ready to make her forget. Lunelle clutched at his back as he kissed her neck, his bare skin smooth to her touch as she ground her hips over his.

Arcas tore at her dress, pulling it down over her shoulders and around her waist. She rolled beneath him to her belly, and he separated from her only to slide the dress off her hips and legs, shedding his pants in the process. He fell back over her, kissing a sizzling line up her spine and straddling her hips. She could feel the length of him resting against her, but he was focused on other things first.

"You're so tense you feel like you're about to burst, and not in a way I'd like to see," he mumbled. He leaned over her, reaching for the candle on his nightstand. Arcas hissed as he dipped his fingers into the molten center, rubbing his palms together as the wax slipped between his skin, glazing them in an oily sheen that smelled like the roses in his gardens.

He ran his hands over her back, the warmth from the oil soaking into her muscles as he leaned his weight into her, massaging the tense knots away. With every movement he made, she felt him graze her backside, the swollen heat of him teasing her. He was on his third round of wax when she snapped, arching her spine so her ass pushed into him, begging for more friction, more movement, more of him inside of her.

"We don't want to play, then?" he hummed, running his hands up her sides, brushing the sensitive skin of her breasts. Lunelle bucked again. "Fine," he sighed, pressing a kiss against the back of her neck.

He leaned his weight over her, his knee hooking behind hers and pushing her leg out, creating space for him.

"Gods," he sighed as she gasped, rolling her head forward and sending her sheet of silver locks over the edge of his bed. He stayed still for a moment, repositioning his arms around her, wrapping his long fingers around her neck, and pulling her face toward him as he hovered over her.

Lunelle took his thumb into her mouth, biting at the soft flesh of a hand that had been spoiled in his palace. Her refreshed irritation with him spurred her on, pushing her hips back as she bit down harder.

"Easy now, starling," Arcas purred, twisting his hand tightly into her hair. The sting on her scalp erased the sting in her ribs. "You don't want to start a game you cannot win."

Lunelle arched harder, twisting her neck to find his hard gaze as his knee pushed her leg further toward her elbow, allowing him to sink deeper and take up more of her space.

That was enough for her.

The way his thighs hit hers, the twitch of his fingers in her mouth, his hot breath in her ear... all of it was enough to destroy whatever pain her misfortune planted within her and send her mind over the edge of the Plutonian cliffs.

His lips claimed her ear, her neck, her shoulder, leaving marks across her entire body as she slowly felt her muscles coil around his.

"That's right," he sighed as she rocked back and forth with him, finally releasing the last vestige of self-loathing keeping her from fully enjoying her distraction of choice. "Take what's yours, Princess."

She pulled his hand from her mouth and shoved it between the bed and her breasts. He may not have been the leader his court needed, but he at least had no problem taking direction. He pinched her soft skin as she rocked her hips faster, taking more.

Arcas leaned back, the pale blue column of his throat stretching toward the ceiling and out of her limited view.

Lunelle closed her eyes, resting her forehead against her arm as he groaned behind her, the sound so delicious she almost forgot she was meant to loathe him. As he pushed her closer to the edge, his grip loosened, the thumb she'd bitten earlier now hovering between her legs.

She pushed her head up, looking over her shoulder. His head leaned back, eyes closed, his lower lip tucked between his teeth as he kneaded her. His throat tightened with the same tension that kept her in place. She watched his thumb swirl a circle around her lower back, hesitating to move lower.

"Do not hold back from me," she said.

Arcas's eyes snapped forward, searching for hers.

"Are you sure, Princess?"

She nodded, the need for more from him driving her onward. Arcas grinned, a darkness welling within his eyes she should have feared, if she didn't know how pathetic he was beneath the veneer of his crown. He leaned over her, that cursed thumb of his slipping lower, but not low enough.

"Ask nicely," he whispered.

"Arcas," she muttered, the pleasure of him quickly drowning in his petulance. He pressed lightly against her, hardly a brush, but it was enough to change her tone as she writhed beneath him, desperate for more.

"You came to me," he said, hovering near her, but not giving in to a second touch. "You *need* me."

Lunelle released a muffled whimper, annoyed enough that she debated if she'd be able to finish the job herself, but just as she began to say as much, a lightning bolt traveled her spine and crackled against the base of her skull as he pressed into her once more.

A satisfied laugh rumbled against her ear. "Ask for more, I'll give you anything you ask for."

"Please," she managed, her teeth clenched tightly against the plea. He did not require her to elaborate on her request. An immediate increase in pressure sent her into another universe entirely. She pushed into the touch, her heart pounding as her vision exploded into white stars. "Arcas—"

"Let go for me, Lunelle," he rasped.

She clenched around him, her entire body dissolving into a rippled spasm that seemed to have no end in sight as he fell forward again, gripping her throat as she cried out. It was as if he wanted to catch the notes and hold onto them in the dark.

Arcas tensed against her, his breathing stifled as he bit at her ear again.

"Where do you want me to—"

"Anywhere but inside of me," she huffed, hardly able to breathe as he pulled away from her.

Arcas collapsed beside her, tangling their legs as she struggled to breathe, the pressure of him gone, the emptiness within her welling into a hot flood of tears at the back of her throat. The pleasure of him hadn't lasted but a second after it was over, the reality of her heartache returning in full force.

"You may stay here tonight if you want to," he offered, stroking her arm lazily.

She pushed herself upright, searching for her dress.

"Not tonight," she mumbled through the wave of stinging pain clutching at her chest.

She was still pulling her dress on when she burst from his room and darted across the palace, the Tether in her chest yanking reluctantly the entire way.

CHAPTER
SEVENTEEN

S ome things were so painful that one could not even risk thinking about them, let alone acknowledging them out loud.

Tethering to her sister's betrothed king after binding herself to him in blood was certainly one of those things.

Fucking a prince she hated—but couldn't seem to stay away from—to fill the void carved by the aforementioned king was another.

She could not tell which sat heavier on her shoulders.

Despite the near-constant ache in her chest begging her to get out of bed, shirk any concept of morality, and run to either of their arms, Lunelle did her best to ignore the alarms ringing against her skull.

Instead, she thought about how irritated she was with her mother as they dressed for the first meeting of the morning. Arcas had promised testimony from a captured Neptunian spy, and Oestera was eager to hear from them.

Lunelle had faked illness for the last three days, and she

knew her excuses as to why she could not attend the daily activities were dwindling.

As Lura helped her slide the morning gown over her chest, Lunelle nearly lost her breath, the ripple of the invisible Tether so unsettling.

"Are you well, Princess?" Lura asked.

"Fine," she muttered.

"You seem... distraught."

Lunelle's eyes flashed to Lura's in the mirror before her. Distraught was one way to put it—she might have gone with something more akin to *devastated* or *so confused I can't figure out which way is Above and which is Below.*

"I have much on my mind," Lunelle returned.

Lura laced up her dress, each tug of the ribbons a brutal reminder that she'd soon have to face the king.

And the prince.

Oh gods.

"Princess, your heart!" Lura's forehead creased with concern, her eyes wide as she listened to Lunelle draw a ragged breath. Of the two secrets shredding her mind, one would strike her dead for revealing, and the other simply made her wish for such a mercy.

"Lura," she breathed, the thought of saying it aloud choking her.

"What has happened?" Lura held her shoulders, searching her crystalline gaze. "Are you safe?"

No. No, she was not safe. She was in grave danger.

Lunelle held her shoulders back, fighting the urge to crumple into a sputtering mess. This was not who she was, not who her mother had carved her into. She rubbed her fingers over the small scar in her palm as if it might release some sort of cosmic wisdom and free her from this spiral.

"Are you hurt?" Lura asked, pulling her hand out between

them. The Moon-shaped cut was small enough—harmless to anyone not looking closely—but Lura *was* looking closely.

Lura softly scratched at the neckline of her dress, shifting the fabric ever so slightly away from her body and revealing the edges of a tattoo Lunelle recognized instantly, even from just a glance.

A dagger and the edge of a crown were inked in silver against her collarbone.

The princess gasped softly as her veins seized with adrenaline. She stared at her maiden, her friend of two decades, watching as Lura's lips curled.

"I don't know the secret passwords," Lunelle sighed, her eyes wide.

Lura sputtered a laugh. "Who bound you?" She held up her own wrist, a barely-there pink scar hovering beneath the fabric of her sleeve.

"I cannot say, can I?"

"You needn't worry about the oath within the rebellion, it's only outside of us that you'll have consequences."

"I did not get a copy of the rules."

Lura sighed. "If you had, that damned prince would have just incinerated it anyway."

Lunelle's brows arched.

"Apologies, Princess—"

Lunelle grasped her hand. "No! No, none of that. No more of that at all. I took the same oath you did, Lura. And I did it in all sincerity. I am not your princess, I am your peer."

"Well, then," Lura said. "What in the Nether are we going to do about the prince?"

Her heart sank. The weight of it was all too much.

"If only that were our largest problem, Lura."

The maiden's head tilted, a hesitation seeping into her smile.

"I will not bind you by blood, but if you tell a single Soul, I will make you wish the oath struck you dead before I did."

Lura bristled, so unused to hearing anything of the sort from this sister. Astra had threatened her with much more for much less.

She nodded. "Of course, Prin—Lunelle."

Lunelle backed away from her, twisting her fingers against her chest.

"The Mercurian king bound me into the rebellion." Just breathing around the sounds of his home court felt impossible.

"Mirquios! Oh, that's fantastic, do you think he bound your sister as well?"

"I do not know," Lunelle mumbled. "But something... else. Something else happened between us."

"Oh," Lura gasped, a shadow passing over her face. "Oh, Lunelle. These things are hard to navigate, I'm sure your sister can forgive—"

"Not that," Lunelle interrupted. "It's worse than that. The king and I... when our palms touched..." Gods, how to say it, how to commit to it? If she said it, she could never escape it. "I believe we Tethered."

Lura's eyes flared, the amethyst swirls darkening as she considered the implications.

"You... you believe? You are not sure?"

Lunelle shook her head. "I do not know what else it could have been! I ran from him immediately, I was so over-whelmed."

"But if you aren't positive... what if it was not a Tether? What if it was just the alchemy between a demigoddess and a man as he bound you? Our blood is not like his."

"What do you mean?" Lunelle sank into an armchair, her

head lighter now that she'd found someone to share her burden with.

"We share blood with the gods Above, Lunelle. We do not bleed crimson like the humans do. There's something within it, something gilded, something that sparks and hums. You've felt it—surely."

Lunelle thought back to her stibnite pieces, how they seemed to sing at her touch.

"I always thought that when—*if*—it happened, I would not be the least bit unsure."

Lura kneeled before her, taking her hands from her lap.

"That's how it should be, Lunelle. There should be no doubt. What if this is all just a misinterpretation?"

"Perhaps," she admitted, daring to relive the moment in her mind.

She'd felt her entire being shift, hadn't she?

She'd heard the way her bones creaked as they moved to accommodate the weight of his Soul within hers.

She'd felt him pace the halls all morning, wandering back and forth, the cord between them ebbing and flowing in response. Hesitating outside her door last night.

Or perhaps it was all in her mind, her sick, *twisted* mind.

What if she was merely assigning a myth to the irredeemable feelings bubbling under her skin when she was near him?

Was she trying to excuse the betrayal of her sister?

"I suppose the only way for you to know is to see him again."

Lura stood, offering her hands to pull Lunelle forward.

She sighed. "I'd sooner tell my mother I joined a rebellion against her throne."

Lura winced. "Start with the king, perhaps."

Any hope Lura had inspired in her chest that it had all been some sort of cosmic misunderstanding disappeared when Lunelle felt the king's anxious energy hovering outside the dining hall.

She'd felt it when he left his room and again when he returned to it. She felt it tense and stretch as he stopped dead in his tracks entering the hall, his bright gaze falling on her.

She felt the shallow breaths rippling from him as he did the calculations and realized how limited his seating options were. But his crown prevailed, the pride woven into his muscles carried him through the hall's doors.

Perhaps he'd convinced himself it was nothing, too.

"...and beyond that, I firmly believe we need to be more considerate of the Inner Courts' sentiments before we make a final decision. If your court does not fully embrace the Plutonians, the Living Courts will feel those ripples in the water—oh. Oh! Oh," Kahlia, the High Regent of Venus, had been deep in conversation with Oestera when they stumbled over their words, their brows arching in surprise at the morning's mysterious tension.

Lunelle had not been fully engaged, she knew, but she heard the startle in their speech. Her eyes flickered to Kahlia's and then followed as they widened and darted between Lunelle and the king as he hovered near the door.

"At any rate," Kahlia recovered and continued. "We cannot move forward if there's any... hesitation... on the princess's side."

Oestera nodded, watching her daughter's face carefully as she sipped her tea, the hot liquid hardly registering to her.

"Good morrow, Your Highness!" Kahlia called as Lunelle

felt the cursed rope around her heart circle her. Mirquios kept a wide berth as he rounded the table and sat between her mother and the other Venusian courtiers.

Five sets of dreamy, lovelorn eyes watched in silence as the Lunar princess and Mercurian king avoided acknowledging one another.

Oestera cleared her throat.

"I understand your concerns, Kahlia. Deeply," she added. "There is plenty for Lunelle and me to discuss on the matter. We will be thoughtful in our decisions."

"Excellent," Kahlia mumbled, the tension at the table pulsating through the morning air.

"Arcas!" Oestera called out as the prince appeared. She stood, rushing toward him as she looped her arm through his, disappearing into the palace gardens beyond the dining hall.

It was just as well, Lunelle thought. She didn't need another man with whom to avoid eye contact.

"I believe we're late for our conference with the Martians," Kahlia said to their courtiers. They all rose in fluid motions, their soft gazes avoiding falling between the young king and princess.

And then they were very much alone.

"Lunelle," Mirquios whispered, his voice tight.

She risked a glance at him.

The second their eyes met, there was no possible way to deny their unfortunate truth.

"Godsdammit," Lunelle cursed, her chest on fire with seething anger, and something else. Something she'd spent so very much of her life pretending she did not have.

Desire.

"Lu," Mirquios said again, leaning forward. His courtiers filed into the dining hall, as well as the rest of the Lunar Court. "I do not know where to begin—"

"You can start with how in the Nether you've managed to Tether to not one sister but *two*," she growled.

Mirquios scoffed, a sound that stoked the rage within her.

"I only... I only Tethered to one," he said. For just a moment, her mind turned over the possibility that she was once again wrong. "Astra... she did not think your mother would approve of her choice of suitors, so we... we concocted the Tether story."

Lunelle rolled her eyes. "My mother invited you expressly to court my sister, you knew she would approve!"

"I did," Mirquios nodded. "That is true. But I *also* knew that if your sister knew that, she'd run off with the next fool, and I did not want to risk losing her to another court. Not all of the monarchs are as bought into the vision as we are. I knew Astra would be safe in Mercury. She has the experience we need from her time in Celene. I thought it was harmless. I never—*never*—would have gone along with it if I'd known! If I..." He swallowed, his eyes softening. "If I had known what I was missing."

Lunelle sighed, the tension melting just a tad in her shoulders. It did not solve any of the problems it presented, but it did ease her overwhelming guilt enough that she could breathe again.

"You and Astra..."

"If you asked her, she'd tell you the exact same story, I swear it. She'd also tell you, while laughing, I'm sure, that romantically... we were not much of a pair."

Lunelle blushed, the delicate rose shade sending a companion heat to his neck.

"I do not need to know the details of your intimate encounters, Mirquios, I assure you—"

"There were none!" he said bluntly, perhaps a bit too loudly. He lowered his tone. "That's what I'm trying to tell you,

Lunelle. We both agreed this was a political move, not one of passion."

"It does not matter," Lunelle said. "Your status does not change with your feelings, Mirquios. You are still engaged to her, and she is still counting on a union with you. I will not be the reason her plans fall apart, I cannot—"

"Understood," he said, waving a hand between them as her voice reached a pitch on the brink of tears. "I have no aims at coming between sisters."

"That aside, I'm practically engaged to Arcas—"

"No," Mirquios muttered. "Not yet, you are not."

Her lips twisted into a delicate pout, the words coming out in a tight whisper.

"But I will be."

Mirquios pushed against his chest. Her sternum ached around her heart as it strained to contain the impulse to reach across the table and haul him to her.

"Surely it will not feel like this forever," Lunelle offered. "So arduous. If you're to marry Astra, you'll forever be in my life in some way. We will be friends, as we are now."

Mirquios leaned away from her, the Tether pulling tight between them.

"Of course," he said.

"It will be enough," she assured him. "It *has* to be enough, Mirquios."

The king did not have a response.

CHAPTER
EIGHTEEN

T he pull of the Tether did not get any less distracting.

If anything, it got worse as the day wore on.

It wasn't just the physical tug she felt toward him, but the emotional complexity that drowned her. It was like she could hear his thoughts from another room over—muted and muffled, but the sentiment relayed all the same. He was feeling just as conflicted as she was.

She'd escaped the torture after dinner, opting to hide in the pomegranate orchards instead of suffering through more drinks and dancing, likely in arms she could no longer think about without feeling the need to vomit.

It was all supremely cruel.

She wandered through the orchard, enjoying the familiarity of the night wrapped around her shoulders until she came to the ancient tree she'd stood before just a few weeks prior. The roots dove underground in thick, wise twists, speckled with fallen fruit.

"Perhaps you were right," Lunelle whispered to Proserpina,

wherever she was. "Perhaps neither Mercury nor Pluto was at fault, but only yourself."

She sighed, folding herself between roots at the base of the tree, tossing her skirts over her feet as she leaned against the withering bark.

"Or perhaps you were the eldest daughter," Lunelle mumbled. "Trapped by the expectations, theirs and yours."

She pushed at the muscles in her chest, their constant engagement starting to wear on her.

"You could have at least warned me," Lunelle said, closing her eyes.

"Warned you about what?"

She snapped her head forward as the prince approached. His evening attire was lined in glimmering silver threads reflecting the moonlight above.

"Arcas," she said, moving to stand, but he waved her off.

"May I join you?"

She nodded as he sat beside her, his tall, slender frame weaving between roots and overgrown grass. His eyes fell to her chest, and for one moment, she worried he could see what she felt, but she realized she was still massaging the sore muscles.

"You've seemed unwell these last few days," he said.

"Have I?" she asked, knowing he was doing her a kindness by calling it so gently.

"I hope that it doesn't have anything to do with the other night—"

"No," Lunelle scoffed. It had nearly everything to do with that night, but not for the reasons he thought.

"Good. I know we are... somewhat attached, Princess, but I would like to discuss formalizing our engagement."

"Oh," Lunelle breathed. "My mother really should be—"

"She and I have spoken. Many times. But I find myself

wondering if you do indeed wish to take the Plutonian throne—"

"What?" she asked, sitting up straighter to face him.

"Where did I lose you?"

She bit her lip. "If we were to wed, Arcas, you would be the Lunar king. I would not be the Plutonian queen. You would forfeit your throne to your sister—you are aware of this, surely!"

Arcas frowned. "I assumed your sister would take the Lunar throne and you'd rule beside me."

She eyed him, baffled. "Forget all of the reasons I would have no need to make such a trade, but why would *you* give up a more powerful throne?"

"*You* have more power in the Lunar Court. I would be an accessory at best."

Lunelle sneered. "For one thing, that's not how it works in the Lunar Court. My father is an integral leader in our society —you've clearly been stained by your father's misgivings about women on thrones. And for another, by your own logic, you'd prefer I become the accessory, then?"

His lips twisted as his face flushed. "That is not what I meant—"

She folded her arms across her chest, the buzzing of the Tether whispering to double down. To wound him. She stood, determined to say her final piece and leave his grasping for a lick of sense.

"Allow me to remind you which one of us is here to beg the other's mercy, *Prince*." She spat the word, her foot digging into the soft ground.

"Lunelle," he sighed, standing from his perch. "I did not mean to hurt your feelings."

"My feelings are fine!" she declared. "It's my pride you've assaulted if anything. I will not be relegated to planning balls

COURTING DEATH & DESIRE

and festivals, Arcas. We are heading for a war, a war the likes of which has not been seen in centuries, and I am poised to lead the most powerful armies in the universe through it. I will not be stepping away from my court for anything, but especially not for a man who does not understand the first thing about duty—a man who not a month ago told me he'd just as soon appoint someone else to his throne because he's too *scared* to do right by them."

She moved to dart into the trees, but he caught her elbow.

"And what of *your* logic then? If you're so offended by my lack of duty to my court, surely you can understand why I might have changed my mind after a certain princess woke me from my stupor?"

Lunelle pulled her arm from his grasp. "If you truly cared about them, you'd do whatever it took to secure their safety. You'd sit proudly beside the Lunar queen and let your sister, who is *more* than capable, lead them to victory. Staying here out of a sense of duty instead of seeking out what would be truly beneficial is cowardly at best. Selfish at worst."

"Yallara is a child—"

She snorted. "And you're so grown?"

Arcas glared, hovering over her, his eyes falling as the wheels turned within his mind.

"My sister is easily swayed by the movements around her, she does not understand their larger implications, she does not understand the long-term impact, and she has no respect for the traditions of our ancestors! My father would turn in his grave if I put her on the throne."

Lunelle grinned, the cracks in his armor showing now. She stepped closer, her proximity cutting off his thoughts.

"Your father? The one you told me in no uncertain terms was a *monster*. Why are you so haunted by his voice? What part of you still cries out for a man who, by your own admission, had no love for his sons? The world that made you is gone—it's burning away by the second. You are well-heeled, Arcas, but even the most loyal dog still sleeps outside."

"I beg your—"

She clutched at his tunic. "Ask yourself why you're so dedicated to earning the approval of a ghost."

"Because!" he roared. "Because. Because I know no other way—"

Lunelle rasped, "Because you know no other way or because you *like* it this way?"

Arcas glared, his eyes flashing even in the dark.

She stepped closer once again. "Power is an addictive substance, Arcas, but it is also corrosive. Things do not have to stay this way simply because you like the way it tastes."

A chill settled between them, charged with spilled ink and smoke.

"And what about you, Princess? Does your mother know she's raised such a progressive thinker?" he whispered.

"She had her chance to disappoint her mother. I look forward to having mine."

She slowly inhaled, her chest tightening as she leaned closer to him, casting a heated stare into his.

"You mystify me," Arcas mumbled.

Lunelle tilted her head, narrowing her eyes.

"If only you'd mystify *me*. I can predict you as well as I can predict the phases of the—"

Before she could finish her insult, Arcas closed the gap between them, pressing his lips to hers and stealing her breath in a way that she didn't find entirely unpleasant.

Lunelle pulled herself away from him, lost on how to breathe, how to see straight. And for a moment, she didn't feel a sick pooling in her chest.

For a moment, she wasn't thinking about... well... a gods-damned thing.

Lunelle thrust herself forward again, tangling herself with Arcas and forgetting everything about everyone except the way he tasted like certain dark things. There was only him. She melted into his touch as his long fingers tore at the back of her dress, digging into the silk ribbons at her waist. He twisted her, backing her into the ancient bark of the tree.

Peeling wood clawed at her hair, but even that felt good in his haze.

His fingers crawled over her, hesitating at her breast before she pushed his hand upward, letting him hold onto her in all the ways she'd secretly craved since she left his bed the last time.

It was senseless—it was *cruel*—to let him give her even a fraction of what she so desperately wanted. To take anything from him at all.

His mouth dropped from hers to her neck, his hips crashing into hers. It was the whisper of her name that sent a despairing wave of reality over her.

"Arcas," she sputtered back, pushing him away.

His breath caught, a whimpered plea escaping in the passion before he grabbed hold of his senses. His chest heaved as he ran his hand over his face, disheveled in a way he was not keen to let go of.

They both gasped for breath in the silence.

There, in the heft of the air between them, there was something else. Something so wildly uncontrollable to her, the urge to unfold herself before him and let him see pieces of her no one else had access to.

It was beyond maddening.

She stepped forward again, holding either side of his face as she examined him, his eyes boring into hers.

"What are you—"

"Shh," she whispered. "I'm trying to convince myself not to fuck some sense into you."

"I'm afraid you've only ever had the opposite effect, Princess," he returned, pulling her into a darker, more tender kiss that twisted spaces within her she had not felt before. His tongue parted her lips, poisoning her slowly, the haze of him spreading through her veins. His hand wandered over her, giving her more space to breathe between touches, to feel the full arc of his movements as he dragged his fingertips across the neckline of her gown.

His fingers slipped below, pinching at her breast, eliciting a soft gasp from her throat that he was quick to replicate.

He traced his lips over her jaw, grasping at her neck. She was lost to him, fully given up on trying to stop this. She *needed* it.

Arcas pressed her further into the tree, his knee slipping between her legs. It was irony in her truest form—the heat of the Ice Queen, revealing that he had any semblance of control over her.

He whispered into her ear, "I wonder..." Arcas dragged a finger across her cheek. "Do you blush like that under his touch, or just mine?"

Lunelle froze.

"Excuse me?"

Arcas pulled his fingertip away from her face.

"I have eyes everywhere, Lunelle. There isn't a room you enter I don't know about."

Lunelle shoved him away from her, the heat in the blood pumping through her chest fizzling at his implication.

"Nor do I mind," Arcas said, shrugging. "You can spend whatever time you wish with the Mercurian."

She could have cleared the accusation. She could have told

him there was nothing—*nothing*—going on between them. Because the truth was that nothing *could* pass between them in the end.

But she liked the way his eyes flared when she smirked.

"I'll be sure to ask him and report back."

Arcas parted his lips but seemed to think better of his next insult. Instead, he leaned forward and brushed his lips to hers one more time, surprising her as she pulled away.

"Good evening, Lunelle."

"Arcas—"

It was almost better that he darted into the trees before she could find anything else to say.

The moment he left her line of sight, the torture of the Tether resumed, burning a hole right through her and suffocating any attempts at justifying her actions.

She should have known it would be even louder upon its return. She should have predicted that yet another tryst with Arcas would only make her feel worse.

But she could not have fathomed the absolute crush of betrayal she felt as Mirquios's movements faded back into her consciousness.

The Tether hummed and twisted as she wandered from the grove, aimless as the fog from the sheer range of her predicaments pulled at her mind. If she hadn't been so overwhelmed, she might have felt the sudden slack on the cord as she rounded the corner outside of her quarters.

"Princess," Mirquios said as she stopped short of him, her cheeks flushing.

Could he feel it? What she'd done? The same way she felt him sigh in pain or tense in irritation all day?

"I was just on my way to bed," she muttered, unable to look at him.

Mirquios stepped closer, the sigh of the Tether too generous, too tempting.

"Lu—"

"Goodnight," she rasped, fighting a downpour as a storm swelled in her chest.

She left him in the hall, where he stayed for much longer than she'd liked to have known.

"You should not be here," Lunelle whispered as she looked up from her book.

They were not in the Plutonian Court in her dream. They were back home, tucked away into Lunelle's favorite corner of the smallest library in the palace. Moonbeams shattered between shelves, warping and wavering in the astral.

She'd been curled up in the armchair she liked best, re-reading the same book of poetry she'd read dozens of times, running her fingers over the bleeding ink in the margins with her sister's bold lettering.

Hiding. That's what she'd really been doing. Though the sting of her guilt was quieter in this plane, it still poked at her as she tried to steady her breath.

"I wouldn't even know where 'here' is," Mirquios mumbled, leaning against an ancient shelf.

She folded her book, setting it in her lap as she lowered her feet to the floor.

"We're in the Andromeda library back home. Not far from your quarters."

He nodded and pointed to her book.

"Any good?"

Lunelle laughed, but it was a curt sound, an immediate reminder that nothing about this was amusing.

"It's my favorite."

"And your favorite tea," he said, gesturing to the simmering pot of chamomile on the coffee table before her. *"Well, favorite non-hallucinogenic tea."*

"Correct," she said.

"And your favorite Mercurian."

Lunelle glanced around. *"Is the commander here?"*

The king winced. *"Ha, very funny."*

"It doesn't hurt as much here," Lunelle said, rubbing at her chest. She could still feel the Tether, but it was a whisper instead of a shout.

"Much easier," he agreed. *"You seemed agitated in the hall earlier. More so than at dinner. Or lunch."*

She heaved a sigh. *"I had an... argument with the prince."*

"Ah," he said. They were both unsure how to navigate the topic —it was clear in their twin hesitation to move forward.

He left his station at the shelf and sat on the coffee table across from her. Even there, where everything moved in slow currents, the air still pulled taut between them.

"Did he hurt you?"

Lunelle rolled her eyes. *"No. It would certainly be easier to hate him if he were as physically cruel as he can be emotionally."*

"But he touched you," Mirquios said. He did not ask. He didn't have to.

"It wasn't uninvited," Lunelle whispered.

The king nodded slowly, a strange blend of envy and anger slipping between them. She felt his attempts to suppress the emotions bleeding into the Tether, but it was not enough to quiet the resounding thought bouncing between their chests.

She was not his. She was not his. She was not his.

"Gods, this is complicated," he admitted.

Lunelle winced. *"Everything is. Arcas... is incredibly complex. I can feel it in him—he wants to do good, but he is so misguided about what 'good' looks like for everyone. I do not know how to get through to him. The moment we get into any serious conversations, we both explode. I fear the only thing that stops us from killing one another is... is—"*

Mirquios eyed her. "You don't owe me any explanations, Lunelle."

"I know. And yet, I feel compelled to share every passing thought with you."

"I worry, Lu. If he found out about you joining the rebels... the volatility you describe... it would be a disaster."

Lunelle frowned. She'd thought of nothing else all evening.

"I can handle myself."

"Of course you can," he said. "But you don't have to. I know that we're in a complex situation. But I cannot stop myself from caring for you, in whatever capacity you'll allow. If you want to be friends, we will be the very best of them. If you want to be enemies, it would be my honor to bare my neck to you. The only thing I can't be to you is indifferent."

Her wide eyes drank him in, allowing the slightest smile to unfurl over her lips. She leaned forward yet again, knowing the danger it put her in. But it was impossible to resist the warmth of him.

"You will make this impossible for me, won't you?"

Mirquios shook his head. "Blame the gods, Princess. I'm merely a victim."

"I cannot allow this to be anything other than friendship," she whispered, desperate to follow her words as they landed on his ears.

"I know," he returned, his eyes locked on hers.

She swallowed—it may have been dulled, but the Tether was not silent. It begged, pleaded for her to close the short gap between them.

"Perhaps we could always have the library," Lunelle said, her

throat tight with every emotion she couldn't stomach. "Maybe dreams could be enough for us."

Mirquios nodded, unable to form much more than a deep sigh. He held out a hand toward her, an invitation she tentatively accepted, the wild heat between their palms so intense she felt it even through the rippling walls of the astral.

It was the most they could give one another.

It would never be enough.

"Read your book, Princess. I'll keep watch," he laughed, sliding from the table to the floor beside her chair. He leaned his head against the arm, handing her the book of poems.

"What are you watching for?" she asked, settling back into her chair and cracking her book open.

"Plutonian princes," he mumbled.

When she woke, the pain began anew, stretching and pulling as she rolled to her side and let a few tears slide onto her pillow like liquid starlight pooling at the corner of her lips.

It was impossible—untenable.

She'd never be able to stand it.

CHAPTER
NINETEEN

"This is brilliant," Kwan said, reading over the message once again.

"I thought so, too," Luxuros responded, sipping from a heady ale Lunelle had already decided wasn't for her—she needed only to see Lura's lips pucker in disgust to know. She watched the commander carefully, the heat of him still hard to trust.

Luxuros had arrived in the middle of dinner with urgent news for Mirquios. He'd darted through the dining hall and pulled him away, the rush of whatever he told his king sending a shiver over the Tether.

They'd left for The Underground immediately after Oestera retired for the night. He hadn't asked her to come along so much as it was simply understood at this point.

"Who would have thought we'd have *two* Lunar princesses on our side by the Equinox?" Kwan smiled and waved at the bartender, sending for another round. The Mercurians huddled against the table, thrilled to break the news to the rebels that not only was Lunelle bound to them, but Astra had already been of great service to their mission in Ellume.

"She is not bound," Luxuros said. "Not yet. We've had a few hiccups with rogue assassins, but I plan on taking her to Ehlaria during the Equinox. Loleena has already offered to bind her—"

"You will not?" Lunelle asked.

Luxuros turned toward her, shifting his large frame next to her king.

His king, she corrected herself.

Lux pulled back his sleeve, revealing a series of shallow scars and a thin pink line in his palm.

"I'm afraid I'll be bled dry by the end of my time in the Lunar Court," he chuckled.

"Bloodmoon won't do it?" Kwan asked.

Luxuros glared at the Plutonian leader as Lunelle snorted —Mirquios arched a brow.

"Long story," Lunelle assured him.

"Loleena will be the best option. I will send word when it's done. Until then, keep chipping away at the prince," Luxuros muttered to Mirquios. As the second round of pints landed on the table, Luxuros began his exit, but Lunelle trailed him out onto the street.

"Commander?"

He spun, his bronzed skin catching the blue flames of the Plutonian streetlamps.

"The assassins..."

Luxuros ran his hand through his dark waves.

"We're handling it, I assure you. Though I'm not sure your sister would even need our assistance."

Lunelle's heart lightened at that.

"She has not responded to my letters," she whispered.

Luxuros stepped back toward her, softening in his stance.

"You would be proud of her, Lunelle. She's handling all of this much better than I would have expected given our first few encounters. But I will be sure to remind her not to neglect the Fire Queen's most loyal subject," he said, winking at her.

As he turned to leave, she wondered for just a moment how she could be considered anything near loyal. The Tether in her chest relaxed as Mirquios joined her on the street, though the wash of nausea in its wake kept her grounded.

"It's about time we had some good news," he said.

She turned to him, folding her arms around herself.

"Luxuros seems to believe you can break Arcas."

Mirquios nodded. "We've had a few conversations around the subject. They've gone better than yours have, I'm sure, but not great."

"I could convince him," she said firmly.

Mirquios eyed her, his lips curling at the edges.

"What?"

"Nothing," he said.

She glared, the ice in her nickname hitting him in the chest.

"It is only... I imagine there's nothing you couldn't convince *any* man of."

She rocked toward him, frowning. "Because of my sharp wit and wise leadership, of course?"

The king leaned forward, the heat of him raining over her. The Tether spun between them, begging them for more, closer, *now, now, now.*

"Of course," he murmured.

She let her eyes linger on that ridiculous smirk of his, framed by eyes that saw far too much.

"Princess!"

Lunelle twisted toward the far-off voice, finding a blur of black and blue rushing over the cobblestone.

"Yallara?" she whispered.

Her face was pained, she was sprinting for gods knew how long—maybe all the way from the palace. Yallara crashed into Lunelle, panting and screaming.

"Get in! Get inside!"

Mirquios did not hesitate to listen to her frantic screams, dragging the women back into The Underground.

"There's a raid coming, they just left the palace, they're heading here!" Yallara grasped at her throat, gasping for air as Lunelle patted her back, two dozen sets of eyes widening as the princess spoke.

"Let's go!" Kwan yelled as the room moved in one chaotic blur.

They'd been through this before.

Mirquios gripped Lunelle's hand, yanking her toward the back of the tavern. She snagged Yallara as they went, wrapping her fingers around the princess's delicate wrists.

Bodies clamored against the small hall, diving down a narrow staircase beneath the city and into the catacombs. No one spoke as Kwan directed them, leading them through the caverns and banging on doors marked with silver roses.

Safe houses, Lunelle realized.

They'd built an entire network of safe houses across the city, and he was letting them know to hunker down.

Mirquios bellowed something in his native tongue, causing the Mercurians to split and fall into a regimented line behind him as he pulled the princesses toward another winding staircase. He gave a final salute to Kwan as the Plutonians continued beyond them, scattering and spreading amongst the various exits to the catacombs. Mirquios did not look back, did not stop moving until they broke through the catacombs and into a quiet townhome, dark and coated in a fine layer of dust.

"The door," he commanded one of his courtiers, who

moved to shove a bookshelf in front of the entry. The rest of the rebels, at least a dozen of them, spread out, some heading upstairs, some lingering in the kitchen, staying away from the windows.

"Sit," Mirquios directed to her, tucking Lunelle and Yallara into a study that had not seen the light of a lantern or candle in months, maybe years.

Mirquios stooped down before them.

"Your only job is to stay quiet and protect her," he said to Lunelle, gesturing to Yallara. "She's our best hope at bringing Pluto into the revolution."

Lunelle glanced at Yallara. She bit back a panic flooding her with the betrayal of one's brother.

"Where are you going?"

He gave her a long, quiet look that said so much, *too* much.

"To make sure your job stays easy," Mirquios mumbled, tapping the shoulder of one of his courtiers, the largest of them. Their boots creaked against the wooden floor, stopping near the front door.

"Lura," Lunelle whispered, a chill jolting through her chest. She looked at Yallara, tucked beside her, and finally caught up to her breath. "My maiden, Lura, I don't see her!"

Lunelle crawled across the study, searching through boots and knees.

She hadn't seen her on the stairs.

"Get back in there, Lunelle, *please*," Mirquios whispered harshly, sitting with his back against the door. "If Arcas barges in here and sees either of you, we're *fucked*."

"Lura was at The Underground, I didn't see her leave," Lunelle said, her heart aching at the thought she was left behind.

"Lura has been part of the rebellion for a decade, Lu. She

knows where to go. The moment Kwan clears us, we'll find her, okay? Now, *please*, please get back from the door!"

Lunelle held her breath as she crawled back toward Yallara —each movement felt like a betrayal.

"When did you join?" Yallara asked quietly, her wide eyes searching Lunelle's.

"Recently," Lunelle mumbled.

"Arcas will kill me if he knows, Lunelle, he will not hesitate—"

"Shh," Lunelle hummed, patting Yallara's knee. "It's my first official Nova assignment to protect you. I would never allow it."

Yallara pressed her lips together, and Lunelle realized just how *young* she truly was.

"What are you going to do about him?" Yallara asked, pointing to the doorway, where Lunelle knew Mirquios hovered.

Lunelle's brows furrowed.

A crash against the back door sent them both jumping.

"It's only Kwan," Mirquios said around the corner. "One knock is stay, three is clear."

"If he finds Lura, he'll arrest her, he'll make a show of it at court. He won't kill her right away," Yallara whispered beside Lunelle.

She only nodded.

WHEN THREE KNOCKS FINALLY CAME, Lunelle had closed her eyes for only a moment.

She jerked awake, Yallara's half-asleep eyes peering back at her.

"How long—"

"An hour. Just an hour," Mirquios said as he stood before her, offering a hand. He hauled her to her feet and helped Yallara up.

"You two should head back to the palace. We shouldn't be caught together."

Lunelle reached for his arm but withheld her touch at the last second.

"Where will you go?"

Mirquios glanced toward the street, now pitch black as the lanterns extinguished themselves in the dead of night. Smoke filled the city.

"They likely burnt The Underground. The Mercurians will stay and help Kwan collect anything salvageable. Go. Get Yallara back and find Lura."

Lunelle nodded, her heart racing at the thought of leaving him. Yallara stepped out of the study, pulling at her sleeves anxiously as she slowly made her way through the hall. Lunelle was nearly at the door when her hand caught in the king's.

She gasped as he pulled her into him.

"Take this," he whispered, pressing a slim dagger into her empty hand. "Through the ribs, harder than you think. Panic is death, Lu."

Lunelle looked at the delicate handle of the dagger—golden, engraved with the Mercurian crest—and back up at him.

"Mir—"

"Go," he said, swallowing whatever else he wanted to say to her. He pressed all of it into the handle of his dagger, hoping it would be enough.

She wanted to lean forward, press her lips to his, she wanted to tell him that if he didn't make it back in one piece, she would crawl to hell herself and strangle him.

But she didn't.

Instead, she pressed the cold steel of the dagger into her hand and slipped quietly into the night, guiding Yallara through the shadows of the city until they were both back in their rooms.

The door clicked closed, and she leaned forward, hesitantly whispering, "Lura?"

Only the darkness whispered back.

CHAPTER
TWENTY

S he waited to hear the footsteps of the Mercurians brush past as they returned. Waited until it was no longer possible that Lura had been with someone else.

Waited—what she did best.

But waiting had not gotten her far.

Lunelle slipped from her room, falling into the shadows of the hall as she skirted toward the end of the Tether. Mirquios was with several other courtiers in one of the libraries, the silence settling heavily between them. Lunelle pulled the door closed behind her, but a hand in the crack stopped her.

Yallara slithered in.

"You two should get some rest," the king said, his eyes fixed on a pile of half-dust documents speckled with ash.

"Lura did not return," Lunelle said. She only looked at him. She only spoke to him.

"Lu," he breathed, rubbing at the back of his neck. "Shit."

"I know where he keeps prisoners," Yallara offered. "I can take you."

Lunelle did not hesitate to follow Yallara, the Tether in her chest twisting and loosening as Mirquios gave his courtiers instructions to await his return and jogged after the women.

Yallara slipped between walls and let them into the servants' corridors, pulling Lunelle gently along in the opposite direction from the stairs to the catacombs.

"They'll be heavily guarded. One of the guards told me they brought back six rebels, four Plutonian. The other two he did not know."

"They burned The Underground to dust," Mirquios said behind them.

"Bastard," Yallara muttered. She stopped at a sharp corner. "They're in the spire. I cannot take you further—"

"I understand," Lunelle said. "Thank you."

Yallara patted her shoulder and faded back down the hall, her inky black waves melting into the shadows.

Lunelle listened to her slippers slow as she found her way back to her room.

"What's the plan, Princess?"

Lunelle pushed her shoulders back, took a cleansing breath, and then charged forward into the spiraling staircase before her.

It took ages to climb, but she felt better with the king at her back. She followed the curve of the spire until they came to a lofted door, flanked by two Plutonian guards.

The first ignored them, the second arched a brow.

"We were informed our courtiers are being held here," Lunelle said, her voice even, flat.

She could feel the thrill in the Tether from Mirquios.

"Who informed you?" the first guard asked, his deep onyx brows thick and overgrown.

"The prince," Mirquios said. "We received word just a bit ago. I could return to confirm with him, but..." The king leaned out from behind Lunelle. "It's a long way down, gents."

They exchanged a glance, and the first guard stepped aside, pushing an ancient wooden door inward.

Two rows of cells lined the small room, five deep on either side. Lunelle darted between them, the bruised and beaten faces of rebels eyeing her as she searched for Lura.

"You cannot be here," Lura hissed from the final cell at the end of the hall. She sat up, her hands wrapping around the bars, shallow cuts bright pink around her knuckles.

"Oh, Lura, I'm so sorry," Lunelle sighed, crouching across from her. "I failed you—"

"You cannot be caught here!"

"Release her," Lunelle declared, rising and pointing to Lura.

The guards looked at her like she'd grown a second head.

"Princess, we cannot—"

"I did not ask," she said, folding her arms across her chest. "The Courts Between do not answer to the Living Courts. This is a Lunarian demigoddess you've tossed behind your bars and I will give you exactly one more moment to consider the repercussions before I let the queen know who is holding her most esteemed maiden."

The guards looked at one another and muttered in a language Lunelle did not understand. The one who had ignored her earlier sighed, rubbing his temple. The second guard stepped forward, spinning a ring of keys around his fingers.

"Why don't you send for her, Princess? We'd like to hear what she wants done with a most esteemed maiden who has the mark of the rebellion carved into her chest."

Lunelle did not flinch as he neared her, hovering just a breath from her face.

"Let her go," a voice rumbled from the door.

Arcas leaned against the frame, his eyes heavy and framed by deep purple bags.

"Your Highness—"

"It's one thing to question a Lunar princess—bold, mind you—but another entirely to question *me*. Release the Lunarian."

The guard sighed, slipping by Lunelle and shoving the key into the cell's gate. Lura scrambled to her feet, looping her arm through Lunelle's as the guard rolled his eyes.

Mirquios moved to leave, but Lunelle was not done.

"Release all of them," she said, holding the prince's gaze.

His lip curled in a sick smile. He stepped closer, his boots scraping the stone flooring.

"Is that an order from the Courts Between?"

She released the tension in her stance, softening as he neared.

"It's a plea, Arcas."

He shook his head, waving his hands to the cells beside them.

"They're a threat to your own power—"

"They're *people* who disagree with you politically. They're only a threat to those who hold power that does not belong to them."

Arcas scoffed, his sapphire eyes blinking slowly as he loomed over her. His gaze slid momentarily toward Mirquios, who looked as if he might lunge for his throat at any moment.

"I see one sister wasn't enough for you, Mirquios," Arcas said quietly. "You had to corrupt them both. Though I'm sure the Fire Queen makes for a much more entertaining—"

Mirquios moved swiftly, darting between Arcas and Lunelle.

"You'll watch your tongue, Arcas—"

"No," Lunelle said, pushing Mirquios aside and closing the gap between them, coming chest to chest with the prince. "Finish."

Arcas's eyes narrowed. "Wh—"

"More entertaining... what? Conversationalist?" She stepped between his boots, her body pressing against his as he tensed. She laughed darkly, a sound she hadn't thought herself capable of making.

"A more entertaining... fuck?" She arched her brow, his lips pressing tightly together as she swallowed the rage back. "That's what you meant, right?"

"Lunelle," Arcas whispered, his breath grazing a loose tendril of silver hair.

"You find yourself in this position quite frequently, Prince. Backed against a wall by a woman you seem to keep in a *very* small box when other eyes are around. I'm good for an accessory. Pleasant to look at. But in the dark of night, when we are alone, whose name do you call out? Who do you go to your knees for, the moment the eyes of the courts are off you? Moreover, who do you look for when things get even a *little* difficult, begging for my wisdom?"

Arcas teetered forward, the pressure between them suffocating.

"Princess," Mirquios said, clearing his throat.

Lunelle clenched her teeth. "I cannot be both your priestess and plaything, Arcas."

Arcas exhaled slowly, agonizingly slowly, his gaze burning so far into hers she thought she might combust.

"Release them," he rasped. "All of them."

The guard bristled. "Your—"

"Now," he demanded, never breaking his hold on Lunelle's eyes. The cells popped open, one by one, until the remaining five rebels were released, their quick steps echoing off the stairs in the spire.

"Leave us," Arcas said, turning to Mirquios and Lura.

Mirquios shook his head, his fingers pushing into his chest.

"It's okay," Lunelle said quietly, nodding toward Lura. "The king will escort you back."

"Lunelle—" Mirquios protested, but Lura's clutched hand around his arm stopped him, shoving him through the door. The guards stepped behind them, slamming the door with a heavy thud.

Arcas turned back to Lunelle, her eyes still locked on his, unwilling to release him like the prisoners.

"Thank you," she said, her tone flat.

"It wasn't a favor."

Her head tilted.

"I see your allegiances have shifted significantly since your arrival."

Lunelle shook her head. He was still so close.

She bit. "My allegiance has always been to my people, Arcas. Perhaps that looks different than I thought a few weeks ago—"

The prince snorted, his eyes darkening as he grinned.

"Whatever you need to tell yourself, Lunelle."

"Why put them down? Why not work with them? I don't understand—"

"Exactly!" Arcas rushed her, pushing her back a few steps into the cold stone wall between cells. The jagged surfaces of the stones pulled at her dress as she gasped under him, his chest flaring in waves of fury. "You *do not* understand. You haven't understood from the moment I met you—how fragile my situation is. How dangerous it is to overturn an entire court on the brink of war! You cannot just wipe the slate clean, there are *real* consequences for everyone here without clear order and rank."

Lunelle squeezed her eyes shut, trying to think, but he drowned her in that strange chemistry once again.

She placed a hand on his chest in an effort to put something, *anything*, between them.

"You would not be alone, Arcas. You would have me, you would have hundreds of people across the courts ready to help, ready to *work*. You carry this entire court on your shoulders, but you do not have to—"

He placed a hand on the wall beside her, moving into her once more, softer this time.

Slower.

"I would have you?" he asked, the ire in his question undeniable.

She nodded.

Arcas leaned closer, his lips brushing her ear, her jaw, sending a cold shiver over her spine. Lunelle swallowed, her chest seizing in an unholy blaze. It was the wrong kind of burn, but a burn nonetheless.

It was *something*.

"By your side, as the Lunar king?"

She moved her hand from his chest to his neck, her pale silver melting into his sky blue. His sapphire eyes flared as they found hers.

"Arcas, I—"

"Oh," he sighed, pushing away from her. "Do not back out now." He paced between the cells, the anger rising back into his throat.

"I'm not—"

He stopped and pivoted toward her.

She saw it—the madness unfold, the desperation as it overtook whatever small piece of him might have wanted to do good.

The desire to maintain his grip over a power he was quickly

losing. The way it erased whatever passion he might have kindled for her personally.

"You will marry me, Lunelle. And you will do so happily because if you do not, I will make sure your queen knows exactly which rebel marched into my prison and demanded her contemporaries be liberated."

Lunelle's face flushed, the feeling in her body dissolving into the ether as her blood rushed in her ears.

"Arcas—"

He towered over her again, hands gripping her jaw as he pushed through clenched teeth.

"And if self-preservation is not enough motivation," he growled. "I will happily go straight to the Court Above and let the gods themselves know their monarchs are folding to this rancid rebellion. Because you know what comes after your throne falls, don't you? They'll never be satisfied until the heads of the gods themselves roll. And I think they'll all find it fascinating which Lunar demigoddess sold them out."

Lunelle pulled away from him, shirking his grasp as her lips snarled in disgust for the boy prince before her.

"I thought you were ignorant, Arcas, but I hoped you were at least redeemable." She stomped toward the door, heaving it open as she spun on her heels. Lunelle inhaled sharply. "There is no saving you from yourself."

Arcas caught her hand, pulling her back into him, venom pooling on his tongue.

"Careful, starling. You know how much it turns me on when you hurt my feelings."

Lunelle wrestled against his grasp, her rage boiling under his fingers.

"That's not you," she spat. "But you're *so* afraid of yourself, I can taste it." She did not give him another chance to grab her, moving swiftly into the hall and down the first set of stairs.

Arcas called after her, "I will be Lunar king, Lunelle! Or I'll be sure to let the gods know who bound you into the rebellion in the first place."

Lunelle froze, her heart shattering as the words snapped from his mouth.

She did not look back before running down the remaining stairs, hardly able to grasp her breath as she felt her entire world start to crumble for not the first time since she stepped foot into this godsforsaken court.

CHAPTER
TWENTY-ONE

Oestera held her breath as her daughter entered their shared study.

"Good morning," she said over her tea, watching as Lunelle sank across from her and leaned into the arm of the sofa. She'd snuck back into her bedroom early that morning and had a hushed argument with Lura, but she'd hoped her mother had not been able to make out the panicked notes of the conversation.

Lunelle's shoulders slumped. A far cry from the posture she normally adopted.

"Lunelle?"

"Good morning," Lunelle finally muttered.

Gods, she sounded pathetic.

"Darling," Oestera said softly, a tone she rarely heard from her mother. "Are you feeling well?"

"Fine," she whispered, choking on the words.

"Is it the prince?"

"It's a myriad of things, Mother. I am tired. I am homesick. I miss my sister."

I fell in love with her fiancé, I let myself think I could love a monster, I've implicated them both, I fucked up, I fucked up, I fucked up.

At the mention of Astra, Oestera sat up straighter, falling back into her role of disappointed mother.

"Your sister does not seem to miss any one of us," Oestera sighed. "She has not responded to a single note to her king in weeks."

"Did he tell you that?" Lunelle asked, her shoulders perking up.

"Tula keeps her eyes on the mail drops," Oestera explained. "You've seemed rather... unfocused these last few days."

Lunelle's eyes widened, a blush creeping over her pale freckles.

"How do you mean?"

Oestera shrugged. "I mean no offense, but we can't afford to be anything other than fixed on our goals here, Lunelle. The news from the Outer Courts only gets more dire."

It landed exactly as she needed it to, right between Lunelle's ribs. She knew she'd been anything but the level-headed leader she'd meant to be. Unfocused was generous, frankly.

"Mother..."

Oestera leaned forward, setting her teacup on the table between them.

Lunelle exhaled slowly, swallowing something painful.

"I've been meaning to make a request of you," Oestera said, her starlight gaze roiling with an unusual fire. "After your trial, when you're to come back through the Lunar Gate, I need you to wait for my signal. Just to be sure all is well."

Lunelle's eyes bounced from the table to Lura, who looked equally as perplexed.

"What wouldn't be well, Mother?"

"Nothing in particular! I just remember from coronations past that sometimes the crowds get a bit raucous waiting for the Lunar champion to emerge, and I want to be sure everyone is prepared."

Lunelle did not buy it, but she didn't have any notion of what Oestera could possibly be on about. And she had more pressing matters to address.

"On the subject of champions..." Lunelle sighed, the pain within her flaring as she formed the harsh threats from Arcas into an easy lie. "I think it's time we formalize my engagement to Arcas."

It was not what Lunelle had wanted to say. It wasn't at all what she *thought* she'd be saying that morning. But it was what she needed to say.

"Are you sure—"

"Yes. At tomorrow's Equinox celebration. Please," she added, avoiding eye contact.

"Is there... a reason for your rush?" Oestera's nose scrunched, her thoughts nearly audible from across the room.

Lunelle glared. "No, Mother. None of that."

Plenty of that, Lunelle thought. But that wasn't her concern.

"Well, if that's what you'd like, I can meet with the prince today. But Lunelle—"

"Thank you," she said, cutting her mother off. She rose and disappeared back into her room, leaving Oestera completely baffled.

Gods, it was painful—horrifyingly painful to say it out loud.

Lunelle could hardly force it from her tongue, but she'd spent all night trying to think of ways around it.

Short of committing murder, her hands were tied—and it had taken Lura a considerable length of time to talk her out of that one. She was losing herself, her mind falling into shambles by the second. She'd been reckless, she'd been foolish, and now everyone would pay the price.

Or, she could suffer, and protect them all.

"Lura!"

The maiden came rushing from the next room over, her lips drawn into a tight line after hearing Lunelle's declaration to the queen.

"I need another pomegranate."

"What?" Lura asked.

Lunelle pulled her long waves into a tight knot at the back of her neck and slipped into a pair of pants, discarding her morning dress.

"I need a pomegranate—I need to have a word with a goddess."

"Lunelle—"

"I know what I'm doing," Lunelle hissed, a tone that Lura had come to anticipate more and more over the last few weeks. Lunelle could practically hear the strings snapping within her ribs.

Lura darted out of the room as Lunelle stuffed the smallest piece of stibnite in her pocket, just for good measure. The energy sparked to life within it, giving her the courage to move. Lura returned with a plump pomegranate and Lunelle's cloak, watching her carefully as she tucked the fruit under her arm.

"I will be back by dinner," Lunelle said as she brushed past Lura and into the hallway, moving swiftly through the courtiers meandering in the garden.

Her chest lurched as she dove into the next hall and around the corner, passing the Mercurians. She knew he felt her rush by, too.

She broke into a jog at the bottom of the endless stairs into the catacombs, avoiding eye contact with anyone who wandered through the underground halls. She pulled her hood lower, making quick work of the tunnels and pathway through the city.

She never once stopped to reassess her plan, if one could call it that.

For the first time in her entire life, she was letting her heart drive her forward, letting it push her up the cracked steps into the glowing Plutonian Sun setting now over the horizon. The cliffs were sparsely populated, a few Plutonians with their fair blue complexions walking along the edges, wondering just how far the fall was.

She paid them no mind as she strolled along the edge closest to the sandy steps, holding her pomegranate in one hand and her crystal in another. She wasn't sure exactly how she spiraled to Proserpina the first time, but Lunelle tried to hold her in her mind—the flowing rose curls, her tan fingers.

Her eyes fell over the cliff's edge, watching the black waters beneath churn inward.

When she'd come before, she carried a curiosity within her. A little glimmer of hope that maybe, *maybe* she'd see something reflected back in those angry waves that might soothe her.

This evening, though, she carried a bitter heart steeped in the rage of a thousand eldest daughters. Proserpina had not helped her before, and perhaps it was because she had not been clear enough, but now she was desperate, and desperation could breed either clarity or chaos.

She prayed for the former.

Perhaps it would be a relief, she thought to herself, edging closer to the crumbling rock bordering the wild sea. *Perhaps it would be a better fate to fall into the watery grave and never resurface.*

Lunelle leaned out over the cliff, her heart dropping into her stomach at the thought of it. She sat, folding her legs beneath her as she let the lullaby of the sea crashing against the rocks below hypnotize her.

Perhaps, she thought again, *it was my fear of jumping that prevented Proserpina from granting my wish in the first place.*

She considered it as she closed her eyes, the sweet relief death might be. Did Tethers follow you into the Court Below? Would the ache ever release?

Would she be damning him to a lifetime of sunken ribs and stilted breaths—never able to breathe through the crushing surf of her?

Ah, there, it was at that thought the dragging began. That tug on the back of her Soul collapsed her inward. She gave herself over to it, letting it sever her from this world and push her into the next.

Her Soul tumbled, falling for much longer than she'd expected, the air around her chilling as she crashed through the surface of another realm. Her lungs filled with frigid smoke —no—water.

She was drowning.

The waves crushed her from overhead, burying her beneath them, sending her spiraling even faster as she fought for breath. The pressure built, a pain searing against her chest, and for a moment, she worried she might have leaned forward and fallen over the cliff before Proserpina could find her.

Just as she thought she might lose herself entirely, her knees clashed into gray sand, sending a shockwave through her bones and water sputtering from her throat.

"Oh," a deep voice sighed. "They never hold their breath."

Lunelle's head snapped forward, the figure before her not

Proserpina at all, but a towering frame of smoke and shadow, surrounded by fathomless black seas.

His eyes sparkled in sapphire, his complexion was that same cerulean hue she'd learned to admire. The same as the man who'd betrayed her.

She stood quickly, flicking water from her hands.

"A Lunar princess... fascinating."

His sharp jaw set as he paced around her in a circle, revealing an iron throne behind him, lit by blue flickering flames.

"Pluto," Lunelle whispered, feeling the God of Death's name bubble to her lips.

"Were you seeking someone else?" He stopped before her, two heads taller than her own lithe frame, and rested his finger on his chin. "Because I certainly heard you calling my name," he said.

"I do not know what I seek anymore," Lunelle confessed, a chill running through her spine. She had surely made a wrong turn through the cosmos, veering into a territory that would only end in more tragedy.

"Oh, come now, Princess. We both know that's untrue. You know *exactly* what you want."

Lunelle chewed on her lip. The gods were powerful, but were they all-knowing?

"I can smell it on you. The desperation. Only Fate and her wicked ways create so much strife in so young a rose."

Lunelle swallowed. Perhaps she *had* called to him. Perhaps she and Proserpina were not so different after all.

Perhaps he could help her.

"I don't know what to do."

"Ah," Pluto said, strolling back to his throne. He folded himself into the cold seat, the black silk draped across his chest catching what little light lived there. "Not knowing what you want and not knowing how to get it aren't quite the same thing, are they?"

She shook her head.

"Do you know what my love's greatest sin was, Princess?"

Lunelle watched as his long, skeletal fingers drew lines over the smooth arm of the throne.

He continued, "She believed her desires were selfish, and not a gift of Fate in and of themselves."

"What—"

"Where do you think your yearnings come from? Gods may be self-centered, but we are not monsters. Fate weaves those threads into your heart, your muscles, your blood—your destiny lives in a million Tethers inside you long before that pesky one in your chest bursts forth."

Lunelle felt both lighter and ready to vomit.

"It's horrifying, isn't it? What we want is already ours, if only we're strong enough to take it." Pluto rested his chin in his hand, his eyes falling over Lunelle and into the ether around them. A soft smile unfolded as a warm light shone and twinkled across the bobbing waves beyond them.

"I'm afraid to hurt everyone."

"Hmm," Pluto leaned back, crossing his leg as he gestured to her chest, the pulsing against the Tether flaring in response. "I wonder which will hurt your king more? Suffering with you, or without?"

He curled two fingers, motioning someone forward.

Proserpina's warmth clung to Lunelle's back as she moved into their space, throwing glittering stars against the shadows. She crossed between them, perching on the arm of the throne. Pluto's hand fell to her hip in a motion so well-practiced it seemed odd that he might ever be anywhere but there.

The goddess leaned forward, holding out her palm. Lunelle offered her the pomegranate.

"Even in eternity, I regret the time I wasted fighting," Proserpina said, looking at Pluto. Between them was a sorrow laced with love and lust, a depth to their feelings that Lunelle worried she understood perfectly. "You can only outrun Fate so long, Lunelle. What is for you will find you, in every plane, in every lifetime. Even if you hide from it."

Lunelle sighed, the sinking feeling within her sparkling with something silver—something like hope.

"Hold your breath this time," Pluto said softly, waving his hand and sending a black wave over her head.

She swept up and over herself with the midnight current.

There was no breath left in her lungs to hold.

CHAPTER
TWENTY-TWO

"Lunelle!" A booming voice sent her back from the edge of the cliff, her fingers reaching for the ache as she righted herself.

She coughed, salty sea water spilling into her hands.

"Lunelle!" Mirquios barked again, a rage within his voice that ravaged her bones. He rushed her, gripping her shoulders as he yelled in Mercurian, by the sound of his dipped vowels.

"Mirquios!" She hit his chest, his eyes wide with harsh words.

He finally found the common tongue phrase he'd been searching for in his panic.

"Are you fucking *insane*?"

She glared and pulled away from him, but his hands only tightened.

"Do you have a death wish?"

She followed his eyes to the edge of the cliffs, the dark brown planes of his face deepened by his anger.

"I wasn't going to—"

"I don't *care*," he hissed, shaking her. "I don't care if other people do it. I care if you—I care if you..."

His bright eyes flickered away, but she didn't need to see them to know what they revealed.

"I was not trying to hurt myself!" she explained, his hands still digging into her shoulders. She shrugged in an effort to loosen his grip, but he remained attached to her.

"I came here before and made an offering to Proserpina," she confessed. "I thought perhaps she denied it because I was too afraid to jump, so I came back, but... it doesn't matter! It doesn't matter." She stroked the king's chest, begging his heart rate to come down.

Mirquios inhaled slowly, his eyes closing as he stepped back, still unable to fully release her, though his fingers held less tightly.

"Arcas knows, Mirquios. He knows we're both rebels. He wants the Lunar throne or he'll tell the gods we're bound—"

"That *fucking* bastard!" Mirquios rasped.

"I know," she said. "I know, but... but I don't know if I care."

Perhaps her wish *had* been granted by the goddess, and she'd been too afraid to accept it the first time. Proserpina had to call in her own love to show her, to make her understand what exactly she was risking.

And what she could not risk.

She rested her hands on either side of his face, cradling him in a way she had not dared before, not even in her dreams.

"Lunelle," he warned, her touch too tender, too hard not to lean into.

"I cannot go the rest of my life without knowing."

The glass wall Lunelle had kept him behind shattered into a billion glittering shards, crumbling across the shoreline as she moved into him. His eyes widened at her motion—he'd been certain she would stay on her side of their carefully maintained line until one of them finally Descended, but a single breath across it was enough to unwind every tortured knot in his muscles.

She'd imagined kissing him to be a slow, noble pursuit.

She'd imagined he'd need coaxing from that stronghold within him.

She'd imagined his regal posture would require some undoing to dissolve beneath her aching palms in ways Arcas never needed.

She'd been so blatantly, brilliantly wrong.

There was *nothing* soft about kissing him. This was a dive off the cliffs beside them—a plunge straight to her death, broken by icy waves that claimed the air from her lungs. Fingers clutched at his cloak, desperate to have him closer, to have him consume every thought she wished she didn't have.

"Lu," he gasped as her lips untangled from his briefly, just long enough to catch any breath she could. "Lunelle."

She shook her head, grasping his face in her cool touch, desperate to hold any piece of him he'd allow.

"Please," she begged, her breath hot against his neck. "Just give me one moment of you, one single moment, and I'll never ask you for anything else, I swear it."

Two ceaseless pools of jade bore into her, wrestling with what a better woman might do. As his gemstone gaze searched hers, Lunelle determined there was no better woman in all thirteen courts she'd aspire to be than the one between his palms.

"Just one moment," she whispered again, a prayer on the sea breeze whipping beyond the cliffs.

Perhaps they could haul themselves over the jagged edges now and be rid of all of this torment. Or slip into the Rift and bang on the Nether Gate to beg sanctuary. He fought every stretch of the Tether between them as he leaned away from her, his voice hardly audible over the crashing waves below.

He brushed a tear away from the crest of Lunelle's cheek as he spoke.

"If I give you one more moment, I fear I'll give every damned one of them to you, Princess. Every single breath between here and my Descent would begin and end with your name. Every step I took from now until my boots crumble to dust would be in service of following you, and you alone." Mirquios tensed beneath her touch, as if she were truly an Ice Queen, chilling him to the bone. "If I give you one more solitary second, Lunelle, I will insist you lay claim to any remaining moments I am allotted."

Her heart swelled with salt and sea air, racing to keep up with the words falling from his lips.

"You will insist?" she asked, unable to choke the bitter-sweet ribbon of tears slipping from her eyes.

"I will," he whispered.

Lunelle battled every voice that warned her to pull back her plea, to unsay the words that begged such eternal notions.

"Then insist," she breathed.

A fractured laugh escaped his throat, tainted by the knowledge that no amount of insistence could untangle this mess.

"I insist, Lunelle," he said, his arms wrapping around her waist. "I'd insist in the face of Pluto himself."

"Gods," she sighed, letting herself press against him for what would likely be the last time—*had* to be the last time. "This is true hell."

"At least we're here together," he said quietly, feathering a kiss against her lips.

Lunelle rested her head against his chest, listening to the sputtering of his heart against his ribs. His chin perched atop her head, and they stood there, frozen, unable to move out of the only moment they could guarantee.

Dread poured from the back of her mind into her lungs, the face of a beloved sister filling her vision and flooding her with sickening guilt.

"We cannot be friends, Mirquios," she said quietly.

"No." He swallowed, the pulse in his throat pushing against her temple.

"We cannot be strangers," she whispered.

"Never."

Her ears heated, prickling with that moment that comes before one does something truly stupid.

"My sister would never deny me this, not if she knew, Mirquois. I know her heart better than I know my own, and she would not hesitate."

"But Arcas—"

"Arcas is an affliction of my own doing," Lunelle sighed. "If he doesn't ally with us, he has no one. Not even the gods will care about him. I am but a political trophy to him, something to play with when he feels insecure, but to you..."

Her eyes dared to find his, her pale cheeks reddened by her near admission.

"To me... you are death herself. The only thing in life that is certain," the king said with a quiet reverence.

Her pulse lit up within her veins, and she wondered briefly if this was how her sister walked through the world, so positively buzzing with *something* in her blood that she felt as if she might burst. She'd never allowed herself the luxury of imagining an alternative, never risked the fantasy of him.

But what if?

What *if?*

"I will speak to my mother this evening," she decided, her

knees aching at the firmness with which she stood on the shore.

Mirquios dropped her hand, his brows arching with confusion.

"What?"

"My mother has stood in my shoes before. Surely she would understand. If anyone could untangle this mess, she could do it."

"Do you really think—"

"I am not thinking at all, Mirq," she laughed.

That was it—that was all she'd give to his doubt. It was all she could spare. She tucked herself into him, not giving a single damn about what it would all mean.

All she could feel was the difference in his touch—the light with which he caressed her, the care. Touching him was not a distraction from what she wanted, it was destiny fulfilled.

"We need to get back," she spoke into his chest.

"One more moment?" Mirquios asked, wrapping his arm around her shoulder again, staring out over the cliffs.

"One more moment," she murmured, lifting his hand to her lips.

CHAPTER
TWENTY-THREE

Dinner had already begun when they returned.

Lunelle felt the prince's cold sapphire stare on her as she slipped into the hall, dropping into the seat beside her mother. The king followed shortly after, an absence Arcas had surely noted.

"You're late," Oestera whispered.

Lunelle nodded in a simple acknowledgement. She would not apologize.

She'd hardly gotten a sip of wine in before her mother rose beside her, tapping the edge of her glass with a silver knife.

"Now that both parties are here," Oestera said, grinning as her eyes fell to Lunelle. "The Lunar Court has exciting news!"

Lunelle choked, the bitter wine catching on her panic.

"Mother—"

Oestera ignored her.

"We've spent these last few months picking apart every possible detail of what it would be like to embrace the Plutonians as the Inner Courts' newest allies. We've aired our doubts and concerns, we've made plan after plan, and I know we all agree that Arcas has demonstrated his dedication to our cause and his rejection of Solar dominance over the Living Courts. I believe we are all aligned on the benefits, and I am thrilled to seal their dedication and welcome Arcas to the Lunar Court beside Lunelle as our Lunar king."

The air in the room tensed, several sets of shoulders pulling taut as Lunelle's face reddened. She could not bear to look at Mirquios's face, she felt enough pain in the Tether.

"There will be no trial, then?" Kahlia asked, their brows arching over their sharp cheekbones.

Oestera rested a hand on her daughter's shoulder as if to prevent her from running.

"We will still hold a coronation trial, of course. It's important to uphold such a sacred tradition. But Arcas will be joining as the sole Lunar champion, as a symbol of our dedication to this partnership."

Lunelle was gone, outside of her body, watching from the depths of the Nether and fighting the urge to vomit. Arcas stood at the end of the table, raising a glass.

His lips twisted into the smirk she saw in her nightmares, the one she'd once thought was enough to take away the pain in her chest.

Gods, she was stupid.

Arcas gestured to Lunelle. "It's my honor, Oestera. A toast to my bride, Lunelle, and her ceaseless dedication to keeping me as honest as she is."

The table raised their glasses as Lunelle felt her stomach turn, her mother's grip on her shoulder tightening.

"We will begin the return to our courts tomorrow, but tonight, we will celebrate!" Oestera declared.

Arcas signaled his servants, who stepped forward with glittering bottles of bubbling wine, filling sapphire flutes. Lunelle finally risked a glance at the end of the table, where two jade eyes held onto the plate before him.

Oestera reached a hand to Lunelle. "Shall we dance, darling?"

There was something in her eyes, something like sadness, that Lunelle couldn't quite understand. She wondered what Astra would see—would a plume of some vivid shade of shame fall over her mother's shoulders before she could spirit it away?

Lunelle sighed, scooting back her chair and slamming the glass of sparkling wine, welcoming the way it stole her breath as her mother led her across the dining hall into the center under a dome coated in delicate blue and violet flowers.

The strings from the quartet shifted as they saw the dignitaries take their places, slowing into something soft, something fluid.

Oestera held her daughter's frame and stepped back as she spun them into a well-worn waltz.

"You could smile," Oestera murmured as Lunelle's muscle memory carried her through a dance they'd performed a million times together.

She did not respond.

"This was what you wanted, Lunelle, was it not?"

She snapped her eyes to her mother's—that cool, icy stare so like her own, and yet they saw everything so differently.

"Yes," Lunelle whispered.

"Then what plagues you?" Oestera twisted them back, Lunelle's pale pink skirts fluttering behind her. The pull in her chest tightened as the king rose and moved toward the floor.

"There's no issue."

"You're sure?" They held still for a moment, and Lunelle wondered—for just one breath—what her mother knew.

What she didn't know was more frightening.

As they turned, Lunelle's spine tightened, the weight of it all settling between cartilage and vessels, flowing through her entire body in the span of two breaths. Tears slithered up the back of her neck, begging her to speak. To drop her mother's hand, to expose herself before Arcas could.

And then he was there, at the edge of the dancefloor, stepping into her line of sight, twisting his blue fingers together as he eased in front of Mirquios.

She hated him.

She'd been so confused, so dizzy over trying to understand him, trying to parse out the facets that might be redeemable. She'd sifted through layers and layers of fear and cowardice, and at the bottom, there was only disappointment.

"Lunelle?" her mother asked again. "This was what you wanted, yes?"

It was in the way Arcas crossed before Mirquios that solidified her resolve.

The way his proximity to the king reeked of danger, and the way she'd do anything to protect him, she felt it in her very Soul. She could not give him the kind of love they both hoped for, but she could give Mirquios the protection she'd nearly taken away by her reckless actions.

She looked back at her mother.

"Yes. It's what I want."

Lunelle stepped back, bowing to her queen.

"May I have the next?" Arcas was beside them as her head came up, his sky-colored palm waiting for hers.

The thought of touching him made her stomach twist.

Perhaps it was like any other pain—all-consuming at first, but eventually, a reluctant companion.

Familiar.

She rested her palm in his, a thin layer of chilled sweat coating her skin as he whisked her into another arc.

He did not wait for her to lead, and she did not fight for it this time—there would be plenty of that in her future.

"I must apologize for my harshness last night," he said quietly as they danced.

Lunelle snorted, a bitter laugh catching in her throat.

"Ah, yes, we've come to the part of the cycle where you confess you're a scared little boy and I find something within the ashes of you to polish into a forgivable gem. I must say, Prince, you're becoming predictable."

Arcas exhaled, his lips tightening as he spun her away from him. He pulled her back and dipped his mouth close to her ear, the sensation no longer intriguing or mysterious.

Only cruel.

"I think you will find that I am not as pathetic as you've decided I am, starling. All I ask is that you leave room for me to surprise you."

Lunelle wrenched her head back, her eyes narrowing into his, a softness to them she had seen so sparingly.

"Your last few surprises have been more than enough for me," she sighed, dropping his hand. She made a swift move for the gardens, desperate for fresh air.

Mirquios was there in moments, the tug on her chest crying out in relief.

"You cannot be out here," she said, cradling herself as she slipped further into the shadows of the towering willows at the far end. Their branches brushed against her back, soothing the ache in her spine.

"I know," he mumbled.

"Just go," she said, the first tear she'd been so desperately holding onto spilling.

"I spoke with Kahlia," Mirquios sighed, standing behind her, fighting the temptation to reach out and turn her toward him. "The Venusians may be able to help. There's a ceremony that some of their hierophants practice to sever Tethers. It cannot do anything to change the feelings, but it could lessen the physical pain—"

"Sever it?" Lunelle spun, the tears flowing freely now.

"I do not want to give you up, Lunelle. But if we have no other option, perhaps it can make it bearable."

Lunelle hovered as close to him as she could stand, resting her hand on his forearm. She crawled her fingers over the slope of his chest, against the silver threads of his tunic, feeling his lungs rise and fall.

"I cannot tell what would be more painful—enduring the ache of the Tether for the rest of my life or only having the memory of it to hold on to. Lura has written to Camaren in Celene, she comes from centuries of historians. She might know something we don't."

"Maybe there is a time, after revolutions and wars, maybe the dust settles—"

Lunelle winced. "It's a nice dream, Mirquios. But it is only that."

"Weren't you the one who said dreams might be enough—"

Lunelle's brows tucked together, her head tilting.

"When did I—"

A half-smile tugged at his lips. "In the library," he whispered.

Pink pooled on her cheeks, warming her face as she leaned into him, hiding her eyes.

"Do not do that," he chuckled, pulling her chin back toward him. "You can never hide from me, Lunelle. I will always find you."

WHEN SHE'D FINALLY PRIED herself from the eyes of the Inner Courts and stumbled back to her bed chambers, she was surprised to find a certain Plutonian princess perched at the edge of her bed.

"Yallara!"

Her onyx waves bounced as she rose at Lunelle's voice, crossing the room and grabbing at her hands.

"Lunelle, my gods, I am so sorry!"

"For what?" Lunelle could think of dozens of things one might pity her for, but not one of them was Yallara's doing.

"I know that this isn't what you intended, that last night things got heated, and he, he, godsdammmit," she cried, falling onto Lunelle's sofa and pulling her into the seat beside her. "I'd always hoped that there was more to my brother than our father's brutal misgivings, but the destruction he caused last night... the pain. It will take Kwan months to rebuild—"

"Yallara," Lunelle whispered, smoothing a tangled curl from her pale face, wet with tears. "I understand your fears. And I will not lie to you and say I do not share them. But perhaps there is a way—with time—that I can influence your brother. I don't believe that he's half the monster he thinks he is."

"Do you really think so?" The sullen blues of her face seemed to deepen with her sorrow, the candlelight clung to her tear-stained cheeks as she drew a slow breath.

Lunelle wasn't sure what she thought. She only knew what she hoped for desperately, and those were rarely the same things.

"I will do my best," she whispered.

"Princesses?" Lura set a tray of tea down on the table before them, her own eyes welled with the frustration and anger of the room.

"If anyone can cause a boy to want to become a man, it's a

woman far too wise for him," Lura said with a quiet confidence Lunelle wished she could bottle. She leaned back into the sofa, maintaining a soft hand on Yallara's forearm, who seemed as if she was finally able to take a full breath.

"Goddess speed to you," Yallara sighed, reaching for a cup. "When you return to the Lunar Court tomorrow, I am calling a meeting with the rebels. I believe there are enough of us within the halls of the palace that, in my brother's absence, we may be able to make strides toward dismantling his advisory."

Lunelle's lips twitched into a half smile, the most she could gather.

"Your brother was right to fear you," she giggled. "You move things along here, and I will move them along with Arcas. If one wise woman can turn a boy into a man, imagine what two can do."

Lura cleared her throat.

"Three," Lunelle corrected, feeling the slightest slip of lightness she'd hold close over the coming months.

"You shouldn't be here," Mirquios groaned when a halo of silver curls appeared in his doorway in the middle of the night.

Not that he'd been anywhere close to sleeping.

She wore less fabric than he was capable of taking in responsibly—just a slip of white silk and a robe left open. Every detail of her sparkled in the flickering lantern light, something they seemed to realize at the same moment. She pulled her robe tightly over her body and tied the waistband, though it wasn't much better.

"I couldn't sleep," she sighed. She'd tried. She'd gone back into that ballroom so bravely, with a smile on her face even though she felt as if she were spiraling back into Pluto's underworld. Yallara and Lura had stayed long enough to convince her not to fling herself from the Plutonian cliffs.

But the moment she was alone again, the pain struck up, flaring across her chest.

"You could at least have worn a very thick cloak," he muttered, rubbing at the ache in his chest. He moved from the doorway and let her in, the war within him seeping into the Tether. She slipped in like smoke, settling quietly into the corner of one of the armchairs near the window. He watched as she peeled back the curtain, spotting the Moon and her contemporaries in the sky and doing some sort of silent calculation.

"What is it?" he asked, sitting gently on the floor beside her. She tucked her knees to her chest and pushed the curtain back further.

"I'm so disoriented after being in Pluto all this time. Just finding my bearings before we return home tomorrow." Lunelle leaned her chin onto her wrist, releasing a slow breath as the tugging in her ribs eased. Mirquios leaned his shoulder against her chair.

Not touching, though the weight of the air between them felt like a tight grasp around their throats.

"What Moon is it?"

She searched the sky, Pluto's many Moons obscuring hers. "Hmm, the Harvest Moon," she replied. "But the next is the Mourning Moon, my favorite." The heft of the words settled on her shoulders. She sank further into herself. "She knows it's coming, the longest night of the year, and she weeps in the cold, but she shows her face regardless."

"Is it the longest night of the year if day never comes?"

Lunelle giggled, a gentle release she so desperately needed. He had a point.

"I suppose that mythology works better in courts like this one."

He was silent for a long moment.

"When we return home, we will figure this out, Lunelle," Mirquios declared.

Lunelle straightened in the chair. "What is there to figure out? My mother has made her decision and she won't change her mind. Arcas has threatened to expose every last one of us if I do not marry him. I do not want to get rid of this between us, and I suspect you don't either..."

He sighed. "Of course not."

They were truly trapped, but there was something gnawing in the back of her mind—a constant whisper between heartbeats.

What if. What if. What if.

She could not let herself follow that trail. It would only lead to worse pain.

"Tell me more about the Moon." Mirquios leaned his head against the leather of the chair as she inhaled, trying to pin a place to start.

"When I was a little girl, my father used to tell me that the Moon was my real mother. That I was a drop of liquid moonlight escaped to the courts, and that he and my mother loved me too much to let me return. I used to cry in my bed, thinking I didn't belong there."

"Lu," he breathed, reaching a hand upward, toward the soft silk falling over her arm, but he thought better of it.

Lunelle had never said her next words out loud, never dared let them pass her lips.

"I think I've always felt like my court wasn't my home, somewhere deep down."

They sat in the silence of what she didn't say—what she *couldn't* say. That she'd never felt settled because, all this time, she'd never had him. That home would always be wherever he was—Moon, Mercury, or anywhere in between.

"Take the bed," he said, pointing to his unmade mattress. "I'll stay in the chair."

"You don't have—"

The fire in his eyes stopped her protest. He was not interested in her independence. She resigned herself to his request and climbed over him, slipping beneath his soft sheets and letting the scent of him drown her as she fell into another world—the dream world they'd created together—her library, where he was already waiting with a fresh cup of tea and a new book.

She pulled her shoulders back, shaking off the misery from the evening.

"We need a plan for tomorrow," she said.

Mirquios waited for her to elaborate.

"My sister will sense what's happened immediately. If we're going to suffer apart, I do not wish to bring her into it."

"Of course," he said, a smirk unfolding.

"What?"

"I like Princess Lunelle, but my gods, Queen Lunelle does something frightening to me," he murmured, his bright eyes dancing as he watched her regal posture return, the desire to protect her sister reminding her just who she was.

"Well, steel yourself. We've got business to attend to, Your Highness."

CHAPTER
TWENTY-FOUR

E verything had changed about the Lunar palace in her absence.

She could smell it in the crisp Autumn air, feel it whispering through the moonblossom petals as they sank to the ground.

She'd parted with the king in the quiet hours of the morning, after a lengthy discussion on how to shield herself from Astra's prying mind, but she still feared the sight of those wild ruby curls.

First on their long list of action items was to find the commander.

Mercury had arrived before the Lunarians—Oestera insisted on an agonizingly silent breakfast with the king and Yallara. Lunelle took full advantage of the chaos of returning to slip away from the Lunar Gate and rush through the halls, Lura hot on her heels.

"I'm to have tea with Ameera this morning to catch up on anything vital we missed," Lura said quietly as they rounded the corner to the Andromeda wing.

"I cannot imagine how long a list that will be," Lunelle muttered. "The king and I are meeting with Luxuros. He's to catch us up on Nova activity in Ellume. We're going to tell him what's happened. Mirquios wants his take on how to handle Arcas."

"Your mother aims to assemble the council in an hour."

"I'll see you then," Lunelle said, parting with her at the end of the hall. Her feet carried her to the library unconsciously. Her safe space—the only space she could think clearly in.

Mirquios and Luxuros were already halfway into a kettle of coffee when she found them behind a row of shelves, dark bags under both their eyes.

"Princess," Luxuros said, rising from his perch on the arm of the couch as his king stood and hovered, his eyes struggling to stay neutral.

She'd forgotten in all their time on Pluto what she looked like under pure, unfiltered moonlight. She was always intriguing to watch, no matter her surroundings, but the way the Moon embraced her, bounced from her pale skin... it reminded her that she was so much more than mere regent.

She was magic in her own right.

"Commander," she said, nodding as she reached for the empty teacup on the table. Mirquios leaned forward, sifting through a pewter box of tea bags until he found a chamomile sachet. He placed it in her cup and added a splash of cream before she could even get her bearings.

"Well then," Luxuros said, a soft chuckle leaving his throat. "I can't *imagine* what urgent matter you two need to discuss." He folded his arms across his chest, his eyes darting between the two of them as they orbited one another on the sofa, maintaining a plausible amount of distance.

But it did not matter.

It never had.

Lunelle sighed. "Luxuros—"

The commander held up his hands. "Please, only tell me what I must know. I can only keep so much from your sister."

"I believe we're all of the same fear where Astra is concerned," Lunelle said.

Mirquios winced. "Here is what you need to know—the princess and I Tethered. Obviously, not ideal in and of itself, but the Plutonian prince has made a bad situation worse. You no doubt heard about the raid on The Underground shortly after you left, Luxuros. That led to us unfortunately exposing our association to Arcas, which he is now using as a threat to force Lunelle to marry him."

Luxuros let out a breath, shaking his head.

"What a fucking mess," he said.

Lunelle pursed her lips.

"Sorry." The commander offered a pity smile, but he was right. It was a mess.

"Arcas is bad enough," Lunelle said. "But then there's Astra's heart to consider, as well."

Mirquios and Luxuros exchanged a look.

The commander tilted his head. "Do you really think your sister would hesitate for one moment if you told her the truth?"

Lunelle frowned. "I know she wouldn't. That's the problem. She'd sacrifice herself the moment she suspected, but I fear what my mother will resort to if Mirquios is no longer an option. She'd likely throw her at Arcas, or another court."

Luxuros buried a pained laugh.

"I'm sorry, I'm just trying to picture a scenario in which Astra does not turn Arcas into a pile of ash within five minutes of meeting him."

His laugh melted into a grimace, a well of thoughts

opening within his chest that Lunelle would have followed if they weren't on such a pressing schedule.

"You know, she might just be the key," Mirquios said. "When she finds out your mother is forcing you to marry him, she'll burn the entire court to the ground for you."

Lunelle wrestled with the way that image pulled at her heart.

"We're heading to Mercury this evening," Luxuros said. "We have to meet with our Nova captain, perhaps Astra could come along and we could catch her up—"

"No," Lunelle said.

Mirquios turned to her, stunned by her clipped response.

"I do not want Astra traveling between courts. The Rift is dangerous for any of us with how much activity we've seen with Solan over these past few months, but she's... it's too dangerous. Astra comes with her own set of risks, too. She can be volatile and short-sighted—"

Luxuros straightened his shoulders.

"Forgive my bluntness, Princess, but you do not know your sister half as well as you think if you fear her safety."

The commander bit back something else, his eyes narrowed in defense of Astra.

Lunelle squared herself to him. "I am sure in your time with her, you've seen her proclivity for flames first, questions later."

Mirquios cleared his throat. "I know that was true of her in her younger years, Lunelle. But the commander has been keeping me well updated on her abilities and the discipline she's developed. You should see the work she's accomplished in Celene alone—"

"What of Celene?" Lunelle asked, confused as she looked to Luxuros.

Lux shrugged. "I do not know anything about Celene," he

said. "But from what I've seen in Ellume and often in response to my own pushing, your sister spends the majority of her energy sparing us the wrath of the Fire Queen, not unleashing it."

Lunelle did not care. She did not care what they thought they knew about her sister, or even if they were right. She could stomach the consequences of her own actions, but she could not stomach Astra paying for them.

"Promise me you will not take Astra into the Rift," she said, eyes locked on Mirquios. "And while we're at it, we cannot ask her to give any more of herself to the rebellion until she knows what's happened. I cannot allow it."

He sighed, the Tether pulling between them.

"Promise me."

"I promise," he relented.

She turned to Luxuros.

"I will make no such promise to you, Princess. I cannot. And I cannot keep your secrets from her forever. You need to tell her tonight. As soon as possible. Or I will, whether I mean to or not."

She eyed the men. Luxuros was the closest thing Mirquios had to a brother, and yet there still wasn't the same cursed blood between them. The fear of losing one another was not carved into their bones the way it lived in ancient markings on hers.

Lunelle stepped toward the commander, her slender frame dwarfed by his as she held his gaze.

"Whatever it is that has passed between you two, whatever it is you think you understand about her... if you're wrong, Commander, I assure you will pray for the wrath of the Fire Queen over her frigid sister."

Lunelle left the library in an icy silence, stilling her heart as she prepared to see her sister again.

LUNELLE WAITED outside the Celestial Hall until the last possible moment to enter. She could see Astra's red halo, feel her uncertainty as she quietly wound her way to her seat at the council's table.

"Ladies," her mother began as Lunelle made it through the first set of seats. "As you all know, Pluto has declared their intentions to join the Lunar Court and Inner Courts as tensions build with Solaris. Solan's armies are gathering in the rings of Saturn and Neptune's seas. We cannot hesitate to send a message of unity."

Lunelle slid into her designated space beside her sister, the sweet florals of her moonblossom perfume like a warm embrace she didn't know she missed so terribly.

Astra's voice immediately slipped into her mind. *There you are!*

Sorry. I needed to freshen up. Lunelle kept her eyes fixed on their mother, her heart locked behind a brick wall the way Mirquios had taught her.

Astra was frantic, and Lunelle could feel the tension building in her chest. *Are you okay? I couldn't even sense you.*

Oestera continued, "In an effort to show our firm support for Pluto's wise decision to join in our fight against the oppression and tyranny of Solaris..."

Lunelle shrugged, doing everything within her power to maintain a casual air.

I'm fine. Just tired. It's a long trip.

That was, unsurprisingly, not enough for her sister.

Everyone is being weird. What are you hiding?

Lunelle sat up, her spine tightening as she realized where

her mother's speech was going, and how much sooner she'd have to confront her reality than she had prepared for.

"It is my honor to announce to you that Arcas, the Prince of Pluto, has joined us along with his court for Lunelle's trial. He'll be the sole Lunar champion, signifying—"

"What?" Astra yelped, her fingers tightening around the arm of her chair.

"What part aren't you clear on, Astra?" Oestera sighed.

Astra's anger echoed in the hall, "The part where you—the queen of 'tradition matters, Astra'—are shucking centuries of ritual by only nominating one champion? The part where you've invited a court full of people who were our sworn enemies until a month ago and then promised your successor to them? Have you lost your mind?"

"Astra," Lunelle said, reaching for her sister.

"Why even put her through a trial if you're going to dictate the outcome? Just plan a wedding instead!"

"Astra Leona, that is enough!" Oestera's harsh yell bounded against the crystalline walls of the palace, silencing any thoughts in Lunelle's mind.

"This is insanity," Astra cried. "How could you do this to her?"

Lunelle silently begged her sister to sit back down, to let her shoulder this burden. Her outburst only served as more proof that Astra was already holding onto too much.

Oestera slowly exhaled, recomposing herself.

"Your sister is not a child, Astra. She understands the role she plays. This is not the time to be soft. If you were more willing to do what was necessary for your court—"

Astra's hands went up in defense, that aventurine ring on her finger glinting in the moonlight. Lunelle's hand involuntarily flexed under the absence of weight on her palm.

Astra's voice dropped to a dangerous tone. "I'm more than

willing to do what needs to be done to further the well-being of my court, something I would argue you have never done!"

The harsh words landed as Astra hoped. Lunelle could see the wince begging at her mother's lips.

"Perhaps you should be down the hall with your intended's court since your allegiance is clearly not to your queen."

They held each other in a brutal stare. Astra broke the silence first.

"My allegiance is to the people upon whose backs you'll fight this war. My allegiance is to my sister and the court she'll have to piece back together after the mess you're making of it."

Gods, Lunelle's heart cracked for both of them. She knew the painful wound Astra was rubbing salt in—she understood it in ways her sister never would.

"You're right, Astra." Oestera returned, a queen defeated. "What would I know about piecing together a broken court?" She would not give Astra a chance to volley another insult. "You are dismissed."

Astra stormed out of the hall, taking her fury with her, but Oestera never recovered. The rest of their meeting was disjointed and sporadic, two things the Lunar queen never allowed herself to be.

The thing Lunelle hated most. Uncertainty.

She made her exit the moment Oestera fielded a final question from a councilwoman, aiming for the bed she'd missed every night for months.

"Lunelle."

Arcas appeared from the edge of the gardens between her bedroom and the Celestial Hall, his expression an unreadable mask.

"I have no interest in games today, Arcas," Lunelle muttered as she brushed by him, ignoring her name as he called it twice more.

For the first time in weeks, she desired to actually be alone.

SHE'D DONE a great job of hiding from the rest of the world for most of the night.

So much so that she'd missed Lura's soft footsteps as they found her in her study, unable to sleep, despite her exhaustion.

"Lunelle?"

She glanced up from her book—not that she'd retained a single word—and was instantly up as Lura's expression sparked a panic in her.

"What's happened?"

"Your sister—"

"Oh, gods, what did my mother do—"

"No," Lura laughed. "Not your mother. Though if she knew, she'd have your sister imprisoned. I was just out in the gardens, and one of the guards saw her leave with the Mercurians."

Lunelle rubbed the bridge of her nose. "Where?"

Lura cleared her throat, her eyes glancing out Lunelle's window at the expansive aurora in the sky.

"The Rift."

"Mother above," Lunelle sighed. She was already on her way through the door and into her dressing room. "That gods-damned traitor!"

Lunelle ripped through her clothing, searching for a pair of pants amongst the gowns and dresses. Her fingers ran over a pair of old riding leathers she'd never put to work, and she wasted no time yanking them on.

"Here's your cloak," Lura said. "And your dagger."

Lura pushed a cool metal dagger into her hand, and

Lunelle's heart stuttered. She knew the handle bore a Mercurian seal.

"Are you coming with me?" Lunelle asked Lura.

She shook her head. "Ameera and I will keep watch here. We'll send someone if your mother comes calling."

Lunelle twisted her long braid into a crown atop her head, pinning it with a silver star before tucking Mirquios's dagger into her boot.

"Goddesspeed, Lu," Lura said.

"Pray for Mercury's foolish king and his asinine commander, not me," Lunelle chuckled darkly.

TWENTY-FIVE

"**S**ir?" The barkeep's eyes flickered from the crates beneath the aventurine slab to the silver-haired demigoddess in the doorway. His heart stopped. He knew her face.

"Your—Your Majesty?"

Lunelle shook her head. "I'm here to see Mirq—the king."

His jaw hung open as he slipped behind the bar and down the stairs to her right. She wasn't sure if she should follow or not, but her chest was so filled with rage as she felt the tug of the Tether below, she didn't care. She'd followed the damned thing through the Rift and into the Mercurian Court's gilded streets, and she wasn't about to stop.

She took the steps two at a time, the commander's deep baritone voice floating up the stairwell.

"You can send her down. She knows why we're here."

The barkeep scooted past her as she hit the landing.

Astra stood just feet from her, but she'd never felt further away. She'd defended Lunelle so fiercely this afternoon, and now she was about to destroy her entire world in return.

A woman in the corner cleared her throat, her deep complexion and glowing green eyes that reminded Lunelle of Mirquios, who held his breath across from Astra.

Maeve, Lunelle realized. She'd heard tales of the Mercurian captain drinking with the Novas in The Underground. Maeve's eyes danced at the sight of the princess, darting quickly between the four of them.

"Well, now. What a strange turn of events," she said.

"We had a deal," Lunelle said to Mirquios, not nearly as forcefully as she wanted to. She was desperately in love with the man, but that didn't make him any less of an idiot.

"I'm not breaking any of our rules," he replied in a tone that caressed her, though she knew she was being managed. Her sister did too, judging by the tick of her freckled cheek.

"Did she walk here?" Lunelle asked, gesturing toward Astra, the rage spilling from her lungs. "I was clear about taking her into the Rift, Mirq."

Astra bristled at her sister's unusual tone, the hardness of the notes sending her stumbling into the commander's arms. Luxuros pushed her back, holding her steady.

"Lu," Mirquios said, a gesture of peace between his hands. Another flare lit her silver eyes from within.

"Good gods, Mirquios. Now you've pissed them both off." Maeve clucked at him as she stepped closer to the edge of the basement. "Who do you put your money on for the final blow, Commander? Fire or Ice?"

"Fire," he said. "Always Fire."

He was ignorant of how far she'd go to avenge any hurt that came her sister's way, so unaware of the damage she'd do to him with a smile on her face.

"I need everyone in this room to start talking, now!" Astra cried.

She was overwhelmed with the loaded silence of their chests, Lunelle realized. Each of them held too tightly to their emotions, creating a tension in the air that must have been worse for her than the symphony of heartache begging to escape.

"As," Lunelle murmured, softening the edge in her tone as she tried to dull the pain in her chest for her sister's sake. "You need to get back home. It's not safe for you here."

Astra groaned. "Mother above, not you, too. I'm so sick of everyone telling me what I need to do with zero explanation!"

"The basement is yours," Maeve said as she exited toward the stairs. "I just got things cleaned up down here, Fire Queen. I don't want return to a disaster," Maeve said.

Lunelle watched her climb the stairs, the barkeep waiting at the top to berate her for bringing so much drama to The Dune. Lunelle crossed the room, falling into one of the ancient armchairs across from Mirquios.

Her chest sighed in relief as his eyes met hers—no matter how angry she was with him.

Astra was not as relieved, understandably.

"If someone doesn't start speaking, I'll volunteer you."

No one spoke as three sets of eyes bounced around the room.

"Very well," Astra muttered. "Lunelle, ladies first."

Shit. Lunelle drew in a sharp breath.

She beamed to her sister's mind, *Before we speak, I need your promise that Mother never finds out about anything you hear.*

Astra rolled her amber eyes. *Not telling Mother things is one of my favorite hobbies, Lunelle. Go.*

She reached for her younger sister's hands, closing the

space between them, though she felt like knives were clawing their way out of her ribs.

"May the Mother bless us," she offered, hoping their old joke might disarm Astra.

"Within and Without Oestera's knowledge." Her sister smiled, the exact effect Lunelle aimed for.

There was no use in delaying it.

"Fine. I don't know where to start!" Lunelle released a breath, letting the tension melt from her shoulders. "Astra, there is no easy way to say what I want to, and I had planned on having a few more answers before we did this—" her eyes narrowed at the king, "—but frankly, we're running out of options and time."

She tried to force the tears back. She hated burying Astra in more feelings that weren't her burden to carry.

The commander spoke up, his gaze cold as it fell to Lunelle.

"Just tell her. She can handle it."

Lunelle nodded toward Luxuros. He'd been clear earlier in the day. If they didn't tell her sister, he would.

She wanted to tell her. She knew she needed to. But what came out was something completely different from what she intended.

"Astra. I don't think Selenia is who we think she is."

"Princess," Luxuros growled, but Lunelle shook her head— she'd get there.

She continued, "I spent a lot of time with the rebels in Pluto. Their captain heard rumors back when Leona died that Selenia sold her out to the Solar God in the Court Above. He didn't know what she got out of it on her end, but the Outer Courts all hold it as common knowledge that Selenia betrayed Leona and Solan, leading to Leona's death."

Astra turned to Luxuros, a burning question on her tongue.

"Does she know about the Shadow Bargaining?"

Shadow Bargaining. Lunelle shivered at the term—it certainly couldn't be a positive thing. Nothing was when Selenia was involved, she realized.

"I figured you'd want to brief them," Luxuros said.

"Shadow Bargaining?" Lunelle rose from her chair.

"Ivonne Bloodmoon was researching Selenia. She thinks Mother is covering up the fact that Selenia traded her Shadow to the Nether Queen for some of her power."

"What would she need more power for? She's already an Ascended Lunar Goddess!"

Astra sighed. "That's where we got stuck, too. Lux and I brought a dozen texts back with us from Ellume, but we can't think of a motive. The Outer Courts believe it had something to do with Leona?"

Lunelle straightened her back, her shoulders still tense with the unspoken secret she could only hold quietly within her chest for another moment. She turned toward her sister.

"Will you show me in the morning? I tried to prod Mother on Selenia a few times, but she always clammed up."

"Of course." Astra's face fell, her heart sinking.

The commander's head tilted, his fiery gaze darting between the women. His lips parted, and Lunelle braced herself.

"There's something else," the commander urged.

"Luxuros," the king warned.

Astra's brows furrowed. "What is it?"

Her silvery stare hit the floor, unable to look Astra in the eye.

"Lunelle," Astra whispered. "You can tell me anything. I'm your sister."

Luxuros rubbed his broad chest, a familiar gesture to Lunelle. Her throat tightened—how many times had she seen the king push at the same spot? He fixed his eyes on Lunelle and Mirquios, waiting.

"She deserves to know," he said.

Lunelle swallowed her pride, her shame, her betrayal. Astra did deserve to know. She inhaled, summoning the bravery she so seldom tapped.

"While we were away, I Tethered."

A sharp gasp escaped her sister. "Oh gods, not the Plutonian!" Astra rubbed her temples, swallowing. She'd been so vocally against their impending union.

"Not Arcas," Mirquios said.

"As," Lunelle whispered, letting the wall within her crumble slowly, showing her sister all the layers of guilt and pain she'd built over the memory of her world falling into his.

She bit her lip as Astra watched them, unsure of what came next. The king sighed slowly as he crossed the space between them and rested a gentle palm on Lunelle's shoulder.

She glanced up at Mirquios, desperate to absorb even a modicum of the calmness in his breath.

He broke the pained silence in the room.

"Astra, I never would have agreed to our deal and put you in such a precarious position if I so much as suspected. I'd crossed paths with your sister a dozen times before we left. I never dreamed..."

Lunelle fought the urge to smile at him. Astra didn't need to see the spark of joy his words kindled, the hazy library in her mind, built just for them.

"We were trying to find a solution," Lunelle whispered. "A way to sever it. We weren't going to tell you until we had a plan." She placed her hand over the king's.

"Oh." Astra sighed, her eyes drinking in the sight of them.

"Astra." Lunelle leaned forward, ready to throw herself on the ground and grovel, but she watched something snap inside of her sister.

Something like relief.

"Oh my gods," Astra shouted, falling into a chair and covering her mouth. A ripple of laughter fell from her lips. "Oh, Lunelle. No wonder you've been so strange!"

Lunelle joined her laughter as the men eyed them, confused.

"The day you told me you Tethered to Mirquios, I felt a piece of me die, Astra. I thought it was because I was losing you... but I think I was losing both of you and didn't even realize it. We've had every historian we know between the two of us hunting for a way to sever the Tether."

"No!" Astra stood, pushing the chair back behind her. "You shouldn't! You can't!"

Lunelle waved her hands. "Well, we certainly cannot—"

"Yes, you can! It makes perfect sense, Lu. You're both so similar, so calm. Like tranquil seas."

"Boring, you mean?" Mirquios scoffed.

"No," Astra said, a shallow laugh bubbling from her as she searched for the right words. "The world needs more of you two and less of my uncontrolled burn, I assure you. And besides, it's not like we had chemistry on our side. I'd begun to wonder if I could go the rest of my life without—" Astra stopped herself, a faint blush crawling over her cheeks. "Sorry."

Mirquios was not offended. "I'd be lying if I said it hadn't been a concern for me, too, Princess. Forever is a long time." Lunelle leaned back into him, his fingers grasping her shoulder tighter.

"Indeed," Astra relented.

237

Lunelle watched her sister's face for any signs of resentment—any hint of pain.

"So you're not angry? Or hurt?"

Astra shook her head, her scarlet curls bouncing.

"Who am I to fight Fate, Lunelle? We signed no contracts, there are no hard feelings on my end. I assume Mirquios told you the truth of our deal? And it's not the first broken engagement Mother has navigated. This is a good thing, my sister."

Lunelle sighed. If only it were that simple—that easy to move forward.

"It's a tad more complex, As."

"Arcas," Mirquios muttered. The name sent a lightning bolt through the Tether. "Your mother is determined to marry Lunelle off to him. She does not know anything transpired between us. I didn't want to erode her trust in you. When the Tether happened, it caught us both off guard. We were so in shock, we didn't speak for three days."

So in shock, Lunelle thought, *that I nearly considered flinging myself off the cliffs into the Plutonian sea just to escape it.*

"Wait," Astra turned toward the commander. "You said she knows why we're here. How!" Astra wasn't asking, she was exclaiming.

A soft grin broke over Lunelle's pale face. "I know you think I am soft and perfectly groomed by Mother, but I have my secrets. The Plutonian rebels contacted me for a meeting when we arrived. I'd heard rumors of their rise in council sessions... I followed Mirquios to their base."

"She forced me to bind her to the rebellion. When our palms touched..." Mirquios mirrored Lunelle's expression. "Between running into one another at The Underground and the Tether, we were both overwhelmed. We decided to deal with it when we returned, but then we were there for so long.

We became good friends, but nothing more. For your sake, Astra."

"No need for details," Astra insisted, a heat rising to her cheeks. Lunelle sighed, trying not to think of how badly she'd wanted to betray her sister in Pluto.

"Lu made me swear I'd tell you before getting you involved in any rebel activity, but when Lux informed me of your run-in with the Lunarian Novas, I may have skirted that rule."

Lunelle scoffed. "I also made him promise not to let you into the Rift."

"That wasn't my doing," Mirq laughed. "The commander insisted."

Astra's eyebrow curved. "You?"

Luxuros remained silent. Lunelle did not miss the curious glance Mirquios shot toward his second-in-command.

"He wanted you to see the Sun, in case you didn't get the chance, depending on what happens next."

Astra's lips twisted. "What *does* happen next?"

"I'm not sure," Lunelle admitted. "I was hoping we could figure it out together."

"I have another question," Astra announced, drawing both Lunelle and Mirquios's attention. "When did my prim-and-proper older sister get so interesting?"

Lunelle's heart lurched, the admiration in her sister's eyes so undeserved.

"I've always admired your spirit and ideas, Sister," she insisted. "I'm just more willing to play the part than you ever were. I knew someday I'd sit on the throne and be able to enact the changes we hoped for, but patience has never been a virtue of the Fire Queen."

Astra's eyes scraped over the shelves of the basement.

"I think I need a second to get my head around all of this."

"I'd actually like a word with the king, anyway," Lunelle

said, her heart beating faster at the thought of being alone with him, unbound to the honor they'd both previously clung to. "I met with Mother again last night before bed. We need to talk about my trial."

Mirquios leaned toward Astra. "If you'd like to see the palace, Luxuros can give you a tour. We'll meet you at the gate in an hour."

"Of course." A sadness slipped over Astra's face.

"My heart broke, Astra. I was ready to conquer the world with you. Never doubt that," Mirquios assured her.

Astra patted his shoulder lightly, her eyes staying on the commander.

"Do not mourn for me, Mirquios. It seems we'll be conquering the world alongside one another, anyway. I'll make sure of it." She squeezed her sister's hand, disappearing up the stairs.

Lunelle counted the heavy thuds of the commander's boots as he followed Astra out of The Dune. A silence fell between them, though she swore she could hear the buzzing of the Tether as if it had sparked to life.

Mirquios did not seem sure what to do with his hands, an air of insecurity she nearly laughed at from such a confident leader.

They'd spent months keeping their hands to themselves—sitting on them if that's what it took—anything to keep the lines between them clean.

But here, in the basement of The Dune, the line had suddenly vanished.

"Lu," he whispered. The sound was a sweet melody to her ears, despite the melancholy notes running beneath it.

"She seemed okay, right?" Lunelle leaned into him, her gentle touch against his chest even more comforting than he'd imagined it might be.

"If Astra is half as strong-willed as you've alluded to, I imagine she'll be onto her next plan by morning."

Lunelle stroked the fine silver threads woven into his tunic. She'd wondered so many times what they would feel like without the sting of guilt clouding them.

"I should check on her—"

"Lunelle," Mirquios disrupted her panic. "She's in good hands with the commander."

"You're right," she breathed, her lungs expanding in jittery waves. "Perhaps *too* good of hands."

"Luxuros did not seem ready to have that conversation," Mirquios laughed.

Lunelle wasn't a child. She knew what came next—she'd stood in this strange sea of tension for so long, waiting for the pressure to drop and the storm to move inland. They'd held themselves back from one another for months, and there was something comforting in always having that line drawn between them.

Now, the possibilities were wide open—hers to take.

"I don't expect anything, Lunelle. I know things are still complicated with the prince, and I would never risk your safety for that."

The king leaned back from her touch, reading the hesitation on her face.

"You could give Astra a run for her money," she laughed.

"I also understand that your feelings for him aren't easily explained."

"That's generous, Mirquios."

He held her hands in his. She enjoyed the pleasant warmth to his touch. She'd been able to tell, of course, standing near him and the brief moments they'd toed the line that she was much cooler than he, but it was always so rushed—so panicked—she never got to marvel in their differences.

"I would wait a thousand lifetimes if you needed me to," he whispered, squeezing her pale hands, so small in his.

It was that admission that made her realize she *couldn't* wait a thousand lifetimes for him.

Lunelle pushed herself forward, wrapping her arms around his strong neck and hanging from him as she moved her mouth over his. The shock melted within a second of tasting him—even sweeter than she'd remembered from the cliffs.

The way his lips moved against hers did something sacred to her heart.

He tangled his hand into her braided crown, the silk strands smooth against his calloused fingertips. She told herself it was just a kiss—to not get ahead of herself—but then a quiet moan spun at the back of his throat and any thought of restraint dissolved.

He pulled away from her, though everything in their bodies begged for less space, at a squeak at the top of the basement steps.

Maeve cleared her throat.

"Don't you have a palace, Your Highness?" she asked.

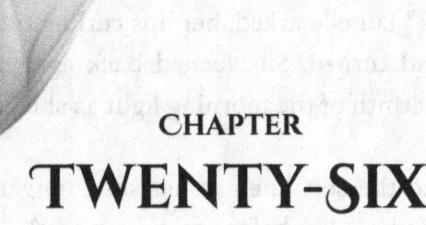

CHAPTER
TWENTY-SIX

"And here I thought the Sun was intense in Pluto," Lunelle said, running her fingers over the lush velvet curtains framing the window—easily twice her height—in the king's bedroom.

The golden Sun broke through the glass and spilled over the Mercurian palace floor, bouncing sparkling rays across her bare feet. She watched as it crowned the city below—a city she'd hopelessly fallen in love with after only a few hours.

A city bathed in golden warmth, just like Mirquios, speckled with pastels and strange flora and gems in the walls she did not yet know the names of.

A city she wanted desperately to call home, she realized.

"I want to come over there, but I don't know how to give up this view," the king mused, lying across the bed and propping himself up on his elbow. With the morning sunlight pouring in behind her, she looked every bit the goddess she was, her silver hair aflame as she brushed it away from her face.

She held her hands out, wondering if perhaps this was how Astra felt when her fingertips caught fire.

"This view?" Lunelle asked, her lips curling into a smile as she twisted and turned. She leaned back against the glass, enjoying the warmth of the morning light as she held his gaze. "Or this one?"

She dragged the soft linen of her shirt upward, letting it slip slowly over her skin before tossing it to the floor. She'd gotten dressed in a hurry before leaving the Lunar Court. She hadn't had time to consider what might come off at the end of her evening.

If she'd had time to plan, she certainly would have included something prettier than the simple white stays wrapped around her chest. She peeled the frilled edges at the center of her back, untying the laces and letting them fall away.

"That one," Mirquios murmured, his mouth unable to fully get around the sounds without swallowing.

His eyes widened as her fingers dragged toward her waistband, peeling the leather of her pants over her thighs. She yanked them off her ankles and basked in the sunlight, warming her body from head to toe.

"Goddess smite me," Mirquios whispered. He pushed himself from the bed and rushed to her. She was unashamed of the desperation that buzzed between them as she wrapped herself around him—to confess how starved for him she was.

In her fantasies, he'd been soft and slow, curling around her like a wisp of smoke. There, in her hands, he was nothing like smoke—he was fire, burning against her as she tangled their bodies into one. He wrapped his hands around her back, taking his time as his fingers traced paths along her spine.

His palm slipped along her side and climbed her ribs like a ladder, gently teasing the soft skin of her breasts.

It wasn't enough.

She made it clear as she arched into him and scraped her teeth against his lower lip. A low, thunderous laugh rippled between them. She loved the notion that he was just as feral for her as she'd been for him since they'd first touched in his room, bleeding into one another as their Souls fused.

"Oh," Lunelle yelped as he moved her back against the window, pressing her against the warm glass. "What if someone sees us?"

Mirquios nipped at her ear. "You deserve to be seen, Lu. They should be so lucky."

Her cheeks flushed as she pulled at his shirt. He shoved his pants as low as he could without abandoning her cool skin, and her hand flew to him like a moth to flame.

She wrapped her fingers around him and pushed her mouth back to his, sliding her lips over his jaw and neck as she sank to her knees.

"Oh, gods," Mirquios rasped as he gripped the window pane with one hand and her silver braid with another. Her hands were everywhere, squeezing, pulling, stroking, and then her lips closed around him, and he nearly wept as the Tether between them pulled tight. The pressure and strain added a strange pleasure to the moment, instead of the unbearable pain of avoiding one another they'd adjusted to.

"Lu," he breathed, his knuckles rosy pink as they curled around the golden pane. The Sun illuminated his dark skin, casting him in a halo she thought made him look much more like a Solar demigod than a Mercurian king.

"Lu," he gasped again, his fist pulling gently against her braid. "Mother above, Princess, if you don't stop, I'll—" He didn't have to finish his thought, she released him with a radiant smile and rose, wrapping herself around him as he pressed her firmly into the window.

Mirquios held his breath as he ran a fingertip up her side. She followed the gentle tip of his finger, admiring the way he dipped into each curve as the Sun danced across her silver freckles.

He leaned into the motion as she wrapped her legs around his waist, marveling at the sigh of the Tether as their bodies melted together. His mouth crawled her neck, the sweet catch of her breath as he nipped her flushed skin his reward.

"Are you sure you're okay with this?" he asked as he nestled against her. They might be out of one mess, but they were still ensnared in a dozen others—she knew this was only a temporary reprieve.

She answered in the form of her heels digging deeper into his back. Sighing at the swell of him against her, she closed her eyes, letting the warmth of the Sun caress her bare shoulders as Mirquios slid into her.

Lunelle whimpered at the sensation, unsure how something she'd done so many times could suddenly feel so wildly different. Her body held his—a sacred note at the end of a hymn, praising every goddess she could name as she tightened her grip on his neck. He moved slowly at first, but that quickly gave way to something much more craven as his arms pulled her closer still.

She pressed into the glass at her back, the feeling of him too intense, too close to rupturing. Mirquios closed his fingers around her throat, pulling her back into him so he could whisper his worship into her ear as he felt the goddess within her crash around him.

She wound like a coil—everything within her pulled together, ready to unleash. He leaned further into her, snagging her ear in his teeth again, growling against her, "Tell me what you need."

Her head fell back, her pulse racing into a rhythm she

wasn't sure was possible. She reached for a hand—any hand, fuck, her own would do if he couldn't reach—but she snagged his fingers from her hip and pushed them toward her breast, flush with blood and heat and desperation.

She'd been asked what she wanted a million times, but no one ever asked what she'd *needed*.

And while Lunelle had learned not to need much, she needed him.

He pulled at her lips with his teeth, losing himself in her, squeezing and kneading and biting and taking any piece of her he could access. When she did finally burst, her cheeks flushed a stunning shade of red as she arched her back, her heavy breaths laced with his name, which only pushed him over the edge.

She gasped as he lost control of himself, a melody of low notes from his throat crashing against her shoulder as his teeth cut into her flesh. The sting of the bite compared to the fullness of him inside her eased the tension of the Tether, buzzing with a different sort of energy now.

"Gods above," he sighed, claiming every breath she managed to take, his kiss just as maddening as it had been on the Plutonian cliffs, but now he was hers to hold.

Hers to enjoy.

Hers.

Lunelle could hardly think. Not a single thread of words stuck to the walls of her mind as her king brought her to his bed, curling around her in an effort to absorb as much of her as he could in whatever time they'd have together.

When she sought out the prince, it was to distract herself from the complete overwhelm of her world. And it had worked for a mere moment. But the quiet never lasted—the safety from her thoughts was only in the thrill of the risk.

With Mirquios, with the other half of her so close and

sharing her breath, her mind was at ease despite the understanding that they had nothing but trouble coming.

But they could face it together.

He tucked his head into her chest as she stroked his hair, a million questions racing across her tongue.

Most of the answers seemed too difficult to find, so she asked the one simmering under her fingertips since she'd arrived back in Lunaria.

"Do you think the commander knows my sister is devastatingly in love with him?"

Mirquios laughed into her skin, the soft reverberation dissolving over her stomach. His bright eyes flashed toward hers, half-closed in her dazed bliss. He sat up, leaning against his headboard, and pulled on her hand, an invitation to climb over his lap as he thought about her question.

Lunelle settled on top of him, her pale skin glowing in the morning sunlight that streamed through the window. Mirquios pressed his lips to her throat, his hands wandering her back. He forced himself to come up for air, though she knew he'd have rather spent every second exploring which spots on her neck made her breath hitch.

"Not to answer your question with a question, but do you think your sister knows the commander is so in love with *her* he can't see straight?"

A quiet smile overtook her lips as she leaned forward, the friction distracting both of them.

"What a mess." Lunelle rested her hand against his neck, feeling the warmth of his pulse as it quickened beneath the surface. "Leave it to the Fire Queen to find herself entangled with a Solarian."

Mirquios leaned into her touch, letting it soothe all of the misery that had built up in his veins like poison for months.

"Leave it to Luxuros to fall for the only woman I've ever met who could go toe-to-toe with his strange mind."

Lunelle sank her hips lower. A stifled groan rose from his throat in return as he leaned forward, pulling her into another intoxicating kiss. How she'd gone so long without the chemistry of this, the depth of sensation between them, she could not fathom.

"Perhaps if we make them wait long enough, they'll sort themselves out," she whispered, hooking an arm around the back of his neck.

"You know," he said between sizzling nips against her neck. "I cannot remember what I worshipped before you."

As she rolled her hips forward once again, she felt the stirrings of his devotion between them, a welcome offering that she would bless again and again, for however long the gods allowed.

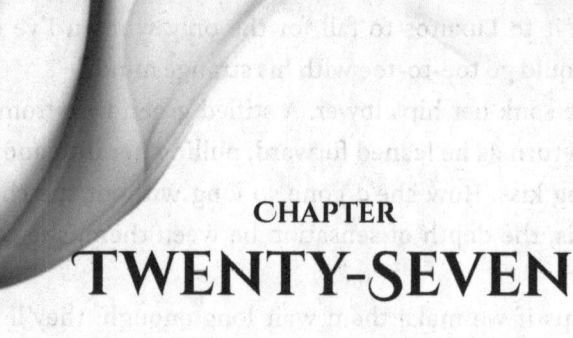

CHAPTER
TWENTY-SEVEN

"O h!" Oestera set her book on the table across from her chair.

"Sorry Mother, I thought I'd be alone here," Lunelle said, her arms filled with books she'd brought back from the Mercurian library.

"I was waiting for you, actually," Oestera said, her face worn from the heightened emotions of the last few days.

"Me?"

Her mother sighed, gesturing to the chair beside her.

"It is honorable, Lunelle, to choose your court over your own dreams," Oestera said, stirring her coffee. "Many simply aren't capable of it. They crumble beneath the weight of a crown before they get their bearings and build enough muscle to hold it."

Lunelle did not understand what she meant by her musings. Her lungs slowly filled with dread as she turned them over in her mind. She sank into her chair, wishing a pit would open up beneath her and take her back to the encounter with

Pluto, where she might ask him why the Nether he'd dared to make her hope.

"It is honorable," Oestera said again. "But honor is not all there is to life."

Lunelle's forehead creased. "Mother, I am tired—"

"Hear me when I tell you, my darling girl, that you and I are not as unalike as I might have thought. As you surely think. I was not much older than you when Leona died and tossed my entire life plan into the ether. Things change, Lunelle. That's all I'm getting at. And if you need to change with them, I would hope you'd have the courage to do so."

Lunelle eyed her mother. She studied the delicate lines forming at the corners of her lips, the fold through her forehead that Lunelle used to imagine Astra carving with her own blade. It seemed so connected to her sister's behavior.

"Do you understand me, Lunelle?"

"No," Lunelle snorted. "No, I do not. My entire life, you have painstakingly and relentlessly trained me to only think of everyone else, never let my will supersede the betterment of my court, and now, weeks away from my coronation, you're unraveling it all to tell me what, Mother? What do you want me to do?"

Oestera's eyes flared.

"That's exactly it, Lunelle. You can't rely on what I want you to do. After your coronation, I will be on borrowed time. I will make my Ascent to the Lunar throne in the Court Above, and all of this will be up to you. Every piece of it. I'm telling you that it's time to consider what you want that to look like."

Lunelle's neck flushed pink with heat. She was exhausted by her mother's riddles.

"That's all I consider, Mother. It's all I've ever considered— and I resent the implication that I'm not doing exactly what it is I believe to be right."

Oestera held her hands up, backing down from the fight in a move that Lunelle had never once seen.

"I was merely offering some understanding, Lunelle."

Lunelle swallowed a bitter laugh. *Understanding* was comical. Understanding was long overdue. Understanding was worthless to her now.

"Perhaps your understanding would be better spent on the daughter down the hall, hmm?" Lunelle arched her brow, knowing that throwing Astra into the mix would swiftly shift the focus from her.

Oestera exhaled.

"If I understood your sister less, perhaps I could give her more."

She left Lunelle to ponder her strange circles, pulling at threads to which she did not see any ends in sight.

"*Explain it again,*" *Mirquios said, his eyes widening as Lunelle held up the diagram she'd drawn.*

"*It's a symbolic ceremony," Lunelle said, the lines of her diagram slipping from the page as her dream struggled to hold the concepts together. "The priestess will lead me through two prayers —the Hymn of the Soul, and the Song of the Shadow. When that's complete, I will offer my Shadow to the Nether queen for the Solstice, typically by placing it into a piece of quartz, and then I will have to reintegrate it in the Court Below to accomplish my trial.*"

"*That's it?" Mirquios said, taking the page from her, the notes bleeding into one another.*

"*Well, I have to find it first.*"

Mirquios leaned back into the sofa. "Does it hurt?"

"*My mother said it's more emotional turmoil than physical.*" *Lunelle poured herself another cup of tea, settling in for the rest of their study session. She'd spent her entire life preparing for her coronation trial, and explaining the ritual to him had made her feel like she just might be capable of it.*

"Say I bribed a priestess to perform the ceremony on me and then snuck into the Court Below... if I completed it... and then beat Arcas back..."

Lunelle shook her head. "You have to be nominated, I think."

"You think?"

She frowned. She did not actually know if that was a prerequisite.

"We should look into that," the king whispered, leaning forward and placing a kiss on her shoulder.

"Add it to the list," Lunelle sighed, resting her head on his.

"What time does Lura typically wake you?" he asked.

Lunelle giggled against him. "If you can rouse yourself, you've got time to get to me."

Mirquios sat up, unsure how to accomplish it. "Pinch me," he commanded her.

"Mirquios!" Lunelle laughed, but she reached for him anyway, pinching his forearm.

"Damn," he murmured. "Still here."

"Perhaps something more intriguing," she whispered, climbing over his lap and wrapping herself up in him. She sank her hips over his, the motion strange and slow in the astral, but at the first sound of pleasure from her throat, the king disappeared from beneath her.

It took him all of five minutes to make it to her door.

BREAKFAST COULD NOT HOLD her attention.

She'd been watching her parents carefully, unnerved by the tension between them.

Do you think Mother and Father are fighting? she beamed to Astra, who was also strangely preoccupied this morning.

Perhaps they were all just drowning in the discomfort between her and the Plutonian prince, whom she'd done her best to stay far, far away from.

What makes you ask that? Astra replied. Lunelle's eyes shifted toward her mother, who looked slightly more agitated than she normally did, and her father, who never looked anything other than happy to be present, a frown wearing lines on his lips.

They just seem at odds, Lunelle sent back.

"Yallara sent a missive for you yesterday, Princess," Arcas mumbled beside her. His sudden comment pulled her from the conversation with her sister.

"Good," Lunelle replied. "I miss her."

"Perhaps she could visit soon," Arcas said. *After he was king,* he wanted to add, Lunelle could taste it.

"Princess?" Astra and Lunelle's heads both snapped toward the end of the table, where Mirquios stared at them expectantly.

Lunelle forced her gaze away from him. He did not mean her. He should not mean her.

"Sorry," Astra offered, her mother's eyes flickering over her.

"I was telling Arcas here what a talented rider you are. He has an affinity for dragons."

"Oh," Astra sighed. "Do you ride?"

Arcas kept his eyes fixed on his teacup. "I don't. But I find them fascinating. We don't have them in the Outer Courts."

The commander leaned forward, his amber gaze rippling across the table.

"Perhaps you could introduce him to Riverion."

"Do not take the prince near that beast!" their mother

254

declared—her tone very much that of an order, not a warning. "You'll forgive me, Arcas, but Riverion has a history of unpredictable behavior around men," she said. Oestera glared at her second-born, she knew better than to risk Riverion's unpredictability around nobility.

Lunelle thought it sounded like a better solution than any of the other half-baked plans rolling around in her head.

"Odd," Mirquios said. "Luxuros seemed to find him quite amiable. I've yet to brave the introduction."

Lunelle's jaw nearly dropped, but she tensed the muscle at the last second, feeling her mother's watchful eye. She was stunned her sister would let anyone near her beast, especially someone she'd sworn to loathe not two months earlier.

Astra Leona, you let the commander meet Riverion!

No! No. Astra found Lunelle's eyes across the table. *Lux snuck up on me in the roost. He threw himself into Riv's claws before I could get the warning out!*

She saw it then, the blush on her sister's cheeks. She should have known better—to leave two such formidable creatures alone for months and expect them *not* to form an attachment... it was rather silly to think any other outcome was possible.

Her father finally looked away from his plate. "I'm sure Riverion would be nothing but kind to you, Your Highness. He respects the worthy. Right, Astra?"

Lunelle bit back a giggle as Mirquios grinned. She knew her father's expressions so well, his every intonation, and he was clearly forming the same conclusion she had. Mirquios could hear the amusement in Nayson's voice as well.

He was fucking with them, but they were too preoccupied with their hands to notice.

Mirquios arched a brow, those bright eyes sparkling with mischief.

"What do you say, Fire Queen? Would I stack up to the commander in your beast's eyes?"

Luxuros reached for another cup of coffee, the heat rolling off him even more intense than usual.

"Only one way to know for certain, my king," Astra muttered.

"The commander can have Riverion's affections," Mirquios said, sipping his tea as Lunelle watched, a quiet rain flooding her heart. "I will not fight that battle."

She had never seen her sister remain quiet at a table for so long. As they went their separate ways for the day, she aimed to get the king alone, but it was Arcas who caught her elbow outside the hall.

He reached into his pocket, producing a pale blue envelope. "Yallara's letter."

Lunelle eyed it, her pulse quickening at the possibilities it contained.

"Did you read it?"

Arcas gave her a crooked smile.

"I was tempted. But no, I did not."

Her heart sank. "I wish I could believe you," Lunelle sighed.

"I wish you could, too, starling."

Arcas pushed the message into her hands, the buzz between their fingertips shocking her and sending her back. He seized his moment, the one she knew he'd been searching for since they arrived. He leaned forward and caught her cheek in his hand, whispering, "As pathetic as it is to admit, I've missed you."

"Arcas," she sighed, pulling from his touch. Pain pooled in his eyes, perhaps surprising both of them. "Do not pretend to care about me—"

"I *do* care about you, Lunelle, despite your clear disdain for me. I do not just miss you in my arms, I miss you in my *head*. I miss your blunt critiques, I miss your disapproving glares, I miss feeling like a disappointment to you—"

"Do not worry to that end," she scoffed. "You are still a grave disappointment to me, Prince."

Arcas could not even pretend to be wounded. He smiled.

"Why does it feel like an honor to be your enemy?"

Lunelle laughed, despite herself, and rested her hand on his chest, adjusting the soft lining on his tunic. The anger she felt dissipated at the concave of his sternum beneath his chest.

Arcas was not a monster. He was an idiot.

"You do not have to be my enemy, you know."

He stepped closer, dropping his tone. "The ally slot on your dance card appears to be filled. I have to find a way in somehow, don't I?"

She resented the thrill it sent through her—the way he closed in around her. Resented the way his lips dragged across her ear and neck as he whispered. Resented the way she both wanted to wring his neck and taste the taut ocean skin that stretched across it.

"You are once again chasing ghosts," she murmured.

It was all she had to say to earn her space. He said no more as he disappeared down the hall.

When his sunken shoulders cleared her line of sight, two jade eyes blinked at the end of the hall as his head tilted toward the study to his right. She glanced behind her, ensuring no one else waited for her attention before slipping into the dim room, teeming with old maps her father liked to catalog in his spare time.

Lunelle's heart beat quickly, and she was unsure if she should feel guilty or not.

She was caught in a strange middle ground between two futures, neither more likely than the other. Mirquios leaned against the desk in the center of the room, the pale wood stained with oil paint—another relic of her father's time.

She cradled her arms around her ribs, hoping to contain the wildness spiraling within her.

He sighed. "You're so far away."

Lunelle glanced down at the space between them, only a few breaths apart, the relief from the Tether no longer stretching over the palace enough for her. Her lips parted to contradict him, but he clarified first.

"In here," he said, reaching his finger between them and tapping her forehead.

"Oh," she sighed. "I suppose you saw Arcas in the hallway."

Mirquos held up a hand, shaking his head.

"I've told you before. You owe me *no* explanations, Lunelle."

She stepped forward, his legs parting to accommodate her.

"But I do, don't I? If we figure out this whole awful mess, if you and I get a chance... you would want to know, wouldn't you?"

Mirquios inhaled slowly, watching her with those kind eyes, always seeing too much.

"You have an affinity for him." He was not asking.

Lunelle's cheeks warmed. "I... I truly am not sure most days, Mirquios."

He reached for her face, her perfectly lovely face, tainted by the shades of gray in her heart.

"Romance was never a priority for me, Lunelle. I watched Tethers do more harm than good in most relationships I grew up near. Among the Mercurian nobility, marriages are political. They're strategic. Tethers are... troublesome. My own mother was wed to my father despite a Tether to a merchant from Saturn. She lived a life of luxury, but she was never once content. There was no love there, no joy. Her heart lived four courts away, and I watched it eat her alive for decades, so I never held much stock in the concept as a whole. I was perfectly content to fake my way through a marriage with your sister if it meant progressing the rebellion forward, because my ideals around love and marriage and commitment had been so poorly honed."

Lunelle leaned away from him, unsure of where he was going as his gaze moved from a painting on the wall to her eyes.

He laughed gently. "And then you shattered every concept I've ever had about any of it. About anything at all."

Her nose scrunched as she absorbed what he was trying to say, what he had not been able to say without the smallest bit of hope before.

"What I am trying to get at, Lunelle, is that this," he gestured to the space between them, the invisible *thing* that they could not deny even if they wanted to. "This is much bigger than any of it. Any of the rules we think we are bound by. You and I... we are bound by Soul and light, nothing else can come close to the intimacy of being formed for one another. Nothing could break it. But it does not mean you do not have desires that extend beyond it."

"I do not—"

"I am genuine, Lunelle, when I say that I *see* you. I see a woman who sets her own desires so far back in her mind that she doesn't even know they exist. But if you wanted more—if you wanted him in some capacity, I would never deny you."

Lunelle was quiet for a long moment, her head swirling as she reached for anything to say that made sense. She left him far too long, his lips dropping into a confused frown.

"...and I just wanted you... to... know that?"

All of her uncertainty, all of the implications his thoughts created, bubbled up from her in a soft giggle.

"So you're telling me that you're *so* enamored with me, you would wholeheartedly allow me to be with a man who may as well be our enemy?"

Mirquios huffed a laugh, circling her hips with his hands.

"I think a few more of your vicious character assassinations, and he might not be so firm in his opposition. You are a quiet observer, Lunelle, but that does not make me blind. That man, whether either of you would ever admit it, would ride into battle for you this instant. I cannot fault him for that. And I cannot fault you for finding a piece of yourself in his touch."

Lunelle rested her hand on his shoulder, her lips pulled tight as she fought back a wave of emotion she did not know how to parse out.

"You are not *mine*, Lunelle. You *are* me. I cannot possess something so deeply woven into my being, nor could I lose it to anyone else. We just *are*—we will always be—in a thousand lifetimes."

She pushed into him, dragging her fingertips from his shoulders to his face.

"You are right. About a great many deal of things."

He leaned his face against hers, enjoying the quietness in her chest for once.

"I only ask that you do not carry his heir," he said softly. "Should this hellish timeline ever straighten out enough that it isn't foolish to do so, I'd like to hold that one thing sacred between us."

Lunelle nodded, stroking the back of his neck. That felt like a fair enough request.

"You speak of an heir as if we'll need one," she sighed. "I hope there will be nothing but love to inherit."

He kissed her—a warm, steady thing that no one else would ever be able to provide for her. The safety, the comfort, their version of infinity.

Lunelle sighed, regretting that she had somewhere to be. "What is it?"

"I'm to meet my sister in the library, we have some catching up to do."

"Come find me tonight," he murmured, pulling at her hips and stealing one final kiss.

"How can I find that which is already within me?" she asked, arching her brow as she smirked at him.

"A cruel goddess," he whispered into her skin. "And yet I cannot help but worship."

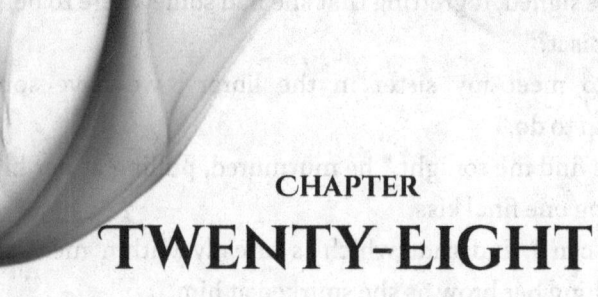

CHAPTER
TWENTY-EIGHT

L unelle was unsettled—she'd spent most of her day reeling after sifting through Astra's documentation from Ellume.

Their hunches, it seemed, were right.

Selenia *was* hiding something, and Oestera knew.

But bigger than that was the note she'd received from Yallara.

> *Dearest Lunelle,*
>
> *In my brother's absence, the movement has gained traction. I fear what he'll do to me when he returns—*
> *if he returns—but you would be proud.*
>
> *Come see for yourself soon.*

It should have been good news. She should have felt excited.

But she could only find dread.

She feared what lengths Arcas would go to when his duty

262

here was done.

"You seem tense," Lura said, moving in circles around Lunelle as she placed a few final pins in her coronation robes. They were velvet and heavy on her frame, with silver Moons embroidered across the hem, exactly as brilliant as she'd always dreamed they'd be.

"Do I?" Lunelle laughed as Lura stuck another pin between her lips.

"I'm sorry, of course you are."

"Astra and Luxuros have uncovered many details that point to the Plutonians being right about Selenia's involvement in The Flare," Lunelle confessed. Lura's shoulders flexed uncomfortably as they spoke.

"Ameera showed me the Shadow Bargaining manual," Lura shared.

"I can't explain it," Lunelle said quietly. "It all seems so wrong, but I can feel in my bones that we're onto something."

Lura glanced at Lunelle with her amethyst gaze, an uncertainty churning within her eyes.

"Your mother has not seemed herself these last few months either, Lunelle."

"How do you mean?"

"Her maidens have been worried about her. She seems... distraught. She and your father have not been sleeping well since Astra's return. They're restless."

Lunelle's head tilted. "I just mentioned to Astra this morning that something seems off. I can't place it. Perhaps something to do with Solan?"

"Perhaps," Lura muttered, leaning back to examine her markings. "All right, you're free to remove them."

"They look gorgeous," Lunelle said. "It's odd, though. They still don't feel like *mine*."

"It will all feel real soon, Lunelle."

The princess nodded, feeling Lura's words bounce off her chest and land somewhere on the floor.

"Psst," Mirquios whispered as Lunelle and Lura walked by the Andromeda wing on their way to bed for the evening.

"I'll see you when you return," Lura said, winking at Lunelle.

She twisted on her heels, glancing over her shoulder before darting into the king's chambers.

Mirquios pulled the door shut behind her and pressed her against it, wasting no time tangling himself up in her. He tasted like tea and honey as her lips parted for him.

"Gods above," the king whispered as her hands snaked up his shirt, her mouth leaving a hot trail across his neck.

"Mirquios!" Lux's panicked voice boomed on the other side of the door, followed by three harsh raps. "Mirq!"

The king hung his head back, pushing Lunelle gently to the side. He cracked open the door, his mouth open to beg his leave, but Lux pushed past him, a wild storm in his eyes.

"He took her," Luxuros gasped.

"Who?" Lunelle asked, her lips swollen and face flushed.

Luxuros paid their indiscretion no mind.

"We were... we were in a dream, and a voice called to her. I do not understand it exactly, but he reached for her, and he took her. She is not in her room!"

"Astra?" Lunelle breathed.

Ameera appeared moments later, her face ashen.

"Commander—"

Lux paced back and forth as he repeated the details of what happened beneath his breath.

"How could someone take her from a dream?" Lunelle asked, her voice rising as panic set in.

"Not someone," Lux said, his eyes widening. "It has to be a deity, yes? Someone much more powerful... we could send for Ehlaria," he said, mostly to Ameera. "She has much more knowledge on the subject—"

"We should tell the queen," Mirquios said.

Luxuros stopped pacing as Lunelle said, "No!"

Ameera stepped between them, reaching for Lux's chest. She yanked at an amulet around his neck, snapping the leather knot as she held it out to him.

"You can find her," she said quietly. Luxuros's eyes searched Ameera's for truths he could not say out loud, but within a moment of the amulet falling away, his head snapped skyward.

"Meet me in Mercury," he said to Mirquios. "I do not know what shape Astra will be in. Gather your medical supplies, Meer."

Meer, Lunelle thought as she looked at her sister's maiden. Ameera was too busy mentally cataloging what she needed to meet Lunelle's gaze.

Mirquios grasped his brother's shoulder. "We'll be there. If you do not return before daybreak, Maeve will activate the Nova response."

Luxuros was gone before Lunelle could catch her breath.

LUNELLE WATCHED the Sun climb over the city below, the morning beams waking the Mercurian Gate.

"Mirquios, perhaps it's time to send for Maeve," Ameera said from a table laden with food no one had touched in hours.

"Yes—"

"No need," Lunelle gasped, taking perhaps her first full breath since Luxuros had come for them, pointing through the window as the commander and Astra faded from the Rift. "He's got her!"

She smacked the king's arm as she raced from the library into the hall.

Lunelle cried, "You found her!" and flung her arms around her sister's neck, desperate to know she was really there, she was safe. "Are you hurt? Who took you? How did you find her?"

She could not stop the flow of questions as she looked between Astra and Luxuros.

"I'm fine, Lu," Astra mumbled into her neck, pulling away from her clutches.

Lunelle dragged Astra down the hall and into the library, even bigger than the one she'd fallen in love with back in Pluto. The morning Sun seeped in through the windows, painting the crimson carpets in shadows and flames. Ameera's eyes widened as they approached, the tension in the air thinning.

"I'm fine," Astra assured everyone. Lunelle had not noticed her sister's warmer tones in the moonlight—the gilded freckles falling over her skin.

She rather looked like the Sun herself.

Gods, she'd fucked up letting Astra out of her sight. She should never have told her about any of this, they would have been none the wiser.

"I cannot believe I let this happen. Anyone could have grabbed you. I told you she shouldn't be in the Rift!" She glared at Mirquios, who gracefully did not argue with her.

Astra sneered. "You sound like Mother."

Lunelle stopped pacing. Of all the things she could have said to justify her pit of loathing, that was the cruelest.

266

"Sorry," Astra apologized. "But I wasn't in the Rift. I was dreaming, Lunelle. It could have happened anywhere."

Lunelle sighed. "You were gone for hours, Astra! The Lunar Court will awaken any moment and we're lucky we aren't bringing back a corpse!"

Her sister sat on the couch, the silver slips of silk and the crown on her head lighting up in the sunbeams.

"I attended a ball with a bunch of deities and drank some wine, Lunelle. That's a Tuesday in the Lunar Court."

Lunelle glared at her king as he scoffed in the corner.

"What did Selenia want?" Ameera asked.

Astra shrugged nonchalantly as if all of this were normal.

"To make a deal."

The blood racing beneath Lunelle's skin seemed to freeze its currents. No deal with Selenia would be worth it—the gods were never fair to bargain with. She kneeled before her sister, searching her eyes.

"What did you do, Astra?"

"She wants me to go to the Court Below with you and Arcas to retrieve something for her," Astra said—the veneer of this being just another night flickered slightly, a tick in Astra's jaw giving her away. "And Mirq," she added.

Lunelle pitched forward, her hands landing on her sister's knees as her head swirled.

"Mirquios?" she asked, unsure if she'd heard correctly.

"In exchange for my help, Selenia will nominate Mirquios as a champion."

The room blurred around her. "What—Astra. No. No!" This had gone far enough already—there was no way Lunelle could allow her to make such a trade on her behalf.

"Lu, it's the solution we've been looking for. If Selenia nominates Mirquios, no one can argue. Not Mother. Not Arcas. It will be seen as a formal decision of the gods."

Astra's words did not soothe Lunelle's tense muscles.

"It's too dangerous!"

"You'll both be there with me," Astra insisted. "When I'm not knocked unconscious by an Ascended god, I actually handle myself quite well."

This sister of hers—she did not know what she was committing to. She did not understand what she was possibly giving up.

For her.

Lunelle pulled her sister into another hug, this one much deeper, much harder to let go of.

"I do not deserve a sister like you."

She whispered the words against Astra's neck, praying they'd absorb into her bloodstream and be worth something, though they'd never be enough compared to Astra's own sacrifice. The king's swift glance to Luxuros pulled her attention. The commander's lips fell into a frustrated tilt.

Lunelle leaned back on her heels. "What does she want you to retrieve?"

Astra pressed her lips together, the answer bubbling to her tongue but reluctant to escape.

"Leona."

The air left Lunelle's lungs. "As—"

"I know it sounds crazy! But she wants to make amends. Leona has never Ascended. Selenia believes that there's been a misunderstanding."

Luxuros crossed his arms, his shoulders pulling together with a lightning bolt of tension. He'd never forgive her if Astra got hurt.

And she understood.

"She can do it," Mirquios said to him. "If anyone can do it, it's Astra."

Ameera leaned forward, her sharp features drawn together.

"And there's no catch? You bring her Leona's Soul and she'll leave it at that?"

Tears threatened to spill from Lunelle's eyes.

Astra sighed, waving her hand between them.

"There's always a catch. I just haven't figured it out yet. But until then, I have her word. She's going to crash your Trial Ball and announce it."

Lunelle giggled nervously, it was the only sound she could make in response to the image Astra's words conjured.

"Oh, Mother is going to hate that."

She could not fault Astra as a grin broke over her face.

"A big part of the appeal for me, if I'm being honest. Now, if you all don't mind, this crown is becoming a permanent part of my skull and I am drunk on the wine of the gods. I desperately need to get home."

"Of course. We can talk more tomorrow," Lunelle said. She crossed the room, leaning into Mirquios's side, drawing any of the calm grace she could from his poised spine.

His fingers brushed hers in a silent prayer.

Lunelle could only see him, only feel him, only hear his breath catching as they both wondered if perhaps they had reason to hope once more.

Astra offered Lunelle one more embrace, her arms circling her shoulders tightly.

"Thank you," Mirquios said as Astra untangled herself from Lunelle. He glanced at the commander, who quietly seethed against the wall.

"Will you make sure Astra makes it back to her chambers safely, Commander? I'd rather she not enter the Rift alone after tonight."

Lunelle waited for the thuds of the commander's boots to fade before she turned to Ameera.

"How much does he hate me?"

Ameera rested a hand on Lunelle's shoulder. "He does not hate you. He envies you. You're allowed to love her as fervently and as publicly as you want."

Lunelle's cheeks heated as Ameera darted into the hall. Mirquios pulled her toward him, looping an arm around her waist.

"He'll never forgive me for this," she sighed.

"I've known that man for thirty years, Lunelle. I believe this is the first time I've seen him scared."

"You don't think..." Lunelle gestured to the Tether singing between them, raising her eyebrows.

"He'd never tell me," Mirquios answered.

"I'll force it out of her after she goes to hell and back on our behalf," Lunelle sighed, her heart aching. He stroked her shoulder in the quiet of the library, pressing his lips to her temple.

"Would you like to stay here tonight?" he asked, his hands wandering her back. "I have a few things I need to tend to, but it shouldn't take me too long."

She leaned back, placing her hands on his chest.

"Believe me, I would. I'm just... I'm a little overwhelmed by Astra. What if...what if—" Lunelle could not bring herself to say the words.

Mirquios understood the implication in her strangled silence.

"We will protect her, Lunelle. Exactly as you always have."

She lingered in his arms for one more moment before heading back to the Rift, finding herself tempted to grip the shimmering sapphire thread above her and make a deal with a certain goddess to protect her sister.

CHAPTER
TWENTY-NINE

The halls were silent as she swept through them. The sconces on the walls burned low, her breath still catching as the panic coursed through her veins.

She'd failed her. She'd failed her sister once again, letting her take on far too much for her benefit. It was unfair of her to even lead Astra to believe it was her job to step in—she should have never created this mess in the first place, let alone let it spiral so far out of her control.

Her muscles burned with anxiety that was begging to go *somewhere*, anywhere but there, anywhere but spinning out in the empty corridors of a palace she wasn't sure she could protect any better than she'd protected her sister.

"Fuck," she muttered under her breath, pacing beyond her own bedroom door, heading for Astra's chambers directly. She could still change her mind.

And she just might have, if only her sister were available. Lunelle hesitated outside her door, and she was glad she did as she heard a high-pitched giggle followed by a rumbling groan from a certain commander's chest.

Lunelle snorted. She should have taken Mirquios up on his offer after all.

She could have returned to the Mercurian Court, it wasn't much of a jaunt. She certainly wouldn't be getting any sleep next to those two. She found herself wandering toward the Andromeda wing. Perhaps she could tuck herself into the king's bed and at least surround herself in his scent for the evening.

Lunelle was midway through the courtyard when she felt something shift in the shadows, a breath holding in the dark. She knew it was him before she spotted his long limbs crossed over one another in the twinkling starlight above. She felt it tug against something deep within her chest. It was not like the Tether—it was harsher. It did not glimmer, but rather curled against her ribs like smoke.

"Princess," Arcas said quietly, gathering a stack of hazy green stones from the table before him.

"What are those?" she asked.

"Aventurine," he said, snorting, the darkness within him painted all over his face. "They're good for mental clarity. And for Mercurian engagement rings," he muttered.

Lunelle leaned over the table, plucking one from his pile. It was a raw version of the carefully cut stone in her sister's ring, a gentle green with smooth facets, cool to the touch.

"Did you find the clarity you seek?"

His sapphire eyes flickered up to her, thick black lashes blinking slowly.

"Perhaps I did." His eyes fell over her fingers, stroking the flat surface of the stone, and traveled up her arm, settling on her face, where he saw it land—what he hadn't said.

"Arcas—"

"Fascinating," he scoffed. "I no longer even need you to speak to hurt my feelings, Lunelle."

272

She hated him. Hated that he was so resistant to change. Hated that he was speaking with such softness now when she knew he would rip it away at the next turn. Hated that she longed to bend forward and soothe the pain within him.

She sat across the table, smoothing her skirts over her knees as she tried to ignore the strange pulsing in her stomach. She only managed to battle it back a few moments before the question emerged.

"Do you think there's a world, in another court, or another life, where we'd have been strung together by Fate?"

Arcas flinched.

"No," he said, swallowing. "The gods have their reasons."

"But what if they're wrong? They're wrong in so many other ways—"

Arcas leaned across the table. "Please," he hissed. "Please, Princess, I cannot take on more pain at your hands. I know you do not trust me. You do not admire me the way you admire braver men, but I am doing my godsdamned best here—"

"Do *better*," she pleaded. "You could do better!"

"I was not *made for you!*" Arcas ground out between clenched teeth, slamming his palm against the table. "I was not threaded to your Soul in some cosmic map of the universe, but that never once stopped me from seeing you as you are and loving you anyway. From the moment I met you, from the *moment* you dared to dress me down, I knew.

"I knew I was being punished for my cowardly heart. I knew I was not good enough or bold enough or, or, or *anything* enough for you! I was a fool to think I might be worthy of even a moment of your time. I am sorry that I was not crafted from stronger stars than this, but I am who I am, and I thought you could—" Arcas stopped himself, hanging his head forward.

He rose, sweeping his stones from the table and clenching his jaw.

"I thought perhaps you could find something within me worth loving anyway."

He barreled out of the garden, leaving her to contend with a heart trapped in the eye of a storm, the weight of his declaration choking her. She listened as his steps faded, each click of his boots yanking at something ugly within her.

Something she recognized.

The pain of an older sibling doing what they thought was right, desires be damned.

The cowardice of hiding behind duty to escape what is difficult.

The reluctance to admit when they've been defeated by forces outside their control.

Fuck, she thought, her breath catching somewhere in her ribs.

It was as if all the darkness in those places he pulled at consolidated at once, falling into a single star that embedded its sharp corners into her lungs, refusing to let her breathe.

"Arcas," she called as she stood so quickly she knocked her chair back into the stone. She left it there as she chased his shadow through the courtyard, breaking into a run as the star rammed its razor-like edge into her.

"Arcas!" she called again, his shoulders hardly visible in the low light of the halls. He stopped outside of the Plutonian quarters, turning with a pained grimace, unsure if he could take another round.

But she did not slow, she slammed against him, sending his back against the amethyst and stone of the palace wall, wrestling every stubborn piece of him into her hold as she gasped for a breath that would not come. The sharp edge in her lungs dug deeper, stung against her as she fought to find his mouth, his shock freezing him against the wall.

He began to say something, but she could not hear him.

She could not hear a godsdamned thing but the air whooshing from her lungs as his arms closed behind her back, fingers ripping at her loose waves to find some sort of control over her.

"Princess," he whispered, hands curling into her, his breath just as short.

Lunelle ignored him, nipping at the edge of his jaw, running her hands through his onyx silk strands. She moaned against his throat, desperate, frantic. Somewhere, on some level, she was aware that he backed her into a bedroom, the sound of a door thudding against its frame nearly breaking her focus.

Nearly.

He twisted her, slamming her against the frame of something, gods knew, as he tore at her dress, shoving it against her hips and ruffling his fingers through layers of lace to get to her.

"Fuck," Lunelle whined, his fingers unforgiving as he sank his teeth into her neck and stroked her, the fury with which they both moved spinning the room into a haze. She yanked at his shirt, needed to get to more of him, to feel the flex of his muscles as he ground against her hips.

"You will kill me," he rasped. "You will *kill me*, Lunelle."

His fingers curled within her, drawing a yelp as her head leaned back against the wall. She could not breathe, could not think, could not see anything but him.

"I need more," she whispered, grabbing at his waistband and the length of him beneath.

The prince's breath shuddered at her touch, his mouth hanging open against her ear as he withdrew his hand, pushing her toward the bed. She hadn't looked at which room he was in, hadn't cared. Nothing mattered but numbing the sting in her chest with the salve of him.

Arcas stripped as they crossed the room, landing on his

back against the headboard, more than ready for her as she flung her dress away. Lunelle climbed over him, his wide hands gripping her hips and guiding her over his lap. Her lips parted at the sensation of him within her, pausing only for a moment to find her bearings before his hands squeezed and pushed her further down.

Her chest ached, the sting spreading through tissue and muscle as he pushed her faster, his head tucked against her neck. Lunelle rocked in brazen circles, pulling at his hair, his shoulder, anything available to her.

Arcas pulled one hand from her hips and clutched his chest as she sped up, desperate to fall apart.

"Look at me," he said, sliding his free hand up her back and pulling her hair into his fist. "Lunelle."

She could not. She could not look at him, for fear that she'd see so much of herself within those sapphire eyes that she'd never be able to look away. He pulled tighter.

"Look at me," he pleaded. "You do not have to say it out loud, Lunelle, but godsdammit I want to see it."

"See what?" she gasped.

"That you *do* love me, in spite of all the hell we've put each other through, and all the hell we're still yet to rain on one another," he growled, pulling her hair tightly as he forced her to face him. She cried out at the sting in her scalp, momentarily able to forget about the pain in her chest as she fought his gaze. Fought his accusation.

Fought the truth as it whispered across her tongue.

Lunelle whimpered, her hands bracing herself against him, eyes closed as his hips drove into hers with such force she thought he was wrong. She would not kill him. He would be *her* death in the end.

"Arcas—"

"Look at me!" he demanded, a crack in his voice breaking her into pieces.

She turned her eyes to him as she shattered in his lap, something so dark, so craven cutting through her chest as their eyes met and she bared it all to him—that she *did* love him, no matter how wrong it was.

No matter how much Fate had already given her in another.

She still wanted more—whether she deserved it or not.

Lunelle shook around him, her entire body drowning in shadows and starlight, a darkness wrapping around them and tying her into knots in his arms. His sparkling eyes, so drenched in pain, widened as something shifted between them, something deep within their spines. His breath came in low groans as he kept moving inside her, the air thickening with something neither of them understood.

A bond as dark as the obsidian of his gaze.

Arcas sucked in a breath through his teeth, close behind her as he mumbled as much into her shoulder. Lunelle wrestled with herself, wanting to feel his release within her, but her head won out over her body. She slid off him, kneeling beside him and taking him in her mouth as he stroked her hair—her name left his lips in an exhausted sigh as she took everything he had to offer to her.

Arcas leaned his head against the headboard, fighting for breath.

"You do not have to say it," he whispered, running his hands through her hair. "But you will always feel it between us, braided between the wisps of our Shadows."

Lunelle sat up, the stretch between them palpable. Her eyes widened as she felt the tug within her, nothing like the Tether she held between the king, but an attachment all the same.

"What is that?" she gasped.

Arcas sighed. "You and I... we may not be bound by Fate. But we are bound by certain dark things that, try as we might, will always seek one another out."

She pressed her hand against the space between her ribs and her stomach, the space she'd hidden him away in.

"Did you know that would happen?"

His sharp gaze narrowed. "No more than you."

Lunelle reached between them, desperate to understand, but nothing buzzed or hummed.

It slithered.

"I do not believe you," she mumbled.

Arcas winced. "Who chased *whom* this evening?"

Lunelle shook her head, attempting to clear the strange sensation away. She crawled over him and off the bed, snatching her dress from the floor, the darkness in her chest delighting in her ire.

"Lunelle," he breathed, leaning over to grab her, but she was already too far away.

"I cannot love you, Arcas. I cannot love anyone who would let their court rot when the right thing to do is within their grasp."

Lunelle ran from his room, burying herself in the king's bed, each breath pulsing with two very distinct, very strange responses.

One that sparkled and begged her to bury deeper within the soft silk of Mirquios's bed, and another that steeped her in ceaseless darkness, drenched with questions she desperately wanted answers to.

She awoke to two strong arms wrapping around her shoulders, sweeping her hair off her neck as Mirquios pulled his quilt over them.

"You're home," she sighed as she rolled over and wrapped her arms around his neck.

His lips tightened into a half smile. *Home* was a loaded concept.

"Is Astra doing all right?" he asked, rubbing her shoulder.

"Well," Lunelle laughed, though the sound was hollow. There was so much within her that ached. "I went to check on her, but it seems the commander was... tending to her needs."

Mirquios closed his eyes and sighed. "Good for him, I suppose." He pressed a kiss to her lips.

"What time is it?"

"It's early, but people are definitely awake. You'll have to be careful."

"Or," she mumbled, snuggling further into him, letting the light of them warm her. "I could stay here forever, and we don't have to deal with any of the nightmares awaiting us."

"Flawless plan," he agreed and brushed her hair away from her face. "I see no issues at all." He eyed her as she inhaled slowly. "Are you well?"

"How do you mean?"

"You seem... weighed down. It's hard to describe. Is it Astra's deal with Selenia?"

Lunelle swallowed the acid in her throat. "Yes."

The king held her tightly against him, the Tether in their chests jumping with a brightness she didn't deserve as he stroked her hair.

"Let her do this for you, Lunelle. For all of us."

Lunelle nodded against him, something deeper than the Tether rolling inside her. She wondered if it was the crushing anxiety of Astra taking on too much, or if a certain prince was awake for the day, storming the palace in search of another way to twist her world on its head.

"I should go before the halls fill with courtiers," she whispered, forcing a smile.

He only nodded sleepily as she kissed his cheek and slipped away from his room, her heart wrapped in both lightning bolts and thunderclouds.

"Oh gods, smite me," Nayson muttered to himself as he came down the Mercurians' hallway.

He stumbled into Lunelle, pulling the king's door shut behind her.

"Father!" she yelped, silver eyes aflame.

"I, uh, well, good morrow, darling." Nayson ran his hand through his hair, desperate for air. His warm gaze was surprisingly hollow as he glanced behind them.

"I was just leaving a note for the king. He is away," Lunelle said sharply.

"Oh," Nayson sighed. "Of course."

She tilted her head. "Are you all right?"

"Better now," he admitted. "You girls certainly keep a man on his toes."

"A family trait," Oestera said over Nayson's shoulder as she passed the mouth of the hall.

"Mother!" Lunelle smoothed her hair.

"Far from your chamber, are you not, Lunelle?"

Lunelle bit her lip. "The king requested a list of Astra's favorite poets. For a gift."

Oestera watched her curiously, her gaze mirroring her daughter's. She was no fool, Lunelle knew, but she also didn't have time to dabble in madness.

"I believe your sister was searching for you in the garden earlier," Oestera said.

It all came crashing back on her—Astra's commitment to Selenia. The guilt fell in sheets of ice down her back.

"Lunelle?" her father asked.

"I should go find her," she muttered, pushing between them and breaking for her bedroom.

LUNELLE HAD LIVED in the murky haze between light and dark for days—floating through every meal and returning to her library as often as possible to avoid everyone and everything.

It was the night before her Trial Ball, and she was tucked away in the safety of her library when the commander interrupted her evening tea.

"Luxuros," she said without needing to look up from her book. She'd learned the strange heat that preceded him well. It prickled at her neck as he sat across from her.

"You've been hiding," he said.

"Correct," Lunelle admitted readily, folding her book into her lap.

"Your king is worried."

"*Your* king is worried," she corrected, sitting up straighter.

"Lunelle."

She huffed a long, irritated sigh. "I am not avoiding Mirquios. I am avoiding... feeling anything. At all. It has been a long few months, Commander, as you no doubt understand."

Luxuros nodded, his bronze waves slipping through scarred hands as he smoothed his hair back.

"I received a note from Kwan this morning." Lunelle perked up at this, tucking her ankles beneath her and fixing her eyes on the commander's fiery stare. "Seems Yallara has reason to believe her brother may be softening in his stance."

Lunelle's lips parted, but no words came. She closed her mouth again. It was much easier that way.

"Kwan says she is to be crowned queen, regardless of the outcome of your trial."

Her eyes narrowed, the confusion settling in the fine lines of her frown. She shook her head.

"What would have changed his mind?"

Luxuros waved a hand. "That's none of my business, Princess."

Her cheeks warmed. She wondered for a moment how much he knew, how much Mirquios had shared with him.

"Once Yallara is on the throne, the pathway to felling Pluto is clear. As are Mercury, Mars, Venus, and Earth."

Lunelle's heart sped forward, the commander's own excitement clear on his upturned lips.

"And the Lunar Court, of course," Luxuros added.

"Of course," she agreed.

Lux leaned forward, catching her eye. "Whatever you've done, Lunelle, it worked."

She smiled tightly, a well of strange feelings opening up in her chest.

"What does Astra think?"

Lux stood, brushing his palms against his thighs.

"Astra is not actually part of the rebellion yet. I thought perhaps you might like to bind her."

"I thought the elves—"

"Didn't work out," Lux sighed, glancing toward the window at the endless night. She saw it then, the strain on him. The weight of loving her sister the way he did. The pain he carried in his heart for her.

"You should be the one to do it, Commander."

His fingertips grazed the leather cord around his neck.

"Is that your blessing, then?"

She arched a brow. "It is a prayer, Luxuros. Don't fuck it up or she'll destroy you." Lunelle sipped her tea. "And I'll help."

The commander laughed, though she saw the heat in his eyes flare.

"I suppose I must express the same sentiment to you on behalf of Mirquios."

Lunelle nodded. "Let us agree to never become enemies then, Luxuros."

The commander offered her a crooked smile before he faded quietly, taking his heated bloodline with him.

The moment she could breathe again, tears slid over her lips, the salty brine swirling against her cup as she silently spiraled in her favorite chair, with her favorite tea, without any of her favorite people.

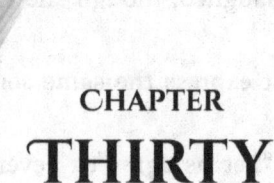

CHAPTER
THIRTY

"**P**rincess?"

Lunelle paced beyond the balcony doors, the fluttering stars of her Trial Ball dress falling like rain behind her as she twisted and turned. She looked toward the hall, where Arcas stood wrapped in a silver tunic to complement hers. Her mother was irritatingly good.

Her heart sparked to life, as did the tender spot beneath her ribs, followed by a sickening churn in her stomach.

"Arcas—"

He reached for the edge of the door, running his thumb over the stone.

"Do not send me away. Please."

She sighed. She was, indeed, about to send him away rather than confront the complex feelings that pulled at her muscles and swirled in her spine.

"I brought you a gift," he mumbled, holding something out to her.

She eyed the box skeptically. "What is that?"

Arcas rolled his eyes, moving closer.

"Just take it, Lunelle," he said. He pushed the small box into her hands, crushed black velvet lining the top. Lunelle cracked it back and held her breath as a delicate silver and sapphire ring caught the flickering light above.

The center stone was flanked by two deep, nearly black crystals, humming to life as she brushed her fingers over them.

"Arcas, I cannot—"

"Even if I perish in the Nether, even if you feed me to unimaginable creatures—which I would not fault you for— you should have it. It is a coronation gift, not an engagement ring."

Lunelle felt that twisted thing within her whisper sweet curses, pushing her toward him.

"It's stunning."

"It was my mother's," he said, testing the line between them as he toed closer to her. "I was going to pass it down to Yallara, but she insisted you have it."

Lunelle arched a brow. "Yallara insisted?"

Arcas's lips twitched into something like a smile.

"She said it would sing for you... does it?"

Lunelle ran her fingers over the stones, their gentle whirring vibrating against her skin. She nodded.

"My mother... she had an affinity for the Descended. They sang to her, too." His eyes dropped to the box in her hand. "I never quite understood it, but perhaps you can hear what I never could."

Lunelle's chest tightened as she closed the box. She glanced over the prince's shoulder at the balcony doors.

"I suppose I should get downstairs," Arcas said, swallowing something she'd wished he had the nerve to speak aloud.

"Arcas—"

"Do not hurt my feelings tonight, starling," he whispered, leaning in and placing a soft kiss on her cheek. It was the most chaste touch they'd ever shared, and yet it felt more intimate than when they were pressed against one another, without a stitch between them.

"Thank you," she said as he left the room. She wondered if he'd heard her—if he knew she was not thanking him for the ring. She could feel his half smile slide down whatever dark portal lived between them as he disappeared.

"What a stunning piece," Lura said over her shoulder, slipping out of the shadows.

"It is." Lunelle stared at the box for another moment before Lura stretched out her hand.

"I'll get it back to your room," she said. "Unless... you wanted to wear it?"

"No," Lunelle said without hesitation. "Not tonight."

"Very well," Lura replied, tucking the box into her pocket. "Last look!"

Lura's amethyst irises swept the princess, every falling star perfectly placed, every white wisp of hair tucked neatly beneath a sparkling diadem.

"We're ready for her," a maiden said, leaning into the room.

Lura gave her princess—her friend—one last smile before gently pushing her toward the door, her heels clicking quickly as she approached the balcony.

"Freeze your face, Ice Queen," Lura called after her, Lunelle's lower lip sucked between her teeth. She released her lip and giggled, setting her shoulders back in a graceful pose.

"Princess Lunelle Silverswan Aurellis, the future Queen of the Lunar Court. May the Mother bless her Within, and Without."

It was a tidal wave crashing over her—all the eyes of the

court at once. She'd been the center of their attention before, but tonight felt different. It felt impossible to breathe.

Each step cracked her careful mask. She was not being seen, she was being looked at.

Her eyes fell on the Mercurian king, Astra's arm tightly looped against him as his fingers clutched into a fist at their shared panic. She did not dare dwell for long, her own nerves screaming at her as she took the final step, and a pale blue hand reached for hers.

The Tether and the echo beyond it both jolted, confusing her gaze as she settled into the crowd. Music struck up, the room spun, and she was once again in the arms of the Plutonian prince. Though, this time, she did not feel sickened by him or an uncontrollable urge to fuck him into silence.

She found something like peace with Arcas. It was not a sparkling gem, and it was not forgiveness, but it was something like it.

"You're going to break my hand, Lunelle," Arcas whispered, a faint chuckle on his breath. Lunelle frowned as they spun, her dress floating behind her. She led him in a spirited waltz, his long legs keeping time with hers as she twisted them into a tight circle.

"Sorry," she muttered, loosening her grip on his palm, eyes scanning the hundreds of faces surrounding them.

When exactly is Selenia supposed to join us? Lunelle beamed to her sister. She'd wanted to sound confident and calm, but even she could hear the panic in her own voice.

Astra's eyes found hers. *We didn't set an exact time. You can do this.*

As they spun again, Lunelle watched as Astra mumbled to Mirquios, his lips pulled into a bitter line. Lunelle snorted. *We may not even have to rely on her. I think Mirq's glare might vaporize Arcas and solve the problem for us.*

Her sister's lips curved into an amused grin. *And that's with my attempts to calm him.*

Lunelle watched as Astra leaned into the king, patting his arm as if he were a scared child. Lunelle knew what he was worried about—not the blue hands that held her, but the chance they might harm her in ways no one else but he understood.

Behind her sister, the commander watched them like a hawk, his eyes on every exit in the room at once.

She wished, for a moment, that her sister had been brave enough to share it with her—the hope they'd found in one another. Astra always had a reason for her secrets, but she was carrying so many at this point, Lunelle had hoped at least this one might spill over.

She had dozens of questions.

Lunelle planted the seed, much like her mother would have, beaming *I only hope you find a love like this one day, Astra.*

Astra didn't even know she did it, surely, but her eyes dropped for merely a breath toward the Solarian at the back of the room.

One day.

As Lunelle swept Arcas across the dancefloor, Astra's ruby curls joined the fray. They were close enough to brush skirts as Astra pulled Mirquios into the center. Something Mirquios said sent her sister's head back in a true, genuine laugh. A sound Lunelle had missed for so long.

She prayed it would be more frequent when they were out of this mess.

Lunelle refocused her attention on Arcas. "We heard some interesting news from the Plutonian captain—"

"Oh, gods," Arcas murmured, stopping mid-turn as the air in the room shifted into something strange, cool.

Whispers tickled at Lunelle's ears, the sudden loss of momentum from Arcas throwing her off balance. She followed the wide stares of the courtiers to an ancient goddess, one boasting the same frigid glare Lunelle knew she fell into.

Her mother was across the floor in a heartbeat, but Selenia was already before her, an ethereal glow with a sick black at the edge—how Lunelle hadn't caught it before was beyond her.

"Lunelle." Selenia reached forward, tilting her chin with ancient fingertips, sizing her up. She felt two distinct shivers within her—one gold, one black, both wrapped in a protective rage.

"Grandmother." Lunelle lowered her head, the tiara atop it suddenly feeling rather heavy.

"What an exciting celebration!" Selenia announced, cutting the music short as the orchestra realized there was a disturbance in the crowd.

Oestera stood beside Lunelle, her shoulder brushing her daughter's in a silent show of *something*. She felt both the panicked pull of the Tether as Mirquios wrestled in his spot and the cool alchemy of Arcas as his hand dropped to her hip, pulling her closer to him. His sapphire eyes flickered to the king's cold stare, the slightest nod between them turning and untangling one of the many knots within her.

Selenia cast a look at her daughter that burned Lunelle's chest.

"No need to stop on my account! I'm merely here to deliver a message on behalf of the Court Above. We've been waiting with bated breath to see who our champions will be, but it seems my daughter has failed to provide much competition for your hand, my dear girl."

Selenia reached for Lunelle's hand, squeezing it as she

spoke. The chill from her fingers ran through Lunelle's gloves, sending goosebumps over her exposed arms.

Selenia continued, "We try not to involve ourselves unless absolutely necessary, of course, but that time has come."

Lunelle's eyes slid to her mother's face, ever the perfect mask of calculated disinterest.

"You there, Mercurian child, look how you've grown under the harsh Sun. Your great-grandmother was just bragging to us at a party about how excited they are for a Lunar queen."

Lunelle lurched forward as her grandmother reached for Mirquios, but the hand on her hip clutched the stars floating from her dress.

"Easy, starling," Arcas whispered.

Mirquios stepped forward, Astra's warm gaze kindling into something brazen.

Selenia pursed her lips. "I understand there's an arrangement made here already, but Astra, my dear girl, surely you understand that bigger games are at play?"

Lunelle watched as her father stepped into her line of vision, his expression a myriad of concern. His fingers danced over the dagger on his hip.

"Mercury has proven themselves worthy of a Lunarian woman already, but perhaps the Lunar Court needs young Mirquios's eyes more than Pluto's... modest offering."

Arcas's breath hitched as he released his hold on her, injured by the goddess's assessment.

Selenia's lips curled in disgust at his visible offense and Lunelle fought the urge to verbally spar with the goddess.

"I suppose only the trial will tell."

Oestera's voice cracked, "Mother—"

Lunelle flinched as Selenia's hand rose, silencing Oestera.

"It is decided. What happens tomorrow is up to Fate."

"But Astra... the Tether—"

Astra played her part well. Her eyes were perfectly terror-struck, and Lunelle wondered if it was impressive acting or the realization that she was about to be truly indebted to Selenia.

Selenia continued, "Sometimes we get things wrong, Oestera. Surely you can understand that. Astra is a strong girl. She'll do whatever it takes to secure her court, will she not?"

Lunelle's gaze tracked a single tear as it slipped over her sister's pale cheek.

"There we have it. Mirquios is to compete in the trial against Arcas, and we'll have a real show to watch in the Court Above. Although..."

She felt their eyes bounce from the Mercurian king to the Plutonian prince, and settle on her. Lunelle held her composure, but the inhale of her grandmother's next breath drove something sharp into her chest.

"One champion is so *very* dull. Two is interesting..." Selenia turned about the room, every step a performance, well rehearsed. Selenia paced before the crowd, drawing out the moment, savoring it. "Three. Three's enticing. You're in quite the predicament, Oestera. The Solar king is mounting an attack, he's already invaded Saturn and Jupiter. Is Pluto *really* the best Outer heir you can do?"

Lunelle's face turned, catching Arcas as his jaw clenched, the Shadows between them reaching for one another.

Selenia's brow arched. "Did you even attempt to find a stronger alliance?"

Oestera rooted into her heels, her lips quaking with a million thoughts she could not say.

"I—"

Selenia had no patience for it. "Spare me, Oestera. Luckily, as always, I've done the work for you. My right hand discovered something *quite* fascinating when your second-born came to visit me."

Lunelle reached for someone, anyone, her hand finding Arcas's as he moved closer to her. She could feel the same uncertainty course through him that flooded her heart, beating loud enough that she knew he could hear it. Could feel it.

Oestera's eyes flickered to Astra, a pain within them Lunelle had never seen before.

"It's always the second-born that breaks your heart, wouldn't you agree, Oestera? You younger lot may not know this—it's not well documented in the Living Courts—but there's only one way to get through the Court Above's gates outside of a Solstice or Equinox. No mere mortal can pass."

Arcas's hand tightened around Lunelle's, her lungs filling with dread. She looked for Luxuros, his jaw set as Selenia spoke. There, in the way his shoulders sloped. In the hold of his chest. She saw the same rigid posture that had been carved into her from birth.

"Now, a demigod has certain privileges. So color me intrigued when a certain commander came to collect my granddaughter."

"Oh," Lunelle breathed, a complex web of thoughts collapsing on itself. She turned against Arcas, looking for Mirquios, the Tether between them shaking with the conclusion they'd both drawn.

"And now that I see you, Commander, the resemblance is *truly* uncanny. Wouldn't you say, Oestera?"

Luxuros stepped onto the floor, his stature so much more than a mere man. More than a soldier or a commander.

A prince.

Selenia frowned. "Well?"

Oestera's lips twitched. Her head tilted, a spark of something in her eyes setting the whole damned room ablaze.

Selenia relished in her verbal dagger, sinking it into her daughter's chest.

"Luxuros Soleras."

Lunelle thought she might be ill. She let go of the prince's hand, pushing away from him, but she felt his fingers grab hold of the back of her dress, trailing her as she bolted toward Astra.

She needed to get to her sister.

Selenia's words only got louder as she twisted the knife.

"The heir to the Solar throne. Two thousand years of trials and we've never had a champion of your lineage for obvious reasons... but it does make one wonder."

Astra, Lunelle sent. Mirquios's gaze found hers as he held Astra back from the goddess.

The commander was a statue, frozen in place, his entire world falling into an infinitely shifting sea.

"You seem confused," Selenia cooed. She grinned as Astra finally broke from the king's grip, her lips trembling as she grasped to understand what had just happened.

Luxuros did not speak.

"No matter," Selenia sighed. "It's settled. You will join your king and the Plutonian prince to compete for Lunelle's hand. Good luck, Commander. Now, we were celebrating, were we not?"

She clapped her hands twice, and that's all it took.

The music crackled back to life, disjointed and not quite right as Selenia cut back through the crowd. The courtiers held their breath for a moment, and then the room burst into hushed speculation as the commander and Astra darted through the crowd.

Someone caught Lunelle's arm.

"Do you've any idea how monstrous Solan is?" Arcas rasped at her. "If he knew—if he finds out you're harboring his *heir*—"

Lunelle ripped her shoulder away from him.

293

"Then go! No one is keeping you here," Lunelle hissed.

Arcas pulled her closer, his eyes scanning the room.

"We need a plan, Lunelle. This just got infinitely more dangerous for both of you! For all of us—"

"I am *aware*, Arcas!"

He squeezed her hand, his eyes pooling with something much more frightening than his cowardice, or his disdain for many of them.

With concern for her.

Lunelle did not hear whatever he muttered behind her as she shoved her way out of the hall and into the gardens. Mirquios had her elbow and Ameera bumped into her shoulder as they froze, the portrait of her sister and the commander hard to bear.

They were Sun and Moon, drowning in one another's untenable light.

"I didn't know," the commander whispered as he grasped Astra's shoulders. Mirquios slid behind Lunelle, resting a hand on the small of her back, a pain of which they'd only scratched the surface. "I never dreamed, Astra."

"I know. I believe you." Astra's hand came to his jaw, but she quickly drew it back, her eyes landing on the audience gathering at the edge of the garden. Lunelle glanced behind her at the sound of shuffling boots. Her father darted from the ballroom, eyes wide as he parted between them.

"Nayson," Luxuros said—a warning to Astra, Lunelle realized. He released his hold on her, stepping as far back as he could.

"As!" Nayson pulled Astra's shocked frame into an embrace, but her eyes never left the ground. "Luxuros? Are you well?"

"I–I don't know," the commander mumbled.

Mirquios's grip on Lunelle's back tightened as the energy

in the garden soared to new heights, her mother's wild eyes sweeping over every last one of them as she charged her sister.

"Astra Leona!"

Astra held her hands up in defense. "We didn't know—"

"What have you done?" her mother asked, the ice in her tone sending a shiver deep into Lunelle's muscles. She'd heard her mother yell at Astra thousands of times, but this was decidedly different.

"What?"

"Why did you go to her? What did you offer her?" All of this spectacle was enough to send anyone into a panic, but her mother's unsteady tone was chilling in a way she'd never experienced.

"I didn't—"

"Do not lie to me!" Oestera's lips curled back, her voice shaking as she yelled. "I can feel it, Astra! What did you do?"

Astra stomped her foot. "I did what you wouldn't! I protected my sister!"

Lunelle's ears filled with the hot rush of shame and agony, her head fogging over as she braced herself on the king's chest. He could feel the pain swelling in her throat, the inky black shades of guilt rushing through her veins.

Her vision blurred as her mother and sister dragged one another down in a screaming match, the anger so thick she could taste the iron dripping from it and feel the sticky blood-soaked words land blow after blow.

Lunelle could have stepped in. She could have stopped her mother. She could have begged Astra to abandon her protection of her, but she could not move. She was a statue, cursed to live within the confines of her stone walls for eternity.

Her mother stormed off, Astra's face a mess with red blotches, her fingers clutched to her palms as the commander stepped to her side.

Mirquios pushed her forward, unwilling to let go of her, but desperate to get to his friend.

"Brother," Mirquios said, stepping into the courtyard.

Lunelle reached for her sister's hand—her poor, singed fingertips warm with angry heat, fighting so hard to keep it all in. Astra's eyes caught hers and it was as if she truly saw her younger sister for the first time.

Lunelle cleared her throat.

"Well. This is certainly more complicated." Her eyes fell on Luxuros's hand, holding onto Astra's arm for dear life. She knew, of course, that he loved her. She'd told him as much to his face. She was not sure if *he* knew just how deeply he'd fallen, but in the desperate grab for her, it was there. Pure devotion. "Much more complicated."

Astra shook off her stupor, pushing her shoulders back as she announced to them, "We need a new plan. A good one."

"I'll get coffee," Ameera said.

"The Solar heir," Lunelle whispered to herself, eyeing the commander once more. She should have seen it. There was something in the air of him, something that can only be bred by years of slapped wrists and sharp instruction. Something her sister had shirked at every chance. She smiled as she squeezed Astra's hand. "I suppose you've always had a flair for the dramatic, sister."

Astra gave a shallow laugh, but it did nothing to soften her fiery gaze.

"We'll meet you in the Andromeda wing in a moment," she said.

Mirquios gave a final pat to Luxuros's shoulder and looped his hand through Lunelle's. There was no sense in pretending at this point—Selenia had blown the court wide open with gossip much more intriguing.

296

THEY BEAT Ameera to the library, folding in on themselves on the sofas tucked in the back.

Mirquios broke the silence first with a startled laugh.

"This is not funny," Lunelle admonished him.

The king shook his head. "No! It is not. I just... I stand a decent chance at losing a second Lunar princess to my best friend now."

Lunelle winced. "You're terrible!"

"Yet you love me still," he whispered.

"I do," she exhaled, fiddling with the stars on her dress as her cheeks flushed with a pale pink. "Luxuros told me of the news from Yallara."

Mirq's head tilted. "Yes, what do you make of that?"

"I do not know what to make of anything," she said. "Arcas gave no indication that he was of changing his mind the last time we—*I* saw him."

Mirquios leaned closer to her, pressing his lips against her bare shoulder.

"You do not have to censor yourself for me, love. When did you... speak with him?" He winked at her.

"Not since Astra struck her deal with Selenia. But surely he would have told me if anything had changed. He would have wanted me to know."

Mirquios trailed over her shoulder and over her neck.

"Perhaps you were such an inspiring *conversationalist* that he could not help but make some different decisions."

She looked at him, his bright eyes sparkling against her pale skin.

He enjoyed this. He *liked* the control she had over Arcas just as much as she did.

Lunelle leaned into him, resting her hand on his thigh.

"I *do* give a good speech," she whispered.

"A very motivational leader," Mirquois sighed as her fingers crawled up his leg.

"You're all going to die tomorrow," Ameera announced as she burst into the library with a tray of tea and coffee. "Perhaps we save the foreplay for after your sister Descends to the Nether and captures your dead aunt's Soul for your probably-evil grandmother, hmm?"

Mirquios tossed his head back with a deep chuckle, moving away from Lunelle.

"I see why the commander likes you so much," he said.

Astra and Luxuros followed, the commander's eyes still sunken with the strange revelations of the evening.

"All right. We've got six hours and a ton of ground to cover," Astra declared, pushing Luxuros into one of the open armchairs. "The newly crowned Solar prince here is damn near catatonic, so once Ameera fixes him one of her concoctions, we're going to figure out how to destroy a goddess."

Mirquios scoffed as Lunelle's lips fell open, the instinct to protest consuming her, but Ameera beat her to it.

"Are you crazy?" she barked.

"Of course she is," Lunelle laughed. "But she's also the only one of us who has a clue where to start."

Astra grinned at her sister, her scarlet curls bouncing as she flopped onto a cushion in front of Lunelle, much like when they were girls and she wanted her hair braided.

Lunelle reached forward and absentmindedly pulled on one of Astra's spirals as she spoke, wondering when she had acquired the thinnest strands of silver at the crown of her head —how it could be remotely possible that they were not still children playing coronation games in the garden.

THIRTY-ONE

"Well, tonight certainly took a few turns," Mirquios said, rubbing at the back of his neck as he returned to the library. They'd spent hours untangling their latest set of complications and finally called it.

Lunelle set her tea on the shelf before her, stretching her legs as she paced in a small circle.

"Is Luxuros okay? He must be a wreck. My sister puts on a brave face, but I can feel her panic."

Mirquios shrugged, sighing as he leaned against the shelf across from her.

"I left him with Astra. Your grandmother not only shocked us with her news, but exposed his lineage to half the courts. His Fate rests in the hands of three hundred courtiers."

Lunelle shook her hands, attempting to dispel some of the anxiety boiling in her veins.

"I truly did not see it coming. I knew there would be *something*, but that was not it."

Mirquios rested a hand on her shoulder. "Your sister can do this, Lunelle. Luxuros can do this. *You* can do this." He stroked her cheek with his thumb, forcing an encouraging smile as she chewed on her lip.

"She's already done too much," Lunelle whispered.

Mirquios's shoulders stiffened. "You speak about Astra as if you've never once fallen on your own sword for her."

"It's not the same. It's my duty to protect her—"

The king huffed a sigh as he cradled her jaw.

"Which of you was the subject of your mother's constant nitpicking, correction, and ire for thirty-some years while the other ran wild?"

Lunelle laughed, but the memories of her sister's constant correction under their mother's watch flooded her mind.

"My mother was hard on her, too."

"Astra has spent the last three years building her dream city away from the eyes of the entire court. Without you, she never would have found her place in this world. You fight for one another, every day, all the time. Her fighting is just a tad more theatrical."

Lunelle leaned into him, resting her head against his shoulder as he wrapped himself around her.

"I really do like this library," Mirquios murmured against her hair. "When I'm Lunar king, perhaps I'll make it my official study."

Lunelle leaned back, glaring. "You can have the throne, but you cannot have my library."

Mirquios backed her slowly toward a shelf, glittering stars falling from her dress as he tangled her into a kiss.

"Perhaps we can *share* the library," she whispered between kisses, losing control of her breath as he poured over her, her shoulders coming into contact with the hardwood behind her. His tongue brushed against her lower lip as his hand ran over her thigh, pushing the starry lace of her skirts higher and higher.

Mirquios blazed a trail from her lips to her neck, finding the space beneath her ear that earned him a muffled moan, the sound undoing any lingering control he might have held onto.

"Are you sure?"

Mirquios froze against her, peeling his lips away from her neck.

"Do I not *feel* sure?" he laughed, pushing his hips into hers, drawing another soft whine from her chest.

"I meant about taking the Lunar throne—about leaving your court."

"Ah," he sighed, dropping his hand from her thigh and bringing it to her face. "Of course I'm sure, Lunelle. Think of what we could do together."

"But who will take the Mercurean throne?"

"No one, that's the whole point, Lu." Mirquios placed a kiss on her cheek, returning to his endeavor to get his hands on as much of her bare skin as possible. "We'll disband it. Luxuros and Maeve can lead them while we work here to do the same."

Lunelle pulled his mouth back to hers, savoring the taste of him as his teeth grazed her lips. He shoved his hands up her sides, gathering her skirts around her hips and dancing his fingertips along the planes of her thighs.

Gods, he blinded her. Everything in her begged to be claimed by him—to sink under his skin and melt into his veins. She wanted to be the blood circulating through his heart, pulsing with every breath he took against her.

His fingertips grazed the underside of her breasts, teasing as if they had all the time in the world.

His voice was so low she felt it rather than heard it as he mumbled against her.

"I want you out of this dress, but you look so divine, it feels like a sin to remove it."

Lunelle pushed the straps of her dress down so the corset

still hugged her breasts, cupping them together in a way he struggled to pry his eyes from.

"Perhaps you can have it both ways," she murmured, taking his lips between hers and shoving his hands under her dress. Mirquios buried his mouth into her neck, working his fingers inside of her, drawing a constant string of moans from her throat as she clung to his back.

Her eyes closed as he worked faster, encouraged by the way her breath caught when he leaned forward and ground himself into her thigh.

"Please," she whispered, her hand pulling at his jacket. "Do not stop, my king."

"Certainly don't stop on my account."

Lunelle gasped as her eyes flew open, Arcas's scoff from across the library yanking her from the edge of release. Mirquios pulled away from her, grasping her hips as he pushed her skirt back toward the floor.

"May we help you, Arcas?" Mirquios did not turn toward him, still pressed into Lunelle's side.

He directed his response to Lunelle. "I was only coming to check on you. I imagine tonight has been difficult," Arcas said. He cleared his throat. "For both of you." He folded his arms, perched against the bookshelf, his eyes locked on hers and hers alone. "I'll come back later," he said quietly, turning to leave.

Mirquios squeezed Lunelle's hip, her eyes still stuck on the prince. She glanced toward her king, the man who gave her so much, but was always willing to give her more. He'd said he wanted her to have everything she wanted—and she saw it in his gaze, he meant it. Even if she wanted a certain sullen prince.

"Stay," she whispered, her heart thundering in her chest at the vulnerability.

Mirquios exhaled beside her, his lips ticking up on a devilish grin.

"What?" The prince's onyx brows tucked toward one another.

Lunelle slid from Mirquios's hold on her, patting his shoulder as she looked to him once more for assurance.

"Anything you want, my love," he said quietly.

She crossed the library, her bare feet padding against the lush rugs, unsure how to communicate what she wanted without spooking Arcas. But, as she drew closer to him, she saw the widened blacks of his eyes—heard the breath catch in his chest.

Some things—most things, when it came to Arcas—did not need to be verbalized.

She stood before him, his chest rising and falling a little quicker than it had a moment ago, and slipped the top of her dress to her waist.

Her intentions were clear, and Arcas had never quite been able to deny her what she wanted any more than Mirquios had. She let her eyes linger on his for a moment longer, and then it was as if all the strings in the air between them snapped and collapsed in on one another.

Arcas crashed into her, his fingers hungry to wrap around her flesh once more—to pinch, pull, and feel the weight of her. She looped her arms around his neck, enjoying the intoxicating duality of his nature as it rained over her.

He tasted every bit as poisonous as he always had, but somehow that venom living in his blood was less bitter, nearly tolerable after this evening. After what he'd given up for her.

For them.

His hands greedily snatched up every bit of skin she offered, all too aware this may be the last time he'd ever touch her.

And then there was the king. Mirquios's strong hands circled her hips, pushing away at what remained of her dress and tugging the closures of her corset violently, setting her skin on fire as he pressed into her backside, his desire for her—for all of her, no matter what that meant—impossible to deny. He placed searing kisses on her bare shoulders, nipping at her skin.

The sharp pain grounded her, made her intensely aware of her body, and kept her mind from floating into the ether as Arcas moaned into her mouth.

She reached a hand back, stroking Mirquios through his pants as her tongue tangled with Arcas.

She burned alive, heaven and hell, her angel and her devil, both willing to do anything to make her sing their praises. Tomorrow would be painful—even if it all went to plan. But tonight, tonight, Lunelle was a queen to her two most loyal subjects.

She released Mirquios, only to arch her spine and shove her ass into his hands, begging for more pressure, more friction, more anything from him. The prince leaned his hips forward, following hers, the pressure of his want just as mind-melting as the king's.

Arcas dropped his lips to her peaked breasts, laying praise against her impossibly soft skin. She wove a hand through his hair—black as night—and pulled gently as he grazed her with his teeth.

"My gods," Lunelle gasped as fingers wound their way down her back and between her legs—she wasn't even sure who they belonged to.

She wasn't sure who she belonged to.

Perhaps that was just it. She didn't belong to either of them.

She belonged to herself.

And perhaps Pluto had a point—if she wanted it, who in the universe would blame her for taking it?

Mirquios kissed her thigh, nipping at her backside as he squeezed against her, rising from the floor and taking her hand. He led her to the sofa, sitting in the corner and pulling her into his lap, her back pressed to his strong chest as she settled between his legs.

Arcas followed, dropping to his knees before her, taking those long fingers of his and crawling them up her thighs. Lunelle pushed against his touch, her cries escalating as her king's hands tickled her ribs and stroked the underside of her breasts, teasing her again.

"Is this where you want your prince?" Mirquios asked, whispering into her ear before biting at the lobe.

"It's where she needs me," Arcas whispered, tracing a blazing path from her knee to her hip, the cool air of the library sending goose flesh over her wet skin.

Lunelle reached up with one hand to caress Mirquios's neck, tense beneath her touch as he worshipped her with his tongue. She twisted the other into Arcas's midnight hair, slipping through her fingers like fine silk.

She pushed him into her as Mirquios pulled back on her thigh with a tight grip—opening her wider to Arcas's torturously slow kiss. The room spun around her. She had to fight to keep her eyes open as the pleasure built between her legs—she did not want to forget a single second of what he looked like.

She pulled harder at his hair, earning a whimper from his throat, a sound that sent lightning through her spine as Mirquios pinched at her breasts. The sharp sensation combined with the prince's mercilessly slow movements against her created such a delicious harmony in her stomach that she thought she might come undone right then and there.

Arcas clearly suspected the same, slowing his pace even

more so he'd have an excuse to stay knelt before her, to earn whatever favor he could from such a divine woman.

"You're holding back," the king whispered to her. "Your silence is always a weapon, but its blade cuts deepest here. Let us hear you."

The way his deep voice vibrated against her neck as he kneaded her body, sending wave after wave of pleasure, drew a high whine from her throat.

"Ah," Mirquios said, a low chuckle thrumming against her. "The goddess speaks."

Arcas increased his pace, adding a finger or two—she could hardly track the movements in and around her at this point—joining in his offering of praise. She unraveled quickly, swirling her hips against his mouth, drawing a low moan from her king as her hips created friction against his lap. She dug her hands deeper into Arcas's scalp, whispering blessings over him as she tightened into a fraying knot, the threads of her shredding into glittering mist.

"Give him what he's earned," Mirquios hummed, reaching his hand gently around her throat, squeezing just enough to send her body into orbit.

Lunelle thrashed against him, against both of them, the library's shelves and walls falling away to dust as the world imploded, and she cried out.

She could feel everything and nothing. It was quiet in her mind for the first time in years. The prince's lips widened into a grin against her thigh, snapping her from her bliss as her eyes found his.

"Is that a smile, Prince?"

Arcas leaned back on his heels, covering his smile as he wiped at his lips.

"Do not get used to it," he muttered, running his fingers through his hair.

"I believe that is a challenge," Mirquios murmured against her, twitching against her lower back.

She sat up straighter, reaching for Arcas's sapphire collar, pulling him to her, and weaved her tongue with his. She could taste herself on him, taste the desperation hidden behind that smirk of his, the need buried deep in his chest to be seen as more than second best.

Lunelle pulled at his buttons, his heart slamming behind them as she plucked each one away. He shoved his pants down to the ground as he climbed beside her onto the sofa and leaned back at her insistence.

As Lunelle crawled over him, he lifted his head toward Mirquios with an uncertain wobble to his lips.

"And you're content to wait your turn?"

Mirquios tossed his head back in a laugh. "Please, Arcas, I know what it is to be inside Lunelle. I won't have to wait long."

She shot him an appreciative smile as she rolled her hips over the hard length of the prince, a feeling she had not dared to allow herself to miss. But here, she could not only admit it to herself, she could revel in it.

She sank slowly, and they both knew that would not do. Arcas's hands roamed her stomach, her hips, anywhere he could grasp as she set a brutal pace. When it had been just them, in the dark of night, where she swore him to silence, she'd wished desperately to be able to tell him how much she saw within him. How much bigger she thought he could be if he just gave up his hold on what he thought he wanted.

He leaned forward, pulling her body flush to his, the shift in their alignment changing the tenor of the sounds between their mouths into something deeper, something less restrained.

"Tell me," he whispered into her ear. It was thrilling— knowing Mirquios heard him. The king's hand drifted over his lap, stroking himself as Lunelle lost control of her rhythm, bucking wildly against Arcas's hold. "What pleases you more, goddess, knowing that you are feared by two of the most powerful men in the courts, or that you are loved by them?"

Lunelle gasped against him, driving her hands into his hair, pulling his lips to hers to stop him from finishing her with words alone.

The weight behind her shifted on the sofa, a third set of clothes hitting the floor. Lunelle was vaguely aware of the sound of her king's breath quickening behind her as he slid between Arcas's legs and pulled her back toward him.

"I did not hear your answer," he said softly into her neck, weaving his fingers into her hair and adding another layer of pleasure to the overwhelm in her spine. He pressed into her back, reminding her that she was still his, too, as he wrapped a hand around her hip and found her center, slipping his fingers between them.

Lunelle's answer only came in the form of a guttural groan as she shook in his arms, the prince's lips pulling tight as he moved to push her off, rolling to the side to finish himself. She reached for him, hardly able to see, but wanted to be the one to bring him over the edge.

As he convulsed in her hand, she found his eyes, holding them for much longer than she'd allowed herself to before.

"Loved," Lunelle finally said. "If I must choose."

Arcas leaned forward, pulling her into a soft kiss, a tenderness she did not expect him capable of.

"I suppose it is good that you don't have to, then." He lay back, breathing hard against the sofa, the pale blue skin of his ribs rippling like the sea.

She backed up a breath and was greeted by her king, patiently waiting, eager for her to bestow some grace his way. He rocked forward on his knees, pushing against her from behind slowly, agonizingly slowly, peppering her sweat-slicked shoulders with languid kisses.

She widened her knees over his lap, straddling him and pitching forward, into the prince's arms as he rose to mirror her. Mirquios ran his hand down her spine, tracing the delicate rivers and valleys between vertebrae, giving her a second to adjust to someone else, to catch her breath before he took it away once more.

He stopped his hand at her tailbone, gently squeezing her hip as he watched her take him in, watched how they fit so keenly together, in a way no one else ever would.

Lunelle inhaled slowly as he claimed his space, relishing the feeling of the Tether between them sparkling and pulsing.

"Tell me how you want it, love," he whispered, Arcas watching her face as her eyes glazed over.

"Slow," she breathed, rocking her hips forward just slightly, just to get her head around where she ended and he began. "Torture me."

Mirquios took his time moving within her, making sure she felt every piece of him, body and soul, as they swirled into one being, one entity.

Arcas watched as her breasts swayed back and forth, her eyes closed against her cheeks, still flush with the red of the release he'd given her. She felt his eyes on her as she told herself to wait, to take her time with Mirquios, before bringing him back into her space.

"Do you want more?" Mirquios whispered behind her.

Lunelle whined, her throat taut with a plea she could not verbalize.

"What do you want, Lunelle?" he whispered into her ear, moving torturously slowly within her. "Do you want me to stay soft and slow? Or do you want me to rouse death herself within you?"

Lunelle shook her head, her eyes opening and falling over Arcas, who stared at her with his lips parted as if about to answer for her.

"Say it, Princess. I can't give you what you won't ask for." He gripped her shoulder in his strong hands, his fingers stroking her neck as he hovered, waiting for her answer. She wiggled her hips against him, begging him to enter her again, but he resisted.

"Not until you tell me what you want."

Lunelle groaned, unwilling to wait a second longer for him to unleash within her.

"I want you to take me. I want to be the only thing you pray to in this lifetime and all the rest."

Lunelle leaned back, capturing his lips with hers as he tightened his grip on her, giving her everything she asked for and more. He pushed her forward, unable to hold his pace and hers at the same time.

All of the moments they never got, all of the moments they might not get, collapsed between them right there, right then. She landed on her hands, her face a breath away from Arcas, who stared with those deeply troubled eyes with a clarity she knew reflected back in her own.

This was enough for her.

This was more than enough for her.

"Touch me," Lunelle pleaded, reaching her fingertips forward and grabbing the prince by his chin. "I need to feel you, too."

Arcas scrambled forward at her plea, his hands capturing her breasts and pushing her back toward the king, claiming her lips as she cried out into his mouth. Mirquios groaned behind her, his grip turning her pale skin red. He looked over her shoulder at the prince.

"Your mouth is better than your hands," he ground out, nearly at his own release. Arcas dropped his lips to her breasts without hesitation, pulling at her flesh with his teeth. One hand came up to his neck, squeezing as she fought for breath against his lips.

Lunelle shattered against them, the king responding to her choked cry with his own string of Mercurian curses, hissing against her shoulder. He panted as he leaned over her, Arcas stroking her hair as she spiraled out of her body and back in, something new buried within her Soul—something made of dark and light.

Arcas fell back onto the sofa as Mirquios cradled her, her breath coming in short bursts. The prince sighed. His grin returned.

"If I am consumed by some hellish beast in the Nether tomorrow, that will have been worth it."

Lunelle laughed, clutching at the king's thighs, attempting to bring herself back to their plane of existence. Arcas rose, pulling his clothes from the floor.

"Well, tomorrow just got a little more complicated," Mirquios sighed.

"Perhaps it just got much simpler," Arcas said, pulling on his trousers.

Lunelle straightened, searching his gaze as it fell somewhere far off.

"How do you mean?"

The prince worked on the buttons on his shirt.

"I never wanted your throne, starling. I only ever wanted you."

Lunelle's heart lurched, that small space in her chest that she'd reserved only for him suddenly taking up a much larger parcel of her lungs.

"Perhaps there is a world where we can all get what we

want." Mirquios held the prince's eyes, a silent understanding passing between them.

Lunelle giggled. "I fear you'll feel differently once you've faced your Shadow."

His lips curled into a sly smile. "I suppose only time will tell." He leaned forward, pressing one final kiss to Lunelle's lips. "You should get some rest. You both should."

Lunelle nodded, feeling so very different from how she had just an hour ago—almost hopeful.

Arcas left the library, leaving only her king, still buried inside her, as they lay on the sofa together, unable to give up on what they thought could be their final evening together.

Mirquios smiled against her neck, enjoying their shared weight as his breath slowed and his heart returned to its typical racing rhythm when she was near.

"We will have many more moments," he whispered. "I promise you."

CHAPTER
THIRTY-TWO

T he temple loomed over them as the Moon climbed over the horizon, an eerie silence settling over their shoulders.

Lunelle stood between lavender pillars, her hair woven into an ornate crown around her foggy mind. Three men towered behind her, each more frightened than the next—but one moved *with* her, the Tether sizzling between them, and another moved *against* her, the wisps of their strange connection tickling her ribs.

"Good morning," Tula said, her silken voice tight as she absorbed the tension between them. "I hope you're all well rested."

Lunelle fought the urge to laugh as two sets of eyes flashed toward her. It was all so preposterous.

"You may enter," Tula said, opening her arm toward the temple. Lunelle stepped softly into the crystalline walls, a bubbling spring in the middle whispering sacred prayers as they kneeled on velvet cushions around the azure waters.

"You've each chosen... or been chosen, rather," Tula

corrected herself, "to undertake a sacred ritual, stretching back to the very first of our Lunar demigoddesses, who built this realm with divine intuition and a deep understanding that to be whole requires a balance of our natures. One cannot love the light without respect for the dark, and one cannot survive the dark without the hope of light. They complete one another. When we are crafted by the gods, they pull our Soul and Shadow from Above and Below, stitching us together with gilded threads. It is up to us to honor them both throughout our lives."

Lunelle's eyes fell across the spring, fixed on the jade gaze of the king as he buried a smile. Beside her, Arcas leaned ever so slightly in her direction, the spring before them reflecting his pale blues. Tula held a long stick of incense over a black candle, waving it between them as she wove through their kneeling bodies.

"Upon our Descent, the Cleaver untangles us once more, giving us time and space to reflect on how our two halves can be reconciled. It is only upon our Souls embracing our Shadows that we can make our journey to the Court Above."

Tula completed her circle, resting the incense on a silver tray, the smoke curling and falling to the temple floor. She lifted a bowl from her table, cradling it in her hands as she stepped behind Lunelle.

"Today, you'll each part with your Shadow temporarily, offering it to the Nether as a symbol of your commitment to maintaining this holy balance throughout your reign." Tula glanced across their faces. "No matter which throne you sit upon."

Tula bent forward, offering the bowl to Lunelle. She plucked a round white palm stone from the top, the cool surface melting into her skin. The priestess made her way around the spring, offering a stone to each of the champions.

She returned the bowl to her table and lifted a gauzy white crystal wand in one hand and a burning bundle of herbs in another.

"These stones will hold your Shadows as they're delivered to Luciela, the Nether Queen herself. Close your eyes, let the darkest pieces of you slip away."

Tula's sweet alto voice rose in delicate notes above their bowed heads. The prayer wrapped around Lunelle's shoulders and warmed her from within as the stone buzzed in her hands.

It was similar to the way her mind spiraled away from her when she found Proserpina, but the drain did not stop at her chest, falling through the veins of her arms and pouring into the stone in her palm.

Her mind swirled, and she felt the buzzing of the Tether fade as she collapsed into herself, falling faster as she heard a familiar giggle.

"We did not think we'd see you again," Proserpina chirped.

Lunelle was not in the midnight seas of Pluto's throne realm, but back in the dim forest with the goddess. This time, Pluto lounged behind her, tangled in a plush blanket as she fed him grapes. The sight amused the princess.

They seemed so light.

She giggled. "I find I'm as surprised as you."

Pluto grinned. "You're but a moment away from taking what you really desire, Princess. *Everything.*"

Lunelle pressed her lips together tightly.

Proserpina tilted her head in response. "You do not think so?"

Lunelle shrugged, her heart shuddering under the gaze of the goddess.

"I do not wish to have false hope."

Pluto nodded, tugging gently on the ends of Proserpina's curls. Something to the edge of them caught his eye, a devilish grin unfurling as he nodded at someone beyond the trees.

"This is the first hope you've had that was true," Proserpina said.

Lunelle's eyes lit, a flicker of something new in her chest, nestled between her two ties to this world. She turned as footsteps approached her left.

"You're late," Pluto said as another god joined their picnic, his face twisted in an eye roll as he reached for a handful of pomegranate seeds. His hand rested on Proserpina's hip as he and Pluto mumbled to one another.

"Go then, Princess," Proserpina said. "We'll be watching."

Pluto tossed Lunelle a wink. "Give my sister my warmest regards," he chuckled.

Lunelle's eyes fluttered open, the spring of the temple gurgling at her knees.

She glanced at the stone in her hands, the white overtaken by a charcoal hue, the center glittering with swirls of gods knew what. She held it to the moonlight above, a glint of sapphire catching her off guard within the silver and emerald tones. She eyed Arcas's stone beside her, a silvery sheen catching as he leaned over the water.

"You may toss them into the spring," Tula said quietly. "Gods be with you all."

Lunelle rose, staring into the water below, sparkling with all sorts of blessings and tears. She let her Shadow fall, sinking to the depths of the Nether, as three others followed.

Her eyes rose to her champions.

They *did* look strangely unburdened in some ways without their Shadows.

Less interesting, she noted.

"Best of luck, gentlemen," she whispered, making a quick

exit at the back of the temple, a cold sweat clinging to her as she tried to control her breath.

"Lunelle," her mother commanded. She hovered at the temple's blossom-laden gate.

"Mother," Lunelle sighed, in no mood to hear more from her after last night. Oestera reached for her hand, pulling her swiftly into the shade of the palace garden as the maidens around them worked to prepare it for the trial.

"What are you—"

"I need you to listen to me," Oestera said, her words sharp. She gripped her daughter's shoulders, forcing her silver stare to fuse with hers. "Whatever happens in the Nether, you *must* not come back through the gate until I tell you to. I know you resisted me back in the Plutonian Court, but it is more important now than *ever* that you listen."

Lunelle shook her head, her heart pounding.

"After what you've pulled with Arcas, I've every reason to do the opposite of what you ask, Mother."

She backed away from her mother's grip, but something frenzied in her eyes, something truly desperate in her fingers caught her.

"I am begging you to trust me, Lunelle. Your sister *needs* to come through the gate first."

"My sister?" Lunelle played dumb, though she could tell without her Shadow, she was hardly convincing herself, let alone her mother.

"I will not force you to confess your plans, but I need you to wait. Wait for my signal, and *then* you bring your king through the gate. Do you understand?"

Lunelle did not, and she would not.

"I am tired of scheming, Mother. It has only dug me further and further into a grave—if you think I would *dare* subject Astra to this—this madness—I will not force her onto a throne she does not want. She's already done enough!"

"I was once a younger sister thrust onto a throne by an older sister who made a mistake, Lunelle." Oestera drew a breath, shivering at the top as she whispered. "And I do not resent her for one second. Not once in my life have I been angry at her for the choices she made. For what she thought she was doing. I am honored to bear the weight of her attempt at taking what she wanted..." she trailed off, her eyes unfocused for a moment.

"I do not understand—what are you saying?"

"Look at me," Oestera pleaded. Lunelle forced herself to connect to her eyes, the pain so clearly still on the surface of her heart. "There are bigger plans at play, Lunelle. Your sister will understand. *You* will understand. Everyone gets what they want this way!"

Lunelle's head was dizzy as she tried to make sense of the words her mother said.

"I cannot tell you more," Oestera mumbled. "I wish to, I will one day. I need you to understand. I need you to trust me."

Lunelle exhaled a long, tortured sigh.

"The only person I trust in this world is my sister," she said. "I only wish to do right by her."

Oestera nodded, biting her lip.

"You and I are on the same side, Lunelle. I need you to search your Soul and see that I am earnest."

Lunelle backed away a step, so unsure of what to think.

"I will try." It was all she could offer.

"That's all I ask," her mother murmured, dropping her hold on her shoulders. "That and... and if you find Le—Leona." Oestera's voice caught on her sister's name. Lunelle had never once heard it on her tongue, not in the decades of dancing around the subject. Moonbeams brushed her face as she watched the maidens string roses across the terrace, lightening the darkness and sorrow cast over Oestera's expression.

"If you see my sister... tell her I hope she can forgive herself. Because my anger died with her final breath."

Oestera cleared her throat, leaving Lunelle in the cool darkness of the temple.

CHAPTER
THIRTY-THREE

"Why am I always letting you into my bedroom against my better judgment?"

Mirquios stepped aside, allowing Lunelle to slip beneath his arm and into his study. She had been pacing in circles for the better part of an hour, awaiting her summons to the Lunar Gate and she could not take the loneliness another moment.

"Because you love me," Lunelle said simply.

His eyes dropped to her hands, twisting together into a knot.

"Gods be damned, Lunelle, I do," he sighed, wrapping her into a soft embrace. He pressed his lips to her forehead. "And you love me, too."

"From the moment you drank that horrifying tea for me," she whispered.

He leaned away from her, searching her gaze, the greens of his eyes even brighter without any darkness within him to shade them. She looked away for a moment, desperate to regain her composure.

320

"My mother wants us to wait to cross back through the gate."

"What?" He released her, unsure what to make of the suggestion.

"She knows we're bringing Astra with us. I don't think she knows *why*, but she begged me to trust her."

"And?"

Lunelle frowned.

"And... I do not know what to do," she sighed, sinking against him.

"If your sister goes through the gate first..."

"She becomes queen."

His brows tucked together. "Well, that's not going to work—"

"It does if a certain commander goes with her."

Mirquios winced. "Solan would set this entire court on fire if he found out."

"I know my sister, Mirq. The moment she realizes what's happened, she'll likely overthrow the entire system anyway. The Fire Queen would live up to her name."

"With Luxuros by her side..." The king paced the small study, his mind working in concentric circles. "If they're here, that would force you onto the Mercurian throne—"

"Would it?" she asked, her brows arched.

Mirquios stopped his pacing, doubling back to her and cradling her face, stroking her cheek with his thumb.

"Temporarily, at least. Is that what you want, Princess?"

Lunelle's lips twisted, though for once, she did not have to think about what she desired.

"More than anything."

He laughed, a low thundering sound as he pressed his lips to hers.

"I would have made you my queen months ago if it weren't

for... well, everything." He waved his hand as he gestured to the unseen chaos that kept them constantly on edge.

Lunelle thought aloud. "With Astra on the Lunar throne, the rebellion would have a clear path to turning the rest of the courts, Mirq. She would not hesitate."

"Neither would the commander. We'd disband Mercury soon after. And Arcas, perhaps—"

"Yes," she sighed. "Perhaps."

Mirquios brushed his fingers over the bridge of her nose. "We will figure out how he fits into our world, I promise."

"This could work," Lunelle breathed.

"This *will* work," Mirquios said.

Three soft raps on the door separated them. Lunelle tucked herself into his bedroom, hiding for what she hoped was the final time. The king pulled back the door to a maiden with a plate of food and a note for him. She set it on the table and disappeared as he read the missive.

"Seems we've been summoned," he said, folding the note into his pocket.

Lunelle stepped back into the room, looking at the plate they'd made for him. A pile of red pomegranate seeds slipped over the edge, bleeding onto the tray.

"One more moment?" she asked, plucking a seed from the plate and letting it roll over her tongue.

Mirquios pulled her into his chest, resting his head on hers.

"You may have every last one of my moments."

THE DUST of the Court Below clung to her lips, much like the salt of the sea below her beloved palace.

Only instead of salt, the Nether tasted like ancient secrets, bitter with betrayal.

Lunelle glanced back over her shoulder, ensuring Astra had made it over her side of the dune.

"She's got this," Luxuros said as they jogged toward a forest of withered branches and gnarled trees. She believed him—believed in her sister—but her heart ached with worry nonetheless.

"Your prince sure ran off in a hurry," Mirquios said, ducking beneath a black oak branch, the wood crackling into decay as he touched it.

"Cut him some slack," Lunelle whispered. "You're here with your best friend and your... whatever I am—"

Mirquios stopped walking. "My Moon, my stars, my sole reason for existing... do you need me to go on?"

"Spare us," Luxuros muttered.

Luxuros trudged ahead of them, a smile tugging at her lips, despite the pain she held for the Plutonian prince.

"I only mean to say that he's alone out here."

Mirquios squeezed her hand. "We will all leave the Court Below in one piece, Lu. I promise."

She nodded, stepping through the heaps of dead logs and overgrown, brittle grass.

"I'm taking the northern edge," Luxuros called over his shoulder, breaking into a jog across the clearing.

Mirquios hopped over a particularly large fallen tree and glanced through the dim forest.

"I don't suppose you have some sort of magical intuition that tells us how to find our Shadows?"

Lunelle's ears heated. "I... I might," she confessed. She turned toward him. "Something strange happened with Arcas the other night."

"You do not have to tell me, Lu—"

"I know, I know. But something.... I cannot explain it, something happened to a darker piece of us... it was not like a

Tether, but not *unlike* it in some ways. I can feel the space it left behind, it's like my blood calls out for it."

Mirquios stared at her for a moment, taking in what she could possibly mean. His eyes swept over her chest as if he might see the shift she spoke of.

"It sings," she whispered. She closed her eyes, blocking out the dull haze of the Court Below, letting her mind drop to that pit in her stomach, that space between bone and blood that waited for him—that swirled with smoke dark as night, but glittered with brilliant sapphire threads.

The tug was there. It was quiet, only a whisper, but she could feel it brush against her ear.

"East," she mumbled, striking forward over the dense decaying flora.

Her king followed without hesitation.

Lunelle followed the ghost of the Shadow within her, seeking the darkness she'd loaned to the sorrowful forest, stretching and yearning to absorb more of itself and feel whole once again. They tore through the macabre woods, branches leaving shallow holds across their cheeks and hands, the silence of phantoms running beside them amplifying the thud of each rock against boot, the *shhhh* of crumbling leaves breaking along their shoulders.

The skin on the back of her neck burst with gooseflesh as something cut into their path—something too fast to identify with her eyes, but she felt it in her Soul.

"Was that—" Mirquios's question cut short as another onyx apparition raced by them.

"That one is yours," she sighed, recognizing the glossy pride of it—the way its shoulders still stood tall even as an amorphous slip of space.

"The other one?" Mirquios barked as he broke into a sprint after the smoke and spirit of him.

Lunelle swallowed, turning in a tight circle as she waited for it to rush through the trees again. A lithe black streak curled at the base of a gnarled tree, springing forward when it sensed her stare. It blew over her like a storm, smelling of desperation and fear.

Her tongue reared back as a bitter note spread through her mouth, slinking down her throat.

"Not mine," she said. But not *far* from hers, she wanted to add.

The same weight on its shoulders, the same stubborn rattle at its core as it refused to accept sacrifice. The same glittering spine of shame, torn between desire and duty, doing what is right and doing what the blood that runs through its missing flesh begs. The same craving to be seen as what it knows it could be, what it might be if only it shed a few deeper hues.

Mirquios dove from a small boulder as he attempted to wrestle his Shadow into place, missing it by just a breath. "Godsdammit," he muttered as he tumbled to the forest floor.

The king sprinted after it, as Lunelle shook her head, attempting to clear the weight of Arcas's Shadow from her chest as it disappeared into the treeline.

She was certain it whispered her name as it went.

"Lu!"

She darted away, casting one more stare behind her before she wove through wicked roots toward the sound of Mirquios's scream, the Tether in her chest lighting up with pain.

He slumped over his leg at the bottom of a shallow ditch, hissing as he cradled his leg. He brought his fingers to his face in the dim of the eternal twilight, stained with a bright crimson.

"I swear to the gods, the damned thing slashed at me!" Mirquios leaned his head back, pulling in a harsh breath as he hauled himself to his feet, reaching out for Lunelle as she leaned over the edge of the rocky ravine.

"Your Shadow did that?" she gasped as she caught sight of his thigh, flayed from hip to knee and weeping beneath shredded leather.

"It attacked, and I fell back. I must have caught it on the rocks. Shit," he groaned as she hauled him back over the crest of the fall.

"Tula did not mention combat," Lunelle sighed.

"No, no, she did not." Mirquios eyed the edge of the trees in the direction his Shadow had taken off. "There! That's you, I'd stake my life on it." He pointed to a movement between the ghostly white trunks a hundred paces away.

Her Shadow did not run. It held.

It demanded to be seen.

Lunelle held her breath and tilted her head, watching the wisps of her watch back. His Shadow slinked behind hers, catching her attention as they both dove deeper into the dark. Mirquios began to run, but grunted as his leg contacted the ground and sent a shock of screaming pain through his spine.

"We have time," Lunelle breathed, looking toward the murky sky, searching for something to anchor her in space and time, but it only returned an endless black. She propped her shoulder under his arm and helped him hobble through the first few steps before he tightened his back and found a motion that allowed him to move swiftly, though the pain only grew more demanding.

"We do not have *that much* time," he sighed. His head already swirled as the blood soaked what remained of his pants. He winced as he struggled to overcome a log, Lunelle waiting for him with guiding hands. "You should not wait for me."

She glared as she pulled him forward, watching the space she'd disappeared into carefully for movement.

"Don't be a fool," she sighed. "We do not leave one another. Ever."

Mirquios nodded beside her, though she did not need his affirmation. She knew it in her bones. They passed through a thickly tangled knot in the wood and fell into a clearing, the ground sharp with rocky soil and brambles fallen from life that perhaps once existed there a millennia ago.

"Yours calls to you," Mirquios mumbled, pushing into the wound on his leg to attempt to stop the flow of blood. "But can you call to it?"

Lunelle tilted her head as she considered what she might need to do—to say—to convince her Shadow to return to her. What might tempt it.

She reached within herself once more, sifting through that hollow for answers. A slight tendril curled a finger toward her, begging her closer.

What do you want?

She was not sure who was asking whom, which way the question flowed, or if it even mattered. She pressed into the shape of the question, leaned into the darkness.

What do you want? she asked her Shadow. She'd spent so long suppressing what her Shadow wanted for the sake of what her Soul needed, she wasn't sure she'd ever considered that it may have a dissenting opinion.

The answer bubbled up easily—instantly.

"Ah!" Mirquios screamed as his Shadow sought to deepen the wound to his leg again. Lunelle's eyes widened as she watched the phantom strike his leg a third time, driving the pain to his bone. His knee hit the brambles beneath them briefly before he sprang back up.

Do not ignore me now, she heard, delivered in an icy chill down her spine as wisps of smoke pulled at her hair, her chin, demanding her attention. She spun back around, pressing her shoulders against Mirquios's, hoping to bring him any amount of relief as he dodged another savage swing.

He was heavy against her, his breath coming hard as he tried to get a hold of his stance.

Lunelle? It was not the voice within her that called her name—it was Astra.

Over here! she called, as if she understood where here even was, grunting as Mirquios landed on her shoulders once more.

"On your left!" he huffed as he hauled himself forward.

She had not expected to feel her Shadow's grip on her jaw, yanking her head, a yelp leaving her throat as nails dug into her flesh.

You will hear us, it hissed, sweeping Lunelle's legs from beneath her and pinning her into the fallen thorns.

Her mind raced back to that answer—back to that truth she'd always known but never wanted to admit. Her Shadow clutched at her hips, her knees, her elbows, forcing her back into the twisted prongs over and over again as she fought to get her gaze on Mirquios. She could hear him hit the ground with a thud, a harsh gasp tore from him as he shuffled against the leaves.

The Shadow atop her refused to entertain the distraction.

She was in charge, like she'd been when she'd taken a blood oath that would change the trajectory of her entire life. Like she'd been when she'd commanded a Plutonian prince to release rebel prisoners, rooted in the darkness that drove her to forsake the nobles that lofted her.

Like she'd been when she'd surrendered to the call within her and shoved Arcas into a wall, refusing to let him slink off into the night.

Mirquios crumbled into a heap beside her, his lungs puffing as his Shadow landed another blow against his neck.

Lunelle ground her hips deep into the sharp thorns, embracing their revenge against her skin as the fuel she needed to throw her Shadow from her, rolling to her right and scrambling to her feet.

I hear you, she thought, *I see you.*

She reached for her king's head, tilting his chin up toward her as his Shadow rounded the clearing, reading for another round. His bright eyes were so heavy, so tired.

She was in charge, like she'd been when she let every rule and boundary—imagined or not, faked or not—fall away at the edge of a cliff and threw her arms around a king that did not belong to her. Could not belong to her.

Unless.

Lunelle smiled, the radiance dimmed in the faded lights of the Nether, but warm all the same.

"We're all making it out in one piece, right?" She yanked him to his feet, pressing her back to his again, taking on his weight as best she could as she watched both their Shadows wind up, haunched against the ether and gathering the darkness around them to launch them forward.

She could have what she wanted, but she could not have it without help.

"Astra!" she screamed, searching for the bright ruby of her sister in the trees. Their Shadows rushed in, two infinite pits of black clashing against their braced bodies.

Her Shadow did not hold back, consuming her as she leaned into her heels. Her eyes burned against the onslaught, Mirquios's muscles flexing against hers as he tried to dodge the viscous rhythm of his own haunting.

A flash of scarlet in the corner of Lunelle's eye grabbed her focus for just long enough that her Shadow wrapped its grip around her arm, squeezing with a ferocity she could not get on top of.

"He's hurt!" Lunelle called to her sister. She could not face her Shadow if she was worried about saving him. Mirquios would always win in that equation. Astra circled them to catch her eye as her Shadow twisted against her, begging for her to give in.

Astra huffed, "Did they tell you how to get them back?"

Lunelle shook her head, Mirquios leaning over her as she felt his slick pant leg stick to hers.

"Tula said something about listening to them! I don't know!" He bent and dodged once more, shaking her as he moved.

Lunelle's eyes snapped forward, peering into the swirls that stung her. She knew what her Shadow wanted—she knew what *she* wanted.

And she was no longer afraid to demand it.

Lunelle wanted to lead the fight against the layers of lies from the Court Above, *and* she wanted to do it from the Mercurian's glittering golden streets. She wanted to be her sister's protector *and* be protected by her. She wanted to bask in the golden light of the Sun, *and* drown in the silver secrets of the Moon.

"You have to embrace them!" The commander's voice bellowed from a distance. Lunelle's Shadow seemed to breathe at his revelation.

"The more you fight, the harder it is!" Arcas called. Lunelle turned when she heard his voice, his tall frame thrown over Luxuros's shoulder.

She did not have a moment to wonder how he found himself there.

Lunelle stopped resisting the touch of her Shadow, stopped wrestling the call to the void of it. She leaned forward, reaching her arms around it, and whispered an apology she didn't know she was choking on for so long.

As the murky blacks and glittering sapphires of her deepest hidden layers melted against her flesh, she knew what it was that she'd wanted all along—she longed to be worshipped by day and death, sunbeams and starlight.

She wanted to hold it all within her, all the versions of herself she was and would be, and she wanted to love them from every angle.

She raised her hand, admiring the depth of color returned to her starry complexion, the rush of cold breath moving through her veins in a gentle sigh. Arcas landed at her feet with a heavy thud, the breath leaving his lungs as she stared at those eyes—those sharp gems, cut just to reflect her.

Mirquios screamed as he lifted his hands to the dim break in trees overhead, searching for whatever light he could find. Lunelle spun, wrapping her fingers around his shoulder.

"Your leg?"

"No!" he barked. "You could have warned me they'd say such horrifying shit," he sighed.

"Mine wasn't *that* bad," Lunelle mused, her eyes sliding back to the prince as he brushed himself off. "But noted for you."

She arched her brow as she turned to examine his wound, the blood clotting and sealing over, but his face paled, the pain was catching up with him.

Astra moved toward them. "What happened to your leg? What happened to Pluto?" she sneered. Lunelle gently helped Mirquios to the ground, his eyes closed against a wave of nausea.

"Shadow," he murmured.

Luxuros scoffed. "Bastard attacked me!"

Lunelle turned to him, prepared to beg for more information, but Astra was already in his face. It was fascinating, she realized, the desire to defend them both, the fear which one might strike first.

Astra beat Arcas to any explanation. "You know you don't have to be the *only* champion back, just the first, right? We aren't barbarians."

Lunelle watched her words undo Arcas's last shred of sanity.

"I don't know! I don't know what's going on!" He flailed his hands between them, the pitch in his voice so familiar to Lunelle. His back was against the wall by a Lunar woman once again, but this one did not have a secret affinity for his weaknesses. "I didn't even want to be here, okay? The queen said that if I came to court the princess, she'd pay off Pluto's debts and help us manage our rebellion! I wasn't even supposed to make it to the trial!" Arcas focused his eyes on Lunelle and Lunelle alone. "She was supposed to announce at the ball that Lunelle is capable of ruling the court without a man and pass the crown to her unwed, but then that goddess changed all the rules, and the commander somehow got roped into this, and I wasn't trying to attack you!"

The prince gasped for breath as he gestured to Luxuros. Lunelle's head felt as if it would cave in at any moment, his words landing like her Shadow's unforgiving blows.

"I wasn't expecting to run into you on the other side of the woods. I can't track you in here, the Tethers are *really* hard to see in such a dull environment."

Four faces froze as they avoided one another's gaze and attempted to piece together what Arcas had just said. Arcas's lips pulled into a tight line, his throat flexing against his next thought, but Lunelle suddenly had the appetite to feel those tendons shift beneath her grasp in a much different way than in the dark of his bedroom.

"What did you just say?" she asked, marching toward him, her chest colliding with his as their Shadows danced against one another, twisting and curling at their edges—welcoming one another back home. Arcas stepped back, flinching as he felt it much clearer here than in the chaos of the other evening.

His lips dropped into a frown, eyes closed against those cerulean cheeks.

"Which part, Princess?"

Astra sputtered beside them, soothing the headache she was surely battling under so many endless revelations.

"Oh," Lunelle spat. "I don't know, Arcas, maybe the part where you can *see* Tethers? Have you known about the king and me this whole time?"

He would not look at her. Could not bear to see the betrayal on her face. He'd implied—more than once—that he knew there was *something* occurring between them. She'd happily weaponized it against him at times. But he'd never come close to intimating that he understood how dire it was for her. The pain of the position Fate put her in.

The agony it caused from all angles.

"Yes. I'm sorry," he whispered. "My mother was Venusian, they can see Tethers."

Lunelle's cheeks heated. She'd been exposed to him in many, *many* ways, but this transcended any of that.

Astra leaned forward, her voice tight. "All... Venusians? And all... Tethers?"

Arcas clenched his jaw before answering. "Yes."

"Oh my gods," Astra gasped, the commander's hand closing around her hip as naturally as his next breath. Orbiting her, as if she were not just something to hold, but the very thing that held him.

Oh.

Lunelle's chest cracked wide open—of *course,* they were.

333

"Are you—Astra? Are you two... *Tethered?*"

Her sister's eyes flitted to the commander and then to Mirquios, sending a fresh wave of feral heat to Lunelle's face.

Astra attempted to move her along. "I think there is much more pressing information that Arcas just dropped on us—"

"Please!" Mirquios begged from his spot on the ground. "Please, just tell her so I can have some *peace!*"

Lunelle spun toward him. "You knew?"

She'd asked him how many times? How many dozens of times had she inquired of his thoughts on their strange alchemy?

"I suspected," he admitted. "They weren't subtle."

Lunelle snorted. "Well, we *knew* they were sleeping together, but you never once thought to tell me you thought they were Tethered?"

He pushed at his injury, drawing a sharp breath.

"We've had a lot on our plate, dear. I assumed Astra would tell you!"

She'd always assumed that, too.

But she had to be forced to tell Astra, hadn't she?

They both set their eyes on the Fire Queen, her face as warm as her fingertips. She balked, holding her hands up.

"Again, bigger things to talk about right now—"

"All that stress, all that heartache, all the worry that my little sister must sacrifice her happiness for me was for *nothing?*" Lunelle's eyes landed on Arcas again, his lips twisting in an amused smirk as he pointed to his chest.

"Oh, we're mad at me again?"

Astra cut in. "I think we're just confused. It's been a hard few months, and we don't exactly know who to trust right now."

Lunelle felt the pain in her sister's words—the whirlwind

of constant betrayal and upheaval must have been tenfold for her sensibilities.

"It really has. Gods, Astra. I wish you had told me how dire this was for you, too. I put too much pressure on you!"

Astra's eyes widened. "No, no, Lu. You've taken the brunt of the responsibility your whole life. I was happy to do this for you, I swear it!" Lunelle could feel Mirquios about to huff an "I told you so" as he held his head in his hands, breathing deeply against the wear on his body.

The commander stepped toward her. "As?"

She sighed, her point still only half-made. "Yes, Luxuros, what is it?"

He glanced at the sky, marking some unseen thing Lunelle could not.

"We've got about half an hour before the gate closes. Do you think you and your sister can hash this out when we're not at risk of getting sealed into the Court Below for three months?"

At that, a wave of clarity washed over her.

"Mirquios is hurt. We need to get him back, but there's no way he should walk on that leg."

The king opened his mouth to protest, but she felt Arcas move before he spoke, the darkness within him shifting gently against her.

"I can help," he said. "Least I can do, I suppose." He reached for the king, and for the first time, Lunelle wondered if perhaps, had she been honest with herself, and both of them from the beginning, they'd be on different sides of a revolution right now. They were two incredibly sharp minds—imagine what they'd accomplish side by side.

"I got him," Luxuros said, pushing past the prince. "You good to get what you came for?"

Astra nodded, resting her hand on his arm. "Just get him back safely," she said.

"Wait for us at the gate," Lunelle said, her eyes shifting from Mirquios to Arcas.

Astra whipped her head toward her. "Lunelle, no. Go with Mirq. I can do this!"

Lunelle had no doubts about that, not a single lingering thought that her sister couldn't do any damned thing she set out to. But they were fighting against the same curses, buried in different places within them, but rotting nonetheless.

"Not a chance," Lunelle said, watching her Soul and Shadow struggle to get the king moving. "We're doing this together."

Astra's eyes settled on her sister, glimmering with a love that no one in all the realms could ever hold for Lunelle—a love that she herself knew she'd put before any man, Tether and ties be damned.

"Let's do this," Astra said, a slow grin spreading over her lips.

CHAPTER
THIRTY-FOUR

Astra glanced at Lunelle from the side as she stared into the murky depths of the woods. They hadn't moved far from the bloodstained patch of forest, Astra's gut stopping her as she held out the locket Selenia had given her.

"Selenia Aurellis," Astra said, a wobble to her voice that surprised Lunelle. She'd so rarely seen her nervous. "We've come to return you to your rightful place."

Astra closed her eyes, the silence heavy between them. Lunelle felt something at the edge of her Soul, a brush against her ribs that reached for something.

Someone, she realized, as a black flash ripped through the woods.

Astra fell back a step, her arm flailing as she gripped the locket tightly. The Shadow circled them, calculating the best way to face the two sisters.

"Steady, As." Lunelle said, rooting her feet into the ground. "Selenia, we've come to claim you!" She let that wisp within her lurch toward the scrambling Shadow as it dipped back into the treeline—call to it. Lunelle drew her in, a stirring in her gut as Selenia's Shadow darted forth.

Astra held the locket higher, her knuckles white as she clasped it, a frigid breeze arriving as a warning that she was close. Lunelle closed her eyes, too, beckoning the tendril of darkness within her—the one that still wondered what life on the throne might be like—to invite Selenia closer.

She *heard* the sound of the Shadow smack Astra's hand, a crack, and *whoosh* as it clasped shut.

Her eyes fluttered open, the locket swinging violently as if whatever was trapped inside had a change of heart.

"Did... did we do it?"

Astra ran a fingertip over the icy condensation forming on the outside of the metal.

"I think so?" She fastened it around her neck. Lunelle wondered what the weight of her mother's mother felt like.

"That seemed too easy," she said aloud.

Her sister laughed, a dark smile breaking over her face.

"I'll take easy at this point. It's what comes next that's going to be impossible."

They started their trek back toward the edge of the forest, but Lunelle's head was steeped in so many thoughts that she could not keep them in.

"What do you think Arcas was talking about?" Astra did not turn back as she responded, climbing over tangled branches.

"I'm not sure, Lu, but the Nether queen... she told me that Selenia was Tethered to the Solar God, Lucian. And that she severed it after trading her Shadow to Luciela for a Shadow diamond dagger—the same one I saw Solan use with Leona."

Lunelle scaled another log, her boots slipping against the peeling bark. She debated if she should add another layer of strange complexities to Astra's heart—how much more could she possibly put on her?

But, hadn't keeping it all from her caused half of this?

"Mother asked me to wait at the Lunar Gate before I came through. She said she'd signal me."

Astra's lips twitched. "Did you tell her what we planned?"

Lunelle shook her head. "No. This was before, in Pluto. She said that she would be waiting beside the gate and that no matter what, I wasn't to come through until she reached out for me. At the time, I thought maybe it was a ritual thing, a symbolic gesture. But now I don't know what to believe."

The mess of skeletal trees thinned as they edged out of the forest, massive gray dunes rising before them. Lunelle froze as she heard something snap loudly behind her.

"What was that?" Astra asked, her eyes searching the treeline. Lunelle felt the heat spark against her fingertips, ready to jump back, but they eased into a quiet, controlled spark.

She walked faster, unsure she wanted to greet any of the Nether's strange creatures face-to-face. Her sister broke into a jog to keep up with her.

"We're almost out, As. Just keep going!" Whatever was at their heels had no trouble keeping pace with them, her Shadow siphoning off her back to get to it.

She leaped forward, over one final fallen tree, and relished in the dusty sand of the dunes beneath her boots. Astra turned as they broke from the forest, shivering as she caught something's eye.

"Let's hustle, Fire and Ice!" Luxuros yelled from the crest of the dune, the Court Below's ravaged onyx gate rising over his broad shoulders. Astra skipped a bit at the sound of his voice, a movement so frivolous for their situation, for her in general, that Lunelle could not fight a wash of warmth over her chest as they climbed the base of the silted dune.

"For the record, I really like the version of you the commander brings out. Mortal enemy thing aside. What are you planning on doing about that?"

Their breaths grew short as the sand slipped beneath their steps.

"Small detail," Astra said, her laugh shallow.

They pushed to the top, their knees aching and lungs puffing. Arcas and Mirquios both watched her with expressions that did something to her chest she couldn't have denied if she wanted to—and in that moment, she wanted to. Her head cleared as she remembered his words earlier, his admission of his scheme. Mirquios winced as Luxuros tied off a tourniquet on his leg. Arcas reached forward to steady him, supporting his shoulder.

"Well," the king said as he hobbled toward the gate. "Are we ready to take down a Lunar goddess?"

Lunelle threw her arm around her sister's shoulders. She still had to carry so much of the burden. Astra turned her eyes toward the king.

"*We* are. *You* are going straight to the infirmary."

Lunelle glanced toward Mirquios as Lux shuffled him over to Arcas, grabbing Astra's hand and hauling her into the Rift.

Lunelle hung back, her heart sinking a bit as she pulled back on the prince's hand.

"Shouldn't we—"

"Were you genuine earlier—did my mother offer to pay your debts to pretend to court me? Was it all just to clear your ledgers? After everything—after *last night*."

Arcas snorted, his lips curling into a crooked smile as he balanced Mirquios's weight.

"If you have to ask, then I wonder which one of us was pretending, starling."

Lunelle's chest flared, the sarcasm too much for her.

"Tell me plainly, Arcas! I can't take more of these games."

Arcas shirked Mirquios's arm away from his shoulders slowly, moving to tower over her.

"Your mother made the offer, and I took it. That is true."

Her lips wobbled, the hurt welling in that space within her, now consumed with Shadows—and not just hers.

"And I was *thrilled* to do it." He reached forward, hesitantly gripping her cheek. She moved to pull away, but he held her tighter. "I was honored to be the great Lunar queen's place-holder if it meant you'd get everything you wanted in the end, no matter where it landed me."

Arcas glanced at the Mercurian king, turning back to help him into the Rift.

"Arcas!"

"You will not have a king to choose over me if we do not see to this wound immediately. You can finish crushing me later!"

Arcas did not wait for her to pull Mirquios into the Rift, hauling him back to the Lunar Gate as Lunelle trailed them. She'd only just gotten her hands wrapped around his arms when they stumbled through the gate. Mirquios lost his footing, collapsing onto the garden's pavers with a heavy gasp.

"Get him help!" Astra cried out. Lunelle could not hear anything—see anything beyond the dense crowd, her only thought was how to get the king back to his feet. Arcas stood behind her, his fingers brushing against her shoulder as maidens rushed forward.

"We need to get him inside," Lura said to Ameera, searching through Ameera's medical kit.

Arcas leaned forward to help the king up as Lura began mixing various powders into a liquid. Lunelle followed behind them as they dragged Mirquios through the crowd, her grandmother's voice rising above the courtiers in a chilling sneer.

"Don't scurry off now, you'll miss all the fun!"

Lunelle did not care what she missed. The halls of the palace were empty as they moved in one mass toward the infirmary, maidens handing Ameera and Lura anything they called out for. Arcas helped push Mirquios's limp frame onto the first bed he saw, the king's eyes half closed as Ameera pressed a tonic to his lips.

"It's for the pain," she said as Lunelle's lips parted. "He will be okay, but he needs to sleep, the repair work will be far too painful awake."

"That's what this one is for," Lura said, passing a thin vial to Ameera. "Lu," she said, grabbing her focus. "You should be in the garden for Astra."

The Tether in her chest burned at the thought of leaving him.

"I will stay with him," Arcas said. "Your sister needs you."

Lunelle found his gaze, like a quiet midnight, about to protest once more.

"Go," he repeated. "We will both be here when you're done."

She swallowed the wave of tears battling to break free. He squeezed her hand once more before she left, running back to the garden where courtiers backed away from the throne in the center, their eyes wide, fixed on the body of a goddess lying still against the stones.

Astra stood motionless, Lux on the ground beside her, as the color drained from her face.

Lunelle's stomach churned—she'd missed quite a bit. Her mother was already well into damage-control mode.

"Aren't we so fortunate that the Lunar queen Astra Leona's first act upon the throne was to defend her court from a premeditated attack by the Solar God Lucian? Hardly a minute into her reign, and she's already proven herself to be a wise and decisive leader."

Oestera turned to Astra, a strange light from within her that Lunelle had never seen before.

"Now, I know this was a lot of excitement for one day, so please, retire to your rooms. The maidens have prepared an evening tea service to help everyone get some rest before tomorrow's coronation!"

Lunelle watched as her mother leaned into Astra, speaking quietly as she fought the tide of courtiers breaking into the palace. She pushed through their baffled faces.

"Mother?" she asked, unsure just how *much* she'd missed. Lunelle and Astra stared at one another as councilwomen flurried in circles around them, responding to a series of orders Oestera barked, her lips curled into a smile.

An actual smile.

She'd orchestrated it all—every second of it—as always. Her mind could not reconcile all of it; the weight of the trades made in the dark confounded her.

"Let's go, ladies!" her mother said, a wild delight beneath the sounds. She swept into the palace, leaving only her daughters to stare after her, both wearing the same shocked expression.

Astra spoke first. "Was she... smiling?"

"I believe so."

A maiden leaned toward them on her way to gods knew where.

"Your Highness?"

Astra pointed toward the palace. "You just missed her."

"Actually," the maiden said, a quiet delight on her lips. "I meant you."

Lunelle could not suppress the astonished giggle as Astra's eyes rolled back in her head. She stepped forward, catching her as best she could, as several maidens rushed to assist their newly crowned queen as she fainted to the floor.

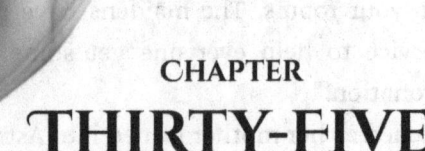

CHAPTER
THIRTY-FIVE

S he followed the maidens toward Astra's room as they carried her through the palace, breaking from the panicked rush to slip into the hall outside the infirmary.

She took a steady breath before stepping into the dimly lit room.

The king was awake, his color looking much better than it had moments ago.

"I thought they were to put you out," she said as she bounded toward him, resting her hand on Mirquios's chest. She felt for the slow breath filling his chest, the gentle beat of his heart.

"It looked worse than it was," Mirquios said, squeezing her hand.

"They were able to close it quickly," Arcas said from a chair in the corner. "Your maidens did not seem too worried about him."

"Thank you for staying," Lunelle said.

Arcas shrugged. "I can stay longer if you need to attend to whatever the fuck put that sister of yours out."

"Careful how you speak about the Lunar queen," Lunelle mumbled, her brow arching.

Both men tilted their heads toward her.

"We all have the same amount of information," Lunelle said, waving her hand. "My mother is assembling the family in half an hour, think you're up for it?"

Mirquios sat up straighter, swinging his legs over the side of the bed.

"If I start now, I should be able to make it," he laughed.

"I've been summoned to help you hobble," Luxuros said, strolling in from the hallway.

"Ah," Mirquios laughed. "And who are you this evening? The Solar prince? The Lunar king?"

Luxuros pushed gently at his shoulder. "I'm your only hope at hearing just how the Nether all of this happened, Your Highness."

Lunelle leaned down and planted a soft kiss on her king's cheek, patting his back as Luxuros pulled him out of the room.

Arcas wandered closer to her. "And who will you be when the dust settles? A Lunar princess? Mercurian queen? Rebel officer?"

Her fingers twisted in front of her, the cast of blood against her leg only now starting to make her stomach churn.

"I don't see why I can't be all three."

He scoffed, tucking his hands behind his back.

"And besides," Lunelle murmured as she circled him, dark shadows beneath his eyes. "Your title is of far more interest to me."

"And what title is that?"

"Precisely," she whispered. "Your sister will be crowned queen if my sources are correct. What does that make you?"

"Free," he replied. "At least, until someone offers to bind me into the rebellion."

Lunelle's heart leaped out of the way for that certain black mist within her, that *thing* that begged her to touch him.

Arcas opened his mouth to speak, but she held up a hand, silencing him.

"I do not want riddles. I do not want guessing games. I need you to tell me truly, once and for all, if you actually intend to commit—"

He was across the room before she could finish her sentence, his lips on hers in a kiss that twisted the very Shadow within her into a knot so tight she did not imagine it would ever breathe again. When he released her, he stepped back, his hand covering his mouth.

"That is all I know," he sighed. "I have no other answers. That is what I can offer to you, and if it is not enough—"

"It is not enough. You know it is not," she gasped between them as his hands grabbed her neck and brought her back into another kiss. Lunelle pushed him away, but he only wrapped his arms around her tighter, melting her into him.

"I love you," he hissed, his eyes narrowed, absolutely horrified to say it aloud. "Is that what you need to hear? Because you *know* it, you *demand* it, and I cannot do a damned thing about it." His hands gripped around her sides, his finger pointing at that space, the one that rested beneath her heart. "We will never have what the rest of them get, what you have with your sparkling beam of light with your gallant king, but I live within you, buried in the darkest night of your Shadow, I am there, waiting, hoping, *dying* to be yours, in whatever capacity you will allow."

Arcas released her from his grip, stepping back, putting space between them.

"And if you must hear it from me, you were right. At every

turn. At every criticism. The Prince of Pluto was indeed a coward, but he left that cowardice with his crown. I will follow you to the ends of the realms, Lunelle. I will listen and learn and fight, not *for* you, but because of you. Because of what you've plucked out of me and cleansed in your divine fire."

He took a sharp breath.

"I have no need for a title or any further clarification between us outside of the scraping of your Shadow against mine. I will be everything to you and nothing at once, and it will be enough."

Arcas's lip twitched in the silence as he stood, bare before her in a way he'd never risked before.

"Well, then," Lunelle said, exhaling slowly as she reached for her boot, slipping her Mercurian dagger from between her ankle and the soft leather, dusted in the Nether's dunes. "I wonder if my Shadow bleeds red or blue?"

He leaned toward her, whispering, "I bleed sapphire and silver."

She snagged his hand, carving the slightest crescent moon into the pad beside his thumb before giving herself a matching mark on her opposite hand from the king's mark.

"Arcas Hydranos, formerly the cowardly Prince of Pluto, you will forsake your regency and fight alongside the people you once ruled. You will seek truth and justice, and you will reject the hierarchy that has oppressed so many. You will never reveal your association or another Nova's as long as we both breathe."

"You forgot that I will bow to only one goddess for the rest of my days," he whispered.

Lunelle giggled. "I will not bind you to that—"

"Please," he whispered. She lifted her eyes to his, unsure if he understood what he was asking. "I will never be yours in the eyes of the gods, allow me to be yours in the confines of an oath."

Lunelle swallowed, the dark space they shared seeming a little lighter now. She pressed their palms together and made the addition.

"Arcas Hydranos, formerly the cowardly Prince of Pluto, now the devoted acolyte of the goddess of death and desire, you will forsake your regency and fight alongside the people you once ruled."

He left his hand in hers for as long as she could allow it, as long as she could stand it before pushing up to her toes and leaving him with one more kiss.

"I have to go check on my sister," she sighed.

"As do I," Arcas replied.

"When will you return?"

Arcas ran a fingertip over her lips.

"The moment you sing for me, starling."

"You're in pain," Lunelle whispered into the king's ear, reaching for his hand as he braced himself against the back of the Celestial Hall, wrapped in finery they'd no longer need by the end of the evening. She flinched as he winced and readjusted his stance.

"I'll make it through this evening," he mumbled. She watched his chest rise and fall with a sharp breath, the pain more than he let on. She felt it tighten between their chests as the sting reverberated.

"I've got a tea that can help," Arcas said, leaning from his station behind the king, his glimmering eyes taking in the swirling courtiers and their half-filled glasses, clinking over jovial whispers that knew nothing of what they'd witness in a few moments.

"Oh, no you don't," Mirquios laughed, the sound deep, rich, like a warm cup of coffee. "Your sister took us down that road once before."

Arcas's lips tilted, a quiet hum in his chest as he pushed off the wall.

"I should take my place, your sister demanded I be front and center."

"Don't fuck it up, Lieutenant," Mirquios said, his fingers closing tighter around Lunelle's. Arcas pushed his shoulders back, appearing that much taller at the use of his new title, the one he'd avoided for so long, and yet rested atop his head much lighter than any crown ever had.

"She can do this, right?" Lunelle asked, craning her neck over the buzz of the ballroom. Her mother and father stood, tolerating Ellume's High Priestess and her ramblings as Oestera glanced over her shoulder toward the moonstone staircase on which Astra would appear soon.

Mirquios's brow curved. "My love, I would be hard-pressed to think of a single thing a Lunarian woman could not do."

She rolled her eyes. "You're biased."

"I'm also right." He pulled her closer, resting her back against his chest as the music quieted to a hush. Lunelle's breath caught at the doors in the mezzanine swung open, revealing her sister, looking more like a queen than she ever had.

Lunelle turned her head to the side, his lips close to her ear. "The robes suit her."

"She'll ignite them before the night is over," he replied.

"Good."

Lunelle scanned the crowd as Astra stepped forward and

began to speak, her voice a steel blade as it cut through the speculation—steady.

Certain.

She felt the same assuredness flow through her veins as her sister informed the court they were no longer—that they would be the first to fall to the Nova Rebellion and become a refuge for the community. That anyone who did not align with their plans was welcome to get the fuck out. She watched as Astra melted her crown over the pristine moonstone balcony, staining it forever with a golden tattoo that would tell generations the exact spot the Lunar Court turned itself over into the hands of her people.

"I promised Luxuros I would bring Astra to him," Mirquios said as he closed a hand around her hip and gave it two squeezes.

Lunelle leaned back into him. "You deserve to see their faces. Stay for one more moment."

He pressed his lips to her cheek as the Ellumian High Priestess's sneer cracked, her voice shaking as she challenged Astra's declaration.

"One more moment."

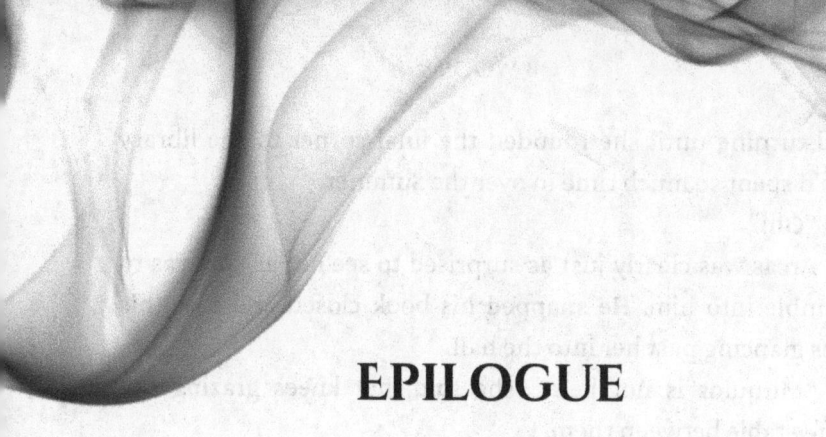

EPILOGUE

"**S**tate your business," the guard said, his pale blue skin reflecting the sky below.

"I have an appointment with the queen." Lunelle pulled at her sleeve, waiting as he confirmed with the queen's officer that Yallara did, indeed, have an appointment with the Queen of Mercury that afternoon.

"Him too?" The guard pointed at Mirquios, hovering behind her.

"I've business in the city."

He sighed, scribbling their names across a ledger and waving them on.

"I'll meet you at the cliffs?" Mirquios asked as Lunelle lingered at the edge of the palace hall.

"Hour, two tops," she replied, squeezing his hand. He began his path through the city to the Novas' newest meeting space.

Lunelle watched as he disappeared into the bustling streets.

She wandered her way through the sapphire halls, twisting

and turning until she rounded the final corner to the library she'd spent so much time in over the Summer.

"Oh!"

Arcas was clearly just as surprised to see her as she was to stumble into him. He snapped his book closed and rose, his eyes glancing past her into the hall.

"Mirquios is not here," she said, her knees grazing the coffee table between them.

"No," he confirmed. "He shouldn't be, anyway. We're to meet at The Pith. I lost track of time."

"You look well, Arcas," Lunelle said, a gentle smile tugging at her lips.

He leaned over the table, dropping those sapphire eyes to hers.

"Come now, starling, you know it's much more fun to hurt my feelings than inflate them."

Lunelle laughed. "I wouldn't *dare* insult a Nova officer."

Arcas stepped around the table and reached for her hand. He held the ring up to the shimmering sunlight, the aventurine dancing in the golden hues.

"It is a lovely stone," he murmured. "It does not sing, however."

Lunelle's eyes rolled as she pulled on the chain around her neck, the sapphire and stibnite ring he'd given her absorbing the light of the room.

He sighed, leaning perhaps a little *too* close to be considered appropriate by passersby.

But they did not understand the strange alchemy between them. The *thing* that would always live in the caverns between their Souls, lurking in their Shadows.

The moments they shared together and with her king.

Arcas's fingertips flared between them, catching her hand for a breath.

"You wear his for all to see, but you keep mine buried in the dark."

Lunelle turned her head, amused at the way he jumped back from her.

"I keep you where you belong, Prince."

"It's Lieutenant now," he said softly, a lightness to his tone that had not been there months ago.

Lunelle pursed her lips—he could not help himself. He closed the distance between them and brushed his lips over hers so quickly she might have questioned if it happened if it weren't for the spiral in her stomach, swirling in anticipation.

"You're late, Lieutenant."

"Yes. And your husband *hates* when I keep him waiting," Arcas murmured, dropping her hand. "Will he be joining us this evening?"

She nodded, a rush of heat washing over her.

"I look forward to worshiping at the altar of you," he whispered before strolling from the room, his sister bustling through the door before Lunelle could draw a breath.

"I'm so sorry!" Yallara said, taking up the space in the room her brother left. "I thought we were meeting in the garden!"

"We can, if you'd like?"

"No, no, sit! I need to hear *everything* about the Nova Court."

Lunelle giggled, leaning back into the sofa, tucking her feet beneath her, listening to the fade of Arcas's boots and tamping down the blush that climbed her neck as Yallara listed off all the changes they were making in preparation to declare the Plutonian Court for the rebellion—a list that Mirquios and she had been tackling in their own court over the last few months.

Her eyes fell on the bay window, the glass cracked as the silver pools below trickled toward the city, and a smile spread across her lips.

HER FOOTSTEPS ECHOED through the catacombs.

Plutonians milled about at the midday hour, running their blue fingertips over the stibnite clusters along the walls. She lowered her hood as she wove between them, the ring around her neck sizzling to life in the underground grave.

She touched it reflexively, a whisper kissing her ear as she did, though it felt too far away to understand it. She quickened her pace, eager to get back above ground.

He was waiting for her at the steps, arms tucked behind his back, jade gaze lighting up as she came into view. Lunelle skipped forward, launching herself into his grasp.

"There she is, the Goddess of Death herself."

"I believe there's a line for that title," Lunelle laughed, peppering his jaw with kisses as he dragged her up the stairs, their boots crunching in the sand. Lunelle pulled him toward the edge of the cliffs, the Sun bouncing off the dark sea below.

It did not look so steep a fall as it once did.

"And you're *positive* we have to do this?" Mirquios clenched his jaw as he peered over the edge.

"It can't be any more frightening than hunting your own Shadow in the Court Below."

Mirquios shuddered. "I'd take dunes to cliffs any day."

"I'll count to three," she said.

"No, not necessary, just… give me a moment," he mumbled, stretching his neck.

Lunelle reached for his hand, pressing his knuckles to her lips. She rubbed her thumb over the band on his left hand, the one she knew had her name engraved on the inside.

"Take as many moments as you need, my love."

Mirquios took a deep breath and then nodded, letting her

lead as she hurled them over the cliff's edge. If that was what Descent felt like, slipping through space with the love of her life's hand around hers, she did not think it all that terrible of a Fate at all.

And when she broke through the surface of the water, frigid but not unwelcoming, she was certain she heard Pluto's amused chuckle, folding into foamy crests and pushing her back to the surface where the gentle Sun kissed her silver-freckled face.

Acknowledgments

If *Rift* was a love letter to little sisters, *Courting Death & Desire* is a love story to oldest sisters, so first and foremost, I want to thank every eldest daughter who has ever set her hopes and dreams aside—especially when no one asked her to.

I also owe *everything* I do to my team at Emrae—Erin, Morgan, and Bailey—but especially Erin, who tolerated a lot of bullshit as *CD&D* evolved from a cute little novella into a full length why choose romance that neither of us saw coming. I can't thank you enough for going on that journey with me and holding space for my ridiculously long text spirals.

Thank you to my beta readers and ARC readers, I appreciate you all so deeply, you have no idea how much it means to me that you all care so much about the world I'm creating. Every comment, review, and DM pushes me to keep writing and exploring the courts, even when it all feels out of reach.

And most of all, thank you to my husband and kids, especially my five-year-old, who is immensely proud of me even if she keeps giving my government name to people we meet out and about and telling her kindergarten classmates that her mom writes adult books.

Someday we'll laugh about that over mimosas.

Love,

CB

MORE FROM CB WOODS

Want a free novella?

Read Nayson & Oestera's prequel for free when you sign up for CB's newsletter at cbwoods.net/risk

EMRAE PUBLISHING

Emrae Publishing challenges traditional and hybrid publishing houses with a profit-share model. With a focus on direct distribution and partnerships with independent bookstores, Emrae gives authors the flexibility of self-publishing with the support of a team that understands them. Their mission is to keep money in the pockets of creatives bringing stories to life while keeping billionaires out of their business.

Discover new voices at reademrae.com